Never Google Heartbreak

About the Author

Emma's first taste of romance came after a BMX championship final, when she was pipped at the post by Bev Batty[1] and found comfort in the arms of a fidgety vegan in a mohair jumper who taught her to snog with tongues.[2]

After graduating from university, she worked as a teacher and travelled around Asia before returning to London and taking up a job designing children's puzzles in an airless office staffed by oddballs and lunatics.[3]

She remained single despite talk of marriage in 1994[4] and actual marriage plans in 2002.[5] Finally, disillusioned and turning her back on love, she became a near recluse in the shadowy back streets of Clapham. One evening she met someone who made her 'feel funny' and found she didn't enjoy being away from him. Luckily he liked her, so they ran away to York where they still live today with their three children, Frankie, Rafael and Lula.

Emma has written and illustrated three children's picture books.[6]

---

[1] An old arch-rival and love enemy.

[2] He later turned out to be weird and had a secret collection of photos of her.

[3] She had various flings with all of them except 'potato head' Stuart.

[4] He joined a travelling dance troupe and therefore couldn't commit.

[5] His third eye told him that their auras were misaligned. He also smelled . . . Okay, he didn't smell.

[6] Really popular with under-threes.

Never Google Heartbreak

EMMA GARCIA

HODDER

First published in Great Britain in 2013 by Hodder & Stoughton
An Hachette UK company

2

Copyright © Emma Garcia 2013

A CIP catalogue record for this title is
available from the British Library.

ISBN 978 1 444 74149 0

Typeset in Plantin Light by Palimpsest Book Production Limited,
Falkirk, Stirlingshire

Printed and bound by Clays Ltd, St Ives plc

Hodder & Stoughton policy is to use papers that are natural,
renewable and recyclable products and made from wood grown in sustainable forests.
The logging and manufacturing processes are expected to conform to the
environmental regulations of the country of origin.

Hodder & Stoughton Ltd
338 Euston Road
London NW1 3BH

www.hodder.co.uk

For my trio of Leos with love and gratitude.

'Look, there's a patch of blue sky over there.'
Maureen Tucker

'*Illegitimi non carborundum.*'
'Don't let the bastards grind you down.'
John Tucker

PROLOGUE: PART I

Rob Waters proposed to me three months after I slept with him. I thought it was one of those whirlwind romances you read about in magazines at the hairdresser's. Five years and two postponed weddings later, I've accepted it's more of a slow burner.

In two months' time, however, we will finally, actually be saying, 'I do.' This time everything's booked: the Blue Room at Burnby Castle near his parents', the reportage photographer and the Rolls-Royce. Rob has been very hands-on, which is great; it was his decision to go with the strawberry brandy snap baskets.

We're keeping it informal. He'll be in a navy blue Hugo Boss suit and pale pink shirt, the same pink as the bouquet roses. My dress is very simply cut with just the right amount of Chantilly lace. I sold the last two meringues on eBay.

We still have to pick out our wedding bands. They'll be platinum to match the engagement ring. It's funny but since he gave me this rock I've never taken it off, not even when he wanted to postpone the wedding the first time (he's scared of churches) or the second (he felt funny about being thirty-five). I suppose I just love Rob Waters. I love him and not for all the obvious reasons like the fact he's incredibly easy on the eye and absolutely loaded. I love the neat way he's put together, his pouty lips and blond curls. I love the way he walks and how he sleeps curled up. I love the way he wrinkles his nose and sniffs when he's concentrating. I've grown to love how he calls me 'Bunny'. I don't even mind when he screams, 'Who's a filthy little bunny?' when we make love. I just say, 'I am.'

He'll be back from the gym soon so I'm making salmon with wild rice and chicory salad for supper, his favourite. I move around the kitchen and find I'm humming to myself. I'm certainly a very lucky girl to live in this fabulous apartment right in the centre of London, the greatest city in the world. I'm young(ish), in love and about to be married. I have everything I ever wanted.

The door slams. He's back early. I go to the top of the stairs. He looks up, ringing bells in my soul with his handsomeness.

'Hi.' I smile. 'Supper's nearly ready.'

'Hey, Viv,' he says, and I know by his voice something is wrong. I go into the living room and wait. He must have had a bad day at work. He steps into the room and just stands there and the look in his blue eyes chills my blood. It's a look I've seen before, twice before. His eyes search my face as he slowly, sadly, shakes his head.

'Oh no,' I whisper, and sink onto the Graham and Green sofa.

'I can't do it, Viv,' he says, and I feel my heart snap like stepped-on ice.

PROLOGUE: PART II

Nevergoogleheartbreak.com – Self-help for Lovers

Rob Waters and I are 'on a break', taking time apart to discover what we want. Well, so he can discover he's lost without me.

Moving out was my decision, a cruel-to-be-kind thing, like cutting back a lovely but straggly rosebush. You only do it to let something more beautiful bloom, and something beautiful will bloom for us when he realises what he's lost and comes to get me back.

So yeah, no, just to be clear . . . We haven't split up; we're on a break – it's different.

Obviously I was devastated when he cancelled our wedding . . . again (he doesn't feel fully grown, spiritually speaking) and I didn't want to leave, but I couldn't stay, waiting like a spider with my wedding-dress web, could I?

I went upstairs that very evening and quietly started to pack. He asked me not to go, but this time something between us felt broken. I just left the dress and the veil hanging on the wardrobe door.

Now I have my own place, a little rented flat in north London. It's fine. It's what you'd call bijou. I was relieved when they finally got the sofa in (by taking the legs off and shoving for an hour). It's funny, that sofa looked tiny at Rob's.

Every day I wake up and remind myself he'll be swinging by any minute, telling me he's made a terrible mistake, he does want to marry me and it's all back on.

Anyway, since I left, he hasn't really been in touch (except to text me to ask if I knew where his hockey pads were) and I've developed a strange fascination. I'm finding myself researching heartbroken people. I'm obsessed with them. I've been collecting the details of other people's break-ups and Googling words like 'heartbreak', 'spinster' and 'dumped', to see what's out there. I haven't been dumped, obviously, but I'm just interested. I can tell you there's a whole lot of misery online. I've also begun to collect self-help books. I spend whole evenings in bookshops browsing through the personal growth section. There are many strategies you can use to help yourself. If only those broken-hearted people online knew!

Then I started thinking about putting all this together on a website. I'm thinking it'll be something hopeful and upbeat, funny even, like an online magazine about relationships. The kind of place where self-help meets heartache, if that makes any sense. I'm thinking there'll be case studies, top tips, an agony aunt forum – even a dating page. I know someone at work who might build it for me.

Yes, so that's what I've mostly been thinking about these past few weeks since I left Rob. It's kind of a project to throw myself into so I don't spend every spare moment pining for him.

I do spend every spare moment pining for him, though. I wonder what he's doing all the time, every second. But I'm not broken-hearted – as I said, we're just on a break. And that's what I think to myself every night as I take his T-shirt from under my pillow, hold it to my face and breathe in the last musky traces of his smell.

I

Case Studies

'That morning I remember he was very keen to have sex. Afterwards I went to work as normal. At about half nine he sent a text: "I'm moving out." That's all it said. When I got home, he'd gone. It was the secrecy that really got me, how he'd arranged everything behind my back.

He took all the cutlery. After two years of living together, he left me without so much as a spoon to stir my tea.'

Debbie, 28, Glamorgan

It's Monday evening at Posh Lucy's, Battersea. We've been scouring the internet for more break-up stories for the website.

'There was a girl I used to work with,' I say.

'Hmm?' replies Lucy, without looking up.

'And she caught her fiancé in bed with their eighteen-year-old neighbour.'

'Nasty.'

'She used to go round to his place after that and hang about outside. Like, every night.'

'Why?'

'So she could see him.'

'Isn't that stalking?'

'And she left little anonymous notes . . . loads of them, Sellotaped to his door.'

'Poor, sad woman.'

'That must take dedication. Imagine that – every night.' I consider going to Rob's and doing something similar, but he lives on a very busy street and I know all the neighbours because I lived there myself for five years.

I pick up the phone just to check a text hasn't come in. 'Ring him,' says Lucy.

'I can't ring him. As I've already explained to you, I'm waiting for him to ring me.'

'So you were about to marry him and now you can't even talk to him?'

'I can't ring him after I moved out, can I? What would I say? "Hi there. Have you missed me yet? Shall I come back? Want to get married?"'

'What if he doesn't ring you?'

'He will. It's about time now. He's had the first week for it to sink in, the second week to enjoy his freedom, go to the gym, watch the rugby and all that, and another week to realise he's lost without me. He'll be calling anytime now. It's text-book stuff.' I glare at her. Making her accept this theory is extremely important.

'Okay.' Lucy shrugs and drains her glass. I finished mine ten minutes ago. I suddenly wish I had a cigarette; it's been quite an intense evening with all these dumped stories. It makes me so glad I haven't been dumped.

Lucy collects up the glasses. 'Want another?' She walks with perfect posture to the kitchen. I consider the gleaming surfaces and unblemished white carpet of Lucy's flat. I read somewhere that the state of a woman's house is linked to her state of mind. If that's true, then Lucy must be mentally extremely healthy. Lucy's always been sorted, though. At university she interior-designed her dorm room. She had a colour scheme, a new colour television, taffeta curtains and scented candles. In my room next door I had a new washbag and thought myself swish. I nearly died when she knocked and introduced herself, with her perfect accent and her 'Fancy a G and T?' I was amazed at how nothing ever fazed her. I called her 'Posh Lucy' and she started introducing herself like that at the Freshers' Ball, as though it were some sort of title: 'Hi, I'm Posh Lucy and this is my little friend Vivienne.'

Anyway, she's done well for herself and she deserves it. She works very hard, so she says. I think of my own place. I haven't actually finished unpacking yet, but I know, even when I have, it's going to be depressing. You know why? Because it's a *single girl's* flat. Nothing against single girls, mind; it's just that I'm not one of them. I might have moved out, but I'm still a fiancée. I'm 'in a relationship'. I rub the skin of my wedding ring finger. It feels naked without the engagement ring.

God, I feel miserable.

A whole month without Rob. I mean, I know we're on a break, but I didn't realise it would be like this. This is a complete cut-off . . . like death.

I put my feet up on the coffee table next to a neatly stacked pile of glossy magazines. My eye falls on the cover girl with her hair blowing back and her caramel lips. 'Women who have it all,' it says across her chest. I flick through to the article. The woman with it all has high heels and an expensive-looking hairdo; there she is in her office, holding up a pen with authority. Next she's lounging with a tray of croissants in satin pyjamas, and she probably hasn't eaten a croissant since the early eighties. There she is crouching on her private beach cuddling three gorgeous kids (although, hold on, is one of them cross-eyed?).

She really actually has it all. Beautiful home, CEO of a blue-chip company, happily married and she still finds time to bake. She's not the kind who sits around waiting for ex-fiancés to call. I start to fill in the little quiz at the bottom.

Are You a 'Have It All' Girl?

Age: Thirty-two – and, as we know, age, like dress size, is just a number.

Relationship: On a break.

How would you describe your relationship on a scale of one to five, five being totally perfect? N/A.

How would you describe your career on a scale of one to five, five being completely fulfilling? Also N/A – what I do for a living isn't really my 'career'.

How would you rate your friendships with the key people in your life? Hmm, key people . . . Lucy and Max, I suppose. My oldest friends. I tick 'good', then change it to 'excellent' in case Lucy sees it.

What you have to do is add up your scores and find the description to fit yourself. The upshot of mine is that I should work out my priorities and set 'life goals'. Of course! Life goals are what I need.

Well, obviously I don't define myself according to whether I'm in a relationship or not, but I have to be honest here and say it's Rob: getting married to Rob, having Rob's children . . . but I suppose I should have 'Get a career' as a life goal too. I'm not a total loser and I've always thought it would be good to become a buyer for Barnes and Worth, the department store chain where I work, before going off on maternity leave.

I'm a product manager in ladies' gifting, and as such I spend my daylight hours putting together 'gift options' so people can buy conveniently for their maiden aunts and mother-in-laws.

Summer rain bubble bath with body lotion set (you get a free toiletries bag covered with raindrops), pop-up brollies, nailcare sets, massage mitts, soft leather gloves, quilted make-up bags, animal-shaped key rings with built-in torches, seasonal headgear, grow-your-own herb kits, mini luxury jam-taster collections. You know the sort of thing.

I glance at the silent phone. It's Rob's birthday this month. Should I call and wish him happy birthday? When do you stop remembering your boyfriend's birthday? I must research this; it's exactly the kind of thing the website should tell you.

Last year I organised a surprise trip to Rome for his birthday. It was very romantic, except he said to not do a surprise trip again because he felt 'hoodwinked'. But I mustn't reminisce about the good times – gritty reality is what I need. Get things into perspective. I pick up one of Lucy's broadsheets.

'Leading doctor says women putting off motherhood are risking infertility.'

I examine the picture of a woman in a suit sadly holding some knitted booties up to her face, with the caption 'Fertility falls off a cliff in mid-thirties.' Oh, now I feel very bad. I stare at the booties woman who's left it too late. She looks like me. Why do they print stuff like this? Why, when women aged thirty-something might be reading? What are we meant to do – run out into the street, find any man who can stand up unaided and get up the duff before the pretty fertility balloon floats away, pulling up its ladder for ever? I throw the newspaper on the floor.

Anyway, I'm not mid-thirties yet. I have years before the cliff thing happens and by then I'll be back with Rob.

Lucy returns with champagne – real champagne, mind, not sparkling wine. She can afford it: she has some big swanky job in a big swanky office in Berkeley Square. It's funny, really – I know the details of her sex life but not so much about how she earns a living. She once sat me down to explain. It was, 'Stocks, shares, market, bull, bear, risk-assessment trading, blah.' She's quite important, I think. I slurp up the winking bubbles.

'I was thinking,' I say, 'we could have a kind of dating page on the site where people are reviewed by their exes – you know, like on Amazon where books get reviewed? You can see what other people think before you buy. It might be fun.'

'Except all your exes think you're devil spawn.'

'Not all . . . do they?'

'You turned Ginger Rog gay, remember?'

'You can't turn someone gay, Lucy. It's not like a cult.'

'That guy from the RAC, then. The one you slept with after he fixed your Mini. He said you ruined his life.'

I stare at her. 'You know, you should be an agony aunt with that knack for straight talking.'

'Hmm, yeah . . . "Ask Lucy". I like it,' she says dreamily.

I pick up the phone and turn it off and on again in case there's a fault.

'Why don't you just call Rob? I don't know what you're scared of.'

'I'm not scared of anything.'

'Just do it, then. Put yourself, and me, out of your misery.'

'Okay, I will.' What I really do not want to do is call Rob. I haven't spoken to him since I moved out. I'm sure the rules of 'on a break' state that I'm the one who left and so he should be the one to ring. I mean, you can't leave someone and then be ringing them up morning, noon and night. Lucy is glaring. Maybe I could just pretend to call him . . .

'And don't do that pretend phone conversation thing where you just say, "Uh-huh," a lot,' she says.

I scroll down to his number and press 'call'. I show her the terrifying display – 'Dialling Rob' – and put the phone to my ear, staring her straight in the eye. Scared indeed – ha! It rings. My heart's jumping like a gerbil in a box.

'Rob Waters speaking.'

I hang up and throw the phone like it's hot.

'Nice one,' says Lucy.

The phone rings. We both look over to where it landed. I scrabble to get it.

'It's him,' I say.

'No shit,' she says, making her eyes unattractively wide.

I jab the button.

'Vivienne Summers speaking.'

'Hi, it's Rob . . . Did you just call?' The sound of his lovely voice makes me ache.

'No, I don't think so,' I say airily.

'Your number came up.'

'All right, all right . . . I did call, but it was a mistake.'

'Oh. So. How are you, Viv? Are you okay?'

'Fine. Very, um, healthy and busy, you know . . . How are you?'

'Great.' There's a pause and I hear plates being cleared.

'Are you eating?' I say.

'Are you going on Saturday?' he says at the same time.

'Saturday? Saturday, er . . .' Yes, good! Pretend not to know it's Jane and Hugo's wedding. Pretend not to care that this Saturday was one of the dates we'd considered for our big day.

'Hugo's wedding?' he says.

'Oh yeah. I'll be there.'

'Me too. Should be a good do.' He's pretending not to care either, but I can tell by his voice he's looking forward to seeing me. We'll be in the same room. I'll make sure I look completely gorgeous. I think seeing me is what he's needed; he'll beg me to take him back. A month apart will have been nothing. We'll sit by a crackling fire and laugh about it one day.

'Actually, I was going to call you about Saturday,' he says.

'Really?' He's going to ask me to go with him. I'll say no, of course; I don't want to seem keen.

'Yeah, I just wanted to let you know I'll be with someone . . . erm, a guest.'

I feel something snag in my throat. 'A guest? Oh. Who?' I say in a strangely high voice.

'A friend of mine.'

'A girl . . . friend?'

'Yeah.' The apology in his voice stabs me through the heart. It takes a second for me to breathe again.

'What kind of girlfriend?'

'What do you mean, what kind?'

'Is she a friend who's a girl, or is she your girlfriend, like, you know . . . a girl who's sleeping with you?' Lucy is making cutting movements at her throat with her hand. I turn away.

'Uh . . . what does it matter?'

'Well, I don't know, does *she* matter? Where did you meet her? *When* did you meet her? Jesus, Rob, I've only been gone a month!'

'Look, Viv, don't get upset—'

'Upset? Who's upset? Not me!'

'I can't really talk now. I just wanted to let you know I'll be there with someone.'

'Me too. I'm bringing someone – not a girlfriend, obviously. No, no. So . . . I'm glad you mentioned it. I was just about to say, you know, to be prepared. Don't know how you'll feel, seeing me with someone else . . .'

'Good. Well, that's great, then – see you Saturday.'

'See you then!' I must hang up before he does. I jab 'end call'.

'Bye, Viv,' I hear him say as I collapse.

2

Rate Your Ex

2 July, 08:03

From: C. Heslop
To: Vivienne Summers
Subject: Re: Rate Your Ex

Vivienne was great. I would definitely recommend her for a date.
She's attractive too – eight out of ten, probably more if she's
made an effort. She's quite a determined person – some might
say stubborn, which did become an issue for me. She's
impulsive, which can be fun but also wearing, and I found on
occasion she was a little clingy.

    Charlie Heslop, 36, London

I would like to point out that this guy, Charlie Heslop, once
slept on my doorstep because he wanted to see what time I
came home – and now suddenly *I'm* clingy? Ugh. Delete.
Delete. We won't have 'Rate Your Ex' on the site: Lucy was right.

But I can't think about the website now, or anything at all,
because . . .

Rob is seeing someone.

I've said it aloud, I've written it down and underlined it,
but I can't take it in.

My thoughts repeat on a loop. Who is she? Do I know
her? Where did he meet her? Was he seeing her before I
left? What size are her thighs? And around again . . . and
whole hours pass and now I'm surprised to find it's
Wednesday morning.

You can't just ring up your ex-fiancée, tell her, 'I'm bringing someone on Saturday,' and expect that to be okay. It's as if he knifed me. I'm stuck in some hellish whirlpool of despair. I can't function. I can't sleep. I've been a zombie at work.

Work! I glance at the wall clock. It's seven fifteen.

Oh no. I can't face going in today. I think I'm coming down with something. My throat feels a bit scratchy, actually, and my stomach's dodgy. I really feel the best thing would be to stay in my pyjamas and walk round and round the flat. I circle the plastic coffee table for a bit, crossing warm patches of sun on the cheap laminate. I rest on the arm of the sofa and gaze out of the window over the rooftops, imagining Rob and this . . . this she-devil. I see them working through the Kama Sutra, laughing at my failings and filling bin bags with leftover traces of me . . . my shower gel, half-empty packets of hair dye, soufflé dishes with burnt-on bits. Down on the street the first commuters are beginning the morning march towards the station.

Oh God, I have to get to work; there's this big meeting today. I have to be there.

In the bedroom I pull clothes from my wardrobe to the floor. My Rob is *with* someone. 'I just wanted to let you know I'll be with someone.' Those were his exact words, the words that sent me to hell. I step into a black dress and struggle to zip up the back. It can't be real. Here was I waiting for him to ring and all the time he's out there meeting someone. I mean, it's only been a month. Didn't he even miss me a bit? Couldn't he have rung, just once? I pull on the buzzing bathroom light and start cleaning my teeth.

He's probably waking up with her right now . . . waking up in *our* bed with her. Thinking this brings on a kind of madness and I quickly spit, rinse and start the pacing again.

Everything in this place is wrong and strange and

frightening. I want Rob. I want our – well, his – beautiful, expensive apartment, our morning routine. He'll be out running now, having eaten his fruit platter and rice cereal. I know the old blue T-shirt he'll wear, how it clings to his chest. Then he'll shower – I know exactly how, hair first, blond curls turning dark under the water. I love to watch him while I get ready. We always leave for work together . . . We always used to leave for work together. That little peck on the cheek he gave me when he got off the train. Who's he pecking now? Her, that's who.

I walk from the bathroom to the bedroom in about five paces and sit on the bed to buckle the straps of my black sandals. I bought this bed only one month ago. I remember thinking how it wouldn't be a waste of money because Rob and I actually needed one in the spare room anyway. Lucy came over to my flat and bounced on it.

'Think of all the shagging adventures you'll have in here,' she said.

'When Rob comes round, you mean?'

'Er, no, I said *adventures*.'

'We have adventurous sex.' I was all indignant.

'What, that time you left the lights on?' she laughed, and I pushed her backwards.

Bloody Lucy. I sigh as I brush my hair. What a fool I've been. A total and utter idiot, sitting here thinking he'd be missing me. I imagine him bringing a girl home, turning the key, opening the door. She's admiring the space that I decorated, lying down on the sheets that I picked out. The pain of it burns. He's mine, my fiancé, my safe future. With him is the only life I know. Our destinies were entwined – he actually said that. I haven't even tried to unravel myself, but hc's out, he's free, running to the next adventure, pausing only to toss a grenade into my life.

Oh God, I feel a panic attack starting. I try to breathe

slowly as I scrabble in my make-up bag for tinted moisturiser. I draw on eyeliner and lipstick, but to be honest my face is so puffy from crying there's only so much I can do.

What about Bob and Marie? His parents love me. Marie knits me a new winter hat and mitt set every Christmas. Does this mean I'll never get to sit in their conservatory sipping sweet white wine from their best crystal ever again? What about the golf lessons Bob promised? What if Marie's already started on the knitting? I walk back into the living room. Oh, when will I see Bob and Marie again? I'd imagined them as the grandparents of my children – kind and patient, grey and bespectacled like in a storybook. They were the only normal, stable thing in my life. Now they're gone. I can't stand it. I throw myself down onto the scatter cushions and sob for the loss of them.

After a while my left leg goes numb. I get up and check the clock. It's half seven. I look at the huge French mirror I thought was cool when I moved in here. Now it seems silly. Rob wouldn't like it. It's too heavy to hang. I thought it looked arty leaning against the wall, but it gives a funny reflection – my thighs are not really wider than my shoulders; I've checked. I stand in front of it now and take a long look: a puffy-eyed, brown-haired girl in a plain dress. I suck in my tummy, open my eyes wide and fluff up my fringe a bit. I wipe away smudged liner. I stand up straight, then collapse into my normal posture. There's no getting away from it, I look like I feel: shit. I need help. Luckily I have Lucy on speed dial.

'Lucy speaking.'

'Hi, it's me.'

'Viv, this isn't a good time.' She sounds like she's holding her breath.

'Yeah, it won't take a minute. I just want to know – how would you describe me? Am I pretty?'

'Yes.'

'In what way? Sexy pretty? Girly pretty? Sophisticated pretty?'

'Sexy pretty,' she gasps.

'Hmm. Vamp sexy pretty, or understated sexy pretty?'

'What would you like to be?' She seems to be panting now.

'Well, I think ideally I'd be . . . not-trying-too-hard sexy pretty.'

'You're that.'

'I'm not, though – I do try hard.'

'I don't care, Viv! There's a man under my covers and I don't want to hear your voice any more.' She hangs up.

I can't believe it. How selfish. Actually, Lucy can sometimes be selfish . . . and hard. I mean, she knows I'm heartbroken. And who's the man under the covers, anyway? She isn't even seeing anyone. I can't believe she's seeing someone and hasn't told me. She's secretive as well as hard and selfish.

I go into the kitchen and stare into space a bit. I think about making coffee. I look around at the pink high-gloss kitchen; it seems so stupid now next to Rob's handmade walnut units. What was I thinking, renting this place? I open the fridge and stare inside. Sighing helps. What do people do in these situations? Probably they go home to their parents and cry and have a cup of tea, but I don't have that kind of set-up. Officially I guess you'd say my mother is a traveller. She got pregnant while still at school and wouldn't ever say who'd done it. She had me when she was seventeen and by the time I was seven, she'd decided motherhood was not for her and 'took off with the gypsies', as Granddad put it. I could go home to Nana, though. Why don't I? I'll ring her. I close the fridge and find my mobile.

It rings out. Where is she? I fall onto the sofa pressing 'redial' again and again. She'll be pottering around the garden dead-heading, wearing one of her linen sack dresses and bizarre cow-toe shoes, oblivious to my pain. I dial once more. She answers breathlessly.

'Seven one eight nine double oh?'

'Nana! I've been ringing. Where were you?'

'Oh? Just . . . here.' She sounds strange, uncomfortable, like a kid telling a lie.

'He's found someone, Nana,' I wail, feeling a flood of sorrow.

'Who has, love?'

'Rob. My Rob.'There's silence. 'Remember we were getting married?'

'I thought you'd broken it off with him.'

'I did, but now he's *with* someone! I didn't expect him to be *with* someone!' My nose fills and I hear my own shrill voice rebounding. There's a clatter like a tin bucket hitting tiles. 'Nana? Are you all right?' I hear muffled giggling. 'Nana?'

'Yes, dear, all okay. Reggie's here and he's just knocked the champagne bucket over.'

'Champagne bucket?'

'Yes. Reg, pick it up – the ice is going everywhere!'

'He's in your house at this time in the morning, drinking champagne?'

'That's right, love.' She sounds pleased.

'It's not even eight o'clock.'

'We've got smoked salmon. We're having a champagne brunch!'

'Brunch? People have brunch at eleven.'

'Do they? Well, champagne breakfast, then.'

This is a cruel new twist of the knife. Everyone in the world is having a great time except for me.

'Well, Nana, I'd better let you go. We don't want my heart-break interrupting your breakfast, do we?'

'Okay, love. Will you call back later?'

'I might.'

'Bye bye, then, sweetie pie.'

I hang up. Sweetie pie? Champagne brunch? This is all the influence of 'Reggie from next door'. He's always round there, especially since Granddad died. He even answers the bloody phone! God. The last thing I need is Nana all loved up. She's not supposed to be having a better love life than me, is she? She's seventy!

I throw the phone into my bag. I should leave for work now. I dither, wondering if I need a jacket. I step into the stairwell, go back in twice for keys and purse before taking the smelly carpeted stairs to the street.

All my thoughts shriek in my head; they all need exclamation marks. It's a nice day, I think. A nice day for a white wedding! Jane and Hugo's wedding! Three days away! What am I going to do? I can't go! But I can't not go! I've already accepted the invitation!

I jump onto the bus just before the driver closes the doors and stand leaning against the luggage racks as we cannon through the streets of London. I was going to pop along to the wedding in my old blue cocktail dress and get back with Rob. Now everything's changed. I've got three days to find a killer dress, lose a stone and get a new boyfriend. It's hopeless. I concentrate on the window displays of passing shops as we jerk towards town, picturing myself in the various dresses I see, comparing myself to this perfect-looking adversary and coming up wanting until it's my stop.

I join the stream of workers and cross Marylebone Road to Baker Street, wondering at each woman I pass, Is that *her*? I cross the street to be swept up by the revolving doors of the Barnes and Worth offices.

I board the packed lift and the doors close. The little arrow of light points upwards and then disappears as the door opens again and a tall man with salt-and-pepper hair squeezes in. I step back to avoid his giant polished shoes. The arrow appears. We're off. No we're not. The door opens again for an apologetic woman in a too-tight jumper. She slides into a corner, standing on tiptoe. Okay, this time. Arrow. Good.

For God's sake! The door opens and I see us in the mirrored tiles opposite, a little crammed sardine tin of people. Some fella with off-putting wet-look gel in his hair tries to board. Now the doors won't close. It takes an age to dawn on him that he's the reason and to get out. The doors close and open again because he's pressed the bloody button.

'No one else can fit in here! Stop pressing the button!' I shriek from behind Salt-and-Pepper Man. A little ripple of excitement passes through the lift as the doors close and we're winched up. The eggy smell of a fart mingles with aftershave. I study flakes of dandruff on Salt-and-Pepper Man's collar, feeling stares on my back. I glance around, expecting a smile or even a comment, but all eyes avoid me. The faces are mute and faintly surprised like shocked cattle.

I don't care. I know not how, but I swear, by the time I leave here today I will have a dress and a plan. I will, I will, I will.

3

Lessons Learned

> **Mooncake:** Can anyone help me? My boyfriend left me and I feel like a pile of shit.
>
> **Alicat:** Poor you, Mooncake. It will get better. I was cruelly dumped last year and know how you feel. All I can say is take it one day at a time.
>
> **Rayofsun:** Never get the letter B tattooed on each butt cheek.
>
> **Mooncake:** BB? His initials?
>
> **Rayofsun:** His name's Bob. (It was a cute and funny gesture at the time.)
>
> **Alicat:** Give up on loving him, but don't give up on love.
>
> **Rayofsun:** Also destroy all the videos of you having sex with him.
>
> **Alicat:** You really will get over this and be so much happier one day.
>
> **Mooncake:** Thanks, everyone. I guess one day I'll feel more hopeful.
>
> **Koola:** Bunch of freaks.

My office is on the thirteenth floor. I say 'office', but it's more 'work station'. We're penned in by felt-covered dividing panels, like cows in a milking shed. I can look over the top down the length of the office. It's very, very grey and the fluorescent lights buzz in a headache-inducing way. I'm sure this building has that sick syndrome thing. I sink into my swivel chair and try to ignore the knot in my stomach.

This morning we're having a 'lessons learned' meeting. We're looking at past product mistakes to see what we can learn from them. My assistant, Christie, is supposed to have put together a table of products from previous ranges that didn't sell and written up the results from customer opinion panels. She begged me to give her the opportunity to present to Snotty, who is the head buyer and our boss. It's a bit like chucking a fluffy puppy into a pen with a Rottweiler, but I agreed – I didn't have time to do it myself anyway.

I watch Christie sashaying back to her desk, her platinum-blonde hair combed into a tight bun, her skin suffocating under dull tan make-up. Red high heels and a blue skirt suit complete a look I'd call 'air hostess'. I guess this is Christie's idea of a corporate outfit.

'Morning!' she sings. 'Have you heard about the cuts?'

'What cuts?' I try to kick-start my ancient computer.

'Belt-tightening here at Barnes and Worth. Cutbacks. Budgeting and all that.'

'Who said?'

'Paul heard it on the radio.'

'Oh, the recession measures.' I try to sound authoritative. 'I wouldn't worry. People buy more useless gifts in a recession anyway, so we'll be busier.'

'Oh yeah!' she says, pleased.

Belt-tightening? I don't like the sound of it. I can't say I love my job, or even like it some days, but it's quite creative and it pays the rent. I definitely don't fancy being unemployed.

'Are you ready?' I ask.

'Well, I looked at the sales figures from last year and picked each month's three worst-performing products.'

'Great.' I switch the monitor on and off.

'Oh, and I've got the customer panel's reactions, so we can analyse them.'

'Do you know what you're going to say, then?'

'What I'm going to say?'

'What you think about the products?'

'Oh, I hadn't thought of that.'

'Well, Snotty's bound to ask.'

I search through my emails. Nothing from Rob. I wonder if he's now sending messages to this new girl and feel a stab. I try to calm myself and think about work, glancing at the list Christie has prepared and making mental notes. My stomach's churning with nervous energy and I'm totally on edge. This meeting cannot drag on. I need to find a dress. I don't care how much it costs, or what style it is; it just has to be amazing – the kind of miracle dress that covers big thighs and accentuates boobs . . . so I hope Christie is organised. I stand up.

'Shall we go?'

She grabs papers and notebooks and clip-clops next to me down the corridor to the meeting room.

We take our places at the large oval table, the vicious air conditioning making me shiver in my sleeveless dress. Snotty arrives, dropping a file of notes down with a slap. Her half-moon specs rest low on her short beak nose and she peers over them without warmth.

'Good morning, Vivienne.' She nods to me and then to Christie. 'Christine.'

'Morning,' we answer together like schoolgirls.

'First off, Vivienne, let me say that I do like to schedule my time, so I would have appreciated an emailed agenda including all the lines we're looking at today.'

I asked Christie to do this; she was supposed to take full responsibility for the meeting. An uneasy sensation prickles at the back of my neck.

'I have a hard copy here.' I slide my own printout across the table. 'Apologies for not emailing it – we were still processing the focus group's results late last night and they affected how the agenda worked out.' Where do these lies come from?

'Well, that's . . . something.' Snotty studies the paper, eyebrows arched. 'Right then, point one: Christine's presentation of the failing ranges.' Her red lips pleat. The hard amber eyes scan Christie.

Christie stands up and begins to read shakily from a crumpled sheet of paper. 'The reason we need to have this meeting today, which I believe is very important, is so that we can look at products that have not sold very well and analyse why they haven't sold very well and then think about how not to do badly selling products again.'

Snotty mutters something like 'Jesus wept' and pours herself a glass of water.

Will I need to buy new shoes to go with the dress? Maybe I could take a long lunch today and go to Oxford Street. I wonder what Rob's 'someone' will be wearing.

Snotty is looking into her lap, shaking her head.

Christie holds up a bath hat and mitt set and reads the panel's comments chirpily. '"It's too old-fashioned" . . . "My gran had a hat like this and she's been dead ten years" . . . "I wouldn't buy this" . . . "Strongly dislike bath hats" . . . "I would expect a product like this in a cheap bargain store, but not at Barnes and Worth."'

Oh my God. Christie is making a total idiot of herself reading out the actual customer comments instead of a nice glossy summary. What is she doing? She's been in so many of these presentations; hasn't she learned a thing? I thought she could do this. I'll kill her later, but right now an emergency rescue is needed. How can I do it without humiliating her? Under the table I dig my nails into my palms.

'"Strongly dislike. What colour is it supposed to be?"' sings Christie.

Snotty presses a manicured finger into her cheek and then points it like a gun. 'And stop. Why you didn't do the customer panel at design stage before we produced five thousand of these "sets" beggars belief.' She picks up the bath hat between thumb and finger as if it were a pair of soiled underpants and tosses it at Christie.

'Tell me, Christine, would you buy this?'

Christie laughs. 'No way!'

'Then who the hell dreamt it up, and who gave it the green light?' Snotty shouts.

There's a silence like the one that happens as an expensive crystal vase topples from a table, just before it shatters. Christie looks at me, her huge eyes moistening.

I stand and pick up the hat. 'Can I explain the placement behind this line? The hat and mitt set were part of the "bathing beauties" range and we went with a fifties screen-siren design. The three other products – pedicure set, bath foam and body lotion, handwash and handcream – did extremely well for us. The customer panels at design stage gave positive feedback to the range as a whole, but I wonder now whether some sort of hair turban and bright sponge might've been better. I actually dreamt it up and, er . . . you gave it the green light.'

We limp on through the morning and through lunch. I try to shield Christie, but the guy who empties the bins could have performed more convincingly. These are our lessons learned:

1. Ensure all products in the range are equally strong.
2. The customer must feel like they are getting a quality product.
3. Christie will be sacked.

We gather up our failed products in silence. I feel Christie's discomfort rising off her like steam. I nod to Snotty and we head for the door, but Snotty calls me back.

'Vivienne, may I have a word?'

'Of course.' Christie hovers at the door.

'Off you go, Christine.' Snotty shoos her with an accessory-bedecked arm. The door swings closed and we sit back down at the table.

'Vivienne, I won't beat about the bush. I've been asked to make cutbacks, and some people in the department are to be let go. I'm looking at everybody' – she stares hard into my eyes – 'but quite honestly I think your assistant, Christine, is inept.'

'It's Christie.'

'What?'

'Her name . . . it's Christie, not Christine.'

'Whatever. I'm letting her go.'

'Right. Can you do that, I mean just like that?'

'Yes, I can.' A sad smile crosses her face as if the burden of this responsibility is killing her; then she sweeps up her papers and stands in a stifling waft of perfume.

'What if I gave her more training? She probably hasn't had enough experience. I probably haven't given her enough responsibilities.'

'Vivienne, it's so sweet of you to defend her, but really, if you're to make upper management, you'll have to get used to this sort of thing.'

'Right . . . It's just that I feel responsible. Today was her first presentation. And wouldn't it be cheaper to keep Christie than to employ a new assistant and train them up?'

She laughs. 'We aren't replacing her.'

'Oh . . . well . . . I think it's unfair.' I clasp and unclasp my hands, feeling my ears burning.

'Okay, look, give her a verbal warning. She can have a

chance to improve. But she'll only get one; next time she's out the door.'

She stands up and I notice her astonishing feet. Phlegm-coloured sandals with pink socks. She holds the door open. 'You'll have the lessons learned written up and circulated by . . . ?'

'Er . . . Let's see now, Friday?'

'Tomorrow. I have a buyers' meeting at nine.'

I sit alone, listening to the air conditioning rattle, feeling as if I'm floating adrift a huge rolling sea. It's okay if you concentrate on the floating feeling, but look around and there are terrifying mountains of water about to crush you. I'll have to work through to finish the stupid report. Today was dress-finding day. On my pad I write, 'BOLLOCKS,' and go to talk to Christie.

She's at her desk, head bowed, a red flush creeping up her neck. In front of her is the pile of failed products and her meeting notes, and I see at the top she's written, 'Do not fuck up,' and underlined it twice. I sit quietly beside her.

'God, that was terrible, wasn't it?' she says.

'Hmm, I suppose it could have gone better.'

'I really worked hard preparing everything.'

'I know.'

'She didn't like hearing the comments, did she?'

'The thing is, buyers think customers are beneath them. She actually winced at that granny comment.'

'Oh God, what did she say?'

'I have to give you a verbal warning.' Christie starts to say something, but then her mouth begins to crumple. 'Hey, don't get upset.'

'A verbal warning. So what . . . how do you do that, then?' she wails.

'I don't know, maybe if I just say "be warned" or something.'

She shakes her head. 'I shouldn't have started with the bath hat. No one likes bath hats.'

I take the bath hat from the pile and put it on. 'I do.' She manages a weak smile. 'Be warned,' I say, wagging a finger.

'Oh God.' She puts her head in her hands and starts to cry.

I whip off the hat. 'Oh come on, Christie, don't cry. You know what Snotty's like.' I pat her back. 'Christie, you're good at your job.' She lets out a surprisingly loud strangled cry. A few heads turn in accounts. 'Christie, come on, this is my fault. I should have told you not to read out the comments.'

'Should you?'

'Yes.'

'Well, why didn't you, then?' She stares, tears glistening.

'I forgot.'

'Thanks very much.'

'Well, I didn't think you'd ever do it, did I?'

She just looks at me with these huge watery eyes and something about her pancake foundation starting to run makes me feel very guilty and bad. Why didn't I check what she was going to say? I thought she could handle it, I suppose, but really I was thinking about other things. I was thinking of websites and relationships and Saturday and the wedding and my Rob with someone else, wasn't I?

Before I know what I'm doing, I've told Christie the whole story, which totally amazes her because we've never even discussed our lives outside the office before, apart from to reply to 'Good weekend?' or something.

'How are you going to find a dress in such a short time? When are you going to get it?' she asks, and I feel a fresh injection of adrenaline making me want to run around in a figure of eight.

'I don't know. Not today, am I? I have to write the report.'

'Oh no!' she shouts, making me jump. 'You need to go shopping!'

'Yes,' I squeak. Wow, how enthusiastic she is suddenly about my problems.

'Could I do the report? No, no, I'm crap at reports so that won't work.'

'It's all right, Christie. I'm sure I'll get it sorted somehow.'

'No, I've got it! My friend Nigel's a fashion designer – well, he's a fashion student, but really talented. He could maybe lend you one of his sample designs. I've done that before now – you know, when I needed a wow dress.'

'Have you?' When has she needed a wow dress? I'm interested for a nanosecond, then remember Christie's style ideas are so fashion forward that she's quite often a laughing stock, like the time she wore white furry leg wraps and everyone kept baaing.

'Thanks, love, but I don't think fashion designers make dresses in my size.'

'What are you? Fourteen?'

'Ten,' I snap. Her eyes shoot to my hips. 'Okay, twelve in some shops.'

'I could ask. The last one he lent me was just amazing, a total one-off. If he has something, he could bring it round this afternoon. He's only at St Martins . . . I'll ask him, shall I? It could be the answer to your prayers.' The answer to my prayers would not be a dress. But then again, imagine if I didn't have to schlep out in a panic and try on every dress in the high street while being lit from above in a smelly changing room . . .

'Okay, Christie. It's worth a try, isn't it?' I look at her expectant face. 'Thanks.'

'No problem.' She smiles. 'Viv, you've made me feel so much better.'

'Good!'

'Hearing about your life has really put my shit into perspective.' She gets up and smooths down her skirt.

'I'm so glad.' I blink my eyes sweetly.

'I'm off to get lunch. Want anything?' I shake my head and watch her leave, then pick up her notes and start the report.

An hour later I've only written the first paragraph. I can't concentrate. Terrible, panic-inducing thoughts keep dive-bombing in like seagulls. I take out my notebook and turn through all the website notes to a new page. I write a title and underline it.

To do (before wedding)
1. dress – get one
2. shoes – get some
3. hair – do something
4. body – ???

Not a very useful list. Oh hell, normally I'd love this – all the preparation and fuss would be part of the fun. But I only have two and a half days and the stakes are so high. I know I should be running up Oxford Street in a shopping frenzy, but I feel frozen, like I'm already beaten. He's with someone else. What can I do about that? What kind of dress can change that? And when I think along these lines, my heart swells up with hopelessness, rendering me a staring, whimpering wreck.

And that will just not do.

I look out of the window at the hazy sunshine. It really is a beautiful day, a day that stretches out long and lonely. The unwritten report hangs blinking on my screen, but I have an uncontrollable urge to go outside. And I don't want to be alone.

What kind of person would have nothing better to do than hang around with me on a sunny Wednesday afternoon?

* * *

Max lopes into the snug of the Crown, wearing jeans and a T-shirt and his old black biker boots despite the heat. He pushes enormous red-framed sunglasses up onto his forehead, where they sit like an extra pair of eyes, and blinks, accustoming himself to the dark. I wave from my little corner table.

'What are you, some kind of bat lurking in here? It's a beautiful day,' he says.

'See, that attitude really annoys me. At the first glimpse of the sun everyone's going, "Beautiful day! Beautiful day!" Running outside doing things they never normally do, flocking to the parks, probably injuring themselves. I always sit inside pubs. I'm normal. It's you that's changed.'

He regards me for a second or two. 'It's worse than I thought,' he says. 'What can I get you to drink? Pint of virgin's blood?'

'I'll have a white wine, please. Large. And don't get crisps – I can't resist them.' I watch him lean on the bar and chat up the barmaid. She tosses her hair and laughs as she pulls his pint. He comes back to the table with the drinks and a leftover smile.

'So what's up with you?' He pulls up a bar stool.

'Weren't you busy painting a masterpiece or something?'

'Never too busy for you.'

'I don't know how you earn a living when you're skipping off to the pub at the drop of a hat.'

'Jesus, you're right. I should go!' He sips his pint and I try the cold wine. He opens a bag of pork scratchings. I watch him put them in his mouth one by one, crunching and swallowing loudly. 'What? You don't like piggy scratchin's?'

'Pork scratchings.'

'Do you want one?'

'No.'

He lifts the pack, pouring the last bits down his gullet, and makes a great show of forming the bag into a small ball that'll fit into the ashtray; then he picks bits out of his molars with his tongue.

'Well, this is certainly lovely,' I say.

'What's up with you?' he asks.

'Oh, I can't think . . . Maybe it's the fact that on Saturday I have to go to a wedding alone and face my ex-fiancé with his new girlfriend.'

He takes a gulp of beer. 'So don't go.'

'I have to go, Max. I, unlike you, honour my commitments.'

He scowls, raises his eyebrows and stares out of the door. 'I'll come with you, then.'

'You?' I laugh. 'It's a free bar – you'd get wasted. It'd be too messy.'

'I'm not doing anything Saturday.'

'Like that black-tie dinner where you showed your arse.'

'I have a suit . . . somewhere.'

'Is it your graduation suit?'

'No. Why, what was wrong with that?'

'I can't believe you're asking.'

He smiles and I notice his chipped front tooth. Why doesn't he get it fixed? Dentists can do wonders these days.

'Well, all I'm saying is, if Daniel Craig's busy Saturday, I'm willing to step in.'

And in my desperation I'm actually entertaining the thought of turning up with Max. Max, my really good friend, who scrubs up nicely if you can stop him wearing trainers or an orange cravat, or both. I can't pretend he's my boyfriend because Rob knows him, but I just can't turn up on my own.

It could work. I'll look dignified. Still single, not needing to jump into another relationship, and crucially, not alone.

'What colour is the suit?' If it's anything other than black, blue or grey, he can't come.

'Navy, with stripes.'

'Pinstripes or deckchair?' I narrow my eyes.

'What do you take me for, Viv? It's a great suit. I look great in it.'

'And you wouldn't mind coming with me?'

'No, I wouldn't mind coming with you,' he says with exaggerated patience.

'Okay, I'll ask Jane if she minds.'

'She'll love me! She single?'

'It's her wedding! Now, you won't forget that you offered, will you?' I scowl.

'Nope.'

'I just want you to stand with me, right? No going off chatting up bridesmaids – and if Rob comes over, you'll have to disappear.'

'Got it.' He mock salutes.

'Thanks, Max.' I pat his knee. 'Thanks a million.'

'You're welcome,' he says, smiling goofily. I pick up my glass and finish the wine, and when I put it down, he's still smiling and staring.

'What?'

'Nothing.' He looks away, and we sit in silence for a moment.

'So . . . I'd better get back.' I stand up and kiss his stubbly cheek. 'Thanks for coming out.'

'I'm looking forward to Saturday,' he calls as I step out into the sunlight.

By the time I get back to the office I feel fractionally better. It could be the wine or it could be that I have Max to go to the wedding with, and that is definitely something. Not going to the wedding alone. A step forward. Good. Things seem a tiny bit less disastrous.

As I get out of the lift I spot Christie in our little work

station, and behind her, hanging up on the roller shelves, is a dress. It's a white and pink dress, and the skirt is made entirely of feathers. She looks up from her non-work-related website.

'You just missed Nigel,' she says, but I don't look at her. I can't take my eyes off the dress.

'Did he make this?' I'm close enough now to touch the frothy white feathers of the skirt. The bodice is the palest pink silk.

'Yeah. Clever, isn't he? He said it's fine if you want to borrow it, but if it gets stained or anything, then you have to buy it.'

I take down the hanger and hold it against me. I've never seen anything like it. Just holding it makes me feel emotional. Everything about it is so well made. The spaghetti straps are satin, and it has tiny buttons all down the back. I feel a little surge of excitement.

'How much would it cost?'

'A thousand.'

'A thousand . . . pounds?' She nods. 'Right. Wow.' I suppose I could just be really, really careful. I mean, it's a wedding, not a rave.

'But it's such an amazing dress,' says Christie. 'Look at this.' She brings up Nigel's website and plays a film of one of his fashion shows. A model bounces down the catwalk wearing the dress with chunky tan heels. The feathers sway beautifully. She looks cool, edgy and not-trying-too-hard sexy. I'm sold. 'It's such a beautiful dress. No one else will have ever seen it.' Christie swivels her chair round to look at me as I hold the dress up to myself.

'Do you think it'll look all right on me?'

'Take it home and try it on,' she says. I hang up the dress, imagining walking into Jane's wedding in it. Could I pull it off?

'It's definitely a wow dress, isn't it?'

'Vivienne, you couldn't get much more wow,' Christie says solemnly. She looks into my eyes and we nod in unison.

At home, three glasses of Pinot down, I'm in the beautiful dress, talking to myself in the mirror.

'Hi. Oh, hi there. I love your dress. This? Thanks, a designer friend made it for me.'

I do a little dance and join in with Paloma Faith on the iPod. The feathers swish and sway and it feels great. The bodice is . . . shall we say, figure-hugging, but in a good way, I think. The only chunky heels I have are black suede, but they kind of work; they contrast. 'Hi, Rob.' I get close to the mirror. My flicky black eyeliner looks wicked. 'How are you? . . . Me? I'm fine . . . Call me.' I walk past the mirror and back again, tossing my hair.

Yes, this is the dress. It definitely is the dress. It's a bloody legend of a dress. I'll tell our children about it one day.

The room grows gloomy as the day fades, but the pale feathers glow magically in the darkness of the glass. The iPod moves on to Ronan Keating now, one of Rob's favourites, a song we once made love to. I say the words.

'When you say nothing at all.' I look at my own shiny eyes. A single tear glistens on my cheek. 'I can't believe I lost him,' I whisper.

I take a sip of wine and a thought glances into my mind like an arrow.

Lost things can be found. A spark of hope begins to smoulder. The fact is, I'll be seeing him on Saturday. We'll actually be face to face. Even if he is bringing someone, we'll still be able to talk. It can't be too late. A little flame burns quietly now. I look at the gorgeous dress and imagine Rob. His jaw drops when he glimpses me; he strains to get a better view and, ignoring her protests, breaks away and rushes over. I cling to the idea like wreckage.

It'll be as easy as falling off a log. I'm suddenly actually looking forward to it.

In a couple of days I'm taking back my man.

4

Top Tips to Look Your Best

'Wear shedloads of make-up and fake tan and have your hair massive.'

Marnie, 28, Cheadle

'Drink a lot of water and get enough sleep.'

Freya, 42, Brighton

'Buy clothes that fit. You aren't an adolescent boy, so why are you wearing their jeans?'

Sue, 33, Lyme Regis

'If I don't eat much for a few days, I look better . . . but then I feel really awful, so don't do that . . . Actually, eat more, and eat things you love, then you'll be happy and therefore you'll look great.'

Ruby, 30, Denham

'If I want to look good, I wear heels. The sound of them is like "Click click, I don't care, click click, sooo over it."'

Rebecca, 25, Teddington

'Just be yourself.'

Your mother

I've been reading a lot of magazines about this and as far as I can make out, what you do to improve your appearance without having surgery is this: lose weight, get your teeth whitened, get a suntan, be well groomed, wear the most expensive designer outfit imaginable and get your hair done. Losing weight and teeth whitening are out – no time. Spray tan would be good, but that's out because it might come off on the dress. Everything else, though, I'm doing. So help me God.

It's Thursday afternoon, four thirty. I'm leaving work early to get to my appointment at David Hedley. I've never been before, but apparently it's the best hairdresser's in London. It says in one of Christie's magazines that all the models go there and also that David Hedley makes his own hairbrushes, so I'm lucky to get an appointment, really. I had to explain about the wedding and Rob and his new girlfriend, and they agreed to squeeze me in. I've also booked a leg and bikini wax at Selfridges' spa for tomorrow lunchtime. They said they'd do my eyebrows for free.

So far, so good. I'll just walk out without anyone noticing. Why does the lift take an age when I'm sneaking out of work? Answer: because the lift also contains Snotty, my boss, and Mole, *her* boss.

'Afternoon, Viv,' says Mole.

'I'm just off to the print room for something,' I blurt.

'Good for you,' she says, and I catch Snotty rolling her eyes.

The lift doors close on my manic grin and then I'm out of there and off to hair heaven.

The salon is all industrial steel and poured concrete with ornate antique mirrors and plush chairs. A stick-thin receptionist in lime-green leggings gives me a drinks menu and asks me to wait on a velvet sofa for my stylist, Mandy. I'm fizzing with nervous energy as I flick through an expensive portfolio of hairstyles. I wish I had the courage for an elfin crop in peroxide blonde, or the face. Fringe or no fringe? Layers?

'Hi. Is it Viv?' A plump woman with her roots showing is

holding out a gown for me. I hope she's not Mandy because by the look of her she could do with a good bath.

'Yes.' I smile.

'Hi, I'm Mandy. I'll be styling you today.'

'Great.' I slip into the gown and follow her to a mirror, where she plays with my hair, pushing it forward, lifting it up and letting it drop.

'So, what are we doing with you?' she asks. The thing is, I hate it when hairdressers ask that. I want them to know what I should have. They should look at me, point and go, 'Soft layers and keep the length through the ends,' or something. Probably not that, actually, because that's what *I* always say. I try to say it this time, but she's pushed all my hair into my face and my chin's on my chest. I remind myself this is the best salon in London. 'You've so much hair!' I try to lift my head. 'Such a lot of hair.' She tilts my head to one side and then the other. 'Very thick hair.' I'm starting to feel like I shouldn't have so much, like there's a limit or something.

'What do you think I should do with it?' I finally manage to ask.

'Do you want to keep this length?' she says, and I nod. She sucks her teeth. 'See, it's very heavy through here . . .' She presses the sides of my head. 'It's very heavy so it's hanging wrong. There's no movement whatsoever. It's very flat.'

'Right.' I didn't know I was supposed to have moving hair.

'We could thin it out on the top, keep the length and pop in a few lowlights for texture,' she says, and by now I'm so relieved to hear that something can actually be done with me that I agree immediately. She nips off to mix up my colour and I suddenly start to feel a bit gloomy. I bet Rob's girlfriend doesn't have such unmanageable hair. I bet hers is all silky and baby soft and smells of fruits of the forest.

Oh, why have I got thick hair? I've never met my dad, but he must be responsible. I'm just cursing my mother for getting laid by some wire-bonced hair bear when Lucy texts.

'*Fancy a swifty?*'

'*Yes but in hairdresser's.*'

'*Okay. Call me when you done.*'

That's good. That means I'll be able to show off my new hairstyle. Mandy returns and offers me a drink. I get a white wine and watch her speedily cover my head with pieces of foil. She's not that bad, Mandy, really. I mean, she must be good to work here. I look around. There are a lot of rich-looking blonde clients being fussed with. I start to relax a bit.

'Do people always ask you if you're going on holiday, Mandy?' I say.

'No,' she says.

'Oh. It's just, I wondered if that cliché thing was true – you know, of people talking about their holidays to hair-dressers.'

'No.' She frowns as if I'm insane.

She's probably concentrating too much to be chatty; obviously she's a total professional. She wheels a circular heater over and switches it on. It rotates round my silver head like the rings of a planet. 'We'll just let your colour get to work and I'll be back in a few minutes. Would you like anything?'

I get more wine. I examine my face and wonder if it looks thinner. I haven't eaten much since Monday. I think I can see cheekbones when I turn my head to the side. I pick up a magazine and read about a woman whose breast implants exploded, until someone with a badge that says 'Daniel' takes me to the sink to get a lovely head massage.

Later Mandy returns and starts snipping. Wet strands fall. I hear the shear of the thinning scissors as they pass my ear. I wonder if she might be taking too much off the top, but I trust her. They do models here.

'What do you think of the colour, then?' she asks. I can't actually see any difference, but that's probably because it's wet.

'It's lovely. Very subtle.'

She smiles and whips out a hairdryer and a huge roll of a brush. I see steam rising from my head as she blasts away. She sprays and teases the sections around my face, shows me the back. I nod even though I suspect my hair might look a bit like a helmet. I don't want to hurt her feelings. She brushes me down and leads me back to the skinny receptionist, who cheerfully takes payment. 'That's two hundred pounds, please.'

I swallow and pass over my credit card. I glance at the bill; fifteen pounds of it was wine. It's worth it, though. It's the best hairdresser's in London. My hair will look great when I get home and mess with it a bit.

'Your hair looks lovely. Are you pleased?' asks the receptionist as I key in my PIN.

'Oh yes! It's great. It's really great. I think it's great,' I say, and for some reason I start to laugh. I give a little wave, stumble out of the door and scuttle away to meet Lucy.

It feels scarily windy around my ears. Are people looking at me funny? Are they looking at my hair? I think a girl back there by the tube might have been. Luckily the place where I'm meeting Lucy is only round the corner; I can get her verdict and fiddle with my hair in the loos. The bar is an underground tavern where the wine is great and they do nice tapas, our usual swifty venue. I clunk down the spiral staircase and spot Lucy at one of the corner tables with a bottle and two glasses.

'What do you think?' I ask her, fluffing up the sides of my head.

'Have you had it done?' She squints as I sit opposite her.

'Er, yeah. It took three hours to look like this.'

'Actually, it is a bit shorter at the top.' She lifts her bottom out of the seat to peer at my crown. 'Oh! Quite a lot shorter.'

'What? Is it?' I feel about and touch some frighteningly tufty layers. 'Does it look all right?'

'It looks nice.'

'Nice? I don't want nice! I just spent two hundred quid.'

'You spent two hundred pounds on your hair?' she asks, incredulous.

'I had a full head of lowlights.'

'You spent two hundred pounds having your hair made slightly more brown?'

'Yes, Lucy, I did.' I pour a glass of wine and glance at Lucy's silky hair, so silky that her ears poke through. How could she understand, bless her?

'Well . . . no, good luck to you. Is that eighties cut back in, then?'

I pick up the tapas menu. 'Poor Lucy. Don't be jealous of my loveliness.'

'But you are so beauootiful,' she says in a Disney way.

'I know, it's a burden,' I say. She raises her glass and we chink. 'Let me tell you about the dress . . .'

We finish the bottle and order another and talk through every aspect of Saturday. How I should be when I meet him. What I'll do if he wants to talk. How I should be gracious about his new girlfriend. And then I take a taxi home and text Lucy to say what a great mate she is. She texts back, '*So are you, babe.*' And I realise I didn't ask her a single thing about her man under the covers.

It's Friday, I drank a lot of wine, I feel rough and I'm late for work – extremely bad since I need a long lunch today for the waxing bonanza.

My hair this morning looks a bit like Tina Turner's wig.

The top layers are so short I can't even get them into a ponytail. The woman must have gone wild with the thinning scissors at the back where I couldn't see. And lowlights? Talk about emperor's new clothes. I try not to cry as I flatten some of it with hairspray, but the back sticks stubbornly up. I look like an ill cockatoo and I have to go.

On the bus I check my diary in case there's something at work I've forgotten. I look at Saturday. I've drawn a big heart shape on Saturday. The day I will win back my man! But also Jane's wedding day, obviously. I'm not sure we'll see so much of Jane once she marries Hugo. He never lets her out of his sight as it is. You try to talk to her about *anything* and he's there fondling her arm or breathing little kisses into her hair. It's very off-putting. He's small and squat; she's thin and petite. It's as if a pygmy hippo in a suit is marrying the fairy off the Christmas tree. Still, they say it takes all sorts and there's your proof. There are no work-related matters in my diary today, though, except I am supposed to be putting together a new range of gifts for Christmas.

A nasty little thought of Christmas without Rob pops up, but I bury it. We might even be married by then. I think about winter weddings – all that white fur and red roses and candles – until it's my stop.

Then it's a dull morning at the office. I can't think straight with the hangover and the nerves about tomorrow, so how can I start anything serious? Christie has declared my new hair 'edgy'. I've added all the loose elastic bands on my desk to a ball I started a year ago and tested the power of the paperclip magnet. I've emailed a few suppliers, played solitaire, and now it's time for . . . drum roll . . . 'the Spa'.

When I get to Selfridges, I take the lift and step out on the top floor into some futuristic clinic, white and green and shiny. Only beautiful people are here. I'm ushered into a

treatment room and into paper knickers before I can spoil
the aura and a stunning-looking black girl appears.

'Let's do the Brazilian first, shall we? Get the worst bit
over with?' She flashes a brilliant smile. I don't normally have
a bikini wax unless I'm about to wear a bikini, which is rare,
but the package and the free eyebrow thing enticed me. Also,
imagine if Rob and I get back together tomorrow and one
thing leads to another and we end up in bed . . . Well, he'll
have a nice surprise, won't he? I mean, he was always saying
I should do something about my wild muff.

'The Brazilian? Is that where you end up with just a
strip?'

'Everything off including underneath, and then a strip or
a shape left on top.'

Underneath? Does she mean the bits that poke out of your
swimming costume underneath or . . . something else?

'*Everything* off underneath?' This seems a bit extreme.

'Yep.'

'Do people like that?' I ask, nervous suddenly.

'Honey, I have nothing at all down there. My boyfriend
goes crazy! He tries to follow me around all day long.' I think
of Rob following me around, begging me to take him back.

'Let's do it,' I say.

'Just bring your knees up and let your legs fall open,' she
says.

I have to say what follows stings a bit. At one point she is
between my legs with tweezers, just finishing off. I'm left
with a perfectly trimmed heart shape for a muff. After that
the legs and eyebrows are a piece of cake. My skin is red
and swollen and throbbing.

'You have a lot of hair,' she says, clearing up.

'Not any more,' I mumble, and hobble out to pay.

*   *   *

That afternoon I keep surprising myself every time I go to the loo. I'm grateful when five o'clock rolls around and I can nip to Boots for some aloe vera.

As soon as I'm home I ring Max.

'Hello.'

'Hi, it's me. You sorted for tomorrow?'

'What's tomorrow?'

'The wedding!'

'Hold on there, baby, I never proposed.'

'Max! Stop pissing about. Jane's wedding. You're coming with me.'

'Okay.'

'You forgot, didn't you?'

'No.'

'So you have your suit, right?'

'Yeah.'

'Okay, what you have to do is, put it on in the morning and wait for me to pick you up in the taxi. I'll be at yours before twelve.'

'Okay. What'll you be wearing?'

'A dress. Why?'

'Well, I might want to match with you.'

'Match with me?'

'You know, like wear a flower the same colour as your dress, to show we're together.'

'We're not together. I'm getting back with Rob.'

'Right. Got you.'

'Right, so . . . see you in the morning?'

'Unless I die in the night.'

'Bye, Max.'

I close my phone and sit for a moment listening to the sirens and the traffic outside. Everything inside the flat is still and silent. I hang the dress on the wardrobe door and place the shoes underneath. I write a 'getting ready' countdown list and place it on my dressing table. I manage to go to bed quite early but struggle to sleep and end up reading self-help books until midnight. 'Hear the roar of the lion within!' Mine's a tiny kitten.

Miaow.

5

The Things We Do for Love

'*I once carried my coffee table down two flights of stairs and into the park. I cooked a full Thai banquet and laid it all out with cushions to lounge on and cold white wine. I waited; I drank the wine; I fed the rice to the pigeons. It got dark; I fell asleep. He didn't show. Someone nicked the cushions.*'

Maria, 34, Battersea

'*I run a small bakery in the city with my boyfriend, Andy. We do these little cakes with alphabet letters on. Well, one day I made a window display with the cakes. It said, "Marry me, Andy." I thought he hadn't noticed, but when I checked the display, he'd rearranged the cakes.*

They said, "Any day."'

Rachel, 30, Liverpool

I wake up to the sound of hammering. It's eight o'clock. The sun dazzles in lines across the blind – a perfect day for a wedding. I pull open the side of the blind and squint into the street. Two men in multicoloured wigs are rolling barrels into position in the road.

I guess there must be some sort of party today at one of the bars on the high street. I pull on my silk kimono bath-robe. In the bathroom I scrutinise myself: I'm looking tired around the eyes, and not in a good 'I've been partying all night' way. I pat on a little cooling eye gel. The packaging claims that it will relieve puffiness and smooth away fine lines. Truly a miracle! And only £2.49. My heart flips when I see the dress hanging by the mirror, the shoes carefully arranged underneath. I feel like a nervous gladiator inspecting my armour, except I have no idea of my opponent.

Briefly I imagine her curled next to Rob, sleeping in post-coital bliss, without the faintest worry to wrinkle her perfect brow. This thought sends my stomach cartwheeling. God! I concentrate on making proper strong coffee, setting the pot on the gas and reading my countdown list while I wait.

8.30	Jo Malone bath
9.00	Body lotion
9.30	Nails – Hard Candy 'Twilight'
10.00	Make-up – sexy
10.30	Hair – clean, smooth, artfully messy
11.00	Get dressed
11.30	Taxi arrives
11.40	Pick up Max
12.00	Arrive at church in good time
1.00	Wedding!

Around the edges I've doodled flowers on stalks with leaves. Christie once told me if you doodle flowers, it means you want to get married and have children. Amazing how accurate these things are! The pot hisses as I pour the coffee. I can't eat anything. I feel like I'm facing the 100-metre hurdles on school sports day all over again.

I pull up the Roman blind at the balcony. The police are in the street, calmly chatting in shirt sleeves and bulletproof vests, their helmet badges glinting in the sun. A guy wanders across the road to join them, so achingly good-looking he's on the cusp of ugly. They're pointing down the road to where a truck is parked. Obviously they're solving some logistical problem with deliveries to one of the restaurants. I wander off to run the bath.

*   *   *

Okay, it's eleven thirty and no taxi. I'll ring them.

'Kins Cars,' says a bored voice.

'Hi, it's Vivienne Summers. I have a car booked for eleven thirty, but it hasn't arrived.'

'Hold on, please, madam.'

I'm blasted with what sounds like 'Greensleeves' played on a kazoo.

'Madam, I've spoken with your driver. He says five minutes.'

'Well, I hope it's no more than that. I have a wedding to get to, you know.'

'Yes, five minutes, madam.'

Okay, it's eleven forty-five. It's fine, it's okay, it'll be here soon. I'll just look out of the window and probably see the car waiting there. Weirdly, there's an unusual number of men milling about. I wander to the mirror again, inspecting my eyeliner. I don't normally wear so much black. It looks good, but is it a bit clubby rather than weddingy? My hair has been blasted into submission and is now passable. The dress looks great, though – cool and edgy.

Shit, it's five to twelve! Where the hell is the taxi? I ring again.

'Kins Cars,' says the can't-be-bothered voice.

'It's Vivienne Summers again. Where is my taxi? It's now twelve o'clock!'

'Hold on, madam.'

Kazoo Favourites has moved on to 'La Cucaracha'.

'Madam, so sorry, your car is stuck in traffic. He will be there in half an hour.'

'No! That's no good! Get me a taxi here now!'

'Madam, so sorry, half an hour is best we can do.'

I feel the breath being knocked out of me. 'Oh my God! What is the point of making a booking with you if you're just going to turn up when you feel like it? I have to get to a wedding and I booked a car for eleven thirty!' Suddenly I'm listening to a kazoo version of 'Nobody Does It Better'.

'Oh God, oh God, oh God.' I run a lap of the flat like a demented goose, before grabbing my handbag and flapping onto the street, feathers flying.

'Let there be a taxi. Let there be a taxi!' I get to the end of the street to find the whole road closed off and blocked with carnival floats. A steel band covers Madonna's 'Like a Virgin'. An Adonis wearing some sort of harness is dancing along the pavement. I grab him by one of his flying straps. 'Excuse me, what's going on?'

He shimmies and pouts. 'It's Gay Pride, darling!'

I look left and right. The floats line up as far as I can see, each one with a different theme. There are banners proclaiming, 'Gay, Catholic and Proud,' and, 'Parents of Gays and Proud.' The truck in front of me, the one with the steel drums, has been turned into a wicker bowl full of gay people dressed as fruit. Two cherries are joined at the head by a green stalk; the bananas in yellow thongs hold a flag declaring, 'Fruity and Funky.' Normally I'd be interested, but why my road? Why now? It's ten past twelve! I call Max.

'Hi, I'm ready. You downstairs?' he asks.

'No! I'm fucking stuck in a Gay Pride march, and I can't get a taxi!'

'Oh shit.'

'We're going to be late! I don't know what to do.'

'Okay, okay. Okay. Viv. We can do this. Where are you?'

'Outside the flat. On the main road.'

'What about if you go down the alley? Is that street open?' I walk to the end of the alley with my head down, phone pressed to my ear, swearing as offensively as I can, and check.

'There are police cars there too.'

'Walk down there and go down the next alley and wait outside that nice deli, okay? That's a cul-de-sac – they won't be going down there. I'll come and get you.'

'You won't be able to get a taxi close enough.'

'Go there and wait for me. I'm coming to get you.'

My heart is thumping. I turn and run down the alley, sending beer bottles clattering and dodging bins. I feel my heels sink into the cracks between the cobbles as I go, and imagine the filth of the street rising up and sticking to my beautiful, delicate dress. The next alley is worse. There's something living in a pile of boxes. I scuttle past, trying not to breathe. I round the corner and walk briskly to the deli.

It's at a crossroads. The streets to my left are deserted, all cordoned off for the march. I look at my phone and a minute has passed, then look again and it's ten minutes.

'Fucking hell! What fucking fuckery!' I feel a film of moisture on my skin and think about crying. I hear the rumble of an engine, turn towards it and a motorbike with two bug-eyed headlamps rounds the corner at speed, the rider in black leather and full helmet. As he gets closer, he raises his arm and circles to a stop alongside me. Max removes his helmet, grinning. This could not get any worse. He expects me to get on the back. No, it *is* worse – I'll have to put on a helmet and get on the back! I shake my head.

'Oh no . . . no way.'

'What? Like you have a choice.'

He dismounts and opens the carrier, getting out a canary-yellow open-face helmet and a huge leather jacket, and offers them to me. I take a step backwards. He gets back on the bike and starts it up, shouting over the rhythmic cough of the engine, 'It's half twelve!'

I grab the helmet, whimpering as I ram it down over my hair and fasten the strap under my chin. It compresses my head, turning my face into a squashed arse. I heave on the heavy jacket. It nearly reaches my knees and the enormous steel cups at the shoulders and elbows dig into my bare skin. I feel sweat trickle down my spine. I scramble up onto the bike, resting my high heels on the footrests. I'm about to arrange the dress when the bike lurches forward and the feather skirt foams around me. We're away and he canes it down the road, overtaking a bus. I'm perched precariously, clinging to his tasselled shoulders. If I try to look ahead, the wind hits me full in the face, splattering me with dust and airborne insects. I can feel something struggling in my right eye. I take cover behind his back, squeezing my arms around his chest like I'm clutching a log in the rapids. This bloody helmet must belong to a child; it's squeezing my head like a vice, but I can smell a spicy perfume over the oil and petrol of the bike, so maybe some pin-headed woman. It's destroying my hair, and the dress is being whipped by the wind over the back of the bike, so God knows what ruin is happening there. We stop at traffic lights and he places one foot down. I notice his shoes; I'm pleased they're smart and clean – thankfully he's made an effort. He lifts his visor and half turns, patting my thigh.

'You okay?'

'No!'

I see close up one of his green-flecked eyes and big nose in profile before the bike leaps forward and accelerates, almost leaving me sitting on the road. I lean into Max to brace myself and stay down until finally we enter side roads and the bike slows. There's the church! It's huge, verging on a cathedral. A vintage Jaguar is pulling up outside.

We skid into the driveway and the bike hiccups as Max changes down a gear, drawing the attention of a couple of grey-suited ushers who hover anxiously at the doorway. I struggle down and prise off the helmet as Max kills the engine. I can hear organ music starting up and the door of the Jag is opening. Jane's dad gets out of the car. He looks so like Hugo it's almost wrong. Max is quietly getting changed beside the bike. I slide out of the heavy jacket, all damp and dishevelled. I try to smooth out the dress and spot a brown

singe in the hem feathers where it's rested against the hot
exhaust pipe.

'Oh shit. Max, look at my bloody dress!'

'What?'

'It's all burnt on your bloody bike.'

At that moment the bride steps from the Jag. She looks
like a beautiful little doll, in a straight-cut sparkly dress that
pools behind her as she moves. The wind catches her veil
and her three bridesmaids in tastefully mismatched black and
white dresses step forward to fuss over it. She holds a bouquet
of tightly packed roses, bound with silver ribbon. I feel Max's
hand at the small of my back as he gently pushes me towards
the church.

'Close your mouth – you look like you're catching flies.'

'No, the flies are all in my eyes because of your bloody
bike!'

We smile at the ushers. I take an order of service and head
into the church, feeling bedraggled. The whole congregation
turns in anticipation when we step into the aisle. Max gives
a little wave and mouths, 'Hi,' before we slide into the nearest
pew.

'We got here, didn't we?' he whispers through gritted teeth.

I punch him in the leg. I try to arrange my dress a bit and
wipe a finger under my eye; it comes away black with eyeliner.
I'm wondering if I can get to a toilet and fix myself up before
I have to mingle when the organist launches into the 'Wedding
March' and we rise as the bride enters and steps carefully
down the aisle.

She smiles and turns her head from side to side, acknowl-
edging her friends. The sparkles on her dress wink and flash
in the sunlight as she walks. I take a moment to inspect Max,
all six foot two of him in a midnight-blue suit with a hint of
pinstripe, white shirt and thin pink tie. His usually unruly hair
is combed back and the curls rest on his collar. He's shaved

too, and he looks . . . really nice. I smile to myself and feel a rush of affection, then the familiar stomach lurch as I begin searching the congregation for Rob. I can't spot him. I bet he got here in plenty of time and is sitting up at the front.

I fan myself with the order of service, and we stand to sing 'To Be a Pilgrim'. I glance to my left and in the row next to me is the most exquisite-looking girl I've ever seen. She's like a stick of caramel. Her shiny hair, only a shade deeper golden brown than her skin, is pulled into a casual ponytail. Her simple but expensive shift dress is toffee-coloured, and perfectly tailored to skim over her petite willowy body. Her classy black slingback heels give just the right edge of sexiness. I suddenly feel like a man in drag. She obviously feels me giving her the once-over and turns to me with a breathtaking white smile. Her feline eyes are the clearest, prettiest blue, and she's hardly wearing make-up. She moves slightly and I catch a glimpse of her partner, and I feel my heart stop in horror. There, standing proudly next to her, singing his little heart out, is my Rob.

I try to breathe through the shock of it and carry on singing, but now I know he's there, I can only hear his voice.

'No foes shall stay his might, though he with giants fight . . .'

I feel faint, a mixture of panic and loss making a wave that breaks over me with a cold sweat. I look down at my scorched hem swinging next to her glossy leg. In a few minutes Rob will see me and introduce me to this beauty and I'll have to smile with my smudged make-up and helmet hair. I can't do it. I have to get out of here. I turn to Max, interrupting his bellowing baritone, and whisper, 'I've got to go.'

'What?'

'Move . . . that way . . . We're leaving.'

He looks wildly around as if something's got him by the leg; then he spots the girl and gawps until I dig him in the ribs and hiss, 'Rob's right there. That's his girlfriend!'

I'm leaning on Max with my back to Rob, but it's like trying to push a bear. A woman in front of us with a feathery hair decoration turns round; the hymn is coming to an end, the organist in the last throes. I'm thumping Max with all my strength.

'Go! Go!'

I feel a hand on my shoulder. I know it's Rob. There's no escape. Oh God, oh God, oh God . . . I suddenly start to laugh as if Max and I are sharing a hilarious joke and turn round, wiping my eyes and saying, 'Oh!' like I'm at the end of a belly laugh. Rob stands in a shaft of sunlight; his golden curls shining, his perfect mouth smiling calmly, his blue eyes full of affection.

'Hello, Vivienne.'

'Rob, hi!' I answer a little too hysterically, making the feathered headdress woman's husband turn round and glare.

'How are you?' he whispers.

'I'm well!'

The girl switches her perfect gaze from him to me. He catches hold of her hand, and sees me notice.

'This is Sam.' He's like a cat presenting me with a dead bird. Look what I've got!

'Hi, Sam.' I smile and she smiles, then frowns as Rob introduces me.

Thankfully the organist starts up with the intro to 'Lord of All Hopefulness' and I'm spared the excruciating explanations. I feel her eyes looking me over and every inch of me cringes. She moves much closer to Rob. They're practically having sex, sharing the one hymn-book. I'm glued to the spot, unable to sing, thoughts madly circling. I'm totally winded and for the rest of the service I can't bear to look to my left. I'm desperate for this to be over.

The bride and groom seem to be in slow motion as they walk down the aisle as a married couple. Jane smiles as she passes and I get the feeling I'm on a shipwreck and she's rowing away in the last of the lifeboats. I'm leaning heavily on Max and he suddenly gives way; we stumble into the aisle and scramble out into the friendly light of the July afternoon, as if tumbling from the mouth of a whale.

I'm breathing in sobs and pushing Max forward; we scarper round the corner until I find a cool wall to lean on, out of sight. I put a hand over my eyes.

'Oh Jesus! Oh my God!'

'I think you're supposed to say that kind of thing inside the church.'

'I can't do this. I really thought I could . . . but I can't.'

I try to breathe, listening to the sparrows fussing in the trees behind us and the chatter of wedding guests. Random exclamations like 'Lovely!' and 'Oh, I know!' flute into the air. My eyes fill up. A tear drops and soaks into the dusty pavement, sending a line of ants into panic. I see Max moving little piles of gravel with the toe of his shoe. I look up, shielding my eyes.

'What am I going to do?'

He smiles and reaches out his hand. 'Come on, my soggy friend. There's a pub. Let's go.'

The Laughing Monk is a refuge for lone men in bad jumpers. A couple of them look up in mild surprise as we enter arm in arm and take up stools at the bar. A television screen shows horseracing with the volume down. The gaunt, unhappy barman looks expectantly at us rather than bothering to speak. I order.

'Two large tequila and Cokes, please.'

'And two whisky chasers,' adds Max.

The barman sets down the drinks in grubby glasses without ice and takes the twenty pounds I offer. He brings a couple of coins for change, all without breathing a word.

I down the whisky; its warmth explodes in my stomach. Max sips his with narrowed eyes.

'Was it that bad, seeing him again?'

I think about this question. 'Bad' doesn't begin to cover it. This Sam girl is a disaster. I look down at myself; the magical dress now seems more fancy dress than cutting edge.

'Max, what do I look like?'

He finishes his whisky, looks me over and considers. 'You look like . . . a lovely bit of coconut ice.'

'You see, that's not the look I was going for.'

'Okay . . . a beautiful marshmallow.'

'Forget it.'

'No, really, Viv, you look gorgeous.'

'Did you get a look at Rob's girlfriend?'

'Yeah, she was all right.'

'She's stunning. He's obviously in love.' My eyes fill up with the shock of saying it. I take a long swig of tequila.

'He didn't hang about, then.'

'Well, you wouldn't, would you, with a girl like her?'

'She's not all *that*, Viv.'

I let out a sob and both nostrils fill up. I sniff and down the drink, slamming the glass on the bar. 'God, I feel so *stupid*! I mean, there was I, thinking all it would take was a nice dress and a bit of slap and I'd get him back. It isn't even a nice dress! I look like a fat fairy next to her.'

A man in a knitted tank top looks up from his paper. I know I'm wailing and this is nearly all the excitement they can bear in the Laughing Monk, but I don't care. Max orders two more large tequila and Cokes. Through the window I can see the church, and a photographer striding about arranging the congregation for photos. A few women in hats are already wandering across the green towards the hotel and the champagne reception.

'Viv, what are you on about – "fat fairy"? You make me laugh sometimes.'

'I don't know . . . I just want him back.' I slump miserably on the bar. Max puts his arm around my shoulders, speaking into my ear like he's pep-talking a boxer.

'Well, if you do – though God only knows why – he's right over there. That girl's no match for you. You're cool and sexy; she's . . . well, she's plastic and corporate. She might be pretty, but you . . . you're the real thing.'

I remain slumped. He nudges my elbow. 'C'mon, Viv, she can't hold a candle to you.'

'Really?'

'Really. Now, let's get one more round in and then we'll go and show them!'

By the time we leave the pub we've introduced ourselves to all the punters and made them aware of our cause. They've agreed that I'm very, very attractive and one man – Norman, I think his name was – said he couldn't imagine anyone nicer than me. So, buoyed by those honeyed words, we hit the reception.

6

Wedding Etiquette

1. *No fighting.*
2. *No stealing cutlery.*
3. *No giving impromptu speeches.*
4. *No sex in the toilets.*
5. *No heckling.*
6. *No histrionics.*
7. *No pole-, line- or break-dancing.*
8. *No getting dangerously smashed.*
9. *No unauthorised singing.*
10. *No talking, texting or Tweeting during the speeches.*
11. *No posting ugly pictures of the bride on Facebook.*
12. *No pets.*
13. *No children (unless a bouncy castle is provided).*
14. *No adults on the bouncy castle.*

'Ready?' asks Max, holding the doorknobs to the reception venue in both hands.

'Never been readier!' I shriek, and he goes to throw them open. Unfortunately we're at the wrong entrance and are directed round the corner by a helpful waitress. We slip into the throng unnoticed.

Max grabs two half-glasses of champagne from a passing tray, necks one and replaces the empty flute with a full one. I do the same. I'm feeling so much better! I look around at the chattering guests but can't see Rob. The hotel is old-fashioned grand, all panelled walls and brocade curtains. The champagne reception is in the grand entrance hall, where the walls are hung with portraits; eighteenth-century VIPs with no eyebrows and staring eyes. From the centre of the room a *Gone with the Wind*-style staircase rises.

Suddenly a kilted man appears at the top of them, holding bagpipes, and begins to play 'Wild Mountain Thyme' as he steps slowly down. Behind him come Jane and Hugo and, oh my God, Hugo is wearing a kilt! The bottle-green tartan rests above his fat knees, below which are thick white socks, tied round the tops with string and feathers. His calves bulge like piano legs. Jane has removed her veil and wears a twinkling tiara. They smile and make their way down to enthusiastic whistling and applause.

Max is shouting, 'Is he Scottish? I didn't know he was a Scot!'

They cut through the cheering guests like celebrities, complete with snapping photographer, and disappear through the huge double doors to the side of the hall. I step back and lean on a decorative radiator cover, feeling a little dizzy; these heels are too high. They are what Lucy would call 'sit-down shoes'. The lone piper appears again at the doorway, finishes the tune with a discordant squeal and lowers his bagpipes to make an announcement.

'Ladies and gentlemen, will you please make your way to the dining room for the wedding breakfast?'

Max links my arm with his and strides forward. 'Jesus, yes! I'm starving.' He pulls me across the rose-patterned carpet and the room seems to tilt. One of Hugo's jovial brothers has been squeezed into a suit and stands by the table plan; we give him our names and he guides us to our table. Max shakes his hand vigorously, saying, 'You must be very proud.'

The round guests' tables are arranged in a semicircle to get the best view of the top table. Ours is out on the edge and I feel momentarily hurt by this – I thought Jane and I had become close, but I suppose we met through Hugo and Rob playing rugby together, so I guess Rob's the 'one'. The entire room sparkles in silver and white, with two swan ice sculptures glistening at either end of it. The ceiling is strung with pearly balloons dangling silver ribbons. The white linen tablecloths are scattered with tiny silver sequins, miniature bottles of bubbles and party poppers. On every table stands a crystal vase of blousy white roses. The place settings are amazing, with elaborately folded napkins and gifts for the guests wrapped in glittery paper. On the back of the chairs, rosebud name cards are daintily attached with tinsel. As I walk to my seat I notice the table across from me, which bears the names Rob and Sam. They'll be sitting directly in my eye-line, then. I feel the euphoric booze bubble evaporate, leaving something sour in its place. I sink into my seat as my stomach tightens and twists. Max is introducing himself to everyone. A goat-eyed woman named Dawn is delighted with him, tinkling with laughter at his every word while her pinched-faced husband fiddles with his napkin. I pull Max's trouser leg and he sits down, finishing his amusing anecdote: 'So I said, it's Tipperary or bust!' The whole table, except pinched-faced husband, laughs hysterically.

Max turns to me, eyes shining. 'What's up?'

'Can you just stop, please?'

'What?'

'Trying so hard to be the life and soul. Why do you have to become more Irish when you're telling a joke, anyway?'

'I don't know . . . it makes it funnier.'

'It doesn't, actually; it makes you look like you've got special needs.'

'I have special needs!' he declares to the table. 'I specially need a drink!'

Dawn acknowledges him with a wanton smile. He points a party popper in my direction and the silver streamers catch in my hair, falling over my face. I look over to Rob's table, noticing with a pang of envy that everyone on it is young and mostly good-looking. He leans close to Sam and places his hand tenderly over hers, speaking in her perfect little ear. She looks down, smiling coyly, then answers something like, 'Me too.'

Max clicks his fingers in front of my nose. 'And come back. Don't look over there – your eyes go like an evil fairy godmother. Here, have more champagne.' He pours it into my red wine glass. There's a pause while I watch the bubbles rise and pop; then he tenderly pulls a few streamers from my hair.

'God, you're a gorgeous creature. Haven't we met before?' He grins.

'No.'

'Are you sure?'

'I think I would have remembered.' I yawn.

'Yes, I've got it. Didn't you graduate from Liverpool University in '01?'

'Might have.'

'Me too! Didn't we . . . ?' He makes a rocking movement with his hips.

'No!' I snap.

'D'you wanna?'

'What, dry hump?'

'No, you know . . .' He repeats the hip thing. I stare at him for a moment.

'You know, I'd love to, especially since you put it like that, but I'm a bit busy.'

The salmon mousse starters are arriving thick and fast. Our waitress, a plump adolescent with incongruous black bunches, dumps them down. A plate rocks in front of me, the cucumber decoration tumbling over. I feel hungry and sick at the same time. I glance at Rob and our eyes meet! My heart flips as he smiles briefly; then he leans to answer a question from a Swedish-looking girl to his left. Sam sits demurely beside him, her hands on her lap. She radiates good manners and taste. Rob often complained about me at parties – I'm too raucous and talkative, apparently. Sam smiles politely as her plate is thrown down and waits for the bride and groom to start eating before she takes a bite. That's good breeding, that is, and I can't compete. I spent my formative years being passed between adults like a relay baton; how was I to learn etiquette? I swallow down the huge glass of champagne and fail to suppress a burp. Max squeezes my knee as he explains the beauty of the Cliffs of Moher to old goat-eyes. She's practically wetting her pants with excitement. To my left is a man called Richard, who's something to do with Granada Television. He turns his long face towards me and attempts to make conversation.

'So, Viv, do you have any children?'

Particles of salmon mousse glisten on his moustache. He smells like a penguin.

'No, because my fiancé went off with someone else.' He pulls back his head as if he's been bitten on the nose. 'Yeah, he just went off with her before I'd had time . . . you know, to . . .'

Richard is at a loss. He starts speaking into the flower arrangement. 'Oh, right. Well, we have three. Our oldest, Josh, is fourteen; he's into music.'

I look around the room, smiling inanely. Jane really looks beautiful and relaxed. Hugo just looks like an overenthusiastic knob, but as I gaze at his razor-burn face and sausage fingers, weirdly, I feel a surge of pity for him. Rob is now feeding Sam with a bit of cucumber from his plate. I feel like he's taken his butter knife and skewered me through the heart. When I move my head, I get a sensation of being at sea. I

smile at Richard, who's still talking, seemingly to an imaginary
friend.

'Then there's Ruby, who's four now . . .'

'Are you talking to me? See, I'm not interested.' I
beam.

'Beg pardon?'

'Not interested in your kids.' As his face crumples in horror
I suddenly feel uncertain and a bit giddy, so I butter a roll.
Richard turns his back on me.

I eat the bread as the starter dishes are cleared and
replaced by plates of roast beef. I chew thoughtfully and
examine the plate. There's a slice of meat looking like the
leather tongue from a shoe, limp yellow spring greens and
a Yorkshire pudding adrift on a pool of gloopy gravy. I grab
the waitress.

'I'm a vegetarian.'

She looks puzzled. 'Oh, we haven't got you down. Did you
order a vegetarian meal?'

'No, but I want one.' I hand the plate of beef to her and
turn back to my bread roll, suddenly starving. I haven't
eaten bread for over a week. Actually, I've hardly eaten
anything for over a week. I take Richard's bread roll as
well.

Max is getting on my nerves with his 'Oirish' act, so I
interrupt him. 'He's been living in England for the past sixteen
years, you know.'

Max clamps his arm tightly around my shoulders,
squeezing me into him. 'Ah, but you never lose it, though,
do you?'

Dawn laughs and Max looks down at me.

'And how are you doing?' He glances at Richard's back.
'I see you've managed to ingratiate yourself with everyone.'

'Let's get more champagne.'

'Are you sure?' He holds up his hand. 'How many fingers?'

'Eleven. Get me a drink.'

People are scraping their plates towards the end of their meals when mine is plonked before me. It's half a red pepper filled with rice topped with a drizzle of mushroom soup. Richard glances at it with distaste. I poke it with a knife and wonder if I can change back to the roast when the lone piper appears beside the top table. Knife hits glass and he is 'praying silence for the father of the bride'. Jane's dad gets to his feet. It's uncanny how much he resembles Hugo; more than Hugo's own father. I examine Hugo's mum – *could* she have had an affair with Jane's dad? Because, if so, surely she should declare it now, and stop Jane continuing a sham marriage to her half-brother. Maybe I'll point that out to Jane later; she'll thank me in the long run.

Jane's dad speaks lovingly of his daughter. I refill my glass. Slides are shown of Jane sitting on a bike and smiling with gappy teeth while he tells an amusing tale of how he taught her to ride a two-wheeler. There's Jane as a teenager with electric-blue eyeliner and braces. Jane's dad tells us how he chauffeured her around town. I wonder if my father would have loved me, or if he ever even knew I was born. I think of my granddad, and how he used to let me steer the car while he pressed the pedals and changed gear. I suddenly wish I could see Granddad just one more time, and feel a bit teary. I glance over as Sam cuddles up to Rob, his arms draped casually around her, his hand gently patting her hip. I close my eyes and take a good few gulps of champagne. Jane's dad is telling us how much he loves his daughter, how proud she makes him, and warning Hugo that she will never back down in an argument. He proposes a toast to true love, and we all stand. Rob and Sam clink glasses and look into each other's eyes. Then everyone sits down and I'm left standing, swaying like a tree in the wind. A hush falls over the room. I hear a sort of crashing in my head as faces gawp. Rob looks straight into my eyes, alarm clanging across his face.

'I would like to say something!' I feel surprised to hear my own raised voice. I glance across to Jane; she looks a bit worried. 'About true love . . . Because sometimes you don't realise . . .' Max grabs my hand, but I pull away. 'You don't realise you've found true love till it's too late, and then . . . it's disappeared.' I look at Rob with what I hope is an expression of deep meaning, and speak directly to him. 'It's not too late for us.' Sam looks as if an old tramp has just flashed her. 'I really miss you, Rob.' There is a horrible silence; then suddenly Max is standing beside me, raising his glass.

'We'd like to propose a toast: to true love! It's never too late!' The relieved guests leap to their feet with their drinks held high as I lock my eyes to Rob's. Voices rise around us.

'True love! It's never too late!' He gazes at me for a few seconds with such awful sadness before slowly shaking his head, and I sink down into my seat.

The excited chatter takes ages to quieten. Hugo stands tinging his glass for all he's worth, but is ignored. Whole tables turn round, straining to get a look at me. I sit motionless, staring straight ahead. My scalp tingles and I feel a heated blush rise around my ears.

Max puts his arm around me. 'You okay?'

I sniff and wipe my eyes with the back of my hand. 'No.' I stare at Sam; she's nodding vigorously with the man next to her; then, catching my eye, she smirks. I stand up suddenly and there is a collective gasp before the room goes silent. She leans back in her chair with a kind of amused expectation on her face. You could hear a pin drop as the room waits for me to speak.

'I . . . I'm just going to the loo.'

The gasps and giggles start up as I walk out, trying to hold my head up amid murmurs of 'That dress!' and 'Ridiculous!' As the doors close on the wedding breakfast I whimper and stagger across the hall to the toilets. The ladies' is tiled in marble, with a brightly lit mirror running the full length of one wall. I see myself walk by, a strange bedraggled ballerina, a doll left out in the rain. I gaze at the reflection: the black eyes stare; the red mouth dominates. I put my hands to my hair, smoothing out the ends and trying to fluff up the helmet-flattened top. I lean my elbows on the little shelf under the mirror and rest my forehead on the heels of my hands. I'm suddenly totally exhausted. I try some vocalisation.

'Oh God. Oh Gooooood.' It feels good, so I try, 'Oh no, oh nooooo.'

I hear the toilet door swish open and quickly lift my head, pretending to apply make-up. It's her! I look at her reflection as I slide on more red lipstick.

'Was that you I heard crying just now?' she asks in mock sympathy.

'No.'

'Oh, I thought I heard someone crying, "Oh no," or something.'

'Not me,' I say chirpily.

She doesn't go to the loo; instead she stands next to me at the mirror and slicks on a little lip gloss. Our faces are so different – she's honey-coloured and natural; I'm ghostly pale and made up to the nines, and next to her my head looks strangely large. I try not to look. She washes her hands.

'It's difficult, isn't it? I mean, you need to use soap to wash your hands, but you don't want it getting into the setting,' she says, gazing at her perfectly tanned hand. There's something sparkly there and I turn my head slightly to get a better look. She stretches out her fingers a little. She's wearing a gleaming engagement ring – pink solitaire diamond, platinum band. I look from the ring to her face and she smiles. 'So . . . it would appear, my dear, that it *is* a little too late for you and Rob after all.'

My insides retreat like a wave before swelling up unbearably.

'You're engaged?' I croak. She opens her beautiful eyes wide and nods. 'You're getting married – you and Rob are?' The shock of it hits me like a bucket of iced water. I'm frozen, lipstick in hand, mouth open in horror.

'I'm afraid so.' She looks in the mirror and slides the band from her ponytail, tossing her silky chestnut hair to one side like she's in a shampoo advert. 'I know what you're thinking. Everyone's saying it's so sudden, but he's insisting, so we're off to get hitched in Bali next month.' She spritzes a little perfume behind her ears and turns to me, head on one side. 'So I guess it's time for you to get over him and move on . . . After all, he has.' She sashays to the door, turns round and gives a little wave. '*Ciao!*'

I'm left gawping at her back. My veins run icy; I can't take this in. He's getting married? Not two months ago he was engaged to me. He's getting married to her after less than two months, but he couldn't marry me after five years? What is he trying to do to me? It's not enough to break my heart, he has to shatter it and then shit on top? Jesus! I'm pacing, making stiletto marks in the beige carpet and shaking my head, trying to comprehend it all. It can't be true, he wouldn't do this . . . but that ring! I can't let it happen; she *can't* steal my future husband. I feel a bit queasy and need to sit for a moment, but I'm even dizzy sitting down. I can hear someone calling me, but the strange thing is, my vision keeps going in and out of focus. I'm peering into the room and then Max is standing there.

'Ah, so this is where the cool set hangs out!' He slides his back down the full-length mirror until he's sitting next to me. He smiles. 'How you doing?'

I squint at him. 'It's the ladies'. What you doin' in here?'

'Just trying to pick up women.'

'Oh.' I grin manically, then remember that bitch. 'They're engaged. She's got a fuck-off ring.'

He looks down at the carpet and pats my leg. 'Why don't I get us a taxi?'

'Engaged.' I shake my head, sending the room sliding. 'She is engaged to Rob!'

'Ah, it'll be a rebound thing.' He takes my hand and gives it a squeeze. 'It'll never last. Have you seen the arse on her?'

'Max! She's about a size eight.'

'Around the tits.'

He looks at me, grinning, willing me to laugh, and I can't help it. We sit on the toilet floor, giggling. The room seems to shift and spin. I stagger to my feet and stand there, wobbling. I offer him my hand.

'Let's get a drink!' He smiles and I suddenly think he's very good-looking.

I'm hoping to sneak to the bar, but we step out of the toilet into a throng of baying women. Jane stands on the staircase, holding her bouquet aloft. The gentle chatter and soft laughter at dinner have been replaced by something sinister; the women shriek and cackle as Jane waves the bouquet madly. A few men hover nervously around the edges. The photographer weaves through the women taking snaps.

'Are you ready?' Jane screams.

'Yes!' howls the pack, and they start to jostle for pole position. I lean on Max as we try to pick our way past – and then I spot Sam. Right at the back, raising her willowy arms up like a beach volleyball babe. Rob leans on the wall behind her, laughing. Something inside me snaps. Something that's been worn down to the thinnest thread just gives way and I'm breaking free from Max and running. If I can just get that bouquet, it'll prove to Rob it should be me he marries. I must not let her get it. She cannot get it – not while there's breath in my body. If she gets it, all is lost. Jane throws the bouquet with a harridan's cry and, airborne, it soars over the hairdos and the outstretched manicured fingers, gaining momentum, flying in a graceful arc and then falling almost directly into Sam's grasp. I jump forward, straining with every sinew. She's concentrating hard and doesn't notice me. Her fingers just touch the stems before I close my hands around it and land on her. She yelps, and as we fall to the ground I feel a sharp pain in my nose as her bony elbow comes down on my face. For a minute there's a struggle as she tries to snatch the flowers from my grasp, but I scrabble to my feet, waving the bouquet high and jumping up and down.

'I got it! I got it!' I run a mini lap of honour in front of Rob and I feel a little flutter in my tummy as he grins. I hold the bouquet as if I'm a bride and swagger over to him.

'That was for you, you know.' I smile my sexiest smile.

'Wow, Viv! Very athletic.' He laughs and hands me a hand-kerchief. 'Here – you're dripping on your prize.'

I look down. Huge red spots fall onto the delicate white roses. I touch my face; my nose is streaming with blood. I hold my head back, pinching it at the bridge. 'Oh God, my nose is bleeding!' I turn round. The baying women are silent, staring at me aghast. 'Er, hello! My nose is bleeding. Can somebody get me some ice?' I turn back to Rob, but he's cuddling Sam, laughing and stroking her hair. 'Hey, you! You bust my nose!' She glances over her shoulder before Rob leads her away, shielding her with his arm. Max steps into the circle of space that has opened around me and hands me a napkin.

'Well, that went as well as can be expected,' he says quietly, and guides me to the door.

7

A Soundtrack for Heartbreak

1. Sorrow
Goodbye, My Lover – James Blunt*
Nothing Compares 2 U – Sinead O'Connor
I Can't Make You Love Me – Bonnie Raitt
Ex-Factor – Lauryn Hill
All Out of Love – Air Supply
* Caution: Contents extremely sad

2. Wrath
See Ya – Atomic Kitten
I Never Loved You Anyway – The Corrs
Survivor – Destiny's Child
I Will Survive – Gloria Gaynor*
Go Your Own Way – Fleetwood Mac
* Enhanced by mucho vino tinto *and a bit of*
a dance routine

3. Healing
Sail On – The Commodores
I Can See Clearly Now – Johnny Nash
1,000 Times Goodbye – MegaDeth*
Believe – Cher
Goody Goody – Benny Goodman
* Avoid if at all vengeful

First there's light poking me in the eyes, then a drilling
sound. My tongue's huge. It's hotter than hell. I try to shift

my body, but there's piercing pain. My desiccated brain gropes for explanations. I've been dragged from a train wreck. I've been beaten up and left for dead in a desert. I'm aware of a weight next to me and feel the warmth of a living thing. As I turn my head towards it, a heavy weight slides inside my skull. I squint into the light and I can distinguish the outline of Dave, Max's cat, in bed with me. Recollections begin to slot into place like cards being dealt – excruciating, full-colour flashbacks.

I slide my hand under the covers. I'm still wearing knickers, also an Arsenal T-shirt. I struggle onto one elbow and my head throbs like a heartbeat. I peer at Dave. He's sphinx-like. Front paws tucked under. He blinks and turns up the drilling purr. Pea-green curtains send a sickly light over Max's bedroom. I've never been so thirsty in my life. Next to the bed are a bucket, tissues, a pint of orange squash and a packet of paracetamol. I seize the pint glass and drain half the squash. My hands are shaking as I press out two tablets and swallow them down with the rest of it; then I lie down again and close my eyes. Dave is kneading the covers with his claws; I push him and he takes this as an invitation and tries to curl up on my chest, sweeping his feather-duster tail over my nose.

'Fuck off, Dave!' I shove him off the bed. He clings on, scrabbling desperately before landing on the grey carpet. Cat hairs set off a sneezing fit and blood clots appear in my hand. The bones of my skull ache, even my teeth. Jesus, I'm seriously ill. I lie back again, trying to dodge pain and not think, but I've seen it and there's no escape. The £1,000 dress lies crumpled across an old armchair, the bodice splattered with blood, the skirt smeared black, the hem singed. On the floor is Jane's trampled, blood-spotted wedding bouquet. It's a *Brides of Dracula* costume. Reality hits me like body blows. Wham, I remember Rob's stunning new girlfriend. Wham, I stood up and made a speech. Wham, wham, the bouquet! Then a knockout blow to the head sends my brain clanging like a pinball . . . HE'S GETTING MARRIED! I feel my heart retreat.

I'm tiny, hopeless, beaten. I stare at an ancient cobweb hanging from the paper shade. I'm searching for a scrap of decorum, perhaps one moment when I wasn't totally embarrassing, but . . . nothing. I hear the flushing of a toilet. Max taps on the door, then appears, in jeans and a faded T-shirt. I turn my head like a dying person to look at him. He smiles and sits on the bed.

'Morning.'

'Help me,' I whisper.

'Is it bad?'

'You wouldn't let an animal suffer like this.'

He brushes my hair from my forehead. His hand feels cool. 'Can I get you something to eat?'

'Urgh. No.' My eyes are filling up. I look down at my hands.

'Dry toast or anything?'

I shake my head slowly. 'The dress is ruined.' We look over at it.

'Well, it'll come in handy for Halloween parties.'

'And he's getting married.' A tear spills.

'Yeah.' He lies next to me, lifts my head onto his shoulder, and we stay like that for a few long minutes. I smell pine washing powder. The curtains shift with the breeze from the ill-fitting window. A dog yaps on the street.

'Did you undress me?' I ask suddenly.

'Yeah . . . You passed out.'

'You took my bra off.'

'Yes, Viv, I took it off.'

'But you left my pants on.'

'Well, I put them back on after I buggered you.'

'Oh. Nice.'

'What do you think I did? I put you to bed,' he laughs.

'Thanks.'

'Don't mention it.'

'I mean, thanks for everything . . . For looking after me yesterday.'

'It was nothing.'

'I made a total arse of myself,' I groan.

'No . . .' He thinks for a minute. 'Okay, yeah, but in a good way.'

I listen to Max's strong heart beating like a fist on a door. The paper shade turns clockwise and back again. I'm paralysed and terrified of my own helplessness. I always know what to do – that's my thing. I just get on with it. Now I'm empty. I'm depending on another person, on Max.

I glance at his face – eyes closed, mouth slightly open, gently snoring. 'Max!'

He jolts awake. 'What?'

'Don't leave me.'

'Ah . . . I never will.' He pats me a little too hard on the head.

'I mean right now. I'm completely gutted . . . and really, really ill.' He props himself up on one elbow, looking down at me and frowning.

'Know this. Laughing boy is not worthy.' I start to interrupt, but he holds up a finger and presses it over my mouth. 'Whatever heinously embarrassing things you did – and, let's face it, there were a few – you still have more grace in one arse cheek than any other girl there. Now say it.'

'Say what?'

'Laughing boy is not worthy and I have more grace in one arse cheek than any other girl there.'

'I'm not saying that.' But I do.

'You're only ill because we drank like whales. What we'll

do is have a huge Sunday dinner at the Eagle and some hair of the dog.' My stomach lurches; the orange squash rises. Max lies back, lifting my head to rest on his chest.

'I'm still gutted. You can't just say, "He's not worthy." I can think it with my head, but my heart . . . it's *bleeding* for him. What's your answer for that?'

'Suicide.' I turn my back to him and curl myself up like a child. He puts his arms around me, speaking close to my ear. 'In my experience of heartbreak, which is great—'

'Who broke your heart?'

'There've been many. Most recently, the girl in the café near Ladbroke Grove tube.'

'What happened?'

'Saw her with a boyfriend.'

'You don't even know her,' I snort.

'I still feel pain. You must *feed* the heart with music and poetry and art.'

'Oh, here we go.'

'Especially country music. The suffering makes your own situation seem much better. Like, "When you leave me, walk out backwards and I'll think you're walking in."'

'I don't believe that's even a song.'

'Well, it is. "Loving you makes leaving you easy." That's a great one. "Lu-u-ving yooo, why d'you make it so hard to do?"' he croons.

'Did you say suicide is the only alternative?'

'Well, it helps to know that other people have suffered too. You're not alone.'

'Have you considered a career in greetings cards?'

'Sarcastic witch. Are you looking for a Chinese burn?'

I'm smiling. Then I remember about Rob. Each time it comes into my head I start to sift through the evidence, trying to convince myself it's not real. I just can't accept it. The man is mine. He doesn't own any underpants not bought by me, or any pillowcases. I realise it must be a mistake and my heart stops clamouring. Then I picture the ring on Sam's elegant finger. He *is* getting married – it is true and it won't go away. I feel my guts squeeze. Max is twirling a strand of my hair round his finger. I shift my position, using his stomach as a pillow and look up at him.

'He's getting married in Bali, you know.'

'Wanker.'

'He doesn't even cope well in the heat. When we went to Sicily, he wouldn't come on any boat trips with me because he needed to lie down between twelve and three.'

'Weedy wanker.'

'It's because he's worried about skin cancer – even with sunblock, he's got very soft skin . . .'

Max is looking at me intently.

'Let me paint your portrait.'

In all the years I've known Max he's wanted to paint me, but I've always refused. I felt it would somehow ruin things, be embarrassing. Now, lying here, empty as a drum, on the rise and fall of his breath, I feel like abandoning myself and being completely in his world – and also I've nothing to lose.

'Go on, then.'

He sits up quickly. 'Really?'

'Yeah.'

'Great! That's great . . . Now?'

'Okay.'

He's up and out of the room as if there's a fire. Then he returns.

'You all right? D'you want anything?'

'Tea. A bucket of sweet tea.'

* * *

After a while I follow him out, deliberately avoiding looking at the wreckage of my dress, or in a mirror, and cross the little hallway into his studio. There's a grey velvet armchair in front of the window. I hear the ting of a spoon in a mug. A virgin canvas waits on an easel. Tubes of acrylic paint are lined up next to a jar of brushes, and some torn cloths give off the sanitary smell of turpentine. The room feels comfortably warm as the morning sun catches swirling dust specks. There's a pile of artefacts and assorted junk in one corner, and a bicycle leans against the wall, some of his recent work propped up near it. I step over to take a look at a striking dark-haired nude. She's lying on a sage-green couch, one of her ivory legs bent at the knee and the other stretched out languidly. Her slender arms make a diamond behind her head. Her tiny breasts are rose-tipped, the colour matching her heart-shaped mouth. Dark green eyes gaze lazily ahead. She's insolent, erotic and breathtaking. I stare at her eyes; there's such power in them. She makes me ashamed to look. Max enters and stands behind me for a moment. I feel his breath on the back of my neck and step aside. He hands me the tea and I take a sip as we both look at the painting.

'Who is she?'

'That's Lula.'

'You never mentioned a Lula. There was a Mary-Jane and a Stephanie . . . There was that awful Patti.'

'Smelly Pat?'

'Yeah, Smelly Pat but not Lula.'

He smiles and shrugs. 'She's just a model who sat for me.'

'She's very beautiful. Are you sure you want to paint me, hung-over and wearing your Arsenal T-shirt?'

'You're very beautiful. And you can take it off.'

'No, thanks.'

'Well, sit down, then.' He gestures to the grey armchair.

The velvet is warm on the bare skin of my legs. He studies my face for a few moments.

'Are you comfortable?' he asks. I nod.

His expression is serious as he sketches; his eyes seem darker. He looks at me as an object, scrutinising the shape of the chair and my body as if he is looking for the first time. As his eyes flit from me to the canvas, the sunlight catches the tips of his dark eyelashes, and his sideburns.

'Did you know you have a tinge of the ginge in you?' He doesn't reply. 'It's because you're a Celtic immigrant, isn't it?'

'Hmm. Yeah.'

I can't get a rise out of him. The warm sun, the smell of paint and the gentle scratching of the pencil are hypnotic. I hold the mug of tea between my palms and watch him working. I feel like I've known him for ever. He was evicted from our halls of residence for brewing beer in the wardrobe, and we met when he set up the Poetry Appreciation Society and I was the only other member for six weeks. We held meetings, drinking cheap cider and reciting poems. I once knew Keats's 'Ode to Autumn' by heart, but now I can only remember one of Max's stupid limericks. I reel it off to him: 'There was a young lass from Herne Hill, who used dynamite sticks for a thrill. They found her vagina in North Carolina, and bits of her tits in Brazil.'

'Ah, the Poetry Society. We were so learned.' He smiles.

An earnest fresher joined the following term: pretty, bespectacled and blighted with pimples that nestled at the sides of her nostrils. This didn't stop Max seducing her and telling me how she howled like a she-wolf in bed.

'Remember that girl who joined? What was her name?'

'Dunno.'

'You shagged her! The one who did the wolf thing?'

'Oh yeah. Jane.' He narrows his eyes, remembering. 'Janet.'

He's squirting paint onto the canvas, frowning, and he doesn't respond. It's amazing, I suppose, that he and I have always remained just friends. I mean, I love him. He's my best friend in many ways and I can definitely see his appeal – he's tall and not bad to look at, but it's just that I know him too well. And he is filthy. He doesn't believe in sell-by dates, and he once had cat fleas and *didn't know*. His idea of gourmet is posh mustard on a ready meal. He thinks fashion is an infringement of human rights. Also, he's told me too much about all the girls he's been with and what he's done with/to them. I know one of his ex-girlfriends still sends him naked pictures of herself and I know he keeps them. On top of that he's an Artist and permanently skint. I watch him spreading paint onto the canvas. He puts down the knife, lights a cigarette and looks at me.

'Mind if I smoke?'

'I suppose not, as long as you know you're increasing your chances of getting cancer by fifty per cent with every drag and killing me as well.'

'That's the way I like it, baby. I don't want to live for ever.' He winks and stands there smiling. I watch the smoke drift into a question mark, curling from his mouth. I look at the red of his bottom lip and suddenly imagine kissing it. I shift myself in the chair.

'Are we nearly done? My neck's aching.'

He throws the brushes into a jar and puts the cigarette down in a lid.

'Yep, done. I think I've got the essence of you.' He stretches both arms above his head, arching his back. His T-shirt rises up and I notice a line of dark hair disappearing beneath his jeans.

'Can I see it?'

'No. It's not finished.' He takes the canvas off the easel and walks out with it, leaving me sitting there. 'C'mon. I'll lend you some clothes. Let's go to the pub.'

8

Take Advice

7 July, 06:11

From: Lucy Bond
To: Vivienne Summers
Subject: Re: Ask Lucy

Hey V,
You know we discussed me being the agony aunt on the website? Well, here's a little sample of my skills!

Dear Lucy,
I recently discovered my boyfriend had been sending texts of a sexual nature to his colleague. When challenged, he said it was 'just a bit of fun'. I then found out the recipient is a forty-year-old man named Nigel, who I rang, and he seemed really funny and nice.
I'm due to marry my boyfriend next year but now I feel confused. What should I do?
M x

Dear M,
Threesome?
Lucy

It's Monday morning, muggy and grey with a light drizzle. I'm coming down with something nasty. My throat feels prickly; my eyeballs ache; there's pressure in my sinuses. I'm wrapped in my blue velour dressing gown, skipping through emails, none of them from Rob. I send a quick message to Lucy: *'Lucy, nice advice to "confused about boyfriend" woman. A threesome. The answer to all our ills. Viv.'*

I need to get ready for work so I slope off to the bathroom and run the shower. I pull down my lower eyelids in front of the mirror – I'm definitely anaemic: there's no colour there at all. Actually, that's very worrying – how am I not dead? I step into the shower, stand under the drilling needles of water and squirt some fruity shampoo onto my head. It's supposed to make you orgasmic. I feel sick. I get out, wrap myself in a huge pink bath sheet and crumple onto the toilet, resting my forehead on my palms. Why do I feel so shit? Max and I drank half a bottle of red each in the pub yesterday, but I was sober when I came home around ten and I went straight to bed. I wrap a towel round my hair and go to put the kettle on the gas to boil. As I'm considering what to wear, an email pings: *'I know . . . am agony aunt queen x'*

I make tea and try to get dressed, but the effort of putting pants on leaves me exhausted, and now it's eight fifteen and I'm going to be late. I lie down with my mobile phone and, with a huge wave of relief, decide I can't go in.

I find a text from Max, sent at midnight. *'You're lovely, you are.'* See, that's why Max is one of my best friends: he just knows exactly what you need to hear and when. I feel my smile fade, though, as I ring work. I'm amazed when Christie answers.

'Barnes and Worth gifting, buyers' department, Christie speaking. How can I help?'

'Hi, Christie, it's Viv. You're in early.'

'Aw, thanks for noticing, Viv. I'm turning over a new leaf!' So she won't be schlepping in at ten and eating breakfast at her desk any more, then. 'Yeah, I just thought it's time to concentrate on my career!' She gives a high little laugh, because this is clearly a joke.

'Great. Good for you. Listen, I—'

'Yeah, I mean, after the verbal warning and that, I'll be honest with you, I thought, Well, fuck it – I'll just leave! But then, you know, I thought about it over the weekend and I just decided, Christie, what you gotta do is pick yourself up and just keep on trying.'

'Oh, right. Well, that's great, Christie. Listen, can you let everyone know I won't be in today? I have a horrible cold and I've got work I can be getting on with here. If anyone needs me, I'll have my mobile on.'

'Oh, that's good.'

'What is?'

'That croaky voice you put on then! It's only me, Viv – you don't have to pretend you're ill.'

'I am ill!'

''Course you are.'

'Actually, I'm anaemic with the beginnings of tonsillitis.'

She does that tinkling giggle again. 'Aw, okay, Viv. I'll tell them you're not coming in.'

'Good. And there's that pile of filing next to my desk. Can you make sure that gets done today?'

'Oh . . . yes.'

'And can you make sure you get the safety reports on the umbrellas, the African-range beads and the nailcare set written up?'

'All of them?'

'Well, you're in early.'

'Okay.'

'That's all for now. I'll ring you later with anything else.'

'Okay. I hope you feel better soon, Viv.'

'Bye, Christie.' I hang up on the cheeky minx.

I lie back on the pillows and put on my blackout eye mask. If I could just sleep for a few hours, everything would be better. But even now as I'm concentrating on slowing my breathing, my mind starts the torment. The light is too bright and the head traffic too loud. I get up, dress and hurry to catch the next train to Kent.

Stepping along the wide pavements of this leafy suburb is like stepping back in time. Turning the corner towards Nana's, I feel like a child. The house stands at the end of a cul-de-sac, spread across the plot like a fat man at the head of a table – pale, shabby and welcoming. I pass a guy pushing a small girl on a new two-wheeler. They glance at me. I remember Granddad holding the saddle of my wobbly bike in exactly that spot, over twenty-five years ago. I crunch onto the gravel driveway of the house, press the bell, peer through the frosted glass of the door and then ring again. I think it'd be more than I could bear if she wasn't in, but I never thought to ring first. I wait in the cloying heat, feeling my cotton dress begin to stick to my skin. She might be in the garden. I step across windfall apples to peer over the side gate, but I can't see her. I ring the bell again, this time half convinced she isn't there; I hold it down for a few seconds. There's a movement; then the shape of her appears, coming to the door.

As she fiddles with the lock I hear her shout, 'Hold on a moment, hold on . . .' Finally she pulls open the door. 'Oh, Viv! Hello.' She pulls me towards her. I feel the jutting bones of her shoulders as we embrace. She takes my face in her hands and there's a light floral scent of hand-cream. 'What a surprise! We were expecting you yesterday.' Funny how she still says 'we'. Granddad passed away two years ago. The morning he died, she took him a cup of tea and chatted to him for half an hour before realising he'd gone.

'I know. Sorry.' She smiles, waiting for an explanation, but there isn't one except me being crap. I wipe my hands over my dress. A beat passes as we stand in the carpeted hallway with the photos, paintings, memories and ghosts.

'Well, you're here now. What a treat.' She searches my face, then puts her hands on my shoulders and pulls me into another hug, releasing me with, 'Come in. Come in! I love to have you home.'

I follow her downstairs to the kitchen, noticing how she grabs the banister tightly with each step, the tendons of her hands standing out like broken umbrella spokes.

'I bet you'd love a coffee!' This way she has of exclaiming a thought like a madwoman used to embarrass me. She'd suddenly stop when we were rushing somewhere and gasp, 'Oh! So beautiful!' because she'd seen a spider's web, or, 'Let's have cake!' when I was concentrating hard on my revision. I think of how ashamed I was to have an old lady collect me from school. I wanted a mum like my friends had, one who wore make-up and high-heeled boots. Every day she'd be there in her kaftan, standing resolutely in the playground even though I'd asked her to wait in the car, and every day I tried to deny her.

The kitchen has a permanent Christmassy, yeasty smell. Dried plants hang from the ceiling above a tiled border of red apples. I slide onto the bench by the huge oak table and gaze out to the garden. The sun is breaking through in patches, highlighting the geranium pots on the patio. Nana whistles softly as she spoons coffee into the machine, an ancient tangle of pipes. It starts up, banging and hissing, eventually yielding perfect cappuccinos. She folds up her blue linen dress around her legs like the edges of an envelope and sits across from me, happily sipping her coffee, leaving the white foam clinging to her upper lip.

'Oh, Viv, the garden's been beautiful. Really, those roses have just gone on and on!'

I put down my cup. 'They're always gorgeous.'

'But this year they've been . . . exceptional.' Her face shines. 'And the fragrance!' I look to the edge of the garden. The lawn has become straggly, the leaves unraked.

'Don't you get lonely here?'

'Oh dear, is this one of those "it's time you went into a home" conversations?'

''Course not! I was just thinking . . . is this how you imagined things turning out?'

She smiles, tilting her head to one side. 'I try not to think of how things might turn out.'

'Don't you regret anything?'

'Not really. I think I've made peace with myself. I've been happy, done my best.' She scratches at a mark on the table. 'Why do you ask that?' She looks into my eyes. 'Do you have regrets?'

'Yeah,' I sigh.

'Oh! I have ginger biscuits.' As she rises to get them, I notice stiffness in her movements and feel a flash of irritation. She calls from behind the pantry door, 'You said on the phone about Rob finding someone else?'

'Yeah, he has. He's getting married.' I rest my chin on my hand to stop it wobbling.

She sits down with a plate of biscuits and looks at me for a while, then speaks carefully: 'And? How do you feel?'

'Terrible. Desolate.'

'Because you want to marry him?'

'I *was* marrying him . . . nearly three months ago.'

She sighs and looks out to the garden. 'Oh, there! Did you see that little wren?' I look up sharply and she puts down her cup and takes my hand. 'Oh, darling, I know this seems like the end of the world. But it will pass, you'll see.' We look into each other's eyes, mine filling with tears, hers extraordinarily blue and bright. She squeezes my hand tightly and pats it. 'In time you'll come to realise just what a cunt he is.'

My breath catches in my throat. 'Nana!'

'What? There are a lot of them about.'

'You can't say that!' She looks pleased to get such a

reaction. I shake my head at her. 'I loved him . . . I mean, love him.'

'Don't you realise what a beautiful girl you are? How funny and clever and warm? You could have another man in a minute.'

'But I want him.'

'I know.' She wipes foam from the inside of her cup with a finger and licks it. 'And knowing you, you'll get him. The question is, then what?'

'I'll marry him and have his babies,' I say quickly.

'Will you?' She looks into the distance sadly.

'Nana, it's different from when you were young. I'm thirty-two, he's the only man who's ever proposed to me, and it's not like there's a queue outside my door!'

'When I was young, you went from being a daughter to a wife to a mother.' She looks over to a framed photo on the windowsill of her and Granddad as a young couple, sitting on a seaside wall. She's holding her hair back to stop it blowing over her face. He looks like he's won first prize. 'Women have much more choice now.'

'Choice . . . yeah. It's not all it's cracked up to be.'

'Well, follow your heart, I'd say . . . even into disaster.' She smiles and stands to clear the cups. 'And there is a queue, Vivienne; you just can't see it.'

I wander despondently into the small sitting room off the kitchen. Granddad's armchair faces the window. A layer of dust dulls the sideboard with the family photos. I pick up one of Granddad and wipe it with my dress. He's smiling in a panama hat. Below it Nana's written, 'Lawrence, 2009' – the year before he died. There are a few of me aged seven after I was dropped off in my pyjamas, never to be collected. One photo is achingly familiar: my mother as a child. I used to keep it by my bed. I smile at that idea now; I thought loving her more would bring her back. I put the picture down. There are a couple of Mum and me together, a rare one where she's smiling.

I hear the doorbell and Nana calls, 'That'll be Reg! I've invited him for lunch.'

Why does this annoy me? I replace the pictures on their dust-free silhouettes and wander back to the kitchen. Reggie appears, clutching a bunch of sweet peas. His solid body seems to clog up the room like over-large furniture. He speaks in a comedy cockney accent. His arrival changes the energy; Nana is chatting and chirruping like a budgie. Suddenly she's preparing lunch.

'I've a nice bit of ham, Reg.'

'Lovely! Hello, Viv. All right, love?' He has the lined face of a lifelong smoker; it crumples as he greets me.

'Fine, thank you.' Nana shoots me a look. I sink down at the table.

Reg looks out to the garden. 'Well, it's a lovely day for it!'

'Hmm.'

'What you doing with yourself today?'

'Nothing much.'

Nana brings plates to the table. 'She's making a surprise visit to her nana, aren't you, love?'

They exchange a look and then turn to me, smiling, and I realise I'm the gooseberry.

'Look, Nana, actually it was just a quick hello. I should go.'

'What? All the way from London!' Reg laughs.

Nana presses my shoulder as if pushing me down. 'No! Don't go, Viv, you've only just got here.'

'I know, but I have things to do, really – and I'll see you on Sunday.' I hug her, closing my eyes to avoid looking at Reg. 'I might even bring Max with me.'

She follows me to the door, looking worried. 'Oh, but I

don't want you to go!' She snuggles into me like a little bird; suddenly she's the child needing nurturing.

'I know, but Reg is here now and I'll see you Sunday.'

'I didn't know you were coming. I could have put Reg off if I'd known.' She looks forlorn.

'Don't worry about it.' I'm secretly a tiny bit pleased she noticed the dig. I step outside. 'I'll see you soon.'

'I love you!' she calls as I walk away. I suddenly can't wait to escape from her life. As I turn the corner and glance back, she waves from the doorstep.

On the journey home, as I lean into the seat of the London-bound train, there's an ugly lump squatting in my gut, something I can't put my finger on. I don't understand why I acted that way at Nana's. I feel really bad now for making her uncomfortable. I guess I just couldn't face being the odd one out again, and maybe it's unreasonable but I expected her to be there for me, no matter what, to send Reg away. Perhaps she couldn't see that I need help. How are you supposed to show your heart is breaking? How do you ask for help? And who is supposed to come to your aid? I realise now that my family and friends didn't think very much of Rob. But just because *they* didn't like him, they're acting as if I shouldn't either, and dismissing my pain. Do I have to wear a banner? 'Warning! Heartbroken. May cry.' But it's not that they don't see it; it's just that they can't help. I have to go through this by myself.

Heartbreak is so lonely, and this is why the website is a good idea. Other people must be feeling like this. The site will be somewhere where everyone on it knows what you're going through. I take out my notebook and jot, 'Chat room, heartbreak hotel?' then immediately feel like a loser. If you're in a chat room like that, you'd have to accept the loss, wouldn't you? You'd have to realise you'd been dumped, that it actually was 'the end'. For Rob and me, it isn't like that. I mean, I know he's getting married and everything, but *he* hasn't told me, we haven't talked.

If I could see him, actually have a conversation, I know he'd realise his mistake. Maybe it's time to swallow my pride and just contact him. I rest my forehead on the window and read the graffiti outside as the train squeals to a stop. An enormous blond youth gets on and despite the carriage being half empty, plonks himself down next to me. I smell stale cigarette smoke and pull my handbag onto my lap, squeezing up to the window. From his earphones comes a loud, tinny beat. He opens a packet of greasy fried chicken in his lap and begins to chew at the flesh, dropping the stripped bones at our feet. I look out of the window as dreary Greater London slides by. The smell of chicken makes my stomach lurch. I look at him pointedly. He smacks his lips, crumples the oily paper and throws that down too. He glances at me and nods. I motion to him to take out his earphones and point to the mess on the floor.

'Oh come on. Who do you think is going to pick that up?'

He looks at the floor and back at me, then speaks in an exaggerated Jamaican accent. 'You can, darlin', and blow me while you down there.'

'Oh very nice!'

He nods. 'Straight.'

'What about the other people who have to use this train?'

He shrugs. 'Man, I don' mind if dey wan' eat dey chicken too!'

'Right. Let me out. Come on, move over.' He slides his legs to the side. I scrabble out of the seat, feeling a blush rising from my neck. I'm furiously trying to find a way to contact the guard when I notice a button directly opposite the boy. I jab it and glare at him. There's a rustle, then a voice.

'Guard speaking.'

'Hello there, I'm in the fourth carriage, I think, and a young man is eating chicken and throwing the rubbish all over the floor!'

'Okay, madam, I'll make sure the cleaner finds it when we reach our final stop.'

'But don't you want to speak to the person? He's still here,' I say, exasperated.

'Madam, the cleaner will deal with the mess.'

'Yes, but what about the person who did it?'

'Nothing we can do, madam.' The line crackles and he's gone.

I glare at the youth and sink into the seat opposite so if the guard comes, I can point him out. He mutters something and I swing round.

'Sorry, what did you say?'

'I saying, you need to chill . . . serious!'

I stare straight ahead, suddenly aware of other passengers looking my way, but when I look up, they avert their eyes. I championed them, sticking my neck out to keep the train clean, and now they're treating me like some sort of freak! I spend the rest of the journey burning with indignation while the youth repeatedly mutters, 'Serious,' like a spell.

Finally I'm home. I close the door and lean on it feeling like I've been set on by wolves. Why did I go outside? I'm obviously mad with grief. I'm out of sync with the universe.

Right now I wish I had a pet. A pretty little cat with a bell on her collar who'd come running at the sound of my key in the door. That would be nice – take the edge off the loneliness. I'd buy gourmet cat food like in the adverts. We'd curl up in front of the TV together. But the litter tray, though – all those little turds covered in granules . . . barf. No, I'm better alone with my pain.

I've decided to contact Rob, so that's something good

– positive action. What I'll do is email him. I chuck my bag down and turn on the computer. The screen flickers into life and my mailbox beeps. I have a few messages – a couple from Christie, one from a catalogue company and one from him! I swallow and lean further in to the screen, heart thumping.

Hello Viv,

I hope you've recovered from Saturday. That was quite a performance!

I'm glad you met Sam. I gather she told you about us getting hitched. Sorry you found out like that. I wanted to tell you myself and had thought to ask you out for dinner or something. So much has happened recently.

Anyway, wish me luck?

Rob

I feel like he's reached through the screen and whacked me in the throat with a bat. I type quickly.

Hi Rob,

Congratulations! I think your new fiancée is a very interesting person.

It would be good to meet for dinner. I would like to wish you luck face to face.

Viv

I should take time to reply, really think about this. The mouse hovers over 'send' and then I just click and it's gone! Good, at least I'm in contact with him. I'm shaking. He's the only man in the world I want and here he is getting married and telling me by email. I mean, 'getting hitched' is so casually put, as if the last five years of planning our wedding was a rehearsal.

He replies immediately.

Where and when for dinner?

He still wants to see me, then – this a good sign, and such a quick reply must mean he's been waiting for me to get in touch all along. I feel a rush of excitement. Now, where would be good for dinner? Not a restaurant – too formal. Nowhere we used to go – too sentimental. I think we need a foody pub, somewhere casual and cool.

How about the Shy Horse on King Street? I've read good things about it. Shall we say Friday 7.30?

Whoosh – sent.

I wait five minutes, staring at the screen, but there's nothing. I open up the messages from Christie, neither of them about work. The first is to say she misses me and she went to our favourite sandwich bar for lunch but didn't get the 'all-day breakfast roll' as she noticed the calorie content, which was more than a gorilla's daily allowance. The second is to say she hopes I'm coming back tomorrow as the sales are starting.

I begin to reply, but hear the soft ding of an incoming message . . . not him. It's a photographer with a link to view photos of Jane and Hugo's wedding. I take a deep breath and click on it.

The bride and groom appear in various poses outside the church. There are a couple verging on the ridiculous, where he's doing a star jump and she's running with the wind in her veil. There's a twee shot of them kissing over the top of a superimposed wishing well. Then I feel a stab as I get to a photo of Rob with Sam, posing in the churchyard. He looks gorgeous, the sun catching his hair; she looks like a model, standing with one leg forward, tummy in and head back. I glare at her, muttering,'You cow, you cow, you cow!' I think I'll print her out and show Christie.

I scroll further down the thumbnails and find myself. There I am, smiling blearily while strangling Max with one arm, champagne glass dangling precariously from my hand. In another I'm staring, devil-like, in the background of the happy couple's portrait. I'm at the table, with smudged eye make-up, mouth open, midway through a bread roll. There's one of Max and me, heads joined at the temple, grinning like goons. Finally, there I am standing holding the bouquet next to Rob and Sam. Oh my God. I'm a pale pink giant next to her, red puffy nose and smeared lipstick. He's looking slightly away, but she stares straight into the camera with a defiant, tight little smile, symmetrical brows, glossy hair, groomed and ice cool. She looks as if she's about to dispatch me with a flick of her skinny wrist. The title of the picture is 'Rob and Sam with friend'. I can't remember it being taken. What kind of photographer takes pictures like that? I drop my head into my hands, cover my eyes and then peer again through my fingers. Yes, it is *that* bad.

Ding!

Fine, see you there.

9

Friends, Favours and Fuck Buddies

How to tell if he fancies you

1. Does he listen to everything you say?
2. Does he comment on your appearance?
3. Does he lick his lips more than usual when you're near?
4. Does he maintain eye contact with you for more than two seconds?
5. Does he smile a lot and laugh at all your jokes?
6. Does he ask if you're seeing anyone?
7. Does he go out of his way to bump into you?
8. Does he try to make himself seem more important/stronger/wiser/ funnier/richer than he really is?
9. Does he text you all the time?
10. Does he try to touch you?

If you can answer 'yes' to three or more of the above, you're on to something.

It's oppressively hot at the office; the air like a thick blanket too tightly tucked. The photo above my computer, of Rob and me, lifts and flicks lazily with the oscillating fan. Visualisation is a skill I have been teaching myself for a few years: in my mind I create a picture of what I want, make it as vivid as possible, add colour and see the picture in animation. It really works and you can use it for anything – to make someone chat you up, make interviews go your way, even to get a parking space. This photo will bring Rob back. It's a close-up of our laughing faces. We were on top of

Primrose Hill and he took it by holding the camera outstretched. The sun makes a halo around his head, his eyes are shining blue, and his perfect smiling toothpaste advert mouth makes my heart beat faster. I kiss my finger and press it to his cheek.

Beside me, Christie is studying the printout of Sam using a magnifying glass. I'm amazed at her efficiency yesterday. She cleared all the filing, wrote the reports I asked for and even made a start on the Christmas gift offer. She's created an impressive mood board, pasting together pictures of the main trends from the autumn/winter fashion collections. It's all luxury folk and animal print with tartan and tweed.

This is obviously the new improved Christie, but alarmingly she's taken to wearing spectacles with clear glass lenses. She says they make her look intelligent; I didn't like to argue. I tell her I'm making tea.

'Tea is full of caffeine, which will dehydrate you. No. Not for me, Viv.' I ask what about coffee? 'Coffee? Coffee is worse!' She wants some herbal brew with soya milk. I wish I'd never offered. Returning from the kitchen, I put her strange-smelling drink on her desk and perch on the other side, sipping my Nescafé. She puts down the magnifying glass and looks up at me with a pained expression.

'She's gorgeous, isn't she?' I nod. 'I mean, I've tried to find a flaw, I really have, but she's stunning, isn't she?' I nod again; Christie looks sadly back at the picture. 'She's really stylish too, isn't she? I wonder where she got that dress.' She studies the picture. 'God, look at her figure! I would kill to have a body like that, wouldn't you?' I snatch the photo away. She looks up in surprise. 'But looks aren't everything. Like you said, she's an absolute bitch. Actually, that's probably just a really good shot of her.'

Avoiding her eyes, I slide off her desk, take the two steps to mine and slump into my chair. I look at the picture, crumple it into a ball and fire it at the bin; it misses and rolls into the walkway, coming to rest beside the pointy shoes of Paul from technology. He picks it up, smooths it out and gives a low whistle.

'He's one lucky fella. I wouldn't mind a crack at that!' He hands the picture to me with a Frisbee-throwing motion. I ball it up again and this time throw it successfully into the bin with a sarcastic smile. He holds up his hands and starts to back out of our little section, but, noticing Christie's legs, he stops.

'Are those fishnet tights you're wearing there, young Christie?' She slides her chair back and stretches out her legs.

'Yes, Paul – stockings, actually.' He puts a fist in his mouth and, with his other hand over his groin, shuffles away. She giggles, watching him go.

'You should report him. That's sexual harassment.'

'Not if I don't mind,' she laughs.

'Well, you should mind!' I snap. She sighs and turns back to her screen.

I look out at white-hot shimmering London. The dome of Madame Tussauds rises above cluttered rooftops. A toy-like red bus crawls along. Outside this window, millions of lives are running their course. People are breathing, loving, eating, fucking, dying. Riding on buses, boats, bikes, taxis and under-ground trains, talking on phones, hustling for deals, queuing for coffee. This world is moving on while I sit here feeling like I've swallowed a great big jagged rock.

I pick up my phone and text Lucy: '*Fancy lunch?*' She replies, '*Could do 1 p.m. for half an hour otherwise can't get away until 3.*' I stare at the words. It seems like everyone else is moving at a different pace to me, cruising along with purpose in the great sea of life while I'm stricken and slowly sinking. I agree to 1 p.m. I skim through my inbox, feeling despondent. I have a lot of work to catch up on and Christie and I need to sit down and decide on the lines we'll put forward for the winter gift range, but I keep thinking of new ideas for the website. I jot down, 'A one-stop shop for the heartbroken.'

Suddenly it seems more important than anything else. I decide I'll nip down and see Creepy Michael in IT about setting up websites. I know he still fancies me since the Hawaiian-themed Christmas party. We won the limbo competition together despite me being nearly a foot taller. I tell Christie I have a meeting and take the lift down to the IT department. The lift door opens and I read the printed sign.

IT Department.

Before you enter, try switching your machine off and on again.

I use my pass to open the door and a wall of air conditioning hits me. There are three rows of desks: first row, help desks, who log your complaint and tell you they'll get back to you Tuesday; second row, maintenance, who'll turn up and plug all your wires back into the sockets, or remove your machine without a word; and third row, hardcore techies, who have their own language and culture. I approach the third row, spotting Michael's glasses glinting in the light of his screen. From the bottom of his chin he seems to have cultivated a rat-tail beard, twisted it and threaded it on a bead. It's the only indicator that he's from the dark side, otherwise he blends with the average, wearing a slightly shiny pale grey suit and sensible shoes.

'Hi, Michael.'

He glances my way, then holds up a hand in a kind of stop sign. He continues his feverish tapping of the keyboard. I watch his small, thin fingers working at speed, a long yellow nail on each little finger, and think of rodents scrabbling in dust. I'm left standing awkwardly waiting.

A bony bloke at the next desk, all in purple with a sparse sandy ponytail, speaks to someone behind him. 'If the veidtsjf system klkafjalkdf is nalkdjal, do we wothg or buyvts?'

It's tomb cold in here and dark like some huge holding tank, smelling of patchouli, stale farts and dusty electricity. No one looks away from their screens for longer than a few seconds. Suddenly Michael pops up.

'Sorry, Viv, can't leave these things. What can I do you for?'

He's one of those blokes who can't stop moving. If he's sitting down, he jiggles his legs or raps his fingers. Standing up, he rocks from side to side or bounces. I explain about my website and give him the notes. He reads through them, shaking and tapping a pen against his teeth.

'Yeah, it could work.'

'Well . . . I was wondering if you could create a site for me?'

'Well, I could.'

'Okay . . . would you?'

'That would depend.'

'On?'

'What's in it for me.'

'Right! What would you want?'

His furtive little eyes dart to my face. 'Well, I'd have to build quite a few layers in there. It's not something I could do using a template.'

'Oh, I see.'

He looks down at the notes and his juddering legs make the desk vibrate. 'I mean, you'd need a lot of pages and links building in. All that takes time.'

He seesaws the pen on his fingers, making a tap-tappety-tap rhythm. I feel my energy draining, like water from a bag. I'm the fairground goldfish left gasping inside.

'So, will you do it for me?'

'Well, I'd want something in return.' He leans back in his chair and smiles without showing any teeth.

'Right . . . well, name it.' I give a high little laugh.

'Dinner. With you. You pay; I choose the venue.'

I'm not sure how much it costs to design and build a website, but I'm guessing it's thousands, or at least a lot more than dinner with Michael will cost, financially or personally. I feel like I'm swallowing a toad, but I agree.

'So when will I see something?'

'Next week . . . and you pay on completion.'

I decide to worry about it then. 'Great! Thanks so much.'

He looks pleased and licks his lips, his tongue darting out like an eel from a hole. I back away.

'Bye bye, Vivienne.' He waggles his fingers and I turn to leave.

Before I round the corner, I glance back and he waves again with a smile. I scarper to the lift, stabbing the 'up' button as if my life depended on it, a creeping horror rising up my back as if I've just lifted a rock and glimpsed the scurrying egg-white bodies of a million underworld creatures.

I shudder as I surface into my grey strip-lit department. Christie is giggling on the phone and she hands me a Post-it message. 'Viv! Snotty is looking for you.' She's made the 'o's of 'looking' into eyes with lashes. Why was Snotty looking for me? She'd never normally come in person. I stand over Christie's desk, miming hanging up the phone, and she starts to wind down the conversation.

'Aw, listen I have to go – boss breathing down my neck and all that . . . No, not the one with the wonky mouth.' Her eyes flick to my face. 'Oh yeah, that one! All right then . . . *Ciao* for now . . . Yes, see you soon, lots of kisses . . . bye . . . bye. No, you go first!' I press down the button, cutting her off.

'Who was that?'

'You know, that Stuart from Printech.' As she gazes up at me I wonder how she keeps the porn star lip gloss in place. She taps a finger to the side of her nose. 'It's not what you know, it's who you know in this business.'

'Is it? Well, you seem to know "Stuart from Printech" very well indeed.'

She gazes into space, lost in memory. 'Yeah . . .'

'Christie! What did Snotty say?'

'Oh. She said, "Where's Viv?" and I said, "In a meeting," and she goes, "Who with?" and I said, "I don't know," and she goes, "Check her calendar," so I did and you weren't down for a meeting, so she said to tell you she was looking for you.'

'Oh fuck.' I check my emails; there's nothing from Snotty and, I note, nothing from Rob either. I'll just tell her I was having technical problems and had to pop down to IT. That's true, really . . . kind of. I feel jumpy as I call her direct line. I know she's on my case at the moment; after Christie's warning she seems to be watching my every move. I get her answerphone, so I leave a breezy message.

We spend the rest of the morning speaking to suppliers, ordering samples and putting together costs. We're thinking of going with red leather compacts, leopard- and zebra-print scarves, and strings of ethnic beads. Then there are scented Christmas candles with Scandinavian folk patterns, clutch bags with tiger stripes, and mini chocolate fondue kits with marshmallows. I realise as Christie leaves for lunch that I haven't thought about Rob for two whole hours.

It's so hot that the lining of my dress sticks to my skin as I lean over a board, arranging photos. We'll present ideas to the head buyers on Monday. It won't be only Snotty this time but Mole as well, who's as impenetrable as a tank. I must warn Christie not to speak – if they smell blood, we'll be savaged.

I meet Lucy in Noodles Quick! near Bond Street. She looks office sexy in a simple white blouse and grey pencil skirt. We share a bench table with some braying tight-trousered young suits. Lucy orders a bowl of pale broth with sea creatures floating among the noodles like some macabre aquarium. I choose a dish called chick-a-doodle; fried noodles and chicken arrive in seconds. She eats with chopsticks, slurping loudly, her head low over the bowl. I pick at my chicken, wondering how to tell her about meeting Rob on Friday. Also, I want to show her the photo I've retrieved from the bin and have her analyse Sam.

I have to shout above the din. 'So, who was under your covers the other day?'

She frowns, sucking up a couple of stray noodles. 'What? Under my covers?'

'Yeah, you couldn't talk because of him.'

She's momentarily confused and then it dawns on her. 'Oh yes. Reuben,' she says dreamily.

'You never mentioned him before. What's he like?'

'Short. Columbian. Amazing in bed.'

I can't help admiring Lucy – she insists that all men she takes home give her at least one orgasm, and if they don't, she kicks them out. 'So . . . will you see him again?'

'Of course. We're fuck buddies.' She smiles goofily and stands up to get some napkins. Her perfect body doesn't go unnoticed. The suits fall into awed silence as she skims past. She hands me a napkin and sits down again.

'So the only reason you see Reuben is to—'

'Fuck. Yes.'

'So you don't eat dinner, you just—'

'We fuck.'

'But do you, like, talk or anything?'

'Not really. We just fuck.'

'All right! Stop saying "fuck". People are staring.'

'So?' She downs her glass of white wine. 'Sorry, love, it's a bit rushed. I have to go in a minute.' I push my plate away and she asks for the bill. 'How are things with you? Are you over the wedding?'

'I'll never get over it as long as I live, and I'm seeing Rob on Friday.'

'Okay, so . . . let me try to work this out – are you one of those crazy women who actually get off on hurting themselves?'

'God! Maybe,' I say, making a shocked face.

She shakes her head. The bill arrives and she puts it on expenses. We step out into the quiet of the street and she hugs me; her hair smells like cocoa butter. She speaks close to my ear: 'Listen, I love you and I don't want you hurt, that's all.'

'I know.' We stand holding each other's hands like lovers at an airport. Then I take out the picture. 'Want to see my competition?' She frowns briefly at the paper and hands it back. 'What do you think?'

'Very nice. Why do you care? You're walking around with a picture of your ex-boyfriend and his new fiancée.' She looks into my face with such pity. 'Let it go, Viv. This will make you ill.' We hug again and she kisses my cheek. 'Let's go clubbing soon. We need a night out.' With that she trots across the road, raising her hand to wave and disappears into her shimmering glass building like a princess into a castle.

IO

Ten Dos and Don'ts to Impress Your Ex

1. *Do use all available resources to make sure you look your absolute best.*
2. *Do not under any circumstances declare your feelings. Be friendly and kind when you meet your ex and make it look like you've moved on.*
3. *Do talk about your social life, a new hobby or a work project. You need to seem busy to be desirable again.*
4. *Do not call your ex repeatedly and do not beg.*
5. *Always be the one who cuts the conversation or meeting short so you leave them wanting more.*
6. *Do not try to French-kiss them or touch them at all, actually.*
7. *Do not bang on about a new boyfriend who is richer/better-looking/funnier/hairier/more well endowed, even if he does exist.*
8. *Don't do anything crazy with your hair.*
9. *Do not cry, make threats or throw stuff.*
10. *When the meeting is over, do not cling to or otherwise try to detain your ex.*

I'm waiting for Friday like it'll save my life and it seems to be stretching further and further into the distance. Why did I suggest Friday? Why didn't I make it Tuesday and spare myself this agony? The answer whispers in my ear. If we get back together and end up in bed on Friday, we'll have all weekend to lie around making love, bringing each other breakfast in bed, reading the papers and taking long walks on the heath. That's why I've stocked the fridge with salmon, cream cheese, strawberries and croissants. I've bought very expensive coffee. I've cleaned the flat and changed the bed sheets.

By the time it's Friday morning, I'm fully prepared. I dress carefully in a sand-coloured shift dress and black pumps. It crosses my mind that I'm trying to copy Sam's look from the wedding, but I delete that thought. No, if he wants classy, I can give it to him. I plait my hair and pin it up, spraying down all the sticking-up ends, and keep my make-up natural. I take a classic black shoulder bag and pack it with the essentials: spare stockings, make-up case, deodorant, perfume, hairspray, breath freshener, toothbrush and clean pants, in case I end up back at his place.

The air is still and warm, and a lacy trace of the moon fades in the pale morning sky. I am filled with calm and peace, sitting with perfect posture on the bus, smiling benignly at a cyclist waving his fist at the bus driver. I take the short sunlit walk to Barnes and Worth, watching myself stride by in the mirrored windows of an office block. I'm a girl who knows what she wants and is about to get it. I should probably have my own theme tune. As the lift toils its way up, dropping workers at every floor, I contemplate my day. Catch up on paperwork, answer emails and prepare for the buyers' meeting. I stroll serenely towards my desk and I'm met by Christie flapping towards me like a twittering bird.

'It's today! It's today! They brought it forward!'

I smile kindly. She will not burst my bubble. 'Good morning, Christie. Come and sit down. What's today?' I move my head carefully, feeling one of the pins in my hair giving way. She follows and I see she's wearing some sort of diaphanous multicoloured batwing toga dress, belted at the waist with what looks like a curtain tieback. 'Wow. Amazing dress!'

'The buyers' meeting is today! They brought it forward!'

I gaze for a second at her stricken face, feeling my fragile veneer of calm shatter and drop like scales. 'What?'

'It's this afternoon!' she squeals.

I hear my own voice, thin and reedy: 'Oh fuck! Oh no! We're not ready!'

'I knoooow!' Christie starts to do a little half-jog on the spot.

We dance around as if the floor is on fire, screeching, 'Oh nooo!' like professional mourners, before scrabbling to the mood boards and ripping open the post looking for samples.

'I've got scarves!' Christie waves a handful of woollen zebra print. They look a bit granny-knitted; I'd pictured chiffon, but I suppose they could be nerdy cool.

'Put them on my desk.' I'm ripping at the brown tape of a package from China. It's wrapped like pass the parcel in layers of odd-smelling paper. Finally at the centre I get a disappointingly small red compact mirror. I open it.

'It's a magnifying mirror! We didn't ask for that, did we?' I scramble to my computer, checking costs against proposed price points and printing out sample request forms.

'Well, that's it. That's all.' I swivel round. Christie sits among shredded packaging, looking like she might cry. 'We've only got the scarves and the compact to show them!' she wails.

'Oh shit. Oh shit! Okay. Check the sample cupboard. Just grab whatever you think might fit and we'll work around it.'

She flaps away like a tropical bird. I return to the spreadsheet, trying to work out profit margins in percentages. I think we can get away with it by showing the mood board and the projected figures, then giving them other possible ideas from the sample cupboard and making out we'd ordered them especially. We can wing that bit. I'll get Christie to prepare samples while I work on the report. I type numbers and the spreadsheet calculates totals. I glance up at Rob's photo. It could all still be okay.

It's not okay. Christie's hands tremble as she stands before Mole, visibly shrinking under her deadpan gaze. I have no idea how to intervene. If I bail Christie out, it makes her look incompetent. If I don't, I look like an imbecile. I study Mole, trying to read her thoughts and wondering about her life. I think it'd be hard to be more unattractive than her. It's like she's made a project of it. She should have a badge: 'Say no to plucking! Let your blemishes shine!' Three raisin-like moles across her cheek, like the stars of Orion's belt, are not even notable compared to the coin-shaped, hairy patch that nestles between the folds of her double chin. It's shocking when it pops into view, riding like a tick on the waves of her skin. Her watery blue eyes regard the sample before her. She begins to unwrap it. Christie shoots me a look of panic and I try to appear calm. Snotty is quiet. She sits, red mouth puckered like a dog's bottom, jotting something on her pad. Mole pulls a tiny pink edible thong from the packet. She opens it out on her blunt fingers like a cat's cradle. She takes a bite and chews thoughtfully.

'I don't think they're supposed to taste really great,' Christie simpers.

Mole slowly grinds and swallows. She turns the packaging over, looking for listed ingredients. 'Extraordinary. What on earth are they made of?'

'Erm, I think just rice paper and flavouring,' Christie answers, pretending to look at her notes.

Snotty, sensing a chance to shine, picks up her packet and turns on her death glare. 'Edible underwear, Christine? Edible underwear? Would you explain how you think this is in keeping with the Barnes and Worth brand?' She smiles conspiratorially at Mole.

'It's just—'

'I mean, have you any idea of our customer base? Have you walked around the store and seen the kind of people who shop in our gifting department?'

Christie looks down at the table, shifting uneasily in her heels. I gather myself to stand up and explain but can't for the life of me think why she chose bloody edible knickers from all the things in the sample cupboard. I know for a fact there was a carriage clock and even a cuddly hot-water bottle in the shape of a moon. Why didn't she choose them? I'm learning, yet again, to check everything she does. I feel a damp film of nervous sweat prickle across my back. I don't care about this! All I wanted was to look good for Rob. On Monday all the rest of the samples are being couriered over. I would have been ready on Monday. Today should have been calm, quiet. I could have focused on the date, on being ready. Now I'm sweaty, stressed out of my mind, and Christie is fucking up. Again.

As I push back my chair, she suddenly rallies, raising her voice over Snotty. 'It's just a bit of fun. A novelty for Christmas and you never know, it might spice up a few lives.'

Mole examines Christie with renewed interest and then starts to laugh, a surprisingly girlish tinkle. She looks at Snotty's stricken face and laughs more. 'She's quite right! I love them! Do they do them for men?' She winks at me, poking her tongue into the corner of her mouth. I smile, inwardly horrified by the image of Mole eating someone's pants off. 'I want samples, ladies, *tout de suite*! I want Christmas colours, cheeky slogans. I want them for both sexes. I want fun packaging, and we need to know what they're made of. Have they been safety tested?'

Christie gawps. I answer no, they haven't.

'I want these in store this Christmas, so get on to it, Viv. Get me costings.' She widens her eyes in my direction, then turns back to Christie. 'Good work, young lady.'

Christie flushes and sinks into her chair.

Mole turns to Snotty. 'This is a good PR opportunity. Let's get on to the press with something . . . Something like . . . "B&W gets spicy this Christmas." You know the sort of thing.'

Snotty nods while writing frantically. I catch her eye as she closes her notebook. She looks quickly away.

We move on through the afternoon, product by product. The scarves are in, but the ethnic beads are moved to the summer range. They go through the figures in detail, studying each profit margin and asking about suppliers. They want the costs down. They want to know how much more they'll make if they buy in bulk or use less ethical suppliers. They send out for pizza at six. At seven they're arguing about the cost of packaging on the chocolate fondue kits. They pick through my brain with chopsticks, selecting details like juicy morsels. I have to leave. How can I leave? I imagine Rob making his way to the pub and finding a seat. How long will he wait? They want to know if there's a supplier of tartan or tweed in China. I say I'll find out. I suggest that we have another meeting when I have more information. They ignore me and continue the bombardment. I note everything down, watching the hands of my watch shift, my heart knotting. We have a few more products to go through and each one is taking at least half an hour.

I'm looking at the door and thinking about bolting when Mole lifts her hands above her head, stretching her back. I glimpse the grey shadow of armpit stubble and expensive black lace through the sleeve of her tent dress.

'Right! It's late. It's Friday. Let's go to the pub and I'll buy us a bottle of wine.'

Christie, high on her edible knickers triumph, claps her hands. 'Yay!' She looks excitedly at me.

'I can't come, unfortunately. I have a dinner date.' I stand, gathering my notes.

'Shame!' thunders Mole.

Snotty walks with me to the door. As she holds it open, she murmurs, 'I would have thought at times like these it would pay to be a team player, Viv. Enjoy your evening.' She gives a disappointed smile.

'Have a good weekend,' I say as she turns back into the room, letting the door close on me. I can't worry about it now. I run to the lift, trying to redo my hair as I go.

The Shy Horse pub clings to tradition. In a street of cocktail bars and minimalist stripped-wood eateries, its cosy red lamps glow reassuringly through diamond-latticed windows. The last clips holding up my hair have collapsed in the rush across town. I drag out the dangling pins as I walk and make what I hope is an artfully scruffy ponytail. I stand for a moment outside the window. I can see a group of girls in strapless tops and heels standing at the bar, a few couples sitting in the snugs, and old blokes on bar stools. Then my heart flips. He's here. He's sitting reading the paper in the next bay. The light warms up half his face, flattering his fine profile and catching his gently tousled hair. His golden skin is complemented by a pale grey suit and baby blue silk tie. Suddenly I'm inadequate. I smooth down my dress and tuck some stray hair behind my ears. I take a deep breath, mentally playing Christina Aguilera.

'I am beautiful,' I say to myself as I heave open the door. The chatter and laughter hit me. The room smells of boozy carpet and wood, making me desperate for a drink. Not my usual Pinot, though – something nostalgic, involving whisky. I feel as if a pulley heaving a great weight has been installed in my stomach. It goes up, smashing into my heart, before thumping down to my guts. I'm standing in front of him now. He hasn't looked up from his newspaper; there's still time to scarper. I get a sudden wild urge to do a monkey impression. *Oh shit, oh God.*

I flash my sexiest smile. 'Hi, Rob.'

He looks up, his perfect face frowning. 'Hello. Finally! You're fifteen' – he glances at his Cartier – 'no, seventeen minutes late!'

'I'm really sorry. Glad you waited, though.' I sink into the chair opposite him and place my hand over his. It's warm and dry. He pulls away and taps his index fingers together. I get a waft of a scent I don't recognise. I bet it's something she bought; spraying her territory, like a cat on heat.

'You smell nice. Is that new?'

'You know, I think being late is the height of rudeness.'

'It is. You're right. I'm sorry, it was unavoidable.'

'Late people have an arrogant disregard for other people's time. I've wasted seventeen minutes of my life waiting for you today.' There's a long silence. In all my imaginings of this meeting, I hadn't prepared for this. I sit, aching to touch him, more sure than ever that I must get him back. I glance at his beautiful face a couple of times, forming the beginnings of sentences in my mind, then thinking better of them. I notice he hasn't, in his seventeen-minute wait, bought himself a drink. That's my 'in'. I lean across the table and clock him glancing briefly at my cleavage.

'Rob, I am truly sorry for being late. I don't expect you to forgive me, but perhaps you'd let me buy you a drink, by way of an apology?' I look into his eyes.

He laughs and he's more gorgeous than ever.

'Well . . . since you put it like that, I'll have a vodka tonic, lots of ice, no lemon.'

Triumphantly, I struggle to the bar and elbow my way into position. I know how to handle this; it'll be fine. Rob has always needed soothing; he needs me to bring out the best in him. Like a salve, I calm him and make him laugh.

I get his drink and a whisky Mac with a cherry for myself. He takes a sip, watching me wince as I sip mine. I'd forgotten these were so strong.

'What the hell are you drinking?'

'Whisky Mac. It's whisky and ginger wine, very warming. I'm feeling all Christmassy.'

'It's July.'

'So?' I look deep into his eyes. There's definitely a spark of something there as he smiles.

'Odd girl, aren't you?'

'Unique. Yes.'

He holds my gaze before his face closes like a trap. He takes a gulp of his drink. He's looking around the room now. He's disengaging. He's resisting.

'Do you want to eat something? They do okay food here, I think. I'm starving, aren't you?' I blurt out quickly.

He shifts in his chair. 'Viv . . .'

'I'll get some menus!' I get up and half jog to the bar. There's a mirror behind the bottles and I watch the reflection of a happy Friday scene: a fat guy desperately chatting up one of the strapless girls. Rob looking at his watch. A small, pink-faced person with a scruffy ponytail. I straighten up, realising it's me, and turn my head slightly to get my best side.

Don't look, I say in my head, that's an ugly mirror. Like those thin mirrors they put in changing rooms . . . only different. I look back at Rob; he's checking his phone. I reach for the menus. Don't lose him! Concentrate. I turn back to the table, composed.

He puts the phone away. 'Viv, I know we said dinner, but I don't think I can stay to eat. I have to be somewhere else.' As his look of sympathy fades, I realise I have no hold on him. He expected to meet me for . . . what? A swift goodbye? A pat on the back and a 'no hard feelings' handshake? He's bloody well arranged something else later! It's amazing how he never fails to be insensitive. I want to tell him I too have a date later, with an oligarch who's hung like a horse, but (a) it's not true, and (b) I can't bear for him to leave. If he leaves, I know my heart will just shatter. Pride has no place in this.

He's finishing up his drink as I touch his arm. 'Please, Rob. Don't go,' I plead.

'Viv.' He pats the top of my hand.

'Just have something to eat with me first.' I meet his eyes. God, I thought I'd be looking into that face on my wedding day and I thought my children would have those eyelashes. He's gazing at me blankly. 'Please. For old times' sake?' I say.

He picks up the menu.

A harassed barman in baggy jeans brings two pies and chips with cutlery rolled in serviettes and a salt cellar with a dribble of gravy down the side. I'm still here with Rob! He's taken off his jacket and tie. He's on his third large vodka and seems to be enjoying himself.

'I love the way you eat, Viv.'

'Really?'

'Yeah, the way you eat like a man. I mean, what girl eats pie and chips washed down with a pint?' I smile, not sure where he's going with this. 'But you do. I like that. I like that you're not forever counting calories and picking at salad.' I think of the citrus and vinegar diet I once tried, of the boom and bust of my eating habits.

'No, not me! It's boring all that, isn't it?' I hope I'm insulting Sam with this. The skin of his throat and the scribble of chest hair just visible above his shirt make me ache, they're so familiar.

I feel a kind of relief, like waking from a bad dream. He's here, it's okay. We chat about work and family, managing to avoid the subject that's sitting like an elephant between us, until he puts down his knife and fork and refuses another drink. He says he has to go. He's meeting Sam and 'a few friends'. I feel a sharp point of pain under the ribs. I've nothing left to hold him here.

'So . . . congratulations on your engagement!' I blurt.

He smiles. 'You don't mean that.'

I line up the beer-mats with great precision. 'No. But I do want you to be happy.' I smile.

'Well . . . thank you.'

'And are you? Happy?'

He looks at me as if measuring the level of pain I can stand. 'I think so.'

Is he leaving the door a crack open with that? Is there a hopeful chink of light to drive a wedge into?

'Happier than when we were getting married?'

'Viv, please. I don't want to go over all that. It's history. I'm with someone else now.'

'Of course. I know. But, well, you're here now. With me. There must be a reason for that.' I hold his hand. 'It must count for something.'

'I just thought I owed it to you to tell you myself, to say goodbye properly.'

Oh my God, this is hard, like being repeatedly punched on the nose. But faint heart never won fair man. I try to keep my voice even. 'I don't want to say goodbye, Rob.'

'I have to go.' He stands up.

'I want us to be together. I think—'

'It's over, Viv.' He brushes the back of his hand gently against my cheek. 'I'm sorry, sweetheart, but you left me – remember?' He slings his glossily lined jacket over one elegant shoulder and saunters out. He doesn't look back.

11

Falling Apart: Part I

1. *Cry your eyes out.*
2. *Howl like a banshee.*
3. *Smash stuff.*
4. *Do not call. You will regret it.*
5. *Don't even think about it.*

The taxi stops at the end of the road. I rummage in my bag for money, pushing aside the spare pants now tangled up with the toothbrush.

The driver eyes me patiently. 'It's not the end of the world, love. It'll all look better in the morning.'

I drip tears as I hand over a twenty. 'It is, actually. It really is the end of my world.'

He hands me the change. 'You take care now, love.'

I nod numbly and limp to the door, whimpering like a wounded dog. Snot and tears drip as I fumble with the keys. Once inside I curl onto the sofa, hugging my knees. A distant scrap of reason reminds me that I left Rob, over two months ago, and I was coping well. But only because I was so sure he'd be back. Now *he* really has left *me*. He hasn't even tried to come and get me. It's final. My mind filters through ideas and scenarios like a flick-book. When it rests on an image of Rob walking away, I howl. Then there's *her*! How can I compete with that supermodel? I can't keep still for the pain of it. I need a drink.

In the fridge I find half a can of flat Coke and a bottle of vodka. There's no time to mix them in a glass, so I swig first one and then the other and pace like a caged tiger. What a fool to think I had any kind of upper hand when actually he never wanted me. He's running down the aisle with someone else, someone *younger*, taking all my white-wedding hopes, having stolen good fertile years of my life, and smashing everything we built.

'I'm on the scrapheap,' I wail, pacing and swigging. 'I've been replaced!' How did I get here? What did I do to deserve this? I let out a big shout and it clatters around the bare walls. I stare out of the window as the vodka burns its way down, at all the lit squares of life in the buildings around me, the homes, the lamps and TVs, imagining the meals cooking, the couples cuddling.

I stand in the dark, feeling as if my heart has popped open like a broken zip and the desperate black of night is whistling through. I crouch by the sofa with my hands around my knees. I'm frightened of being alone. I don't know how to cope with the terror of it.

'It isn't fair!' I shout. 'I can't do this!' I rock backwards and forwards and call out to him. I shout at him as if he's asleep in the next room and then as if he can hear me across the city.

I swig more vodka as I sit in the light of the strange greenish glow from my phone. I say his name and whisper it. I pick up the phone and find his name in the contacts. If I could just explain to him, just hear his voice, he'd come. He wouldn't let me suffer; surely he'd see. I get his voice-mail message:

'You've reached Robin Waters. Unfortunately I'm unable to take your call. Please leave a message after the tone, or press the hash key to be put through to my secretary. Thank you. Goodbye.'

That lovely, lovely voice. I just want to hear him say my name. I hang up and redial.

'You've reached Robin Waters . . .'

And again. And again. And again and then a few more times.

12

Falling Apart: Part II

1. *Stand before a mirror, naked, take a deep breath and say in a very calm, quiet voice, 'I am a warrior princess and I deserve love. I will be stronger and better next time.'*
2. *Repeat above.*
3. *Get a pet or a plant, anything, nurture something.*
4. *Take up a new sport.*
5. *Redecorate.*

When I open my eyes, I'm looking directly under the sofa. There's a gold hoop earring I've been missing, a plate, dust and a balled-up sock. My head feels like a walnut in the jaws of a nutcracker with my brain the rattling, shrivelled contents. A headache fizzes behind my eyes. I lie in a shaft of hothouse sun burning from the window with the wool fibres of the rug scratching my face. I roll onto my back. Dust specks circle and fall beneath the glass dome ceiling light. To my right a vodka bottle sparkles like mountain water; I push it upright with my fingers and the remaining splash gathers at the bottom. Oh hell. I drank a lot of vodka.

I try to recall the evening. I think I just came home and drank myself blind. I mean, it wasn't a high point of my life, but at least I didn't humiliate myself. There's comfort in that. I lie still, concentrating on my body, feeling the double whammy of grief and hangover kick in, and I'm aware of something pressing into my left shoulder. I move to the side, trying to keep my eyeballs still, and I find my phone. I lift my head a little and squint at the display. I called Rob *ten times*! I drop the phone onto my chest. Pain crackles in my head, forking into my eyes like lightning. What a total and utter loser. Why, why, why do I get that dially finger when I'm drunk? It only ever leads to disaster – like the time when I tried to get back with my childhood ex, Ginger Roge, who's now gay.

The phone vibrates, buzzing with a chirpy tune. I fumble with it, pressing buttons randomly. *Make it stop. Make it stop.*

'Hello?' I rasp, like a witch.

'Hi, it's Rob.'

A crazy banner unfurls, screaming, 'He wants you back!' Be cool, be cool.

'Yes? How can I help you?'

'Well, you could start by not repeatedly ringing me and then hanging up.'

'Oh, did I? Sorry. I must have sat on the phone without the keypad lock thingy on.'

'Right, well . . . you okay?'

'Me? Yes, fine.'

'I thought you might have been upset. You know, after last night.'

'No! I'm fine – just off for a run.'

'A run?'

'Oh yeah. I try to do half an hour a day now. Loving it, actually.'

'I can't imagine you running, Viv.'

'Yeah, I'm just warming up. Got to watch those hamstrings.'

'Well then, I should let you go. You won't keep ringing me, though, will you? Sam wasn't too pleased – we were watching a film.'

I feel my heart rip like an old rag.

'Noooo. No, I won't.' There's a sob brewing in my throat, gagging me.

'Anyway, look, while you're on, I have a few bits and pieces of yours . . . I just wondered what you'd like me to do with them.'

'Bits and pieces?'

'Uh, just photo albums, a couple of plants from the patio and the red chair.'

'But I bought the red chair for you. You love that chair.'

'Yeah, uh . . . Sam's not a fan. She's redecorating. Quite keen to be an interior designer, actually.'

'Really?' I imagine her falling off a high ladder. A tear trickles down my cheek and soaks into the parched rug.

'Anyway, you have a think and just text me what you'd like done with the stuff, yeah?'

'Righty ho.' *Righty ho?*

'*Ciao* for now.' He hangs up.

'Yeah, *ciao.*'

I lie on my back, letting my face get soaked with tears. There's no sobbing or wailing, just water. I wonder how long it's possible to cry. I wonder if it's in *The Guinness Book of Records*.

13

Will I Ever Get Over It?

Patticake:	I broke up with my boyfriend two months ago and I thought by now I'd be feeling better than this. Any tips on how to get over him?
Swedishblonde:	Ask yourself, Was I really in love with this man, or do I just love the idea of being with somebody? Do you miss his particular smell, or his way of walking, or are you just annoyed because you're alone?
Golumismyex:	To get over him you need to get under someone else.
Prettylacey:	So many men and so little time. Get yourself out there, angel. Get busy. Join clubs. Have a makeover. Pretend you're over it and eventually you will be.
Golumismyex:	Ask yourself, Will I care about this a year from now?
Voodoowitch:	I can make you a powerful love spell to cause your desired one to fall deeply in love with you again. I also sell a wide variety of wax effigies . . . but you must obtain a hair from his head.

Since I'm not basking in rekindled love, encircled within the arms of my fiancé, I'm out clubbing with Lucy. I'm quickly realising there is nothing so depressing as clubbing in London on a Saturday if your heart is broken. Where do these people come from? It's as if the city has been sucked dry of its usual population and filled with people in fancy dress. The clubs are packed with tourists, day-trippers and fun-time goons on the pull. Lucy has brought me to Nite Spot – apparently the cheesiness is ironic and therefore über-cool. When I suggest we might just go to the pub, she shrieks, 'Action!' She's 'taken me under her wing', so here I stand in her high heels with a watery Long Island iced tea, feeling as animated as a hollowed-out log.

'Right, Viv, is there anyone here you fancy?' Lucy snakes her hips in time to the beat. I stare gloomily around the room. There are groups of men loitering by the dance floor where the girls shake out moves like lap dancers. Occasionally a lone wolf breaks away and begins to gyrate suggestively next to one of the girls and is either ignored or encouraged. The whole scene is only missing a David Attenborough voiceover.

Lucy is now shimmying up and down in her clingy, sparkly dress, singing along to the music about break, break, breaking someone's heart. 'Well? Spotted anyone?'

'Yeah, you.' I dance a few comedy moves in front of her.

'No, I'm serious. If you had to shag someone in here or die, who would you chose?'

'Still you.'

'I mean a man!'

'I know what you mean. I just don't feel like this is really helping.'

'Because you're not even trying!' She hands me a tequila shot. I finish it in three sips while she downs hers in one, shouts, 'Yee-ha!' and slams her empty glass on the bar. 'Right, choose, or I'll tell the barman you want to fuck him.'

I glance at the grinning Polish guy tending the bar, then hurriedly scan the low tables, eventually spotting a guy with glasses and a kind smile.

'Okay, him over there.'

'In the black shirt? Nice!' She smiles at a male model in a studded belt.

'No, over there, sitting down. Glasses. Kind-looking.'

'Oh my God, you *are* joking!' She looks at my face. 'You're not joking!'

'He looks like he'd be nice to talk to.'

'You don't want to *talk* to him, Vivienne!'

'Don't I?'

She holds my arms and then pulls me close. 'Oh, you poor love. When was the last time you were screaming in sexual ecstasy?' She makes it sound like an everyday occurrence, like buying milk.

'I don't think I've ever—'

'Just as I thought. Tonight we'll fix that, my lovely. Let's get more shots!'

We're on our third round of something that tastes like Benylin when I get it – I'm feeling a tingling beginning in my stomach and radiating outwards to every extremity and I'm also . . . so pretty! We move onto the dance floor and I slide up and down back to back against Lucy. As I twirl round I know that every girl in there wishes she'd worn a polo-neck jumper just like me. Then someone is dancing close to Lucy and I'm spinning on my own. The music is so great I just have to *move*. Large black shoes shuffle in front of me. Someone's dancing with me and he's feeling this groove too – his legs, in black trousers, step to the beat. I look up, see a stripy unbuttoned shirt, then an enormous Adam's apple. I grab the back of his neck and shout, 'Amazing!' in his ear. He nods, touching my waist. I grab him again and shout, 'Adam's apple!' He holds my waist and dances closer to me. I notice his big nose. I like it! The tips of his fingers are beginning to touch my bottom. I dance back a few steps and point at him, shouting, 'Cheeky!' He shimmies up close to me and I feel his breath on the side of my neck. I smell soapy aftershave. Lifting my hands above my head, I snake my hips. I'm *the* most desirable woman in the world!

Now he's behind me, unmovable, like a wall. The bass is vibrating, the lights moving, and he's holding my hips, pushing them around. It's a bit weird, actually. His lips brush the side of my face. I turn to move away and he locks them on my mouth, using an uncomfortable suction to hold on, and I feel the mollusc-like tip of his tongue, probing. I pull away, turning my head, and he suckers onto my neck.

'Uh, don't do that,' I shout. He tries again, this time sucking up my ear like a hoover fish. 'No, thanks!' I shriek, and dance a little more, aiming to casually lose him. He smiles and makes another lunge for my face. I see the wet mouth looming as I dodge away.

I find Lucy dancing with the model guy. She's swaying close to him with her eyes closed. She sings, 'Make love and dance . . .'

I shriek, 'Toilet!' in her ear.

I'm trying to pee while holding the door shut and balancing to avoid the yellow-splattered seat. It's not easy in heels. Lucy is shouting from next door.

'I'm taking mine home – he's hot! What about you?' I'm out of the cubicle now, but Lucy is still peeing strongly. She didn't get the nickname 'Hoss' at uni for nothing.

'Christ, no! He's like something from *Star Wars*!'

'Not in a cute way?'

'He's like a face-sucking alien.'

She finally emerges, still pulling down her dress. 'You ready to go, then?' She smiles naughtily. She's pulled, so end of evening.

'Er, no. I want to dance.'

She looks disappointed.

'You yourself said I needed a good night out. It's only one

o'clock.' I glare at her as I pull open the door, but as I turn I come eye to eye with the freaky face-sucker. He lunges towards me, lips puckered, tentacles reaching. I only just manage to slam the door in time. I lean back against the wood, feeling like Sigourney Weaver. 'I can't go out there!' Lucy tuts and pulls open the door, but he blocks the way, lurching wildly.

'Look, buster, my friend isn't interested.' He smiles vacantly. 'Can you move, please? She's not interested.' She turns to me. 'I don't think he speaks English.' I peer around the door-frame and his face lights up, wet red mouth winking. I slam the door on him.

'What are you doing, Viv? We can't stay in here.'

'No . . . he'll be gone now.' I open the door confidently, but he steps into the space, looming over us. There's only one thing for it – I need to say something science fictiony. Something fit for a face-sucking monster. I step forward, holding my hand up in a stop sign.

'You will let us pass!' I say solemnly.

He hesitates. I keep my hand up and repeat the command, avoiding eye contact, until he writhes away like a scalded snake.

At the end of the night I think I might have to find a therapist. See someone. Maybe I'm depressed. As the slow dance plays I stand on my own, while Lucy smooches around the floor with Model Man. He's rubbing her bottom; she's massaging the back of his neck. The lights go on and I feel suddenly exposed and hot in my jumper. I feel like Lucy's mother who has come to collect her in a Fiat Panda.

The cloakroom can't find my jacket and I end up being crammed into the back seat of a speeding minicab listening to the squelch and slurp of Lucy and Model Guy exploring each other. They've insisted on dropping me home. Every now and then Model Guy breaks off and asks me a polite question like, 'How long have you lived in London?' while sliding a hand up Lucy's dress. I rest my forehead against the steamy window, watching kebab shops and taxi ranks zoom by. A girl in a strappy black dress clings to a lamppost and vomits on her shoes. I imagine the kind of evening Rob and Sam have had: dinner somewhere exclusive and expensive, champagne, sparkling conversation and then home. And I've turned myself inside out with jealousy and pain.

14

Family and Friends

1. Do you have a support network of people to lean on when life gets tough?

a. Yes, I have a large circle of friends and a loving family.

b. No, even my work colleagues have stopped listening.

c. Yes, but I can't let them know what a fool I've been.

2. Do you believe a problem shared is a problem halved?

a. Yes, it's always better to open up about what's worrying you.

b. No, I can't think of a single person I'd share a problem with.

c. There are no problems that can't be fixed by a party.

3. Do you have a special person in your life to help you to discover your true worth and potential?

a. Yes, my closest friends.

b. Yes, my ex.

c. I have no worth or potential.

Answers

Mostly A – you are making healthy choices. Making some new happy memories with family and friends will set you well on the road to recovery.

Mostly B – you may need to make some connections with the outside world. Do not mope alone. Do some fun stuff.

Mostly C – seek professional help.

Sunday morning is a time for lovers. There's not a radio programme that isn't devoted to it. Why do people ring up to say how 'in love' they are? Who are they trying to convince? It's really pathetic, actually.

I'm practising stillness of body and mind. It's chapter four of *Find Your* Own *Way, Be Free*, about quietening the mental voices and achieving a peaceful soul. The author photo shows a woman with the kind of neat hair you can trust. Her smile says, *I know*. I'm in bed realising that keeping still is actually very difficult. I'm approaching what I think could be the beginning of stillness when Lucy calls.

'How are you?' she asks.

'Pretty shit,' I say, without moving my jaw much.

'Shitter than yesterday?'

I think about this. I've never before considered levels of shitness. 'Probably less shit than yesterday. How was it with Model Guy?'

'Unfeasibly small penis.'

'Oh.'

'It was a good night, though, hey? And you pulled!'

'Yeah . . . hideous . . . Actually, is there something about me that attracts other life forms?'

'I think they just pick up your scent. So, fancy coming to a singles' lunch today? It's at the Jug and Goblet. Everyone gets off their heads, goes crazy and you will not go home alone. Guaranteed!'

'Wow. That sounds amazing, but I can't.'

'Why?'

'I don't want to.'

'So, what will you do instead – mope around your flat, gazing at pictures of Rob?'

'No.'

'Study pictures of Rob's new girlfriend? Make yourself a barbed-wire shirt? Stay in bed reading self-help books?'

I glance at *Find Your* Own *Way, Be Free*. 'I might.'

'Viv, come on. You have to get a life!'

'Actually, I'm going to Nana's.' I'll call her in a minute – it'll be all right.

'Oh, very rock and roll.'

'I've invited Max.' I'll call him too.

'You are living the dream!' I'm not sure why she thinks this tough love thing is helping. It crosses my mind that she might be heartless.

'Don't you have to meet your fuck buddy today or something?'

'No. That's the idea of a fuck buddy. You don't *have* to do anything.'

'Oh.'

'You all right? You sound weird.'

'Oh yeah, I'm fine. Talk to you later.'

'Later.' She hangs up. I listen to the fizzing drone of the handset and wonder what comes next and how long it will take. After a while, when nothing happens, I drag myself to the kitchen and pull open the fridge. The shelves grin. I take out a packet of smoked salmon. I read words like 'finest' and 'wild' on the recycled packaging. It was full of promise on Friday. I hold the pack in my hands like a prayer book, gazing through the kitchen window at the summer sky. I slide the glass up, looking down onto the back alley where discarded pizza boxes and empty cans have collected. I see a used condom lying flabbily on top. I examine the salmon I was once so hopeful about and let it drop. It falls among the Saturday-night remains, a nugget of wholesomeness in the wasteland. I get the cream cheese and the croissants and hurl them out too. I take the strawberries and fire them one by one into the sky. A couple ricochet off the windowframe and roll onto the floor. I consider the champagne, then grab it by the neck and rip off the foil. There is no pop as the cork slides out. Rob told me it's vulgar to pop. To think – before he educated me, I used to pop *and* cheer. Leaning against the worktop, I swallow down a flute of blush bubbles. Then I let the last of my glasses drop onto the kitchen tiles. It smashes, sending shards scattering spectacularly. I close the fridge door with my foot and shuffle off to get dressed.

Max arrives early. This is not his natural behaviour. He's even combed his hair, and when I kiss him on the cheek, I notice he's shaved and is smelling of some weird citrusy scent. His jeans are clean and he has on a shirt I've never seen before – blue checks. I look him up and down.

'Look at you!'

'What? What's wrong with me?' He looks around as if I just shouted, 'It's the cops!'

'Nothing's wrong.' I smile. 'You look quite nice.'

'Well, you know nanas, they like this kind of thing, don't they?' His grin is a bit like a pirate's with the chipped tooth.

'Nanas do?'

'Ah, shut up, Viv. What have you come as, anyway?'

'Me? Er . . . a girl who hasn't done her washing and has had to pick from the back of the cupboard.' I know my three-year-old bleached jeans make my arse look enormous, and the sleeveless blouse is less 'retro floral', more 'sad loser'.

'Fancy a drink?'

'Have you any whisky?'

'No. Anyway, it's Sunday morning.'

'Anything then.'

'I've got champagne. It's pink.'

'Grand.' He follows me into the kitchen. 'You rang me on Friday. I tried to call you back.' My cowboy boots crunch on the shattered flute. Max doesn't mention it. 'You all right?'

'Yeah.'

'Yeah? Because you sounded not all right.'

'Rob wants to get rid of that red chair.'

He nods in a way that shows he has no idea what I'm talking about.

'I bought that chair for him . . . We went for a walk on this really perfect autumn day and we passed a little junk shop. We went inside and I spotted the arm of this chair under a pile of stuff. It was such a lovely tomato red.' I glance at Max. He's staring at the floor. 'It was almost orange, really. We got the guy to drag it out and there it was, a perfect old reading chair with a wingback. I secretly bought it for his birthday and I had it re-stuffed and cleaned and all that. He loved it. Now his fiancée doesn't like it, so he wants to know what I want to do with it.'

'Tell him to stick it up his arse.'

'Just like that, though. What do I want doing with it? Unbelievable. And it's made me realise – it's not that he didn't want to get married; he just didn't want to marry *me*.' I stare at Max's face, trying to concentrate away the tears, then slowly turn my gaze to the living room, sniffing and imagining the chair there. 'I can't have it here. It'd be like a big fat ghost sitting in the corner, reminding me. But I can't get rid of it . . .' I hear my voice waver and wonder why this whole chair thing has become so huge for me.

'Look. I'll go and get it off him and keep it at mine until you realise that you love the chair but that he's a cock-end. Then we'll bring it here and have a chair party.'

'God. What would that be like?'

'A chair party? Well, it would involve you and me and the chair and not many clothes . . .'

'No – what would it be like to realise he's a cock-end?'

He puts his arm around my shoulders. 'Ah, Viv, I promise one day you'll be so adored you'll not give a shit.'

I rest my head on his shoulder. 'You promise, do you?'

'I do.'

* * *

Nana's street is shaded green by the summer trees. The pavement shimmers in the early heat. As we approach the house she throws open the front door and stands on the step in a full-length peacock-blue sundress, her twiggy arms outstretched.

'Max! Max Kelly!' she calls like a Shakespearean actress.

He reaches for her, doing a side-to-side dance. 'Hello, Eve.' She seems small as a child in his vigorous embrace. 'Good to see you.'

'Max, you look so *well*. Doesn't he look well, Viv?'

He turns to me, grinning like a goon.

'Yes, I suppose he does,' I mutter.

'I am well, Eve. And how are you keeping?'

'You know, I can't complain. Now . . .' She leads us into the house and downstairs to the heat of the kitchen. I smell a joint of beef roasting. She kisses me and fusses over drinks. Max's presence is making her giggly and silly, and I feel a flash of embarrassment. 'You take this lovely man out to the garden, Vivienne, and I'll bring out a tray.'

We push open the French doors and step onto the sunlit patio. The stones are cracked like a crumpled roadmap, and spread with moss. A rusting table and four chairs are shaded by a tattered canvas umbrella. Max turns his face to the sun and puts on sunglasses.

'It's looking like a beautiful day,' he says.

'You're very popular.'

'Yeah, well, me and Eve go way back.'

I tut, feeling childishly left out. 'She should do something about the garden,' I mutter, and climb up the three bowed steps to the sloping lawn. Max follows. We brush past straggly, scented jasmine, and I stop for a moment before Nana's angel statue. She stands in the centre of the lawn. I look at her beatific gaze and I'm seven again, whispering secrets to her sad stone eyes and hanging daisy chains on her wings. I used to think if I talked to the angel, my mother could hear. Bless me. Fruit trees shade the dappled lawn and windfall apples shine through the long grass, giving off a faint sickly perfume. We wander to the end of the garden where old roses tangle together, their blousy heads nodding with the attention of bees. 'I really love English roses,' I tell him. I watch his suntanned hand as he brushes the underside of a peach-white bloom.

'Me too,' he says. I glance at his face. He's smiling down at me, eyes full of warmth and humour. I turn back to the roses. He shifts on his feet and says, 'I'll go and help your nan with the drinks.'

I turn round as he bounds down the steps. Taking off my boots, I walk barefoot on the cool damp grass and wander past the forgotten vegetable patch back to the angel.

'What do you know?' I ask her, touching the tips of her chipped fingers.

There's shouting and laughter coming from the kitchen; then Nana steps out wearing a wide-brimmed white hat, followed by Max in a straw fedora, carrying a tray at shoulder height. Nana shades her eyes and calls to me, her voice becoming comically loud and posh.

'Viv, look, we've gone all Riviera! I've made margaritas!'

Max stands behind her, grinning; his white teeth and tanned face with the dark curls escaping the hat at the sides make him look like a wicked Greek waiter out to seduce susceptible tourists.

'You're both ridiculous.' I step onto the warm patio and we sip cocktails under the umbrella. Max lights a cigarette and Nana picks up the packet.

'May I?'

'Sure.' He slides over the lighter.

'You don't smoke!' I exclaim.

Her face scrunches up as she inhales. She holds the cigarette awkwardly away from her, its filter now smeared with coral lipstick. She gives a little cough as she exhales.

'Well, it's something I've always wanted to take up, but I've been waiting until I'm seventy.' She sits with her skirt hitched up, sunning her thin, veiny legs.

'Why would you do that?'

'Well, it can kill you, you know,' she says, taking another drag, this time coughing the smoke straight back out. 'In any case, I don't think I like it. Would you like this back, Max?'

He leans forward and takes the cigarette from her, putting it out in a saucer. 'Is there anything else you want to try, Eve? Hang-gliding? Class-A drugs?' he asks.

'Drugs, most definitely. Especially that one that's good for arthritis. Hang-gliding, no, but perhaps a balloon ride. I'd like to have got married in a hot-air balloon.'

'She's such a show-off! You're scared of heights, Nana.'

'But that's the beauty of a balloon – you don't have to go very high and you can't fit many guests in the basket.'

'It's genius, Eve! When I get married, I'll do it.' He refills our glasses.

'Who's going to marry you?' I snap.

He looks up from pouring. 'There are scores of women after me, don't you worry. I'm just choosy, that's all.' He winks at Nana.

'Good for you, Max!' she squeals.

'Well, Max, you're many things, but I'd never have said choosy.' I lean back with my drink, laughing at him.

'Ah, but there's a lot you don't know about me, Vivienne,' he says quietly.

'Is there?' I smile.

'Yeah.' He puts down the jug and turns his face to the sun. I shiver suddenly, goose bumps rising on my arms. We sit quietly for a while, listening to the buzz and twitter of the garden before Nana declares the roast ready.

'Although it's the very last thing you want on such a hot day.'

In the kitchen we decide to turn lunch into a cold buffet. Max makes a salad out of the roast potatoes with mayonnaise and French mustard. I make up something weird with the carrots, grating them and adding coriander and orange juice. We eat it with slices of cold beef. Nana interrogates Max with her mouth full.

'So, Max, tell me about your paintings. Are you planning any exhibitions?'

'I show a few all the time – a little gallery in north London takes them.'

'And do they sell?'

'Occasionally. I pay the rent, anyway.'

I think of his scruffy flat, calculating just how little he must sell.

'What about commissions?'

'Not so far. I'm hoping to be part of this art show they're doing at the Academy. If I get selected, it would be great exposure.'

'I remember one you once showed me – a naked man holding a cat. It was very striking.'

'That was part of my first show. I sold that one.'

'I think it's amazing to have such talent, Max. You must never give up.'

It's strange to hear Max talk about his work like this. It seems he has ambitions. I've always told him to get a proper job.

He glances at me. 'Viv thinks creative people are skint losers.'

'I never said that!'

'Vivienne, I'm surprised at you.' Nana frowns as Max laughs.

I try to defend myself: 'I like your stuff. That painting of Lula is beautiful.'

'Thanks. It's not the best. That comes when you really feel

something for the subject, like there's an energy coming from them . . . then something beautiful is possible.' He smiles at me. His eyes seem incredibly dark. I look away to the garden, my cheeks burning. I'm surprised to find that I want him to be talking about my portrait.

'Phew, it's so hot today!' I move my chair back into the meagre patch of shade.

'Well, Max, I was hoping you might do a little sketch of me this afternoon.'

He turns his eyes to Nana and I feel as if I've been given a rest from electrocution. 'Sure! Do you have paper?'

I clear away the plates as they settle into their roles. The artist with his jeans rolled up, revealing hairy, skinny legs, sketching silently as the model poses, gazing out to the garden. I fill the sink and wash pots, looking out to the patio. She takes off her hat. He rips off a page. So typical of Nana, suddenly producing a sketchpad and pencils like that. They occasionally rest for a few moments and I hear snatches of easy chatter; what a pair of flirts they are. I change the water and start on the pans. She's looking straight at him now. In the sketch there's a ghost of the young beauty she was. A pan lid slides from the drainer and they both turn.

'Hey, you! Any chance of a drink out here?' Max shouts over his shoulder.

'There's cold white wine in the fridge, darling,' Nana adds.

I take out the bottle and glasses, and pick up one of the sketches. The smudged lines hold the essence of Nana. 'These are good.'

'I hope he's made me beautiful.'

'I can only draw what I see.' Max throws down a pencil and pours the wine.

'And you can't make a silk purse out of a sow's ear,' she adds.

There's cheese instead of dessert. Nana brings out a Brie, and setting the board down in the sun, she cuts herself a huge slice, scraping up the oozing middle and nibbling the rind. I think she looks very contented these days. I close my eyes and let the sun bathe my face, half listening as she chats to Max about travel plans.

'. . . then we thought about Santander. Reg has never been.'

'I love that northern coast,' says Max.

'Did you say Reg has never been?' I keep my eyes closed as I speak.

'Yes.'

'So you two are going on holidays together now?' I sit up.

'Well, yes.'

I slump down again, sighing.

'Is there a problem, Viv?' she asks.

I open one eye, then shut it again. 'No, not at all. It's just . . . well, Granddad doesn't seem very long gone, for you to be off having fun with someone new.'

'Two years he's been gone, Viv. Two years is a long time to be lonely.'

'Well, maybe it's just me. I still miss him, that's all.'

'And so do I. But I'm still alive and while I am, I'll jolly well make the most of it!' She stands up, gathering a few plates, and stalks off to the kitchen. I hear the click of a lighter.

Max exhales a curl of smoke. 'Oh dear,' he says.

'What?'

'Looks like you've upset your nan.'

'Well! This whole thing with Reg is ridiculous.' I glare at him. 'She flirted with him even when Granddad was alive, you know.' Max's face is calm. I glance to the kitchen but can't see Nana. 'I think she started seeing him not long after the funeral.' I sit back, feeling the heat of the day blazing on the top of my head while he finishes his smoke. 'And she's never said anything. She's never announced it. They just sneak around.'

'I wonder why.'

'Because she feels guilty!'

'Or . . . maybe she doesn't want to hurt you.'

'It's got nothing to do with me.'

'Well, you're right about that.' He smiles. I stare out to the garden, feeling stung. I feel the muffled throb of a headache pressing against my temples. Why should I care if Nana and Reg are spending time together? I want her to be happy. But I feel betrayed in a way I can't explain. Max wouldn't understand; he has parents, two of them, alive and still married, and four mad sisters and hundreds of nephews and nieces. They all love him with a neediness and longing that makes him avoid going home. My home and family history are a fragile glass and Reg is tapping at the edges with a hammer.

I struggle to get to the heart of my feelings, and just when I think I can explain, the sense escapes, leaving half a thought like a discarded tail. I give up and go into the kitchen in search of water. Nana is putting away plates in the dresser and I notice her hands tremble as she reaches up to a top cupboard.

'Can I help?' I ask.

'Nearly done.' Crockery clatters onto the shelf and I stand awkwardly beside her. She closes the glass door, breathing slightly heavily with the effort of the stretch. She turns to me and smiles, her blue eyes full of understanding, places a hand on top of mine and gives it a little squeeze.

'We'll have to go soon,' I say.

'Just as you like, love,' she says, and strokes my face with the backs of her fingers.

The heat of the day seems trapped in the feverish London streets. The smell of things fried mingles with the fumes and dust. Max walks with me towards the tube. I tell him I don't need an escort; he thinks I do.

He's talking about getting away from the city, taking a sabbatical, a motorbike pilgrimage. 'Why don't you come with me?' he asks.

'I don't have a bike.'

'You'd ride pillion, dummy.'

'Where'd we sleep?'

'Under the stars.'

'What, together?' I make a face.

'Okay, I'll sleep under the stars alone; you can check into a five-star hotel.'

We turn the corner; I look up to the open kitchen window of my flat, thinking how Rob would kill me for being so careless about security.

'A five-star hotel with a spa,' I say as we get to my door. I struggle a little with the lock and when I turn round, Max has stepped back into the street.

'Oh. Are you not coming up?'

'No . . . stuff to do.' He smiles.

'Like what?'

'Like plan the "stars and spas" trip.' He starts to walk away, leaving me standing on the doorstep.

'I'm not coming!' I shout at his back.

'Ah, you say that now . . .'

I watch him go, sauntering out of view like a great bear. I feel like he's taken the sunshine with him.

15

Moving On

It's important not to idolise your ex. Focus on their weaknesses and make a list of everything you didn't like about them. Read the list every time you start to miss them.

'My ex-boyfriend Shaun always said my feet made him feel sick. He used to make this joke about me swooping down and picking things up with my talons. I just look at my feet and remember him laughing and poof! I stop missing him.'

Becka, 20, Harrow

'My ex-girlfriend wanted me to sleep with her and her eighteen cuddly animals. I'd wake up in the night, rammed against the wall, with all these glass eyes staring at me. I honestly don't miss her, especially when I think of that evil monkey.'

Simon, 25, Leeds

'If I miss him, I just go, "Spotty back, spotty back, spotty back."'

Tanya, 30, Newcastle

'The best thing is if you just go out with someone else. Anyone will do – just get out there and get back in the saddle.'

Katie, 39, Staines

It's Monday morning and I arrive at work with a feeling of doom, but I can't put my finger on why. Everything is as it was when I left before the weekend – grey carpet, striplights, overloaded desk – but it feels like I'm walking to the guillotine. I see Christie isn't in – so much for her new leaf. I look out at the perfect summer sky; a white vapour trail arches across the clear blue. It's a gift of a day, a day for picnicking with a lover, for waterskiing across a lake, or driving to the coast in a convertible . . . if I weren't completely and utterly alone.

I look at Rob's photo, at his perfect smile. A smile that's no longer mine. I pull him off the pinboard and drop him in my drawer. 'Goodbye, my love,' I whisper, and close it. Right, I will seek out every shred of myself that's still waiting for him and give it shock treatment. I'll let him go. Even the thought of it makes me want to howl.

I turn on the desktop. It complains I didn't shut down properly, then pings up the spreadsheet I was panicking over on Friday. Friday! I was so full of hope then. I was seeing him that night. How a weekend can change everything . . . Now I have no future. I'm desolate. All I have is work. I'll throw myself into that. I write, 'Slogans for edible knickers,' on my notepad and check emails. Two from suppliers, one telling me the tartan we chose for the purses is out of stock. The other says the candles with Scandinavian patterns on are made by prisoners in Norway. They wonder – will this fit with Barnes and Worth's ethical standards? I think about this. Prisoners have to do something, right? It's not like we're harvesting their organs or anything. I'll need to check it before we order. I go to make coffee using the wall-mounted water boiler, thinking how Rob once told me they spread legionnaires' disease, and search the fridge in vain for any milk labelled 'Gifting'. I use the one labelled 'Accounts. Do not even think about it!' instead. Just as I'm rinsing the spoon, I hear Christie giggling. I step from the kitchen and find her talking shoes with Snotty, who has today teamed leopard-print popsocks with zebra-skin sandal-boots.

'No, I think just go for it! Life's too short,' gasps Christie. They both turn to me and the conversation dies.

I smile. 'Morning!'

'Good morning, Vivienne,' says Snotty, and she squeezes Christie on the shoulder before she walks away, leaving me gawping after her.

'I think she's taking this whole animal-print thing a bit far, don't you?' I say.

'I think she looks all right today, actually,' says Christie.

I feel panic, like a buffalo suddenly finding itself far from the herd and hearing growling in the bushes.

'What's going on?' I ask as we walk back to our desks.

Her cheeks flush. 'Nothing.'

'What? So you're great mates with Snotty now?'

'No, it's just—' She plonks some papers down on her desk.

'What are those?'

'Oh, Viv. Ruth, I mean Snotty, asked me to have a breakfast meeting with her this morning – you know, to come up with ideas for products.'

'A breakfast meeting?'

'Yeah, and she brought croissants.'

'Croissants?'

'Yeah, those ones with chocolate in.'

I stare at Christie. What is Snotty doing having meetings with my assistant behind my back and discussing creative matters that are my concern? Something's going on. She wanted Christie sacked last week. All I can think is that Mole likes Christie and after the meeting on Friday she must have set this up. Snotty doesn't like anyone. A scarlet rash creeps up Christie's neck. She opens her mouth to speak, then thinks better of it.

'So did you have a good time in the pub on Friday night?' I ask.

'Yeah,' she squeaks uncertainly.

'What did you talk about?' We stand face to face and I start to tap my fingers on the desk.

'Well, the pub was rammed and Marion – Mole – knew nearly everyone in there. It was a right laugh, Viv – you should've come.'

'Uh-huh, uh-huh, and did you discuss work?'

'Well, a bit.'

'Right, so, what was said?'

She starts picking bits of fluff from her chair. 'They were talking about the Christmas offer and how there might be career opportunities for me because I have such good ideas and everything.'

'Yes?'

'And that's when Snotty asked me to have this meeting.'

'And did she offer you any career opportunities?'

'No, we just talked underwear really.' She can't look at me.

'I see. Well. All I would say is, be careful, Christie. Remember, "Ruth" will only ever look after herself.' I see her face fall. She's deflated and I'm holding the pin. I know that whatever's going on, Christie won't have a clue. It's not her fault; they've made her a pawn. She looks down at her Mary Jane heels. I smile at her, suddenly sorry. 'I'm sure they will offer you something, though . . .'

'Well, they said *your* work has been missing the mark recently . . .' she fires after the bell. 'Yeah, they said you've had your eye off the ball for a while now . . . that you let personal matters interfere with your work.'

'Did they?'

'Yeah.'

'And what did you say?'

'I said you've been through a difficult time recently.'

'Right.' I feel something scratch in my throat. I stare at a poster about fire regulations behind Christie's head, trying to will away tears. 'Okay, Christie. Give me a moment and then we'll have a meeting about our range. All right?' I turn to my desk, staring at the screen and swallowing hard.

What's wrong with me? I must not start crying! I'm furious that they discussed me in the pub like that – I know I've not been as committed as I might normally be, but I have been dealing with a personal crisis. Would they cut me some slack if I were actually getting divorced? I'm losing the love of my life here, I can barely cope with tomorrow, so forgive me if I'm not *so* interested in Christmas gifts . . I blow my nose and a new email pings onto my screen.

> Good morning, Vivienne,
> The website is ready for your perusal . . . when I see you.
> Mike

This is all I need. How has he managed to make even his email seem creepy? I reply quickly.

> Hi Mike,
> Thanks so much! I can't wait to see what you've come up with.
> I'm in meetings all morning, but are you free after lunch?
> Viv

His reply appears almost instantly.

> See you tonight after work. 6 p.m.

Is he expecting me to buy him a meal tonight? I had thought the website would be up and running before I 'paid'. What choice do I have? I owe him, and a Monday-night dinner is less painful a sacrifice than any other day. I agree and, feeling like I've just made a deal with the devil, I close the email and print out our product spreadsheet. Missing the mark recently? Not any more. I swivel on my chair to face Christie's desk.

She senses me there and quickly shuts down a fashion website.

'Are you okay to meet now?' I ask. She turns round, nettled.

'I think so.'

'Good. So, edible knickers, then?' I smile encouragingly.

'Actually, I want to handle that line myself. The buying team think I should bring something from idea stage to store shelf on my own.'

'The buying team?'

'Yes.'

'Who, Snotty and Mole? S and M?'

'That's right.'

'Well, then, isn't that a great plan? May I ask if you've found a supplier?'

'Not yet.'

'Okay, did you come up with any slogans?'

'Yes, actually. I have a few that I think could work.'

'Would you like to share them with me?'

She seems to loosen up a little, even smiling as she picks up a notepad. 'Well, there's "Hairy Christmas" – it's a play on merry Christmas, but because it's going on pants, it'll be close to pubic hair . . .'

'I get it.'

'Then there's "Suck it and see." And "Deck your balls" – that's for the men's range,' she reads.

'Right . . .'

'Then I was thinking of variations on traditional Christmas food. I mean, it won't be these actual ones, but I thought things like instead of mince pie we could have "Minge pie", instead of Christmas pudding we could have "Christmas pussy" . . .' she says, with a straight face.

'Or maybe instead of Christmas turkey you could have "Last turkey in the shop"?' I laugh.

She looks up to the ceiling, chewing her pencil thought-fully, then frowns. 'No, Viv, I don't get that one.' She looks at the notepad. '"Cranberry saucy"?'

'What about just "saucy"?'

'See, the point you're missing, Viv, is the theme. It's Christmas food.' She speaks patiently, as if to an imbecile. 'Anyway, those are my ideas for now. I'll let you know if I need any more help.'

I search her face, looking for a scrap of the Christie I recognise, but Snotty has replaced her with an android.

We carry on through the morning, finalising the range. Christie dodges anything I try to delegate, saying she has to concentrate on her own 'line'. She's calling it 'pantalise'. Because it sounds like tantalise, she explains. She's being really very annoying, so I insist she cover the decorative candles and check out the 'made by prisoners' issue; then I'm left with the other ten products. It will be good to keep busy – it'll keep my mind occupied. I'll be heroic, working all the hours. Everyone will be amazed. A daydream of Rob in Sicily, on our last holiday, rolls golden and honey-coated through my memory before bursting like a pretty bubble as it hits the wet pavement of reality. Real life: work, and a date with creepy Michael.

The lift doors open and there he is, leaning greasily against the marble foyer wall with studied confidence, one of his legs juddering. I have the urge to dart past like a startled deer and disappear into the undergrowth of home-bound commuters, but instead I walk slowly across the gleaming square. His darting eyes clock me, but bizarrely, he pretends he hasn't seen. He looks round casually, both legs now bouncing at the knee. He greets me with fake surprise when I'm standing in front of him, leaning forward, taking me by the elbow and kissing the air next to my ear. I take in the faint vegetable smell of his breath and a hint of spice on his collar. He avoids eye contact and nods towards the exit; then there's an embarrassing scuffle as we approach the revolving door and end up squashed in the same segment, shuffling round in silence and being spat out into the warm, rushing evening.

'Where are we off to, then, Michael?' I ask breezily.

'Mike.'

'Sorry . . . Mike,' I say. He stares off down the street, eyes narrowing as if assessing a combat zone, then turns and faces the other way.

'I think drinks at O'Malley's first,' he replies with a little satisfied gasp, then walks away, taking quick, short steps. I run a bit to keep up and fall in line beside him, thankful that I'm wearing flat shoes; his eyes are level with my throat. I glance at his rat-tail beard as he stares straight ahead.

'O'Malley's. I don't think I've ever been.'

'Oh, you'd know if you'd been!' He sniggers into space.

I look down at the pavement, at my sandals and his scuffed synthetic loafers. We walk against the crowd, buffeting our way through. At times he walks ahead along the kerb, never checking to see if I'm following. At least we don't look like we're together, walking like this. I feel a strange combination of anxiety and dread, mixed with a pinch of curiosity. I remind myself I had nothing better to do this evening and that it's important to get out of your comfort zone – it says so in *Find Your Own Way, Be Free*. Also, I must remember he's done me a huge favour. I catch up with him as we hit the pavement again.

'So, Mike, how's the site looking?'

'All right.'

'I can't wait to see it.'

He looks at me sideways, like I've tried to trick him out of a windfall. We lapse into silence until he comes to a stop in front of some formal-looking black railings. Concrete steps turn downwards to a wooden door. He skips down like a gameshow host and I see the white of his scalp through his thinning hair. I take a longing look at the golden sunlit evening, like taking a last breath before plunging underwater, then follow.

He pulls at the door and we're hit by the muggy belch of an underworld bar, all dark wood and burgundy upholstery. My eyes adjust to the murky light and I make out figures hunched in booths around the walls; here and there the glint of a facial piercing. Behind the bar a beautiful obese brunette leans, her skin shining white as a cream cheese in the gloom, her chalk-smooth bosom contrasting starkly with a shiny black corset.

'All right, Mike? What can I get you?' she calls as we approach.

He glances at me triumphantly. He orders a pint of bitter, takes his glass and moves off to a booth, leaving me to get my own drink and pay. I slide into the bench opposite with my vodka and tonic.

'I've had her,' he says, licking beer foam from his upper lip and nodding towards the bar.

'Well, she's very pretty.' I nod.

'I love big girls.'

I feel the table vibrate with his shaking legs and take a big gulp of vodka. I look around the room and back at him, smiling thinly.

'You're probably not big enough for me, but you've got a good-sized arse on you. I like that,' he elaborates.

'Thanks, that's . . . er . . . nice of you to say.'

'No problem. You're not stacked enough in front, though, strictly speaking.'

'Oh.' I feel the skin of my inadequate cleavage crawl. My striped T-shirt keeps me covered up, but it's clingy. I catch his eyes darting away from my nipples. His bony fingers tap a beat on the table and he looks around with shoulders hunched, nodding his head to a beat only he can hear. Then he laughs suddenly, a sort of bray ending in a giggle.

'You're not comfortable here, are you?'

'I'm fine.'

'It's mad in here.'

I look around at other people quietly drinking, thinking there must be something about to happen that I'm not aware of. Maybe a bell will suddenly ring and we'll all have to swap trousers and do the Macarena.

'Mike . . . about the website . . .'

He quickly throws down a slip of paper with a web address written on it. 'All on there, for your . . . perusal.'

'Great!' I reach for it, but he snatches it back, his scrabbling fingers catching my hand.

'Not until *I've* had a good evening, sister!' He smiles. 'One thing you should know about me is this: I know women. I know what you're like.' He taps the side of his nose and shakes his head. 'If I give you what you want up front, you're going to run off home as soon as you can, aren't you?' I stare at him. Does this mean he regularly bribes women to go out with him? Knows they'd avoid him like chronic candida if he didn't have a carrot on a stick? He jiggles in his seat. 'I've got what you want' – he taps his pocket – 'so you give me what I want. That's only fair, isn't it?'

'I wasn't going to run off home!' I laugh. 'I just thought we might talk about the site, that's all.' He stares at me like a wolf outside the chicken pen. 'And you wanted a meal, right?' I feel the need to clarify suddenly.

'That's right. Chinese banquet, I think.' He smacks his lips.

'Well, that's fine.' I down my drink. 'Shall we go?'

'Not until the belly dancer's been on.'

* * *

Quite a lot of vodka later, I'm sitting in the Golden Garden, feeling a warm sense of goodwill and chatting excitedly to Michael about facial hair. He has a closely trimmed patch of whiskers just below his bottom lip, above the long, beaded beard.

'Women love it,' he claims. He spins the turntable round so that I can reach the crispy fried seaweed. I take some with plastic chopsticks, and add a spring roll from the red dragon dishes.

'What kind of women love facial hair?' I screech.

'*Real* women do.' He grins. I laugh and the caramel-coloured ducks in the window seem to sway and dance. He sucks up chop suey, gathering escaping noodles from his chin with his tongue. I stare at the tongue; it seems obscenely long. I stuff my face with prawn balls. He leans forward conspiratorially. 'They call it my clit tickler,' he giggles. I look at his glistening whiskers, imagining. He suddenly flicks out the tongue.

'Oh my God!' I scream with my mouth full, then begin to choke on a bit of prawn. Mike leaps up and starts hammering me on the back with such force that I feel my eyes might pop out. I think he's winded me. I manage to nod and gasp, 'I'm okay!' before he stops and returns to his seat. I take a sip of water.

'I thought I'd have to do the Heimlich then. I'm advanced first aid trained,' he tells me.

'Mike, you're everything a woman could ask for! First aid trained and . . .' I can hardly complete the sentence '. . . you have a clit tickler!' I'm obviously hysterical. I can't stop laughing and he's laughing too, spraying bits of noodle. We sit like a pair of giggling children, quietening and suddenly hooting again. Someone approaches our table.

'Viv! Hello. Having fun?' I turn and look up, wiping my eyes. Rob stands over us, bemused. In an instant I'm sober and nothing's funny. I spot Sam hovering in a sparkly dress, her Bambi eyes wide and innocent.

'Hi! Rob!' I clear my throat.

'I thought someone was going to have to throw a bucket of water over you two.' He smiles, eyeing Michael.

'Oh, Rob – this is Michael, a colleague.' I turn to Michael. 'Michael, this is Rob, a . . . uh, a friend, and his fiancée, Sam.' I feel like he's holding the bucket.

'All right?' says Michael. Rob looks from me to him and back again.

'Well, nice to see you,' he says formally, and places his hand in the small of Sam's back, guiding her to the door. Her stilettos click like a thoroughbred's hooves as she takes a few steps. 'You'll let me know about collecting your stuff, then?' he adds. Sam tosses her chestnut mane and looks over her shoulder to check my reaction.

'Sure. What about tomorrow?' I reply, staring at Sam.

'Tomorrow?' He checks with her; she smiles in my face. 'Tomorrow's fine, Viv,' he says. 'See you at, say, seven thirty, then?' I nod. He looks at me for a moment and smiles a little intimate smile. I watch them leave. He says something to her and she laughs as they step into the night. I turn to Michael, feeling my insides deflate. He's scooping up baby squid with chopsticks; it's disgusting.

I shiver as we pick our way through Chinatown and Michael drapes his jacket around my shoulders. We pass the fart smell of decaying bins outside the back of restaurants. He's walking me to the tube, trying to persuade me to stay at his place. Apparently he has an aquarium I should see.

'You can walk three hundred and sixty degrees round the outside of it,' he says as we arrive at the gaping mouth of Leicester Square station.

'Michael. Thanks for a great night,' I say, meaning it. He stares at me. 'I mean that.' I peck him lightly on the cheek, feeling a buzzing energy emanate from him. No wonder he can't keep still.

He takes the slip of paper with the web address from his pocket and hands it to me. 'That, sister, is one great website. Check it through and we'll get it live, yeah?'

'I really appreciate it.'

'And listen, that guy back there, the one that floored you?' He shakes his head. 'He isn't a good guy.' I smile at him and feel my eyes fill. 'He could have just walked out. Instead he twisted the knife.'

I hold his hand in both of mine, feeling scaly skin and ridged nails. 'Thanks,' I tell him, and watch his black eyes casting about, looking at passers-by and occasionally settling on me before darting away again like flies, and I understand this small shred: the most unlikely people can become saviours in dark times, and the small kindnesses they offer can matter like life and death.

16

He Loves Me Not

If you hear any of these lines, he's definitely breaking up with you. Walk away with as much dignity as you can muster.

1. It's not you, it's me.
2. You're such a sweet girl . . .
3. I just need time to find myself.
4. I'm just not ready for a serious relationship, or a casual one, or any relationship . . . with you.
5. You're better off without me/too good for me/beneath me.
6. I'm moving away/don't have long to live.
7. I can't see you any more. This whole thing is just making me ill.
8. If you were slimmer, had red hair and didn't have the deformed toe, I think I could love you.
9. I think I'm allergic to your saliva.
10. I want to be free to find someone who agrees with me about things.
11. It's not your fault. I just feel I don't want to see your big fat face any more.
12. If I were ready for love, it wouldn't be with you.
13. If you wanted sex more often, I wouldn't need to sleep with anyone else.
14. I find the smell of you off-putting.
15. My ex is haunting me.

I'm standing outside my old home, looking up at the lit window, my heart flipping like a fish on a deck. It's okay. I can be calm. I'm just here to get the last of my things and leave, that's all. So why did I just spend forty quid having my hair blow-dried? While I watch, Sam flits into view and tugs at a curtain. *Intruder! Get out of my house!*

I hesitate at the heavy front door, touching the brass number 7. Lucky for some – that's what I said when we moved in and we kissed on the doorstep. Now there are two round box bushes in Italian terracotta pots; neat, ordered, symmetrical and nothing to do with me. I pick up the lion door-knocker and let it fall. I wait like a ghost, hearing a muffled shout and feet thumping downstairs. Rob throws open the door wearing a striped apron over a pale shirt, no tie. A thermal of curry powder and frying chicken floats into the cool street. He smiles and I'm stunned at the shining health of him. I stare at his perfect jaw, at his fallen-forward curls that make him almost too handsome. I lean to kiss him, but he's already bounding up the stairs.

'Come up,' he says, like I've come to read the meter.

Standing in the living room, I see she's moved in. It's suddenly frilly and ornate. There's a patterned lamp with ugly glass beads hanging around the base. Hairy cushions like yetis' bollocks are scattered on the sofa. Steam billows from the open-plan kitchen. I glance in at copper pans and fridge magnets with slogans about wine making you a better cook.

'Very homely,' I say.

'Uh yeah, so all the stuff is in the spare room – take anything you want and the rest we'll just clear out.' He shifts from one foot to the other.

'Clear out?'

'We're turning it into a nursery, you see.' He runs his hand through his hair, unable to look at me.

'Is Sam pregnant?' I almost choke on the words. He looks uncomfortable. 'Don't spare my feelings.'

'No, but she . . . we want to try on honeymoon.'

'Oh.' A lump clambers up to my throat like a poisonous toad.

'Look, sorry, Viv – there's no nice way of doing this really, is there? It's a bit like ripping a plaster off, isn't it? Best done quickly.'

'If you say so.'

I know I've no pride; it's both a good thing and a bad one. I make a show of myself because of it, but on the other hand I don't take offence too much and I can't hold grudges to save my life. Right now, though, it's a bad, bad thing; at the epicentre of my pain, barely able to keep it together, I'm arranging to clear out my stuff to make space for her *nursery*.

I want to scream at him. What about my babies? I want to demand he give me back my late twenties, but to get out alive, I must cut them off like a trapped limb. He shows me to the spare room where the relics of another life are piled like wreckage around the upended red chair. I step among the discarded things; it's like walking in a dead woman's attic.

'You don't want this?' I pick up a framed photo I took of him on top of Mount Snowdon. He looks at his feet. I walk a little further into the room. 'Or this?' I throw a designer candlestick onto a cardboard box stuffed with letters, photo albums and other detritus of our relationship.

'Viv . . . come on . . .'

I realise I can't hold it together; it's like digging poison from an infected wound – with a spoon. I'm losing it. A sob catches in my throat.

'Uh, sorry . . . this is difficult.' Christ! Pull yourself together. All thc books say don't show emotion. But I don't care what the books say – this is real and I can't help myself. 'I . . . I've made a mistake. I don't want it, any of it. Just clear it, or whatever. Burn it!' I turn to leg it down the stairs and escape, but he's right behind me and catches my arm as I get to the door. I swear I see *her* scuttle across the landing like a mocking little elf.

He holds me firmly by the shoulders, making me look into those startling blue eyes and driving home the misery of losing him. I can't stop my face from crumpling inwards, even as I tell myself, You will not cry.

'Viv, baby, don't.'

I let out a silent sob. He hugs me, pressing his chest and hips against mine. I can't believe he doesn't miss this.

'It's really over, isn't it?' I gasp. He looks surprised and then embarrassed, but doesn't answer. 'Rob! Don't you miss me even a bit? Don't you feel *anything*?' I breathe in the savoury scent of his neck like an addict.

'It's very . . . sad,' he offers finally, stiffening, pulling from the embrace with a pat on the back.

'And that's it? It's me, Rob. Don't you know me any more?' I look into his face, but he looks away down the street.

'What do you want, Viv? What do you want?'

'I want you!' I try to smile through snot and streaky mascara, and reach out to brush my fingers against the side of his face. 'Don't you understand? I've always wanted you, ever since we met.'

He sighs, holds my face with one hand and rubs his thumb over my mouth, smearing my lipstick. I close my eyes, waiting for his kiss. I feel his breath tingle against my ear.

'I'm . . . not free,' he whispers. I search his eyes, but they're as cold and flat as glass. 'Sorry, Viv.' He squeezes me like a murderer pushing the knife good and deep. I break free.

'Don't say you're sorry,' I sob, and make a sound I've never in my life made before, a kind of raspy howl. I run into the night, half hoping he'll catch me again. As I reach the corner of the street, I glance back at the house, but the door's closed. Sam's pale face peers from the window, her mouth a perfect crescent.

17

Sleeping with Friends

Loopyloo: I really, really fancy my best friend. I can't stop thinking about him and he says I'm acting weird. Shall I tell him and risk the friendship?

Raraskirt: Ooh – tricky, I know. I just went ahead and slept with my best friend and now he's my hubby!

Figmonster: That's so cute, Rara. Loopy, I'd say do it if you think you can handle any and all of the possible outcomes!

Loopyloo: I'd hate it if he wasn't my friend any more, though.

Monkeybiz: No, do not do this thing you are contemplating.

Figmonster: That's a bit black and white, don't you think, Monkey? Just tell him but don't expect anything. Not telling him could spoil the friendship and you might regret it.

Monkeybiz: There is no wisdom in this. Friendship is sacred.

Loopyloo: I get what you're saying, but I need to do something or I'm going to burst!

Monkeybiz: You are young, but you will learn.

Figmonster: Yoda? Is that you?

I wobble away, wounded, stumbling past streetside bars and packed restaurants, to the Embankment and the slick brown Thames. I lean over the wall with its carp statues, breathing in metallic saltiness, watching the water suck at the shingle. I think of a museum exhibition I once saw of things dredged up from the soft clay riverbed: the remains of a girl who'd died in childbirth, a tiny skeleton trapped inside hers. How sad it was. Life is just so sad. Lonely and cruel and sad. I stare at the water, letting my vision blur. Boys on skateboards clatter past; 'Do it!' they shout. A party boat trawls by, flashing green and red to a thumping beat.

I turn away and start walking north, closing my mind up like a shuttered shop. I can't think about what just happened; instead I concentrate on the rhythm of my steps. I'm rounding corners, hit by channelled winds, jogging across lanes of traffic, dodging proffered flyers, papers and invitations. I go underground and take the tube, rattling ten stops, then surfacing into a light drizzle. I take the short cut through a maze of run-down back streets until I'm standing outside Max's building.

I hold the buzzer until the door clicks. Thank God he's home. I'm inside with the smell of damp plaster, looking up the spiral stone staircase. I begin the slow climb to his flat. He answers his door in threadbare jeans and an ancient Ramones T-shirt.

'Ah, it's you.' He looks past me with the shiftiness of a fugitive before guiding me in. I stand silently in the shabby square of his hallway. I hear the rising and falling intonations of a football commentator coming from the TV.

'Were you expecting someone?'

'No . . . it's just . . . sometimes people, uh, pop in unexpectedly.'

'People?'

'Yeah.'

'What, like female people?'

'Yeah, or police people.'

I stare at his throat, thinking up scenarios where this might be likely. He smooths his hair and shirt, pulls up his jeans.

'So, what's up?'

'I just wanted to see you.'

'Great. Well . . . never fight that feeling.' We stand for a moment in silence. 'Want to come in, then?' I nod like a dumbstruck child. He slings an arm over my shoulders and we go into the kitchenette. 'You okay?' he asks.

'I'm . . . I . . . No.' He glances at my face as he opens a bottle of wine with a naked-woman corkscrew. I watch as he squeezes her legs together, then releases them. The cork pops out.

'God! If she was real, she'd be in hospital.'

'If she was real, she'd be a millionaire.' He winks and looks around for glasses; finding a mug and a small goblet-like vase, he pours, handing me the vase. I take a sip and breathe in a heavy woodiness. It's rough wine, but I swallow more, gratefully.

'What's up?' he asks again.

'Am I a nice person?'

'Well, I *am* biased, I know, but . . . honestly? You're terrible.'

'I feel . . . broken . . . like, damaged. Rejected. Like an egg with a crack.'

'Okay.'

'Like my shell is breaking and something heavy and horrible is about to flop out over the floor.'

'Flop away, baby,' he grins.

I stare at his chest, feeling a huge low swallow me up. I look at his kind face and burst into tears. He steps quickly across the lino, throwing down his mug to grab me as I fall.

We watch the second half of the match eating takeaway Thai food. On the narrow sofa, I lean against him, dipping spring rolls into sweet chilli sauce. Dave sits at my feet, blinking his eyes hopefully.

I feel Max's heart drumming against my back, his hands loosening and squeezing my neck, his fingers smelling of soap. His breath tickles my ear, raising goose bumps on my arms and making a flyaway hair dance and catch the flickering light of the screen. I feel his body tense as the roar of the crowd gets louder.

'Ah, come on! Fucking defence!' he shouts, and squeezes my shoulder too hard.

I'm stunned at how much I've cried. We finished the wine sitting on the kitchen floor and now I feel tired and heavy. I sigh, closing my swollen eyes. I'd almost forgotten the physical pleasure of leaning on another person's body, the essence of another life so close, the solidity of muscle, the rhythm of breath and heartbeat, bone resting against bone, blocking out the terror of 'out there'. I rest in the moment, breathing in the musk and tobacco of his T-shirt, letting my mind float, and I glimpse a kind of peace.

'Viv. Come on, it's late.' I open my eyes; Max is kneeling by the sofa. The TV has been switched off, the takeaway trays cleared. 'Shall I call you a cab?'

I sit up slowly. Ugh, the cab ride home, the darkness of my empty flat. I look at the face of my friend, the line of his jaw, his dark eyebrows like bold brushstrokes, and I know I'm not leaving. 'Don't make me go out there.'

'Stay,' he says. 'I'll sleep on the sofa.'

'Can't I just sleep with you, in your bed? Can't I just *be* you for a while? It's really lonely and shit being me.'

He smiles. 'Viv, always remember, you can sleep with me whenever you like.'

'Not sexually.'

'You can sleep with me anytime, sexually or not.'

'That's very neighbourly of you.'

We go to his bedroom; he straightens the covers and

finds me a T-shirt to wear. 'I'll get water,' he says as I change and slide between the cool sheets. I turn towards the wall, closing my eyes and feeling the soothing relief of not facing this night alone. He gets into bed beside me and fidgets. After a minute the light clicks out. I listen to his shallow breathing and the distant rumble of a night bus on the main road. I try to consider the implications of being in this bed with Max, but all I know is I can't be on my own.

'Max?' I whisper.

'Hmm?'

'Give us a cuddle.' He shuffles up behind and puts his arm loosely over my shoulder, keeping his body away. I nudge him with my elbow. 'A proper cuddle.'

'I can't.'

'Why?'

'I have an erection.'

'Oh . . .'

'I'm sorry, but I just got a glimpse of your arse as I lifted the covers. Don't worry, you're safe, but if you don't mind, I'll just keep to me own side of the bed.'

Outside I hear girls shriek and start to sing. I listen to their voices trailing down the street, then the quiet. I can't rest. I'm alert, distracted by the presence of Max: the male essence of him gently lying so close, the size of him, the stubble, the weight of his arm. The idea of just turning over and quietly loving him seeps like ink. I feel my skin come alive and burn with the possibility of it. My mouth feels dry; I moisten my lips.

'I do mind.'

'What?'

I hear our hearts beating hotly in the dark and swallow hard. 'I do mind you staying on your own side.'

There's a pause and I hear his breath get heavier. He

turns onto his back and speaks carefully. 'What are you saying?'

I open my eyes, making out the grainy grey shape of the window. My heart hammers in my throat. I turn over, resting my head on his chest, lifting my bare knee over his hairy legs, skimming the hardness pressing against the cotton of his boxers. I lift my chin and put my lips against his face.

'I want to be with you.' I kiss him again at the side of his mouth. He turns, slowly lifting himself onto one elbow, and brushes his lips gently against mine. He hesitates and I gaze up at the outline of him, the curls of hair and the cross of his shoulders.

'Are you sure?' he whispers.

I kiss him, tasting toothpaste. The tip of his tongue brushes my lips and I feel myself melt and flow. I move closer to him, touching his face, feeling his heart beat. His hand strokes over my thighs, pushing up the T-shirt, sending currents of excitement darting over my body. I feel an irresistible heat pulsing between my legs. I arch as his hand grazes the lace of my pants. He stops.

'Viv. Are you sure?' he breathes. I brush my fingers over his boxers and his cock leaps.

I breathe close to his ear. 'Max . . . just fuck me,' I whisper.

It's morning. I'm not at home. I think of Rob, waiting for the familiar stab in the heart. It comes, but it's deadened. I open my eyes to the green glow of Max's sunlit curtains. I stretch my legs out to the bottom of the bed, finding my balled-up knickers with my toes. Max shifts in his sleep, stretching his arm over my waist. I examine the relaxed hand, the long fingers and clean, square-ended nails, the remnants of paint in the creases of his thumb. I let the fact that I've slept with Max sink in, expecting panic. But I feel totally calm. I slept with Max! I don't feel strange. I'm here, naked, in his bed and my mind is . . . at ease. I look at the lines of his palm, this hand, a hand I know so well. I put my own hand into it and he squeezes gently. The sex with him was so easy, like taking a cool drink of water in the desert – healing and natural. I listen to his dozing breath and wriggle around to face him.

'Morning,' I whisper. He sniffs, still sleeping. I study his face: the dark pelt of his eyebrows and the curl of his lashes, the curve of his mouth, the large straight nose. I've looked at this face many times, but never *looked*. The small scar near his ear is new to me, so is the pock-mark in the cleft of his chin.

I twang his lower lip and he grabs my hand, smiling, eyes still closed. 'What you doing?'

'You've got quite big ears, haven't you?'

'Hmm.'

'They get bigger with age, you know.' I lean on one elbow, rubbing my eyes, then look down at him. 'Hey!' I shout.

His eyes open and focus sleepily on me. 'Hello. What do you think you're doing naked in my bed?'

I snuggle into his neck and breathe in a male smell, pepper and earth. 'Hiding,' I reply. His fingers trace up and down my spine. 'What time is it?'

He reaches down for his phone and squints. 'Coming up to eight,' he says, patting my shoulder.

I gaze at a warm wedge of sun turning the bedcover pale and consider rushing across town to work. I stretch onto my back. 'I'm not going in.' He caresses my arm and we lie in the warm room, listening to snatches of breakfast-show music blaring close then fading from passing cars, heels drumming towards trains, buses hissing.

He turns to me and strokes my hair. 'Viv, about last night . . .'

'Don't say anything.' I pull the duvet over my head.

'Are you okay with it?'

'Yes.'

He pulls it down. 'Are you sure?'

'Why, are you going to give me my money back?'

'No returns or refunds – did you not read the small print? I mean, I don't want you to think I took advantage or anything.'

'You didn't. I started it,' I reassure him.

'But I probably shouldn't have let you. You were upset.'

'Max, shut up.' I flick him on the nose.

'So . . . you're okay with it?'

'God! Yes! I said yes, didn't I? Why? Are you not okay?' I peer at him, eyes narrowed.

'I am very, very okay.' He looks tenderly over my face and I realise I'm grinning like a monkey. 'Geeky.' He smiles. 'I'll get us some coffee.'

He rolls out of bed and I watch his bare arse as he swaggers to the kitchen, admiring his broad tanned back, even feeling affection for the ugly tiger tattoo on his shoulder. I lie back, smiling to myself. I slept with Max. I slept with Max and it was good. I slept with him and I think I might like to do it again. As long as I stay here basking in his warm energy, nothing can hurt me. It's like some kind of force field. I try to concentrate on the concerns of yesterday, the struggle and heartbreak, but my mind bounces back to Max, to this bed and last night.

He returns, still naked, with a tray. I can't help but notice his penis bounce against his thigh. We sit in bed with half-filled mugs of strong black coffee. He spoons sugar into both, then downs his in two gulps.

'It's a kick in the head, isn't it?' he says. 'I don't get tea drinkers.'

I play with the curls at the back of his neck. 'You know, I've always thought you have lovely hair.'

'And all these years you never said.' He squeezes my leg; I watch his tanned hand on my pale skin, aware of electricity spreading to my toes.

'I'm sure I must have . . .' I feel his fingers trace over my thigh, stroking and stopping, returning. I move my leg slightly, allowing him higher.

'Well, I'll let you off. There are lots of things I didn't say before that I guess I can say now,' he murmurs.

'Yeah? Like what?'

'Like how gorgeous you are.' I look at his dark eyes wandering over me. He kisses my ear. 'How delicious you smell.' I feel a tingle travel from my neck downwards. His hand moves over my chest, circling my breasts, and he gazes at them, his eyes as black as pools. 'How beautiful you are.' I lie completely still, barely breathing with desire, with the weight of him over me, amazed at the effect he has on my body, feeling myself instantly melting for him. 'How many times I've dreamt of fucking you.' He moves my legs apart and I feel him push inside me slowly. 'And how I've always loved you. How I love you, Vivienne Summers,' he says into my neck.

Standing naked before the bathroom mirror, I inspect my wanton self as I speak on the phone. My hair stands in matted peaks at the back; my lips are red and bitten, my chin stubble-scratched.

'My nana is very ill,' I say to Snotty's voicemail, 'and there's only me to take care of her. I think I'll need a couple of days, but I'll ring tomorrow . . . Sorry again, thanks, bye.' I zip the phone into my bag, feeling briefly uncomfortable, wondering if Nana is actually okay or if this lie could be somehow tempting fate. I turn on the tap and the shower splutters into life, blasting a curly black hair to the drain. The room fills with steam and I step under the thudding jet, letting it hammer my back. I turn my face into the flow, spitting water from my mouth. What am I doing skipping work, shagging my best friend, refusing to go home? I find a thin scrape of soap and wash the smell of sex from my tingling skin. Max said he loves me, but something about that makes me uncomfortable. I can't deal with love. I feel alive and a bit reckless and I have what Lucy would call a freshly fucked grin. I've fucked Max! And who knew it'd be so good? But I can't think about love. I just want to feel good. I deserve to feel good without thinking about anything else, don't I? I step out of the shower and cold drops of condensation drip on my shoulder from the cheap ceiling tiles. I wrap myself up in a crispy towel and step into the bedroom.

Max, still naked, sits on the edge of the bed, strumming a guitar. His eyes are narrowed, and a cigarette dangles from his lips.

'Oh no, not "All Along the Watchtower"!' I smirk, remembering how he humiliated himself in a talent show at uni. How serious he was. People threw things.

'It might have been. Now you'll never know.' He lowers the guitar to his lap and puts out the cigarette.

'Isn't that all you can play?'

'No, I also do "Happy Birthday".'

I open the window to clear the smoke. Cool air rushes in, sweet and clear despite the London traffic. The sun's a pale eye in a white sky. 'It's going to be a hot day.'

'So, how will you spend it, Miss Summers?' he asks. I step from the towel and use it to rub my wet hair.

'With you, I thought.'

'Ah. You presume that I'll just drop everything because you're at a loose end?' He gazes over my body.

'Yeah.'

'Okay, I will.'

I walk over to him and kiss him on the lips. 'Thank you very much. And I feel like seeing the sea.'

'Let's do it.' He leans to kiss me again, but I dodge away.

'So lend me some clothes.'

We walk along Brighton seafront arm in arm. The heat strokes the turquoise sea, calming it like a cat. The water glitters, occasionally gathering itself up and crashing to shore, scattering pebbles and sending children squealing. I'm wearing Max's jeans and T-shirt with yesterday's heels, feeling faintly stupid as we pass bikini-clad lovelies on rollerblades. I notice he doesn't even glance their way. He wouldn't lend me shorts; we came down on the bike.

'I want to get everything seasidey,' I say.

'Like cockles and mussels, alive, alive-o?' He stops by the cockle van.

'Uh, no – they look like genitals.'

'I love 'em!' He buys a tub, scooping up dripping yellow-grey bodies with a wooden fork. He waves one in my face, saying, 'Mmmm, fishy!'

'We have to have fish and chips in the paper, candy floss and ice cream, and you have to win something for me on the pier.'

'That's your definition of seasidey?' He laughs.

'So what's yours?'

'A deckchair on the beach, a few beers . . . and a tub of genitals.'

'We have to get a stick of rock.'

'And a lewd postcard.'

I frown at his profile as he marches along in his biker jacket, the wind in his hair. 'What's *wrong* with you?' I say, and he laughs, putting his arm around me. We go down to the beach and pay for two deckchairs, setting them up to face the sun. He lies back and lets his arms flop, lifting his face to the sky. I roll up my jeans and wonder about taking off the T-shirt, weighing up whether or not my bra looks enough like a bikini. I watch a fat lady in a frilly bathing costume hobble over the pebbles, her lumpy legs like roughly sculpted clay. Some young men half wrestle in front of a beautiful Spanish-looking girl. I turn to study Max and something flickers in my heart. His large straight nose and wide smiling mouth definitely make a sexy combination, but it's more than that. I'm so at home with him, there's no awkwardness between us. I brush my fingers over beach stones, gathering one up.

'Oh my God, this stone looks exactly like your head!'

He opens his eyes and squints. 'It's way better-looking than me. That stone could be in films.'

'He just never had the ambition and now he's all washed up.'

'Funny!' He closes his eyes again. I aim bits of gravel at him, missing each time.

I watch the waves rush over the shingle, letting the rhythm soothe me for a while. After a while I hear a light snore.

'Max! Go and get fish and chips,' I whine.

He stretches his back. 'Will I bring them down here?'

I nod, shielding my eyes from the sun. I watch him clamber comically over a bank of shingle and up the steps to the street, then focus on the shimmering horizon beyond the pier edge. I close my eyes and sigh. London and all its waiting worry is a world away. I know I'll have to face it, but not today. I think of Rob, like pushing my tongue into the wound of a lost tooth. It aches, there's the pang of something missing, but it's no longer life-threatening.

Max wins a luminous orange orang-utan in the sitting-duck shootout on the pier. It has Velcro hands and feet, and when I refuse to carry it, he arranges it around his body where it clings like a manic grinning baby. He calls it Maurice and buys it a doughnut. At the end of the pier we sit in a bar drinking glasses of cold beer and looking out to sea. I feel his stare, turn and smile.

'What?'

'I'd love to sketch you now.' We look into each other's eyes like a cliché.

'Max, I feel scared to leave you,' I suddenly blurt out, taking his hand. 'Like you rescued me or something, and if you let me go, I'll have to face up to everything.'

'I won't let you go.' He squeezes my hand. 'You'll be the one to decide.'

'You know I'd never hurt you. I don't want . . . what happened between us to mean you get hurt.' I feel my eyes unexpectedly fill and put my hand to his neck, pulling him to me and pressing my lips on his. 'But I've been . . . I am a bit lost.'

'Viv, don't worry,' he says, taking my hand. 'It's cool. I know you haven't made your mind up.' I squeeze his fingers. 'I'm in no hurry. I've loved you for ages already . . . from the moment we met.'

'That's because you don't really know me.' I pull a geeky face.

'I know you.'

He looks into my eyes. I glance away and lean back in my chair. He takes a drink. I look back at him and he nods once, raising his glass.

On the journey home I cling to his leather-clad back as we speed through the rolling Downs. Maurice the toy orang-utan clings to my waist, one leg blowing behind, free in the slipstream. I feel a drunken kind of freedom until the cluttered streets of London begin to close around us again like a trap. Max stops at a mini-market to get supper and I stay by the bike while he goes inside. I check my phone for the first time today. Christie has called, Nana has called, Lucy, then Christie again. I listen to the messages.

'Hi, Viv! It's only Christie. Just checking you're okay. I've looked in your diary and you had a suppliers' meeting down so I've cancelled it. Let me know if there's anything you need me to do. Bye!' Shit, I forgot about the bloody suppliers' meeting. But I'll rearrange it. I mean, I'd have to if I really was ill, wouldn't I?

Then it's Nana. 'Hello, darling. Listen, I think I might have done a bad thing. I called you just now and you didn't answer, so I rang your work number. They seemed to think you were with me because I'm ill! I wasn't sure what to say, so I just hung up. I'm terribly sorry if I've caused any trouble. Could you give me a little tinkle because now I'm wondering where you are . . .'

She rang work! She never rings work. I feel the familiar tension rising. This is bad. There will be reprisals.

Then it's Lucy, talking and eating something. 'Hi, it's Luce. Listen, call me. I want to know how it went at Rob's. I hope you got your stuff and kicked his arse. I just had the most amazing experience with Reuben – he did this thing with his tongue and a little rubber device he's got and oh my God! Anyway, call me.'

I look into the shop; Max is queuing. Lucy having great sex is not news. Me having great sex, however . . . I watch him putting the shopping down for the till girl, smiling and saying something. I notice how she cocks her head and fiddles with her ponytail. Max is actually what you'd call hot, and I really fancy him suddenly after all this time.

It's Christie again. 'Hi, Viv, me again. Sorry to bother you. Just wanted you to know that some old bat claiming to be your nan rang up. I told her she can't be your nan because your nan's ill in hospital and you're with her. Then the cheeky cow hung up! So I don't know what that's about. Anyway, Snotty's on the warpath and wants to know when you'll be back in. Call me!'

Thank God Christie answered the phone – anyone else and I'd be busted.

I call Nana. The long rambling of the answer machine clicks in, beginning with Nana speaking to someone in the room: '. . . not sure about it . . . Hold on, I think it's on . . . Hello? Hello, you've reached seven one eight nine double oh. There's no one here at the moment. Uh, this is a recorded message. You can leave your name and number and I will ring you back when I'm home . . . Is that it? It didn't beep . . .' I tell the machine to tell Nana not to worry, I'll call and explain soon.

Max appears with a bag of groceries. 'I got dinner.'

'It's a yam.'

'Yeah, I liked the look of it.' He tosses it in his pannier. 'What happened? You look like Daddy said no to the pony.' He pulls his helmet on.

I hold up the phone. 'Just . . . life.'

He takes the phone, chucks it into the pannier next to The Yam and starts the engine. Then he mounts the bike, manoeuvring it backwards with his legs, and motions to me with a jerk of his head.

'Get on, darlin'.' His eyes crinkle inside the helmet. I tuck myself in behind him, resting my head against his back, and we take off with my worries flapping behind like big black birds.

The dusty light in Max's place is fading when we walk in. Dave blinks from the sofa but doesn't move. Max lights a tatty lamp and a couple of candles; then I wander into his studio while he gets drinks. On the easel is a new painting. A large arresting canvas, a woman's back and huge bottom, bold brushstrokes of purple, gold and green. The face turns slightly to the right and the straight nose contrasts with the voluptuous curves. One sloping breast points upwards. I'm transfixed by the womanliness and grace of it.

Max appears at the doorway. 'You like that?'

'I love it.' I turn to him. 'Are you selling much?'

He hands me a glass of wine. 'More than before.'

'So, how much for this one?'

'Er . . . two grand, to you.'

'Two grand?' I stare at the colours, wondering at how he's painted the light.

'All right, call it a straight grand and I'll deliver.'

'I was thinking it's worth more.'

'Ah, I'm shit at negotiating.'

'Don't you have a dealer or something?'

'I'm working on it.'

'If you're selling more than before, you must be doing okay.'

'Well . . . before I wasn't selling any.'

I wander further into the room stopping to admire his painting of Lula, her ivory limbs and distant gaze. Max follows. 'You've slept with her.'

'No.'

'I can tell by the way she looks. She's sated.'

'Not by me.'

'I don't believe you. You seduce all your models . . . it's obvious.' I hate sounding like a jealous child.

He shakes his head. 'She's insane.'

'Cute insane, though?' I look at the beautiful pert mouth.

'Uh, more chop-off-your-bollocks insane.'

'And where's the portrait of me?'

'Not here. It's in the show.'

'At the Academy?' He nods. 'Max!' He stands grinning, his arms hanging loosely by his sides. 'That's amazing!'

'Yeah.'

'I'm in an exhibition!'

'You are.'

'You'd better not have made me ugly.'

'I couldn't really do much about that, to be honest.'

I put my arms around him. 'So you're not such a sad loser after all, then?'

'Ah no, I still am.' He grins.

'Yeah, you are,' I say. He rests his forehead against mine. 'Congratulations.' I touch my lips against his.

'For what? Getting into the exhibition, or pulling you?'

'Er, you have not "pulled" me.'

'Haven't I?' He squeezes my bottom.

'No. I pulled you, actually.'

'Whatever,' he says, and I kiss him gently. He responds. 'I can't believe you're here. With me.'

'Well, it *is* unbelievable . . . You are one very lucky guy.' I kiss him, opening my lips a little. He lifts my T-shirt and I help him get it over my head until I'm standing in my bra. He turns me round and unclips it, slipping off the straps and kissing my shoulders as it falls. He slides one palm over my belly button. I shiver. He lifts my hair and kisses the back of my neck.

'You're beautiful,' he whispers, close to my ear. His hand slides under my belt, the fingers exploring and discovering my wetness. I feel my breath coming in short gasps, as his fingers press against me. 'My beautiful friend,' he murmurs as he unfastens my belt. 'I can't believe you're mine.' The jeans fall to the ground and I kick them away. I hear him taking off his shirt, then feel the warmth of his chest against my back and still his hand is kneading and sliding between my legs, making me gasp, bringing pleasure in waves. I look up at the easel – the gold and purple buttocks, the pointed nipple and secret smile. Max leans over me, biting my shoulder; I'm pushed forward and I steady myself on his table, my hands clanking against jars of brushes. I feel him stroke my bare bottom, feel the warmth of his breath there, light butterfly kisses. I hear his belt buckle coming loose, the rush of fabric as he undresses. He doesn't speak as he moves close behind me. I'm shivering with anticipation as I push back into him and he takes me there in the studio, under Lula's jealous gaze.

Afterwards we lie down on the dusty floorboards and I'm shaking. He puts his arm around me and lights a cigarette with the other hand. Something about it is too practised and I suddenly feel foolish.

'Do you always do that?'

'What?'

'Smoke after sex.'

'No.' He kisses my hair. I try to pull away, but he holds me close.

'How many women have you had in here?'

'Millions.' I turn to look at him, but he's gazing at the ceiling. 'Yeah, they all fall for the tortured artist thing . . . I put out a few cheap canvases and boom, they drop like flies.' I try again to wriggle out of his arms, but he's got me wrapped tight. 'I think I've had every person who's ever set foot in this studio – men and women.' I see him smile as he exhales a curl of smoke. I thump him on the chest, making him cough.

'Don't tease me.'

'Viv, what do you think I am?'

'I don't know. I feel a bit vulnerable.'

'Well, don't. I can't believe my luck.' I curl back into him and we watch the last of the daylight fade. He strokes my arm. The air is warm, but I have goose bumps. He gets up, lights some more candles and pulls a musty throw around us.

'Max?'

'Yeah.'

'Got anything to eat?'

He stretches. I watch him get up. He looks down at me and smiles. 'I'll see what I can do.'

I stay wrapped in the throw and study my emerging reflection in the darkening window. I'm naked here in Max's studio, enjoying myself. Fucking hell!

He fetches bread and cheese, and goes back for wine, laying a little picnic out on the floor. I can't stop staring at him. He's slicing the cheese with an enormous carving knife. He looks up and I'm aware I'm smiling in wonder at him, ready to hang on his every word.

'What do you do with a yam?' he asks. 'Do you know?' I shake my head, watching him carve a wedge of bread. He places it in front of me and lays the cheese on top. Then he fills the little vase glass for me. 'Cheers,' he says in his soft Irish accent, looking into my eyes. He seems incredible to me now, with the light making his bare skin glow. His eyes full of humour and sex and . . . life. I'm suddenly aware of a power shift, like he could kill me just by being a bit cool.

He flashes his wide, sexy smile. 'What's up?'

'Nothing. Just . . . you.'

'What?'

'Just . . . who knew?'

'Me. I knew.' He laughs.

'All that time . . .'

'But you didn't know.'

'So why didn't you tell me?'

'I did – all the time.'

I think about this and realise I've always known he fancied me a bit. I'd just never thought of him that way. A struggling artist wasn't my idea of a catch and anyway, he did this to other women, women who rang and cried to see him again. How can sex change the way you view someone? He's still scruffy and disorganised and . . . poor, but as I look at the curve of his shoulder, the messy studio, the beautiful canvases, I see only his talent.

In the morning I wake early. It's bright outside and I dress while Max is half awake. Before I leave I go to kiss him. He pulls back the quilt, growling.

'Stay with me.'

'I have to get to work.'

'Come here.' He pats the bed.

'I have to go. Come round later.' I stroke his chest.

'Stay with me.'

'I'll cook something for us.'

He rolls onto his stomach and puts his hands behind his head as I look for my bag. 'Don't go. I'll die.'

'I'll call you.' I smile.

'Vivienne!' he shouts as I walk across the bedroom. 'VIVIENNE!' His roar makes Dave leave off licking his arse. He's sitting next to the savaged body of Maurice the orang-utan, and blinks disdainfully as I close the door.

A summer morning in north London is just cranking into life. Commuters rush to the tube; a delivery van with trays of croissants idles outside the coffee shop. I think about work, mentally compiling a to-do list, waiting for the familiar panic, but get nothing. I think about Rob and I remain calm. I know it's a total cliché, but for the first time in months, I have a spring in my step. I'm exhilarated. Max has woken me from a nightmare and I realise that when I'm with him, everything is proper and brilliant and in colour.

18

Are You Compatible?

1. Do you genuinely like each other and seek to spend time in each other's company?
2. Do you take it in turns to play the role of the lover and the loved?
3. Are you both able to say sorry and talk about how to move the relationship forward?
4. Do you both laugh at the same kinds of things?
5. Are you able to talk about money without fighting?
6. Are you both willing to change any habits that upset each other?
7. Do you have similar expectations and life plans?
8. Are you any of these zodiac combinations: Leo + Aries, Taurus + Virgo, Gemini + Libra or Cancer + Scorpio?

Answers
Mostly Yes – highly compatible (yay).
Mostly No – don't bother (boo).

I'm at my desk by eight. The office is deserted. I've only missed one day – what could have gone wrong? I read my emails. Nothing from Rob. A couple of suppliers can't come in with the prices they promised. A competitor has bought up all the tartan there is in the world, and Snotty wants to see me first thing. I leave a wheedling message on her voice-mail, mainly to let her know I was in at eight.

Pretty soon I find myself gazing out of the window at the

blue sky. I look at my phone to see if there's a message from Max. There is.

'*Vivienne! You ravaging beauty. I smell you on my skin. M x*'

I feel my body respond as I text back: '*Have a shower! V xx*'

I open a spreadsheet and look at some costings, trying to work out if we can still afford the product range as it stands, but my mind begins to wander. I decide to have a proper look at the website. I haven't had a chance to explore it until now. I type in the link that Michael gave me and a webpage design appears; the title in dark blue, joined-up font stands out against a pale grey background. The home page is striking, with its 'Top tips' choices. I click on 'How to end it' and there's a list and a forum where you can post your own story and advice. I click on 'Date my ex' and there's a photo of Michael. He stares out solemnly, reminding me of a high-school murderer. I find it hard to believe an ex of his has written this profile: '*If you like sex and good times, then this guy is for you. He's all about fun, and he's really well hung.*' I cruise the heartbreak forum where break-up emails are posted. There's the 'Ask Lucy' page with my life story laid out as this week's example. I'm getting more excited with each page. I send a message to Michael, thanking him and asking how soon it can go live. He replies, '*Live now ;)*' I type the address and there it is!

I click the 'What's on your mind?' forum where there's an open thread, to post a message to Max: '*It's been two hours. Are you dead yet?*' I text him the address of the site, telling him to check it out.

It's nine now and desks around me are filling up. I close the page like I'm folding up a secret message and go back to checking emails.

There's a new one from Snotty. '*Come to my office now, Vivienne.*' She sent it at eight fifteen.

She's speaking on the phone as I sidle up to the glass wall of her office, but she waves me in. I take the chair opposite her desk, open my pad and smooth down the first sheet, placing my pen on top, trying to look efficient and in control. She sits with her legs bent round one another like an aniseed twist. The sunshine from her panoramic window highlights a fluffy down on her heavily powdered face. I glance at her feet; today she seems to be wearing a hybrid of a sandal and an ankle boot over tan nylons that show the seam at the toe. Something about this reminds me of my nana – a flashback to the sweaty, flesh-coloured popsocks she used to leave scattered around like dead mice.

Snotty looks at me without expression, her red lips pressed into a line as she listens to the caller. I look around the neat office, surprised by a couple of books about assertiveness on the shelf. Outside the buildings shimmer in the heat. I think of Max, suddenly flashing back to him on top of me.

'Vivienne!' Snotty declares as she hangs up the phone. 'I'm glad you could join us.'

'Morning.' I smile.

'Is your grandmother better?'

'Much better, thanks.'

'Yes, she *sounded* well when she rang yesterday.' She smiles; her eyes glitter.

Now I'm confused. Who the hell did Nana speak to? 'She rang here?'

'Yes, she did. Looking for you.'

'Well, she gets a bit . . . confused.'

She smiles for the longest time, looking like a crazed cat. When she speaks again, her voice is comically low. 'Vivienne, if I thought for one minute you weren't telling the truth, you'd be out of here. There are many people who'd be grateful for your job and yet you seem to think it's beneath you.' It's like being fifteen, in the head teacher's office. I feel my cheeks burn. 'I've noticed a distinct falling-off in your performance recently. I know you've been having a hard time in your *personal* life . . .' she smiles condescendingly '. . . but even so.' There's the frozen-face grin again; it's a moment before I realise she wants me to speak.

'I understand what you're saying—'

'What I'm saying is a verbal warning,' she snaps.

I open and close my mouth. 'Right, okay. What, because I took a day to care for my nana?'

'No, because of your recent performance.'

'Can you be more specific, please?'

'Yes, I can.' She takes out a file and reads dates followed by things like 'arrived late', 'called in sick', 'left early', 'forgot a meeting'. 'Shall I go on?'

'No.'

'So to be absolutely clear, this is a *verbal* warning, then follows a *written* warning, and then we'd be within our rights to *let you go.*'

'Is this instead of making people redundant? Just sack them? It's easier and cheaper that way, is it?'

'Vivienne, I don't appreciate your tone . . .'

'You know I've worked hard in this position. You know that.'

'I'm referring to your performance *recently.*'

I stand up. 'This stinks.' I open the door. 'It stinks,' I repeat as I stalk out. I feel a fury beat red in my chest and climb to my throat. A verbal fucking warning? What kind of place is this? How many times have I pulled something out of the hat and saved Snotty's reputation? I stride back through the office and faces pop up from behind the grey work station screens, then hide again like rabbits. Paul from technology sticks his ferrety nose up.

'Morning, skiver!'

'Fuck off, Paul,' I snap, making him chortle like a schoolboy. Finally I get to my desk. Christie sits typing; her hair is coiled in two plaits, one over each ear, and she's wearing silver eyeliner – her version of space-age chic. She turns to me, smiling. 'What the fuck went on yesterday, Christie?' I demand, wiping the smile off her face. 'Because I've just been given a verbal warning.'

She looks confused, then concerned. 'I didn't know about that!' She swivels her chair round, shaking her head. 'I know how you feel, though, Viv – I've had a verbal warning.'

'I know! I gave it to you!'

'I suppose that's justice or something, then.'

'Did you speak to my nana yesterday?'

'No.'

'Yes you did, Christie! She rang the office – the old bat?'

'Oh, I thought it wasn't her.'

'Well, it *was* her. How did Snotty know?'

'Oh!' She holds up her finger in a eureka gesture. 'That's probably because she was standing right behind me when I took the call. I think she thought it really was your nan.'

'It was!' A frown momentarily crinkles Christie's brow. I sink into my chair, fury turning to despair. 'Look, don't worry about it, Christie,' I sigh.

'O-kay.' She holds up her hands. 'Only I got into trouble yesterday as well.'

I rest my chin in my hands, studying her. There's a silver tip to each of her eyelashes. How long did she spend?

'I presented our ideas for the pantalise range. The knicker slogans? Well, Snotty didn't like any of them. She said they were offensive. Went a bit mental, actually.'

'*Our* ideas?'

'Yeah, you know, like "Hairy Christmas" and that.'

'Yeah, *your* ideas.'

'Well, I did clear them with you, and "The last turkey in the shop" onc was your idea.'

'Tell me you didn't actually say the words "last turkey in the shop" to Snotty.'

'I can't tell you that . . . I did say it.' She blinks.

I look around the office at the familiar backs of heads of the accounts department, the buzzing lights and humming air conditioner, then back at Christie's blank-as-a-sheet face. I think of Snotty calmly listening to the slogans and I feel a kind of hysteria fizzing in my nose. I'm smiling, then laughing, then snorting, hardly able to speak. 'Did you say . . . "Deck your balls"?' I squeak.

'All of them.' She's deadpan. I clutch my stomach, feeling tears in my eyes as I imagine it. 'What? It's not funny, Viv.' I nod my head, trying to catch my breath, sighing and wiping my eyes. I look at her for a moment with a straight face.

'Last turkey in the shop!' I cry and I'm off again. It's a good few minutes before I turn back to Christie, but when I do, she looks a bit upset. I sober up. 'It's okay,' I lie. 'We're both in the bad books, but we'll get out of it. Don't worry, Christie. All right?' She looks doubtful. 'All right?' She nods. 'You and me are the dream team of product management and if they can't see that, well . . .' I can't think how to end the sentence. 'Well, that's their problem!'

'Okay.' She smiles.

We high-five as I remember the facts; we both have warnings. The company are making cutbacks. But I'm optimistic.

I take a deep breath and call Nana.

'Seven one eight nine double oh?'

'Hi, Nana.'

'Darling! Listen, sorry about yesterday, ringing up your office. Did you get into trouble?'

'Not really. Who did you speak to? Can you remember?'

'The girl who answered seemed a bit of a dimwit.' I glance at Christie's carefully parted hair, feeling a rush of affection. 'She was at cross purposes with me, and then a rather frosty lady came on, asking all sorts of questions.' I rub my brow. 'To be honest, I didn't like the sound of her.'

'No. Well . . . it's probably better if you don't ring work.'

'I did try your mobile, but when you didn't answer . . .'

'Nana, I spent the day with Max. I told them I was with you, that you were ill,' I whisper.

'Oh!' she whispers back.

'Why did you ring? Are you okay?'

'Oh . . . I just had a little pain in my chest and got frightened. It's all fine now, nothing to worry about.'

'Are you sure? Did you ring the doctor?'

'No, no. Reg came round and we had a little brandy and it calmed right down. So, how did you come to be skipping work and spending the day with Max? Details, please.'

'Long story.' I smile.

'Well, bring him along on Sunday.'

'We'll see. Listen, I've got to go. Speak soon.'

I put down the phone and lean back in my chair. My mind jumps to yesterday, to Max's studio, remembering the longing, reliving the moments with him. The thought of him has my heart hammering like I'm a schoolgirl with a crush; it's insane. I click on my website, opening 'What's on your mind?'

> Vivienne Summers,
> Had I the heavens' embroidered cloths,
> Inwrought with golden and silver light,
> The blue and the dim and the dark cloths
> Of night and light and the half-light,
> I would spread the cloths under your feet:
> But I, being poor, have only my dreams;
> I have spread my dreams under your feet;
> Tread softly because you tread on my dreams.
> I want you. I've always wanted you and I never
> want to stop wanting you. M

I close the page quickly, then open it and read it again, feeling warmth rising inside me. I think of his sexy fingers typing those words and imagine escaping, running away with him, to some bohemian world where our lives are spent practising love and art. But I'm terrified of falling in love with him. I remember the short time when I was with my mother in a shitty bedsit with nothing. I know very well that romance can't pay the rent and love definitely does not keep you warm. I think of Rob and the life I'd planned. The pain of losing that secure future still hits me like a punch. Jesus, I'm pathetic, letting loneliness and lust blind me.

No, it would be nice to get all carried away, but poetry and dreams can't replace the secure future I lost. Now I'm probably about to lose my job. I'm just confused, that's all. A lot has happened and the best thing is to just behave calmly and try to see everything in perspective. I need time to think about things. I close the site without replying and concentrate finally on work.

It's six when I leave the building. The street is chequered with sunlight and shadow. I duck into a little deli on the last corner before the station and pick up lovely food like tiny peppers stuffed with cream cheese, artisan bread, expensive salami and wine. I've always wanted to do this – buy sexy food. I imagine a picnic with Max. I know I should just slow down and think, but I'm only getting some bits in to be prepared. I'm not a slave to impulse. Probably I'll cancel him and spend the evening alone. Definitely I'll write out all my life goals and the pros and cons of fucking my best friend.

Then I feel a little tremor imagining his tanned body naked in my bed, how he'll look against the starched white cotton, and I just can't believe how he affects me.

I just make the tube, squeezing between a well-padded woman and the sliding doors. I check my phone, reading his messages.

'*What time will you have me, Mrs? M xx*'

'*What have you done to me, you witch? I can't work, I can't think! M*'

'*Vivienne! My heart! M*'

'*I want to taste you again . . . M*'

Oh, some of them are a bit rude. I look up into the pink face of the woman as the train rocks out of the station. Her eyes flutter up from my phone; she raises one eyebrow and smiles. I swallow, feeling flushed as I look out to the backs of passing mansions, wondering what I've started and wanting this delicious anticipation to last for ever. I text him.

'*I should probably just have an evening alone – to sort my head out. V*' I wince at how mundane it sounds.

'*What kind of word is "should"? There is no "should". Do what you want,*' he replies. Then, '*What do you want?*'

I answer without thinking: '*You.*'

'Have a good evening,' the train woman says as I step onto the platform. I stalk off. As the train lurches away I look up and meet her eye again. She winks.

I'm scarily out of control. I can't wait to see him. There are schoolgirl butterflies in my stomach. This is definitely not sensible. It's just lust and will end in disaster, but I'm powerless. I'm going to have to let things happen and see how I feel later. I take a few running steps, sliding in my heels, hurrying across the sunny road and turning into the side streets on my short-cut route home. I'll have a shower as soon as I'm in, wash my hair and use that expensive body lotion Lucy got me for Christmas. I'll wear that long summer dress – Max said he liked it once. One more block of houses. I turn into the back alley and see my building. There's someone waiting in the doorway.

He leans on the wall in shirt sleeves. The light glows on his tanned arms and glances off his platinum watch strap. His profile is like a classical sculpture as he searches the street ahead. His straight nose, pouting mouth and designer shades are fashion-shoot perfect. I stop walking. I stand and stare. He's shining like gold outside my door and I fear the blade he must be hiding, bracing myself for a fresh stab. He turns, sees me and straightens. He's lifting his hand to wave. He's calling to me, like in my dreams.

'Hi, Viv.' He smiles that little-boy smile.

'Rob!' I say. 'What are you doing here?'

19

What Women Want*

Well, since you ask . . . [takes deep breath] Breakfast in bed, weekends away, clean sheets, candles, oral sex, Manolo Blahniks, a phone call, a cleaner, leisure time, a cuddle from behind, a man who knows how to drive and can reverse with one hand on the steering wheel, a man who can fix things and knows how to entertain a baby, big shoulders, a plan, someone with a good working knowledge of female anatomy, whispered dirty talk at dinner, someone funny, a great book, a comfortable bra, love letters, flowers, raindrops on roses and whiskers on kittens.

* Valid today only

Rob walks slowly towards me, reaching out and pulling me into an embrace, clinging around my waist. I stare over his shoulder, holding up the grocery bags until my biceps burn. He breathes in my hair. I pull back.

'God, I've missed you, Viv.'

'Uh . . .' I say. I try to ignore him, unlocking the door as my heart thumps in my throat.

'Can I come up?' he asks. I turn round. It is definitely him. He's here. He wants to come into my home. What do I do? What do I do?

'Okay,' I reply.

As we climb the stairs I hear his expensive brogues swish on the cheap carpet. What does he want? Why's he here?

Does my bum look okay? I open the door and he takes a few steps inside as if entering a gallery, inspecting the shrine of my life. Then more steps, heel toe, heel toe across the wooden floor. He turns on one foot like an actor.

'It's nice, Viv. Very . . . shabby chic.' His unasked-for verdict.

'Thanks.' I glance at his eyes, the sparkling blue of them. He's watching me intently. 'Did you want anything in particular?' My voice seems tiny.

'Yes,' he says, 'you.' I put down the shopping, rubbing my hands together and waiting for a punchline and pain. 'I realised it when you came over the other day – it struck me like a thunderbolt. I want her, I thought. I couldn't stop thinking of you. I can't bear to be without you. Let's get married, Viv!' Suddenly he's on his knees, holding my old engagement ring, the solitaire diamond throwing shards of light. I always loved that ring and seeing it again feels like seeing an old friend. I want to snatch it and scuttle away like a sort of Gollum character. He walks on his knees towards me. I close my eyes and open them. He's kneeling there before me, smiling, dazzling me. I wonder if I might be hallucinating, if I've overheated or something. I touch his hair. It's real.

'Please will you get up, Rob?' I say. He stands now, holding the ring up like a hypnotist. I take two steps to the sofa and perch on the arm to steady myself. 'What about Sam?'

'It's over. It's you I want.' He sits next to me and takes my hand. 'I'm so sorry I hurt you.' I stare at his handsome face. Maybe I've been hit by a taxi and I'll wake up in twenty-four hours in A&E. Maybe it's all a joke and Sam is giggling somewhere, watching via webcam.

'Is this a joke?'

'I've never been more serious in my life.'

'Because it's not funny. I won't have you taking the piss out of me.'

'Marry me, Vivienne.' He waits. I stare.

'I don't know what to say.'

'Say yes!' His face is alight, unnerving, with the white toothy smile and the perfect jaw. I take in the familiarity of this face I've loved and longed for and feel something shift in my heart.

'It's a bit sudden . . .' I say.

He stands up and strides to the window. 'Oh come on, Viv! What do you want? You said you wanted me back and here I am on bended knee! I really don't know what else to do . . .' He leans against the windowsill, ankles crossed.

'You can't just walk in here and say you want to marry me.'

'But I just did.'

'Well, it doesn't work like that.'

He lifts his head, looking at the ceiling, and laughs. 'Okay, I'm sorry, there I go again. You tell me, my darling. You tell me how it works, Viv.'

'I don't know.' What the hell is going on? I feel my heart thundering.

'You want me to beg? I'll beg. I'd cut off my bollocks with a rusty bread knife if I thought that's what you wanted.'

'No! No need for that. I don't know. I was trying to get over you just a minute ago.'

'Don't you see? I'm sorry. I'm so sorry for everything and I'm here to make it all better.'

'But you can't really make it all better – not just like that.' I snap my fingers. He just leans and smiles. I look at him, look away, look back, and in that glance I see all my dreams of a life with him. I see us when we first got together, when he wasn't this big corporate guy, he was just Rob, my Rob, wearing jeans and trainers. He used to be funny. We had plans. We were getting a dog. We'd already named our four kids (although I was never sure about Horatio). We planned to learn gardening and grow our own salads. We even started a herb wheel on the patio, but they all died. Where did that guy go? I look at Rob now and hardly recognise him in his designer suit.

'I'm real. I'm here. I'm not going away,' he declares, patting himself.

'I need a drink,' I mutter, half to myself.

He reaches in his bag and pulls out a bottle of Bollinger. 'Let's open this. I had it chilled . . . I knew you'd say yes.' He uncorks it expertly and I remember I smashed all my flutes. I slope off to fetch wine glasses.

What the hell is going on? If I drink his bubbly, am I accepting his proposal? And what about Max? I stand in the kitchen, frozen, clutching the glasses. 'Shit!' I whisper to the dishwasher. 'What's he doing here? Fucking hell!' In the living room he clears his throat and I hurry back.

'To us,' he says, chinking his glass to mine. I look at the sparkling drink, then into his incredible eyes.

'You think we can just go back to how we were?' I ask.

He takes my hand and kisses it softly. 'No, not like before. I didn't love you properly before. This time I'm going to make you the happiest woman alive. I promise, Viv. Nearly losing you has changed me. I was wrong and I see that now.' I'm motionless as he moves closer, stroking my hair. 'I'm really sorry.'

I smell the familiar salt of his skin. He kisses my eyelids. His warm breath is on my mouth and he kisses me gently on the lips, then again. Light tender kisses. Kisses I've longed for.

'You hurt me. I don't know if . . .'

'We hurt each other, babe. People in love do that.' He kisses my mouth again and this time I respond, like an alcoholic falling off the wagon. I kiss him, feeling a twist in my stomach like swallowed acid. He holds my face. 'Let's go away some-where. Let's just hop on a plane and fly away.'

'What, somewhere like Bali?'

'Well, there are two first-class tickets going spare. Five-star hotel, with spa, for a fortnight – we might as well enjoy it.' He smiles. I realise he's serious.

'Don't think I fancy Bali, Rob.'

'No. I suppose not. Well, we don't have to decide now.'

I step back. 'Don't say "we". Just slow down, will you?'

'Sorry! Sorry, Viv. You're right we need to talk it all through. I know. It's just I want to make up for lost time.' I stare at the darkening window. This is surreal. He sits down and puts his feet up. 'You were right to leave me, darling. It was just the push I needed.'

I can't believe it. How many times have I pictured him here? Lived this moment? Yet now I feel . . . a bit annoyed.

'I'm just going to the loo,' I announce, and scarper. I rummage in my bag, find my phone and call Max.

'What's up, sexy?' he says.

'Max. Listen, something's happened, so don't come over, okay?'

'Are you all right?'

'I'm fine.'

'Sure? You sound a bit . . . strange.'

'No, no, I'm okay, it's just . . . Listen, I'll explain later. Don't come – I won't be in.'

'Okay, whatever you say . . . but I miss you.' I squeeze my eyes closed, listening. It will be all right; I'll explain to Max later.

Rob taps on the door. 'Viv! Who are you talking to? Come on, I have a surprise for you!'

I lean against the wall. 'I miss you too,' I whisper, and hang up as Rob hammers harder.

'Viv!' he shouts. I open the door. 'Who were you talking to, darling?'

'Just myself.' He takes my hand and leads me back to the

sofa. He's arranged the deli food I bought on the coffee table and refilled the glasses. Next to my glass is a beautiful turquoise box tied with a white bow.

'Open it,' he says in an emotional voice. My hands tremble as I untie the bow. I lift the lid and inside find a soft drawstring pouch. I glance at him; his eyes are shining. He watches me loosen the strings. A filigree chain falls like liquid in my hand, an emerald-cut diamond pendant sparkles. I look at his stunning smile.

'Put it on.' I unclasp the chain and hold up my hair while he fastens it round my neck. The diamond falls heavy against my skin. His eyes flick from it to my face and an image flashes, of Max lying over me, his dark eyes and broad shoulders.

'I can't accept this . . .'

'You have to: I got it for you. It's one of the perks of being successful – I get to shower my girl with jewels.'

'Your girl?'

'Yes. Are you going to be my girl again?'

'I can't. I don't know.'

'Well, listen, just keep the necklace anyway, a token of my esteem. I insist.'

I look at the floor.

'Thank you, Rob, but I . . .'

'Kiss,' he says, pouting.

I lean towards him and he's pushing his tongue into my mouth. I feel his hand graze my breast. I back off and sit up, touching the cool weight of the stone with my fingers.

'This diamond, it's an emerald cut, isn't it?' I ask, and sip champagne.

He slumps back. 'Probably.'

'It's very lovely.'

'It's two grand of lovely, Viv.'

I finger the chain. 'Are you sure you want me to have it?'

'That's why I gave it to you.' He takes my hand. 'Viv, can I stay tonight?' He looks into my eyes. 'She's moving out, you see, and it's better if I'm not around.'

'Oh.' I think of the day I moved out and almost feel sorry for her. I look at this gorgeous man returned to me and search my heart, weighing up my feelings, willing them to be unchanged. But he seems smaller than I remember, diminished somehow. In my heart Rob was a god, but here is the flesh-and-blood person breaking up with his fiancée, like a stranger with the face of someone I loved. It can't be that I don't love him . . . It's the shock, that's all – after everything we've been through.

'Actually, I need somewhere to crash for a couple of days. I mean, I could go to a hotel, but . . . Viv, I want to live the rest of my life with you, so why not start now?' I look at his hand holding mine, remembering how I felt when he first proposed. I was bloody over the moon. I was the happiest I'd ever been. I wonder if I could feel like that again.

'Rob, of course you can stay . . .'

'You angel!' He kisses me again. I try to feel something, kissing him back with my eyes open, looking at the perfection of his long lashes against his cheek, feeling his tongue pushing against mine . . . but I can only think of Max. I pull away.

'What?'

'We'll have to take things slowly.' He drops his head and my throat tightens with a familiar panic. He might leave! I might lose him again. 'But I'm glad you're here,' I add quietly, and he smiles like a schoolboy who's first in the queue at the tuck shop.

We eat with knives, forks and plates. With a pang of guilt I think of the sexy picnic I'd planned and find I have no appetite. He puts some love songs on to play on the computer, lights a few tealights as if this is his place and settles down to tell me about Sam, as if I'm an android who feels no pain.

I stop him. I don't want to know how he met her a week after I left, how she dazzled him or about her mung bean diet or her silly friends.

He talks about work – he's due to make partner this year and is well on his way to becoming a millionaire before he's forty. I watch the sun fade at the window and feel part of my soul fly out over the rooftops, straining towards Max, like an anchored kite. Rob's phone rings, a sound like a buzzing gnat.

'Sorry, I should take this,' he says, flipping it open while putting it to his ear in a smooth and practised movement. 'Rob Waters.' I look around the dusk-darkening room, listening to his voice drop. 'Okay, calm down.' He walks out into the hall. I tidy up the plates, running water into the sink and sliding them in. I watch them float to the bottom and check my phone. There's a message from Max.

'*Can you call me? Are you okay? Are you being held in the rafters by a hairy gorilla? I think I should come over.*'

I reply quickly. '*I'm fine. Please don't come. I'll explain tomorrow.*'

I wander back into the living room where the computer is playing a soulful melody, a woman singing throatily about her lost lover. I turn her off and hear Rob arguing, hissing something. I think I catch 'Don't you even fucking try it!' then 'You wouldn't dare.' I walk slowly around the room, muttering to myself.

'I can't believe he's here! He wants to get back together!' I finger the diamond pendant, sliding it along its chain. I could just step back into the life I'd planned, a life of security, married to a gorgeous rich husband. I'd be hosting huge dinner parties in an enormous kitchen somewhere. There'd be children and dogs . . . and Max gazing adoringly . . . I mean Rob – *Rob* gazing adoringly. I rerun the image, replacing the children, realising they'd all looked like mini Maxes.

I look down at the alley, watching a cat that's not unlike Dave with its tawny tiger markings. It pads along the brick wall, then stops and looks right at me, sending some spooky energy buzzing from its eyes, lasering me to the spot, before disappearing into shadow. What is Max doing right now? My mind keeps returning to him. I really miss him and obviously that's because of the situation, isn't it? It's not exactly ordinary. He's my lovely friend and we just slept together. Of course I'm going to be thinking about him a bit. But really, if I want my old life back, I should concentrate on Rob. Another circuit of the room; he's talking urgently to someone. 'If she thinks . . .'

I log on to nevergoogleheartbreak.com, getting a buzz as it appears. God, Michael did a great job! I check 'What's on your mind?' Nothing new, but I read Max's words twice over. I think I'll send him a reply. My phone rings, the display flashing 'Lucy' just as Rob returns looking rattled. He motions for me to hang up. I shake my head and he rolls his eyes as I go to the bedroom.

'Hello? Hello?'

'I'm here, Luce.'

'Fucking hell, you're a hard girl to pin down! Where've you been?'

'You wouldn't believe it. Guess who's in the other room right now?'

'Uh, Father Christmas? Jesus?'

'Rob!'

'Oh.'

'He's asked me to marry him!'

'Original.'

'He's left Sam and bought me a diamond necklace.' I pause. There's silence. 'So I'm a bit shell-shocked! I'm all over the place . . . don't know what to do.'

'Say no. He's had his chance. Kick him out.'

'I told him he can stay while she moves out.'

'Ugh. Grim.'

'That's what I love about you – you're so girly, so understanding.'

'Sorry. Can't stand the guy. He's not good for you, babe.'

'Also I've slept with Max.'

'Fuck!'

'A couple of times. Three, actually.'

'Really? You and Max?'

'Yeah.'

'Well, spill – what was he like?'

'Very good, as it happens.'

'I knew it! I knew you had it in you.'

'But now Rob's back.'

'Oh please, don't tell me you're even thinking about it with Rob.'

'I don't know what to do.'

'Come on, girl, it's obvious – get rid of Rob. He's a loser and you've always loved Max. Since uni.'

I chew the side of my thumb, thinking how simple she makes it sound. I play with my new diamond. Lucy was always going on about how much Rob earned, saying he was too thick to deserve it. I feel foolish for discussing it with her suddenly.

'You don't really know Rob.'

'I do. He's a total knob.'

'Any-wayy . . .' I change the subject. 'What about you?'

'My God! Reuben! He's blowing my mind.'

'Really?'

Rob knocks on the door. 'What're you doing, babe?' he shouts.

'Listen, Luce, can you do lunch tomorrow?' I whisper.

'Tell him you're on the phone!'

'I'll call you tomorrow. We'll do lunch, okay?'

'Not okay.' I hear Rob's footsteps moving away from the door.

'It's okay, he's gone,' I tell her. 'Go on, yeah? Reuben . . .'

'Viv, he's just the best lover . . .'

'I'm glad you're happy. I have to go. Meet me tomorrow?'

In the living room Rob is at the computer, typing. Sensing me there, he quickly shuts down, gets up and puts his arms around me.

'Who was that?' he asks, dropping kisses on my neck.

'Lucy.'

'You still friends with *her*?'

'Yes.'

'She's a bit of a slag, isn't she? She came on to me once.'

'Well, she's only human. Did you see my website?' I nod to the computer. He releases me and flops onto the sofa.

'No. Your website? I was just checking a legal thing.' He rubs his nose and sighs.

'Work?'

'No, Sam thinking she can get her hands on my money,' he says to the table. 'If you and I get married, there'd have to be a pre-nup for sure.' He gazes into space. I lean against the wall, watching him. What does he mean, 'if'? A minute ago he couldn't live without me.

'Aren't they for celebrities?'

'They're for anyone who doesn't fancy being taken to the fucking cleaners.'

'Oh.'

He studies me for a second. 'Come here, you.' He smiles. I sit beside him and he takes my hands in his palms, cool and smooth. I look at our feet. His cashmere socks with my bargain-basement nail polish. Our roles are so familiar. He's to be adored, since he has the power, the money and the looks, and I'm supposed to be happy and grateful. I guess this is who I was for five years, and now I'm . . . well, I'm surprised to find I'm not like that. After a while he lifts a strand of hair away from my face. 'Viv?'

'Hmm?'

'Have you . . . been with anyone else?'

'What, since we split up and you moved in with Sam and were about to marry her?'

He laughs a little but keeps watching me, puppy-eyed, waiting for an answer.

'What?' I say.

'I need to know.'

'Why?'

'Just . . . have you?'

'No, I sat here every night embroidering your name on my underwear.'

He squeezes my fingers. 'What about Max?'

'What about him?' I feel a blush spreading down from my scalp, like I've been caught shoplifting.

'Have you . . . you know, with him?'

I stand up and walk across the room, putting the coffee table between us. 'I don't want to talk about this, Rob. I mean, it's really none of your business.'

'Well, technically it *is* my business. We're getting back together, so . . .'

'We had five years together, you asked me to marry you, then said you weren't ready for marriage and then got engaged to someone else. Now you say you want to marry me again.' I stare at him. 'You've bounced my heart around like a balloon. I'm just about coping with you being here. I am not going to discuss who I may or may not have fucked while you were away, all right?'

'Fair enough.' He laughs. 'You must have, though, with an outburst like that!' I look at his white-toothed smile. He's reclining, relaxed, legs apart, enjoying himself. He looks me up and down. 'We are getting back together, though, Viv. You know it and I know it. You never could resist me.'

'You're very sure of yourself.' I pick up a cushion and throw it at him. 'And I'm glad to see you're getting comfortable on that sofa, because tonight you're sleeping there, sunshine.'

20

Ten Break-up Commandments

1. Thou shalt face up to thy ex and be firm and fair.

2. Thou shalt not use any cheesy one-liners.

3. Thou shalt do it quickly.

4. Thou shalt not let them catch you with someone else.

5. Thou shalt not call. (Thou can't make it better.)

6. Thou shalt explain thy reasons honestly but shalt not get dragged into discussing the ins and outs . . . again.

7. Thou shalt not have sex for old times' sake and then break up again.

8. Thou shalt not accept gifts/dinner invitations from someone thou is dumping.

9. Thou shalt not resort to name-calling or shouting, no matter what is said; rather, thou shalt remain calm.

10. Thou shalt not hit anyone with a stiletto.

Wow. Two men want me. I've always dreamt of being in exactly this situation. Well, not exactly this situation – my dream involved knights and jousting, or something like that.

It doesn't feel as good as you might think. I can't deny there's a certain thrill about the idea of it, but actually, really? It just feels a bit shit and dishonest and I feel crap and cowardly.

Max sent a text at midnight: *'Keep tomorrow night free for me, beautiful. I have a surprise for you. M x'*

God, I must go and see Max. I'll have to sit him down and explain to him, tell him I just need time to sort myself out. He'll understand, surely. He'll be patient.

Rob left a note by the front door this morning: '*I'm taking you out tonight. Wear something special.*'

He was long gone this morning before I really woke up. I found his washbag squatting by the sink and a pair of his shoes left like a brand by the door. I thought if he came back, it would be the same as before – better, even – but now I'm questioning whether it can work. It's not the same and definitely not better; it's weird.

It'll just take time to find a new way to be together, I guess. If in fact we're supposed to be together . . . I think of Max.

I get on the bus to work. London streets whizz by in bursts between stops. The sky is yellow-grey, the air warm and fuggy, like my head. Is there some way I could see both of them this evening? Like meet Rob first, then go and see Max? I call Max, letting it ring, but there's no answer. The bus trundles on past the green apron of Regent's Park, the joggers following the yellow pathways, the tourists queuing for the sightseeing bus. We pass the top of Marylebone High Street; I count the Ferraris and think of Rob. We hiss into Baker Street and I get off at the next stop, trotting past Angelo's, not stopping for coffee – we have a buyers' meeting first thing – and cross two lanes of traffic to my building. I check my reflection in the dark glass doors – I was going for Audrey Hepburn classic chic, but now I wonder if the neck scarf might be a bit much.

I catch the lift doors as they close, making people inside sigh. A wiry-haired man jabs the 'close doors' button as if it discharges banknotes. I glance apologetically around the cramped space and spot Michael. He's grinning, nodding and chewing gum all at the same time and he's pressed up to the soft ham-shank arm of Mole. As the lift pings at his floor I notice him squeeze her thigh. He nods at my wondering face as he slides past in a cloud of patchouli and I watch him swagger across the landing before the doors close. I turn to Mole. She smiles; there's lipstick the colour of congealed blood on her teeth.

'Hi, Viv. Twelfth floor, isn't it?'

All eyes turn to me.

'The meeting? Yes.'

They turn to her.

'Let's hope there's breakfast!' she booms. I smile and study the lift controls. The light passes slowly through two to ten and the lift empties. It hits twelve and we walk to the meeting together. She's quick on her surprisingly small feet, stepping daintily in red velvet pumps.

'So do you know Michael, then?' I can't resist.

'Do you mean in the biblical sense of the word?' She laughs her tinkling laugh. 'Yes, as it happens, I do know Michael. Very well, actually. Do you?'

'A bit.' I want to gag.

'Well, he's certainly worth knowing!' She laughs again. I get a disturbing mental picture of them locked together, rolling like puppies across a satin bed while something by Barry White plays in the background.

Despite the air conditioning, the meeting room smells of stale bodies. There's a forlorn trolley with flasks of instant coffee, hot water for tea and a plate of sweaty pastries. Mole makes black coffee with an apricot Danish in her mouth and sits overflowing from a chair at the top of the oval table. She opens a card folder and throws down a pile of printed agendas.

'Be a love and put these out, would you?' I put one next to each chair, glancing at the items as I go. First up for discussion is 'Redundancy'. Better be on the ball today. Christie and Snotty arrive within a minute of each other. Snotty, in a shocking wrap dress covered in tiny yellow stirrups, popsocks

with a love-heart pattern and green suede sandals, nods to
me. Christie looks cool in a black vest and satin harem pants.
She settles next to me, wafting summer flowers.

'All right?' she whispers.

I point to the agenda. She pulls a face.

Mole begins. 'We've been asked to draw up a schedule for
redundancy. While we are undergoing the 'reshuffle', we need
to cut costs. This means no more market research or taxis
on account or lunches for suppliers. We will cut the range
by a third and concentrate on public relations.'

'Viv, I want you to handle the press. I want something
from the range to be featured in all the Sunday supplements
and at least three of the glossies.'

'How are we fixed for freebies?' I ask. Snotty makes a note,
which makes me nervous. 'I mean, they kind of expect it.'

Mole nods. 'Do what you have to do to get coverage.'

Snotty underlines something. She places her pen down
purposefully and begins to talk through the range item by
item, explaining which lines will go. 'The edible underwear
. . . we will go ahead, but not with the ideas already put
forward. Viv, we think even though this is Christie's project,
you should oversee it.'

I nod, feeling humiliated for Christie. I glance left but she
seems unscathed, writing, 'Fake tan,' and, 'Nail varnish
remover,' on a shopping list.

'The Scandinavian-print candles are a no,' Snotty continues,
and Christie sits up suddenly and writes on my pad.

'I ordered ten thousand!' She draws a worried face next
to it.

I feel my chest tighten as I write back, 'Did you check the
"made by prisoners" issue?'

'Forgot,' she replies and draws a sad face.

Oh fuck. I feel the skin on my neck prickle. 'Cancel it!' I
scribble.

'I signed it off already!'

I take a deep breath, looking around the meeting room. I look at Snotty and think about the verbal warning. I suddenly feel like laughing. Shall I interrupt her and calmly explain we have fucked up again and now ten thousand unethical candles are on their way to the central warehouse? Speak. Say something.

'Uh, about the candles . . .' Snotty looks up over her glasses. 'I was under the impression that we were going ahead with them, so I think they're already on order.' I smile.

'Then cancel them,' she snaps.

'Well, of course we could, it's just that House of Fraser are doing a great candle offer, so I think we should match them with a candle in our gift range. These are better – and cheaper.'

'House of Fraser are?'

'Oh yes,' Christie pipes up. 'With glitter and Christmas spices in, and when you burn them, your whole room goes all Christmassy.'

'Our candles, on the other hand, are chic. They're minimalist – fitting in with current trends in interior design. I think they're featuring in *Living Today*'s next issue,' I lie, but I do know a subeditor at *Living Today*. Snotty looks at her spreadsheet and scribbles something.

'Okay, we'll do two thousand and see how they sell through.' Oh shit – we're toast.

I look at Mole picking her way through a third pastry. I watch Christie doodling spirals over her notepad. I look out of the window at a square of blue sky. I feel a rush of excitement thinking of Max and remind myself about Rob. Rob, the love of my life, the person I've thought about non-stop for months wants to take me out tonight. I will go, of course, but . . . I really would love to see Max. I wonder what his surprise was going to be . . . Snotty drones on, and I try to feel enthusiasm for how we'll package the leather compacts and which gifts to do in the three-for-two range, but I find myself far away. Choosing what to wear on my date tonight and agonising over who to go with.

Public relations call. I hate them. I have to try and sell a story about our meagre Christmas range. The sauciness of the edible knickers! The fashion-forward accessories! I must not make it seem desperate, even if we are about to go belly up like a stranded whale on High Street beach. I have a list of magazines and contact names and I scan it for people I recognise. I think I know a girl called Donna from the *Sunday Read*. Wasn't she the one talking weddings with the gorgeous boyfriend at the Valentine's press party? I'll call her first.

'Donna Hayes?' She takes me by surprise. I expected a machine.

'Oh, hi, Donna. It's Vivienne Summers here from Barnes and Worth.'

'Hi.'

'Hi there. We met at the B & W Valentine's do. I don't know if you remember?'

'Oh yeah . . . it was a good night.'

'All that pink champagne had to be drunk by someone, right?'

'Hmm, it was fun.'

'And how's that gorgeous fiancé of yours?' There's silence and I wonder if I've accidentally cut her off. 'When's your big day?'

'He . . . er . . . I . . . er. We're not together.'

Oh shit. I draw exclamation marks next to her name. 'I'm sorry,' I say.

'Yeah, turned out he didn't want to get married.'

'Oh no.' This is going horribly wrong. How can I turn the conversation around to edible pants?

'But he's getting married to someone else now. I mean, five months after we split up.' Her voice is taut.

'That's exactly what happened to me!'

Forty minutes later, Donna from *Sunday Read* has agreed to do a story about nevergoogleheartbreak.com. Great news! But it's not work. It's almost lunchtime and I jot down possible headlines: 'B&W gets saucy this winter', 'Knickknacks, knickers and B&W'. I call Graham from the *Weekend*. I'm sure he'd be interested in the story, especially if we did a photo shoot with male models in pants.

'Graham Jackson . . .'

'Hi, Graham! It's Viv Summers from Barnes and Worth.'

'. . . is unable to take your call at the moment. Please leave a message or try again later.' I leave a message about two possible stories, but realise after I've hung up that again I spent a bit more time talking about my website than B&W. I'm becoming obsessed. I think we need a thread about dating two men at the same time – maybe I'll start one. I'll break for lunch now and then phone every paper on the list this afternoon and really push the Barnes and Worth thing.

The phone buzzes. Lucy. I bet she's thought of somewhere amazing for lunch.

'Hi, Viv. Listen, do you mind if we do lunch another day?'

'Yes, actually, I really do mind. I need to talk.'

'It's just . . . I have a lot of work to do and I can't stay late tonight. I'm meeting the Love God.'

'So you're putting your own sexual fulfilment before our friendship.'

'Yeah, I suppose I am . . . sorry.'

'You're a crap friend.'

'I know. I am. I'll make it up to you, and anyway, you only want to talk about Rob, don't you?'

'Yes, so?'

'Well, all I would have said is get rid of the jerk. What else?'

'Well, Max.'

'Go for it.'

'Oh well, fine, then. I'm obviously over-complicating things.'

'Don't be cross with me. I think I'm in love!'

'Good for you.'

'It's a big deal! He's amazing, Viv. Sexually he's the male equivalent of me, except he has lubricant and cock rings.'

'That's great! Is that great?'

'It's like he brings you to the brink so many times and when you finally come, your eyes nearly pop out.' I'm about to get a running commentary, and I'm not sure I can face it. 'He does this thing with his tongue—'

'You know how you don't want to hear about Rob? Well, I don't want to hear – *again* – exactly how and where you've had a multiple orgasm. I don't care what he does with his tongue or how big his cock is. It's just . . . boring!' There's a long pause. I wonder if she's still there.

'No. *You* are boring, Viv.'

'I'm in the middle of a crisis and you don't seem to give a shit.'

'Of course I give a shit, Viv. I've been trying to support you for months. But now I've found someone, finally, and I want to talk about it. You're always in the middle of a bloody crisis!'

'I am not.'

'You *like* being in a crisis.'

'You take that back!'

'I won't.'

'God. You are just so selfish! I know you don't exactly like Rob, but I thought you at least liked me.'

'You know what? At the moment I really don't.' She hangs up.

I can't believe she just hung up on me. Shit, shit, shit. I think I might cry. How selfish is she? But I knew that, didn't I? All through our friendship it's always been me fitting in with her. She's the successful one. She's the one with the more important love life. My issues are just amusing to her. She . . . she just belittles me. She dismisses my feelings, that's what she does. Well, I'm not ringing her back. Always in the middle of a crisis? At least I don't use sex like a drug! I grab my purse, deliberately leaving my phone behind, in case she calls. That'll teach her. I won't answer. I take the lift down, spin through the revolving doors and trot down the street to the flagship Barnes and Worth store.

Mooching about the make-up department, I immediately feel better. Pah, bloody Lucy! I need a new lipstick for tonight. I fancy something a bit sparkly, actually. A man at Chanel with unbelievable eyebrows convinces me to go for a purply red with matching nail polish. Next I spot a lingerie display. One navy satin bra with bright pink ribbons and matching panties later and I'm ready to go back to work. In the lift there's a woman with something of my nana about her. I think of chatting to Nana about Max versus Rob, but I know what she would say, and anyway she hasn't been too well recently so I don't want to worry her. I must call and see how she is, in fact.

I'm at my desk writing, 'Ring Nana,' at the top of the press list and underlining it when my phone flashes a message. That will be Lucy apologising.

'*Hi, Viv. Forget about tonight, then, I guess. M*'

That's weird. What does he mean? I call him.

'It's Max. Leave a message.'

'Hi, Mr Mysterious. I don't understand your text. Where are you?'

I hang up and call again in case he didn't hear the phone, but still no answer. Forget about tonight? We haven't even spoken today. Is he sulking because I didn't reply to the text last night? I really wanted to see him and I really need to talk to him. I call again, but it goes straight to voicemail. I hang up. A strange dread creeps over me. I wonder if he knows about Rob . . . I leave another message.

'Max, call me. It's urgent.'

I'm sitting at my desk trying lipstick on the back of my hand when Christie returns, plonking down a paper cup full of foul-smelling brown broth.

'What the hell is that? It looks like drain water.'

'Ah-ha! Miso soup with seaweed and tofu jelly. It's sooo good for you.'

'It's making me gag.'

She slurps from a plastic spoon and shiny green tendrils slither over her bottom lip. I look out of the window, worrying about Max. I hope he's okay and not pissed off with me. God! This whole situation is a mess and I have no one to talk to. I turn back to Christie.

'Rob came back last night.'

'Oh my God!' She gives up with the spoon and lifts the paper cup, momentarily obscuring her face, then leaving a gelatinous line on the bridge of her nose.

'You have something there.'

She dabs her face with a tissue. 'What happened? He was marrying that model girl, wasn't he?'

'They split up. He wants us to get back together.'

'Oh my God, and he's really rich, isn't he?'

'Yeah.'

'And totally gorgeous, isn't he?'

'Yeah.'

'God. Lucky you, Viv.'

'You think?'

'Yehuh.' She scrapes globs of jelly from the bottom of the cup. 'I wish I could find someone like that. I mean, it's every girl's dream, isn't it?' I smile at her. She produces a mirror and checks her teeth for seaweed. 'So you're getting back with him, then?'

'Don't know.' I sigh.

'Oh my God, I'd bite his hand off!' She applies sparkly beige gloss, making her lips look sugar-coated. She peers over the top of the mirror.

'Would you?' I ask her.

'Yeah! I mean, it's a no-brainer,' she says without a trace of irony.

I'm wearing a new clingy black jersey dress and high heels, trying to fasten the diamond necklace. The taxi driver buzzes the intercom, making me jump. Calm down, calm down. It's just a date. Right, check my teeth for lipstick and pull on a jacket not long enough to reach the hem of the dress. No, Rob won't like that – go without. I step carefully down the stairs and settle into the back seat of a waiting Mercedes, adjust the gusset of my new knickers and ask where we're headed.

'No, no, ma'am! The booking says it's a surprise.' He smiles in the rearview mirror. A little pine tree dangles there, giving off the synthetic smell of toilet cleaner. We pull out into the traffic and head towards the West End. 'Is it your birthday, ma'am?' He smiles, showing teeth like a burnt-out forest.

'Uh, no.'

'He just wants to impress you, then!' I imagine Rob waiting somewhere, wanting to impress me, but I can't see it. This kind of thing is second nature to him. He never doubts his ability to impress. A random thought pops up about sending the taxi to Max's. It's unnerving that he's not answering any of my calls or texts. He never doesn't answer – he's much too nosey. I bite the side of my thumb and rack my brains. I haven't done anything to upset him, so actually he's just being bloody rude.

I'll concentrate on Rob. I'll try to relax and enjoy the evening with the man I love – well, used to and might still love.

The car pulls up at the double doors of a Soho restaurant. Someone in a navy suit opens the door. I find my purse to pay.

'No, ma'am,' says the driver. 'It's been taken care of.'

'Oh, right,' I mumble.

'Have a nice evening.' He smiles. I climb out onto the pavement and the someone opens the restaurant door. I step onto a walkway of industrial steel overlooking a cavernous room packed with tables and echoing with voices and laughter. There are huge spotlights highlighting pipes that snake up the walls and over the ceiling. A ridiculously good-looking guy smiles at me from the cloakroom. The walkway curves to the right and forms a balcony spanning the length of one wall. A bar of brushed steel is tended by sleek men in starched white linen. Rob is sitting at one of the tables. I feel a bolt of nervous energy as he puts down his glass and stands to greet me. As we kiss hello I wish I'd worn lower heels; we're embarrassingly eye to eye. As usual I'm shocked by the beauty of him as he looks up from under his eyebrows with that little-boy charm.

'You look beautiful,' he says, pulling out a chair. 'Two vodka martinis.' He speaks to the hovering waiter without taking his eyes from me.

'Actually, I'll have a white wine, please!' I call to the waiter's retreating back. 'Can I have a dry white wine?' I ask Rob.

'No. You're not down the local. I want tonight to be special.'

He takes my hand, rubbing his thumb over the back of my fingers. 'I wish you were wearing the ring.'

I pull my hand away, feeling told off already. 'I can't.' Then seeing his disappointment, I add, 'I will . . . soon.'

'I want the world to know you're mine, Viv.' He reaches for my hand again, stroking it as if a genie will appear. I smile. I'm not his, though, not any more, and this thought makes me so sad I bury it quickly. It will take time, that's all, to love and trust him again.

I look down into the pit of diners. White-jacketed waiters scurry between the tables and an open-plan kitchen. In the centre, a maître d' on a kind of podium conducts the whole thing.

'This place is amazing. I've never been before.'

'It's members only.'

'That'll be why, then.'

'Eight grand a year.'

'Wow. When did you join?'

'Uh, about two months ago, I think.'

Our drinks arrive in heavy dimpled glasses. The waiter arranges them and sets down dishes of dry salted almonds and some sort of curly baked biscuits.

'*Salud!*' Rob says, lifting his glass.

I sip the ice-cold liquid. The chemical smell of it nearly knocks me out and pure alcohol grabs me by the windpipe. I take a handful of biscuits to compensate, but they're powdered with hot chilli. I hold the martini, taking a deep gulp, and swallow the hideous mixture with my eyes watering. I smile at Rob and he laughs.

'An acquired taste, no?'

'Actually, I really like it.' I smile and take another gulp of martini to show him. I have a sophisticated palate – I once ate oysters. I swallow it down with a shudder. His eyes are full of amusement; he pushes the biscuits towards me.

'Want some more?'

I glance at the bowl, spotting the thick red powder now. 'No, thank you.' I smile.

'Oh, Viv, you are hilarious!' He takes my glass and looks into my eyes as he downs the drink in one. With his other hand he signals to the waiter. I watch the perfect skin of his throat tighten as he swallows. He licks his lips, staring at me, before turning to order. 'The lady will have Sancerre.'

'And a glass of tap water!' I add. The waiter nods and actually backs away before turning round. Rob looks at me and shakes his head.

'What?' I ask.

He lifts my hand to his mouth, turning it and smelling my wrist. 'You smell amazing,' he murmurs, and I want to laugh. I must focus. He takes my diamond pendant between his finger and thumb. 'This looks cxquisite on you.'

'Thank you. An old friend of mine gave it to me,' I joke.

'He must be a very, very good friend,' he croons, and I get a weird, hunted feeling.

The wine arrives and we're escorted down the staircase and handed over to the maître d'. He lets his eyes trail over me before smiling knowingly at Rob.

'Good evening, Mr Waters. We have your usual table ready.'

'Thanks, Patrick.' Rob winks and presses a folded banknote into his hand. We follow a mincing waiter, picking our way through tables, and are ushered into a booth at the far side. Rob slides onto the artfully aged leather seat opposite me and immediately orders more wine and starters for us both. I gaze around at the coliseum-like space, feeling faintly irritated. I know he's only trying to impress me, but since when did he bclong to a place like this, with a 'usual' table?

'It's a great table,' he says, closing his menu.

I smile. 'Your usual, it seems.'

'Well, I am a member here, as I said, so I come all the time. I mean, it wouldn't be worth it otherwise.'

'And here's me thinking you've brought me somewhere special,' I laugh.

A coldness passes across his face. 'This is fucking special, Viv. Been somewhere like this before, have you?' A little fleck of spittle hits my cheek. I use the damask napkin to dab at it, and when I raise my eyes to his, he's calm again. He reaches under the table and holds my left knee as if warming his hands. 'Vivienne, all you need to know is you're my life . . . Soon to be my wife.'

'That rhymes,' I say stupidly. The hands slip from my knee. He glances across the restaurant and a muscle in his jaw jumps.

'Viv, look, forgive me. I'm trying to show off, I suppose. I see you're not impressed.'

'No, I am. I really am. I think I just miss you. The old you before all the . . . success and everything.'

'But I'm successful now. It's who I am.'

'I know.' I look down at my hands. 'Remember the pint and pasty days?'

'I'm still the same person.'

'Carpaccio of octopus with juniper . . . madam?' The waiter sets down an artfully arranged plate. 'Sir?' Rob flicks out his napkin to make room for it. He takes up his knife and fork and cuts into what looks like thinly sliced tripe. He crams it in, making a white rosette on his lips.

'Delicious.' He takes a sip of wine. 'The Sancerre complements it perfectly.'

I look down at my plate and feel exhausted.

The meal drags on. Each course is a kind of test of wills, with Rob ordering things that are exotic or raw or both. By the time we get to dessert, which involves some sort of rare egg-yolk jelly, my stomach is spinning unhappily. Finally he signs for the bill and we're escorted to a waiting cab.

I look at Rob. He's trying so hard to impress me, I see that, and I decide I'm bloody determined to have a nice time. If we both relax, we might find our groove again.

I must stop my mind wandering back to Max. I've checked my phone and there's still no message from him. It's strange to be worried about him. I mean, with Max, I've always been the one with the power, but here I am desperate to hear from him, just like all the girls he's ever been with. I answered the phone to one once, who said she'd walk into the sea if he didn't talk to her. 'Let her,' he'd said, adding, 'She won't,' when he saw my face. I spent half an hour talking to that girl, trying to make her see what a dick Max is. Now I am that girl . . .

As we climb into the back of the taxi, Rob says he has a treat in store; I've no idea where we're headed. I look out as Piccadilly Circus passes, feeling the charge of excitement I get from central London. My head's woolly with the wine. Rob spreads himself languidly across the seat, his profile occasionally lit by oncoming headlights. He casually pats my thigh.

'Did you enjoy your meal, darling?' he asks.

'It was very nice.' I smile.

'Are you going to say thank you?'

I turn to check if he's joking. 'What?'

'I said, are you going to say thank you for the meal I just paid for?'

I feel myself blush. 'Didn't I say it at the restaurant?'

'Nope.'

'Well then, thank you, Rob, for a lovely meal.'

'Good girl,' he murmurs. I turn back to the window. His hand rests on my thigh like a tarantula. The taxi edges left out of traffic and shoots along like a freed thing, jolting me suddenly back into the seat. Rob looks at my low-cut dress where the diamond necklace now bounces slightly and smiles, meeting my eyes. I smile too, rearranging the folds of my dress. What is the matter with me? I just want to run away! This is the man I've longed for, the man I've cried over for months. Now he's here doing just what I wanted him to do and I don't feel anything except irritation. The taxi pulls up. It's a moment before I realise where we are. Rob takes my arm and we walk into a courtyard. There's a kiosk where he buys champagne and then we're among a crowd of people at the front desk of a gallery. I notice posters about an exhibition.

'Where are we, Rob? Is this the Royal Academy?'

'It's the Summer Exhibition. I want you to choose a piece and I'm going to buy it for you.'

'Oh no. I can't go in.'

'It's busy, I know. But there's a "Meet the Artist" thing tonight apparently. Probably full of celebrities. What did you say?'

'I'm feeling queasy. Could we take a walk or something?'

'Don't be silly, Viv. We will be walking – around the gallery. I know how you love art, so I arranged this as a surprise for you. Hnnn?' He pats my arse.

'I think it might be something I've eaten. I feel a bit hot.'

'Come on, you'll feel better in a minute.' He guides me forward into the first room. 'Most of the artists will be here. It's very interesting to see who did what.' We stand before a huge egg of blue glass.

I scan the room, looking for Max. This must be the surprise he meant in his text. He was going to bring me here. He wanted me with him and I didn't even bother to reply. Shit! How could I be so stupid? This was so important to him and I didn't even realise. And I was wondering why he wouldn't answer my calls. I feel my heart hammering.

Whatever happens, I must not bump into him while I'm with Rob.

I look around. Apart from two canvases in yellow and blue, the room is full of sculptures. If we stay in here, I might avoid him.

'God, I love sculpture.' I squeeze Rob's arm, slowing him down. We stop at a tall rusted metal figure. The contorted body seems to be melting, turning into ridges and dropping into a pool of salt. 'Amazing,' I say. 'I think it's a comment about humanity.'

'Bit bloody ugly, though. I mean, would you want it in your living room?'

'I don't know. I think it's beautiful.' I scan the room.

'You serious?' He looks at me. 'I was thinking more of a pretty painting. Let's go through there.' He gestures with his champagne glass towards thc arched doorway of another room, packed with people.

I fan myself with the guide booklet. 'Phew, I'm feeling a bit faint.' All around are 'Meet the Artist' posters, photos of smiling, groovy-looking artists. I hope to God we don't meet one. I sink onto a bench. 'Must be the booze.'

Rob frowns at me. 'What's the matter, love? You didn't have that much.'

'I think I just need some fresh air,' I say. He looks around the gallery and spots another doorway.

'Let's try through there, less crowded. Come on.' He pulls me up. I search the doorway: a small group of collectors and critics gather before a huge canvas. I walk forward weakly, guided by Rob's hand on my back. As we approach the entrance I scan the crowd. A man in a tweed suit moves a step back and my heart jumps painfully as I think I see Max – a tall figure dressed in black jeans and shirt, dark curls combed back. The man moves again, obscuring my view. I stand still.

'Oh, I don't think we'll find anything in here,' I say. 'It's not really our style.' Rob grips my arm, pushing me forward.

'Well, let's have a look, shall we?'

'Ow, you've got my skin!'

He loosens his grip, sliding his arm around my waist instead. Tweed man steps aside. Max turns, glances in my direction and then away before realising what he's just seen. When he turns again towards us, what I see in his face just kills me: anguish, hurt, disappointment and then fury. He strides towards us, pushing people out of the way until he stands in front of me. He searches my face murderously and I feel like the shittiest person on earth.

'Max!' I reach up to touch his face, feeling Rob's arm tighten at my waist.

'Don't even dare to look at me, Vivienne, while you're with him.' His lip curls like a snarling wolf's.

'It's not what you think, Max. I've been trying to call you today . . .'

'What do you care what I think? What kind of fool do you think I am?' His eyes dart over my face. I touch his arm, but he shakes me off.

'Don't talk to my fiancé like that!' says Rob, and Max turns on him.

'Don't you say a fucking word, right? Or I swear you'll swallow your teeth. This is between her and me.' He stares at me like I'm a monster suddenly revealed.

'What have I done?' I feel tears prickle.

'You have betrayed me,' he says quietly, looking from me to Rob and back. 'Good luck to you both.' I catch the pain in his eyes as he turns away and walks quickly through the crowd, leaving me shaking with shock.

'Well, that was a bit much!' smiles Rob. 'I thought he was a friend of yours.' I break away from him, trying to follow Max. People are staring and tutting as I push through.

'Max, wait!' I shout into the crowd, but I can't see him. I turn round, searching the room, the artwork and gilded frames becoming a blur. 'Max!' I shout again. But he's gone.

21

Love Potions

Love cocktail #1 – the Heartbreak Breaker
Pour one measure of vodka into a glass with two spoonfuls of
sugar and fresh mint. Crush with the end of a rolling pin, top up
with ice and a dash of soda water. Add a squeeze of lime and
shake. Voilà, no more heartbreak!

Monique, London

Love cocktail #2 – the Seducer
Pour one measure of tequila into a tall glass. Top up with ice,
ginger beer and lime juice. Stir and serve to your victim.

Lizzie, Braintree

Love cocktail #3 – the Sex Bomb
Mix two parts Baileys Irish Cream with one part brandy and
pour over ice. Alternatively, sit naked in a high-backed chair
cradling a tumbler of Scotch and see what comes up.

Caroline, Perth

At home, slumped on the sofa, I'm feeling very bad. There's a dragging in my tummy – is it booze or dread or both? I run through the gallery scene over and over, trying to see things from Max's point of view. He wanted me with him at the 'Meet the Artist' evening, of course he did, and I should have known it was tonight.

Maybe he was angry because I didn't respond to his text immediately, and that's why he told me to forget about tonight and wouldn't answer my calls. And then I turned up at the gallery with Rob . . . But something doesn't fit. It's just not like him to be touchy.

Well, anyway, I can't think of a reason why he wouldn't even talk to me, and then his reaction when he saw me – it was like he hated me! And now he won't answer the phone, so I guess I'll have to wait until he's calmed down. I'll find out what I've done and I'll just apologise forever until he speaks to me.

Bloody Rob bloody Waters. Making me go in there when I said I didn't want to. Where is he, anyway? I'll just rest my eyes a bit. Feel a touch queasy.

I keep thinking about Max, and the pain in his face when he walked away, and hating myself. I know he thinks I turned up with Rob on purpose. He actually thinks I'd do that. I've really hurt him, that's what I've done, and that's just what I never, ever wanted to do.

Rob appears and hands me a brandy. I shake my head and the room tilts. Bugger, I must be completely drunk, but I feel sober. He sits beside me and strokes my hair.

'You all right?' he asks softly. I nod. 'I'll complain about him. Get his fucking shit paintings removed from the gallery.'

'No!'

'Upsetting you like that, just because we're back together again.'

'We are not . . . It wasn't about that.'

'Listen, shhh, you're here with me now. It's all okay. I'll look after you.'

His beautiful face is close to mine, his eyes smiling, a faint smell of cologne. Trying to focus makes my eyeballs ache. He kisses my cheek. I can't show how much I care about Max, how much I want to run out of here and find him. Even if Max doesn't care about me, I have to explain to him how I came to be in the gallery with Rob.

Something jagged in that thought sticks – what if he doesn't care about me? I can't imagine Max not caring. Of course he bloody does. But why did he treat me like that? Maybe I was actually right not to get involved with him for all those years.

'The trouble is, he's very passionate,' I say out loud, surprising myself.

'Hmmn, don't worry, Bunny,' whispers Rob. He's kissing my neck. His hand moves slowly up a leg, under my dress. I watch the hand as if it's touching someone else. I lean my head back, but the room lurches sickeningly. I lean forward again.

'I'm so turned on right now,' he says to my thighs.

So all that shit Max said about loving me? He doesn't love me. If he did, he'd have answered the phone today and told me why he was pissed off. He just cancelled this evening with a text! That's not how people who love people behave.

Ugh, there's a horrible acid taste in my mouth. I'll get up in a second, go for a glass of water. Rob is tracing little circles over the pink ribbons on the front of my new undies. I was right to get them. So pretty. Twenty per cent staff discount, too. Rob really does have beautiful hair, all falling forward like that. He's kissing my leg now. He looks a bit like a bird pecking corn.

I betrayed him! How did I betray him? He was the one who said, 'Forget about tonight.' He was the one who dumped me! To refuse to speak to me is just really childish. If I keep squinting to the left and try not to think about that horrible octopus I ate, then I might feel better. Rob is on his knees between my feet undoing his trousers. He pulls down starched white boxers. It's quite a nice view. Handsome.

The phone rings and my heart leaps. That'll be Max! Right – let's have it out and clear the air. I move to get it, but Rob holds me back. He kneels over me and I suddenly notice he's holding his cock in his hand.

'Come on, Bunny. Suck me,' he murmurs. I glance at the phone, then back at Rob.

The machine clicks in.

Objectively he is definitely a perfect-looking man, with his tanned legs and flat muscular stomach. I feel like I'm watching myself from far away and I'm vaguely aware of being tired and really sad. He rests one hand on the wall behind the sofa while the other guides his cock towards my face. I look it right in the eye. I don't recognise it any more. That soap smells new. It smells expensive. I think I hear Nana's voice leaving a message as I open my mouth.

22

Wisdom

'You are beaten to earth? Well, well, what's that? Come up with a smiling face. It's nothing against you to fall down flat, but to lie there – that's disgrace.'

Edmund Vance Cooke

'And don't spend your time lookin' around for something you want that can't be found when you find out you can live without it and go along not thinkin' about it.'

Baloo the bear, *The Jungle Book*

There's no getting away from it: vomiting at work is a bad way to begin a day. Afterwards I sit up in the toilet cubicle to check how I feel . . . head pulsing, poisonous stomach ache, eyeballs burning and . . . why does it have to be so hot?

One thing I do well with Rob is drinking myself into oblivion. He eggs me on, though. Urggh . . . I can't think about it without retching. I should be ashamed of myself, and I am. Utterly ashamed. I mean, what's wrong with me? Is this what they call 'off the rails'? I flush the toilet, roll back and lean on the door. Oh God, there's no toilet paper. Maybe I have tissues in my bag. I feel the shape of my phone in the inside pocket and check for messages. You never know, maybe Max has called. But no – nothing. I call his house phone.

'It's Max. Leave a message.'

'Please, Max, talk to me. I feel terrible . . .' I wait in case he picks up, but there's only the hiss of the open line. 'I'm so, so sorry. I want to explain everything. I need to see you. Max . . . I . . . I miss you.' I hang up and blow my nose on an old receipt.

Rob was in my bed this morning. I can't remember how that happened. I wonder – did we? I stare at the toilet panelling until the geometric pattern swims, and try to blink it still until I hear someone come in, the click of heels and humming. The cubicle shakes as she slams the door. There's an ankle, ginger with fake tan, and a plaited rope sandal with wooden sole showing under the partition.

'Christie?'

'Hello, who's there?' she sings.

'Help me.'

Aspirin in lemonade is Christie's remedy. I sit at my desk, miserably sipping, while she flirts with Paul.

'No, I've never had a pearl necklace,' she says.

'Go on, you must have done.'

'No. I find pearls a bit old-fashioned for me, really. I don't think you should wear them in your twenties.'

Paul is turning red trying not to laugh.

'Christie. Ignore him. He's being filthy,' I interrupt.

'Oh. I don't understand.' She gazes at him with heavy mascara eyes.

'Of course you don't. I'll explain later.' I lay my head on the cool tabletop.

'Vivienne! I don't know what you are on about. We're talking jewellery here.'

'Yeah, and I'm Angelina's body double.' I wonder – if I close my eyes, would that be better? Ugh – no, no. I concentrate on a fixed point.

'Looking a bit peaky there, Viv. Rough night, was it?' I turn my eyeballs to look at him. He grins, stoat-like with his small head, long neck and sloping shoulders.

'Mind your own.' I smile nastily.

'Observe, Christie. Alcohol abuse – not clever, definitely not pretty.'

'How are you still here? Go and *technologise* something. Isn't that what you claim to do?' I rasp. He laughs, blows a kiss to Christie and slopes back to his desk. The lemonade and aspirin curdles dangerously in my stomach. I find a packet of crackers in my drawer and nibble one, wondering at Christie's nautical outfit as she checks her email.

'Oh no. Mole wants to see us as soon as we get in.' She spins round. 'Do you think it could be about those candles? They get delivered soon.'

I look at her, then out of the window, wondering if I should throw up before I go.

'Don't worry, Christie. What's the worst that can happen?' I slide from my chair and start walking before I fall down. 'Let's go and see what she wants.'

Mole is a triangle in moss-green linen. She looks relaxed, chin in hand, squinting at her screen. We linger like fools at her open door before I knock.

'Come!' she calls, and gestures with a fat hand for us to sit. I will not look for the neck mole, I will not. She studies her steepled fingers as we settle into chairs, then looks at us with measured sympathy and – there! – it bobs into view like a poo in the sea. I'm drawn to it, fascinated by the hairs, until I think I might be sick on the table. I shift in the chair, swallowing hard.

'Now, you two, I wanted to speak to you together because you are a team, are you not?' Christie is nodding and smiling as if she's about to receive an award. 'It's about the planned redundancies.' My heart thumps painfully. Mole's pale eyes flit from me to Christie, looking for a reaction. The cherry-red lips look too small for her face and plastic, like she won them in a cracker.

'I don't think I'd like to. I won't be taking voluntary redundancy,' Christie blurts, glancing sideways at me. I feel a film of moisture prickle my skin and try to concentrate on the edge of Mole's desk. If I keep my head still, I might not need to hurl.

Mole takes a sip of water, swallows slowly and presses her chest as she suppresses a couple of burps. 'No, love, you won't be.' She grimaces, looks at some papers on her desk, then back at us. 'There are no *voluntary* redundancies as such . . .'

'Oh, that's a relief! I've already booked Thailand,' squeals Christie.

'Look . . . I'll come out with it straight. Can you girls give me one good reason not to sack you?'

Wow. Now that I wasn't expecting. Christie looks at me, then back at Mole. I keep my head still, staring straight ahead.

'What did you say?' Christie clutches the sailor collar of her blouse.

'You know the company is trimming the fat.' Mole looks searchingly at my face and I move my eyes to meet hers as my stomach churns. Try not to think of fat. Don't think of fat. I swallow hard, tasting the lemonade-aspirin concoction. 'Well, you two might be the fat, so to speak.'

'We're the fat?' asks Christie.

'Yes.'

'We're the fat,' she repeats, mulling it over. 'Oh.'

'I'm sorry,' says Mole. 'We've been reviewing your performance. The over-ordering of the candles' – I feel Christie shooting me a look – 'the stupid underwear slogans, the absenteeism . . . I could go on, but I won't. I'm now giving you both a final warning. Any more fuck-ups and you're out.'

'I don't think they can do that, Viv. You can't do that!'

'You're free to meet with human resources to discuss any concerns, of course.' A shadow passes over her brow as she slides two envelopes across the table to us. I know I'm in trouble if I don't remain absolutely still. 'In the meantime we've laid out our terms here.' She studies me. 'Have you anything to say, Vivienne?'

'I think I'm going to be sick.' I stand up clutching my mouth and run.

The written warning letters lie unopened on our desks. I upturn the wastepaper basket and put my feet on it. Sometimes if you're actually sick, you feel better. I can now face a cup of tea.

'I can't believe she had the cheek to call us fat. I mean, have you seen the size of her? Big fat cow, she is . . .'

'Shhh!'

'Well! And the whole candle thing was my fault. Why d'you get a warning?'

'Because I'm supposed to be managing you.' I sigh as I open the letter. Why have I been so crap? I read we are to have no more absences without valid sick notes. We have to find creative ways to sell through the candles over the year. We are to prepare detailed files on each of our products for their perusal. It's not looking good. 'It's not that bad – at least we still have jobs.'

'I have to pay for Thailand.'

'And I have to pay the rent.'

'You're all right; you've got a rich fiancé.' For a minute I can't think what she's talking about. Then I realise she means Rob.

'You can't rely on a man,' I mutter.

'Yeah, but I bet you're glad he's back, though, aren't you?' I think of the shock of waking up with him naked in my bed. How I sneaked to the bathroom and put on pyjamas. I remember his cereal bowl left in the sink and how he'd soaked the bathmat. How have things come to this? I close my eyes, feeling incredibly tired.

'Viv?'

'What?'

'I bet you're thanking your lucky stars, aren't you?'

'Something like that.' I look across the office at the bowed heads behind grey partitions. I should thank my lucky stars. Start thanking them right now. Thank them that this is not my future because I have achieved every girl's dream: just like Cinderella, I've bagged a rich, good-looking man to take me away from all this. 'You don't love him!' something inside me shrieks, before being overpowered like a kidnapped hostage. No. I love him. I do, and the huge advantage of loving him is not having to worry right now. Wasn't I feeling despondent about this job anyway? Wasn't I embarrassed, even, by what I do and wishing for something else? Well, here it is – a rich fiancé . . . jackpot.

But . . . There is no but.

I'm just staring out of the window thinking about this when my phone vibrates across the desk. It's a number I don't recognise. Max! Well, he could be using a payphone.

'Hi!' I answer.

'Vivienne, it's Reggie from next door.' He doesn't live next door to me. What a way to introduce himself.

'Hello.'

'It's about your nana, love.' I hear the shake of age in his voice, silly old bugger. 'Listen, I'm calling from the hospital. I think you'd better come down.'

'What's happened?'

'Well, she's . . . she's in a bad way.'

'A bad way?'

'Yes, they're keeping her in. Pneumonia, they say. She wouldn't let me get a doctor . . .'

The train to Kent shudders, stopping at every windblown station on the way. Scrubby back gardens and lopsided swings, extensions with patio doors slide by.

Nana will be all right. She's tough. I can't remember her ever being ill. She had a fall and they discovered the arthritis, but never anything like this.

People die from pneumonia. Old people die from it. They go into hospital and never come out.

But Nana isn't old. She just turned seventy. They say sixty is the new forty, so . . . And she'd never smoked a cigarette until the other day. Her lungs are strong.

But she is too thin. She's actually underweight. I've been thinking a lot how frail she is recently. The thought of my life without her slides over me like a terrible shadow. She's always been there. My mother left me on her doorstep when I was seven and she took my hand and never let go, reassuring me through everything. I think of how calm and loving she was when I was sixteen and thought I was pregnant. Even when Granddad died, it was her consoling me. My eyes fill; she's been the only constant in my whole life. I've always relied on her love, and her kindness. She's the kindest person anyone knows. Everyone says how kind she is. I start to recall a million examples of her kindness, going back in time and gathering them up like magic powers, making her brighter and stronger in my mind and pushing away that shadow until the train reaches the end of the line.

At the hospital, Reggie bear-hugs me. I feel a bone in my spine crack as my eyes draw level with his hairy ear. He's been crying.

'Where is she?'

'Ward twelve.' I search the information board. 'She's uncon-scious.' His wet eyes blink from pits of wrinkles.

'How long has she been in?'

'Since the middle of last night.'

'Why didn't you call me sooner?'

'She said she'd left a message. She told me not to bother you, especially at work.' I set off jogging along the pastel corridor, following the signs to ward twelve. I turn left, bashing into a huge man and crushing his bunch of sad chrysanthe-mums. The ward is locked. I try the door twice, rattling it before spotting the intercom system. I press the buzzer and a woman answers.

'I'm here to see my nana . . . Eve Summers – is she in there?' The voice tells me to wait. Moments later the ward door opens and a dark-haired nurse in blue uniform steps out. I go to hold the door open as she calmly presses it closed.

'Hello. Is it Vivienne?' she asks softly.

'Yes. My nana has pneumonia. I was told she's in ward twelve. Is this twelve? Is she in there?' The nurse guides me lightly by the elbow towards a small table and chairs near the door. I sit clutching the flesh-coloured upholstery.

'I'm Claire, one of the nurses on duty today. I just need to talk to you for a second, Vivienne, and then you can go and see your nana.' I try to smile, feeling very small and out of control. The institutional smell of boiled cabbage wafts along the corridor. 'Are you all right?' she asks.

'I just want to see her,' I say, feeling my lip wobbling.

'I know. I have to tell you that she is quite poorly. We're treating her with antibiotics, so she has a drip in. She also has a drip for fluids.' She looks carefully at my face. I nod, but I can't look at the sympathy in her eyes. 'And we're giving her oxygen to help her breathe, so she has a mask on.'

'Will she be okay?'

'She's stable at the moment. I'll get the doctor to speak

with you as soon as he comes in.' She squeezes my hand and her forearm seems strong and capable next to mine. She is heroic and useful to society and sensible. I feel a hot stab of shame thinking about the last twenty-four hours of my life.

'Is she awake?'

'She's not conscious.' I look at the shiny pink floor. 'All right, now I just need you to sterilise your hands and we'll go through.' She presses a code into the keypad on the door and it clicks open.

The ward is pale green and hung with blue curtains the colour of overalls. It smells of shit and antiseptic. Beds line each side and in every one of them the husk of a person lies, like something left behind in a web. I glance left and right as I follow. These people have nothing to do with my nana – why have they brought her here?

We stop beside a skeletal man, his skin nut brown like he's been unearthed from a sarcophagus. He peers balefully over his oxygen mask. I stare into his yellowed eyes and try to hide my horror with a polite smile. He nods. The nurse pulls back curtains from around a bed and there she is. My nana. My vibrant, dotty, busy nana on her back, hands palm down at her side, the stillest I've ever seen her. My breath catches in my throat.

'Would you like a cup of tea?' The nurse presses my shoulder.

'Uh, yes, please.' I feel a tear slide down my face. I slip into the visitor's chair and take her hand, crying softly as I rub a thumb over the mottled skin. Her poor arthritic joints. Her almond-shaped fingernails look strangely bare without the crazy nail polish she loves. It's the first time I've squeezed this hand and it hasn't responded. I kiss the skin, cool and smooth as marble. Tears drip and I wipe them away. The white oxygen mask covers her nose and mouth; her eyes are peacefully closed. I touch the side of her face where her skin folds.

'Nana.' I kiss her forehead, brushing aside her hair, and sit, pressing her hand to my face. I gaze at the slow rise and fall of her chest. Liquid drips silently from a bag into a tube taped into the crêpey skin of her arm where a bruise is blossoming. I look at her wristband. *Eve Summers. DOB 07.05.42*. This person, so precious to me, this Eve Summers, she's the anchor in my world. 'Why didn't you let the doctor come?' I wipe my eyes again. 'Reg said you wouldn't let him get the doctor.' I kiss the knuckles of her hand. 'Now look at you – you've ended up in here.'

The nurse brings a paper cup of tea. 'Okay?' she asks.

'When will she be awake?'

She looks at Nana thoughtfully. 'It's hard to say. I'll get the doctor to speak to you as soon as he's on the ward.'

She smiles and the curtains swing behind her. The respirator hisses and sighs as it fills Nana's lungs with breath, but there's no sign of her spirit. I lay my head next to the blanketed legs and close my eyes.

'Get better. Get better, okay?' I tell her. 'Don't leave me.' The heart monitor beeps softly. 'Don't leave me.'

It's dark when I step outside the hospital. The last of the visitors spread out across the car park, engines starting up and headlights sweeping across the pavement as I make my way back to the station. I hate to leave her here, but they wouldn't let me stay. Outside the world seems hostile and cold.

I start thinking about Max, wishing he was here, wishing he'd brought me on the bike and was waiting for me now with his big smile. I root in my pocket and turn on my phone. There's a message from Rob: *Working late, angel. Don't make supper.* I delete it and call Max.

'It's Max. Leave a message.'

'Max, it's me. I . . . just called to, you know, say hello and see if you're okay . . . so call me.' What am I going to say?

My nana is in hospital. Please feel sorry for me? I hang up and walk slowly down the station steps to wait on the deserted platform, where a lonely wind rocks the squeaking 'London bound' sign.

The flat is in darkness as I turn the key. It's after ten. I find a packet of mushroom soup and boil the kettle. I turn on the laptop and type 'pneumonia' into the search engine, then make a list of questions from my research. It seems septi-caemia is the biggest risk – twice as likely in those over sixty. The doctor didn't mention it. Is that a good sign? I pour hot water onto the granules and stir. Mushrooms like flakes of leather swirl to the surface. Back at the laptop I type in 'nevergoogleheartbreak.com', wondering if Max has been in touch. I go to 'What's on your mind?', and there's been some activity. The last comment was posted yesterday: '*I agree it is harsh, but then no one wants a sap!*' I scroll up, looking for Max's name, but I have to go all the way back to his poem. Underneath someone called 'smileycat' commented, '*Beautiful! My favourite poem.*' Then someone replied, '*This guy is a joke! He's shit poor and has only his dreams? Keep 'em, babe, they won't pay the rent! How embarrassing and overdramatic, quoting poetry! M – stay away from me, I've made a mistake. I don't want you or your dreams! Vivienne.*'

I read it again. My name. I'm shaking, staring at the words, trying to figure it out. Only someone logged on as me could use my name. I try to remember the last time I was on the site . . . I read Max's poem at work. Did I leave the site open? Could it be Michael? He could have overridden the password and logged on as me, but why would he? I imagine Max reading it, then find the text he sent. '*Hi, Viv. Forget about tonight, then, I guess. M*'

I type, hammering at the keys. '*Max, I didn't write this! I don't know how or who but someone must have logged on as me.*'

The cursor blinks. Whatever I write is pathetic. I get my jacket and run out of the door.

I call Max, redialling when his answer message kicks in. I take a cab to his place. What must he be thinking? First I tell him not to come to my flat, then he reads that message, and then I turn up at the gallery with Rob. My lovely Max. How hurt he looked. I replay the gallery scene over and over, feeling the pain of it sharply each time until the taxi pulls up.

I jump out, leaving the door open and the fare unpaid. The engine idles as I press the buzzer of Max's building. I hold it down. I press it in a rhythm. Press and wait. Nothing. I run to the back of the building and look up at the kitchen window. No light. His motorbike's missing. I try the front door again, holding the buzzer then jabbing it. The taxi driver leans across the passenger seat.

'Hey, love. The meter's ticking here! Want me to wait?'

I stare up at the dark, empty windows of Max's building. 'I'm coming,' I say.

As the cab turns in the road I look up again at the blank window, feeling desolate. It's dawning on me that Max could actually have left. I mean, he could be gone. I imagine my life with him not in it, and it's rubbish.

23

Getting Back with Your Ex

> **Roadkill:** I'm thinking of getting back with my ex-boyfriend. He keeps asking if we can meet. I've been really lonely without him, but I'm worried it might not work out. How do I stop us splitting up again?
>
> **Looneytunes:** Morph yourself into a different person?
>
> **Spidercat:** You don't say how long you've been apart, Roadkill. If you've had enough non-contact time, it might be possible to start afresh; if not, though, you'll just end up going over old ground.
>
> **Debbo:** I'd say be careful what you wish for. My ex moved back in after six months apart. After about twenty minutes I realised I couldn't stand her.
>
> **Gringo:** I thought if I split with my gf, I'd get lots of sex with other women. When that didn't happen, I got back with my ex. It's not long term, though.
>
> **Spidercat:** It's not long term? Really? You are an irresponsible twat, Gringo.
>
> **Gringo:** Whatevs.

What the hell is that godawful caterwauling? I sit up in bed – what time is it? Six a.m. on the clock. Rob is singing in the shower. I get up and call the hospital. No change, they say – she's still unconscious. I sit on the bed and stare into space.

He appears like a shaving-cream advert, wrapped at the waist in a towel, trailing wafts of steam and shower gel.

'Hey, Bun,' he booms. 'Did I wake you?'

I rub my forehead. 'Rob, how long are you staying?'

He stops drying himself and studies me with a sympathetic little frown, as if I must be insane to ask. He sits beside me on the bed. 'What's the matter, Bunny? Are you cross because I worked late?'

'No.' He tries to kiss me. I stand up. 'I just think there's lots unresolved between us. I don't think we can sort this out with you living here. Do you?' He drops his head. 'I mean, when is she moving out of your place?'

'I wanted to talk to you about that,' he says, making puppy eyes.

'Did you write something on my website?'

'What?'

'My website. Someone has written something pretending to be me. I left it open here the night you came back. You said you never looked at it, but I can't think who else it could have been.'

He cocks his head. Water sticks to his eyelashes. It drips from his hair onto his bare tanned chest. His eyes shine incredibly blue in the filtered sunlight.

'Okay. You got me.' He raises his hands.

'What?'

'I did it.'

'You did it?' I suddenly don't know what to say. I have a strong desire to shove him in the face. 'Why? Why would you do that?'

'Well, I don't want that Max making a play for you, do I? Writing poems to another man's chick like that – it's not right. Who does he think he is with all those flowery words? I want you all to myself. No loved-up poet is getting the better of me.' He flashes his dazzling white smile.

I stare at him. 'He didn't write the poem; he was quoting Yeats.'

'Yes, thank you, I knew that.'

'I can't believe you!' I spit. 'I can't believe you would mess with my life like this.'

'Listen, Bun, I love you. It's that simple, and I'll beat off any rival. It's like bears—'

'No, it's not like bears! How dare you?' He comes across the room and puts his arms around me. I push his chest. His perfect biceps tense as he holds me tighter. 'Get off!' I punch him on the shoulder.

'Bunny, come on . . . I'm sorry! I'm sorry, okay? I love you. I shouldn't have done it.' I struggle and his towel falls off. I glance at his body, distracted for a millisecond. He is definitely drop-dead gorgeous and he knows it – even now, posing. 'It was very wrong of me. I see that now.'

'It was evil! How did you get like this? How could you be so controlling and mean?'

'I don't want to be mean.' He manages to look shamefaced.

A terrible thought drops into place, like a coin in a slot. 'Did you know he'd be at the Royal Academy? Is that why we went there?' He purses his lips and smiles. 'Jesus, Rob!'

'I'll admit it was a bad thing to do, okay? I Googled the guy and saw he'd be at the gallery and I just couldn't resist. I did it for us. You need saving from yourself sometimes!' he shouts at my back.

I storm to the kitchen and slam the coffee pot on the heat, so furious I can hardly breathe. How could he do that and think I'd be okay about it? I go to the laptop and jiggle the mouse. Nothing. No word from Max.

The coffee gurgles; I stomp back to the kitchen and pour a cup. Rob appears fully dressed in a lilac checked shirt and well-cut dark grey trousers. He stands close to me, watching, saying nothing. I'm burning with rage and can't look at him. Then I burst into tears.

'Oh, baby bunny, don't cry!'

'This is not okay, Rob.' He eases the coffee from my hands and pulls me in. I find myself blubbing onto his checked shoulder.

'I'm sorry,' he says. 'I'm sorry.' He squeezes me. 'I'm such a twat. Listen, I'll ring the guy. I'll tell him it was me.' I push him away. 'Hell, I'll even buy one of his scribbles if you'll forgive me.'

'You have no idea what you've done, have you?'

He looks at his watch. 'Come on, Viv.'

'You have no clue about friendship or trust or love or . . . or anything good, have you?'

'Well, that's a little unfair, don't you think? I love you.'

'No you don't, not really.'

'Viv, look, everything's okay. It's not cancer, is it? I know you're pissed off, but everything's okay. I'm here now . . .'

'It's not okay. Nana's in hospital, I think I'm about to lose my job, and now, because of you, I've lost my best friend. Everything is definitely *not* okay.'

'What do you mean, you're losing your job?'

'Oh, trust you to pick up on that first.' I scuttle away to get dressed, quickly throwing on a dress and boots. I clip back my hair and splash water on my swollen eyes. The last thing I need is a stupid fight. I need to get to the hospital. Rob knocks softly on the bathroom door.

'Viv?'

'What?'

'Can you come out, please?' I open the door abruptly, making him jump. 'Listen, I want to talk to you. I've phoned work and I've got half an hour.' I snort at the generosity but follow him to the sofa anyway. 'Now, I know I've put you through a lot, and I'm sorry. I'm truly sorry, Viv. But I want to be with you. I know I'm going about it the wrong way, but we can make this work.' He takes a stray piece of my hair and tucks it back into the clip. 'We can.' I look at my clasped fingers. 'Hnnn?' He's holding the diamond necklace in an open hand. 'Here, put this on.' He clasps it at my throat like a flea collar. 'Property prices are plummeting, so I'm going to sell my place.' I look into the hypnotising blue of his eyes. 'Now, what I'd like to do is to move in here with you and we'll get married as soon as possible.' I feel a scream of 'No!' building inside, but what he's selling here is something I've longed for. His voice is soothing. He pats my tummy. 'Then we can get a baby in there, all right? And don't you worry about your job – I mean, it was hardly a *career* and you won't need to work . . . unless you want to. I can support you, Viv. I can give us a good life; you'll never want for anything. We'll have plenty of money and you'll be pregnant very, very quickly.' God, how easy he makes it seem. I could just surrender, roll over and have everything I used to dream of. He squeezes my thigh.

'I . . . I can't talk about this now. I have to get to the hospital,' I reply.

He drops his head. 'Yeah. I have to get to work.' He grabs his jacket and opens the door. 'Think about what I said, though.' He steps out, then bobs back in again. 'And chin up. I'm here for you. Give my best to your granny.' The door slams and I listen to his footsteps do a rhythmic jog down the stairs.

I pick up his half-finished coffee and hurl it at the door; it slams against the painted wood. Two china halves bounce, leaving a dripping stain.

'I would, but she's unconscious,' I say quietly.

I sit for a moment, staring into the street. The sunlight glances off buildings like some sort of code. How will I ever make Max see I had nothing to do with this?

But . . . I did have something to do with this. I am responsible, aren't I? I let Rob in. I could have turned him away that night, but I didn't and he's still here. So of course it's my fault Max got hurt. He won't understand. I hardly get it myself. I walk around the room, trying to think of ways to make it better. I'll make him talk to me. I'll email him. I'll camp at his place. Then I notice the flashing answer machine. I stand over it, hoping for Max's voice, take a breath and press 'play'.

'Hello, Viv darling, it's only Nana. Listen, I'm not feeling too well. I've got these dreadful chest pains and have been a bit dizzy. Anyway, Reg thinks I should go down to the hospital . . . Viv? Are you there? She's not answering . . . Bye bye, my darling . . . Lots of love.'

I listen to it again with tears in my eyes. Of course. Nana's message! There she was trying to speak to me, sounding so scared and brave, trying to ask for help, and what was I doing? I shudder at the memory and leave for the hospital.

24

Love

'When love beckons to you, follow him, though his ways are hard and steep. And when his wings enfold you, yield to him, though the sword hidden among his pinions may wound you.'

Kahlil Gibran

'Love is when the person they see in you is better than the person you are, and you really want to close the gap.'

Jem, 19, Poole

'Try not to anticipate love; it's never how you think it will be. I once made a drama of it. But I've found love to be calm and gentle, and passion quiet and deep. Bliss comes from the certainty. My love is the staff that I lean on after one of life's hard climbs. He's constant and true, quick to forgive and easy company. His beauty is in his dignity, his faith, his maleness and his way of moving. He makes me laugh and laughs with and at me. This never changes and it's been forty years.'

Rose, 62, Yorkshire

'Hello, it's Vivienne Summers calling. Just to say I won't be coming in today . . .'

'Hello, Vivienne.' Snotty picks up, interrupting the answer machine. Bugger!

'Oh, hi. Morning I—'

'You're not coming in, did you say?' she snaps.

'No. My nana is in hospital.'

'Really? What is it this time?'

'She has pneumonia.' Speaking that somehow makes it more real and brings a huge lump to my throat.

'Really?' she says again, bored.

'I need to be with her.'

'She's quite a sickly woman, isn't she, your nan?'

'So I won't be in.'

'Okay!' she sings in a threatening kind of way and hangs up.

I press 'end call'. I'll worry about work later.

Morning time on the ward feels busy. The bed curtains are tied back. Nurses are clearing away after the night shift. I wonder about Sarcophagus Man as I see them stripping his bed. I spot Reggie there at Nana's bedside, holding her hand. I wait behind him for a second.

'I was thinking of cutting back the rhododendron, but I didn't. I know you like those flowers, my darling.' He strokes the back of her hand with his big rough paw; then he starts singing: '*Dum de dum . . . exchanging glances . . . hmm hmm, what were the chances . . .* That cat you keep feeding was back this morning. Looking like it'd lost a pound and found a penny . . . Suppose I'll give it something if it's still there later.'

'She can't hear you, you know,' I pronounce.

'Oh, hello, Viv.' He looks up from under straggly brows. 'I don't know . . . s'pose it helps me, to think she might.' He smiles nicotine yellow. I go to the bed, pulling up the covers and arranging flowers. I kiss her cheek; her skin is dry and warm.

'How long have you been here?'

'About an hour.'

'Well, go now if you like. I'm here.'

Something skids across his eyes and he glances at Nana. 'No, I think I'll stay a bit.' He smiles. 'I promised to sit with her. She hates hospitals.'

'Yes, I know.' I hover over him. 'I'll get another chair, then.' I hear him crooning again as I walk across the ward. Why can't he just get the message and let me be alone with her? I drag the chair to the other side of the bed and take her hand, kissing it. 'Has the doctor been round?'

'Not yet.' He gives a sad little smile, like I'm the intruder.

'Why didn't you call a doctor out to the house before she got so ill?'

'Ah . . . she wouldn't have it.'

'Should have made her,' I mutter, frowning at the purple around the drip-feed needle.

He smiles again. 'You know you can't *make* Eve do anything.'

'*Persuaded* her, then, or something. I don't know. But she shouldn't be in here.'

'You're right.' He rubs his blunt thumb over her wrist and kisses her hand. I suddenly want to slap him away. I should be the one looking after her.

'Tell me something, Reg: were you and my nana carrying on while Granddad was alive?'

He sits back, draws in a breath. Good, a reaction. 'I've always loved her, Viv. Since the first day I saw her.'

'Yeah . . . that's not what I asked.'

'She loved your granddad.'

'He was away quite a bit, though, wasn't he? Did that make it easier for you? Did you wait until your Alice had gone, or didn't that matter?'

A little pulsing vein appears at his temple. 'Now's not the time, Viv,' he almost whispers.

'I think it's the perfect time. You're sitting here like she's the love of your life!'

The respirator shushes. Someone on the ward is coughing up liquid.

'She was . . . is. We were talking about getting married before all this.'

'Oh Jesus! Now I've heard everything! What for?' I almost laugh.

His rheumy old eyes look longingly at her. 'Well, Vivienne, if you're asking that, you've never been in love,' he says softly. 'You don't know.' He shakes his head, getting to his feet. 'You don't know.' He walks out.

Now I've got what I wanted: I'm alone with Nana, but the stupid man has made me feel bad. Getting married! She would have told me. I try to shake off a hollow feeling, so I stand up and brush Nana's hair a bit. It's greasy. I'd like to wash it for her. I look at her bare lashes, thinking I'll buy her a little make-up to have when she wakes. As I smooth out the covers and a wet drop lands on her neck I realise I'm crying.

I do know about love. I know how it feels to love someone and how it feels to think you might lose them.

Later I wander through the corridors, following my nose to the hospital canteen. I should eat something, I suppose. The hot food sweats, colourless and miserable. Everywhere people are dribbling soup and shuffling with trays. You really would think that a hospital canteen could be a bit more uplifting. Shouldn't it be painted orange and be bursting with fresh stuff and health food? Shouldn't you get a free wheat-grass shot with every alfalfa wrap?

I get coffee and a curling white sandwich, find a seat alone and begin redialling Max and listening to his answer message. The third time it clicks in I speak.

'Hey, Max, it's me. I'm guessing you don't want to talk to me – I'm sharp like that. But I was wondering if you'd let me explain. Also, some stuff has happened and . . . well, I could do with a friend and you are my best friend. I take it you still want that position? Ha ha, er . . . Please, Max, give me a call.'

As I flip the phone shut, something catches my attention,

like a swan on a duck pond: a beautifully cut dress of burnt-orange silk, long tanned limbs and glossy hair. She waits by the till to pay and tosses her head as she turns. Rob's ex-girlfriend, Sam.

Oh fuck. I look down at the table, hoping she didn't notice me, but from the corner of my eye I see she's coming this way, sashaying in classy sandals, leaving a trail of magic and putting roses in the cheeks of the half-dead as they watch her. I wouldn't be surprised if she had a posse of songbirds and Bambis in tow. I hear her heels as I study the sandwich's ingredients panel. Click, click, click. Keep walking. Walk on by, sister! She stops. I wait.

'Vivienne, isn't it?'

I set my face to pleasant surprise before I look up. 'Hello?' I enquire. Like I'd not remember her!

'It's Sam. We have Rob Waters in common. We're both his exes.'

'Oh yes! Except I'm not . . . No, we're back together.' God, this is sweet! I enjoy the little wrinkle that appears between her eyebrows. 'Yeah, I think he finally realised he couldn't live without me . . . Probably needed a real woman, so . . .' Why oh why oh why am I not wearing the engagement ring?

'Is that right?'

'Uh-huh. You see, in a way, we never really broke up. Sorry, you know, that things didn't work out for you, though.' I smile sympathetically.

'Don't be,' she says. 'I don't know what he told you, but I ended it with Rob last month.' She puts down her egg salad and inspects a perfect nail. 'He took it quite badly, poor thing, but you see, I fell head over heels for my gynaecologist.' She gestures towards the canteen counter to a beautiful man in doctor's whites, his skin perfectly blue-black, like he's carved from ebony.

'Oh.'

'How funny to run into you, in this dump of all places. It's a teaching hospital and Troy's lecturing this morning; then we're off to France for a long weekend.'

'Oh. Troy.' Why doesn't she just fuck off now?

'And I was going to confide . . . Rob is the meanest guy I've ever met, but I suppose I shouldn't now. To think, he used to make me say thank you whenever he took me for dinner!' She giggles like a tinkling crystal bell. The doctor strolls over. With every move he oozes sex. His smile is stunning. He curls an arm around her, his dark hand appears on her hip and I suddenly imagine them having sex. It's very beautiful and erotic and exotic . . . et cetera.

'Hello.' His voice is so gorgeous I'd like a tape of him saying my name.

'Hi there.' I give a small wave, trying to be casual, but blushing to my roots. She doesn't bother to introduce us, just smiles into my eyes and collects her salad.

'And by the way, that necklace you're wearing? Rob gave that to me. I didn't have the heart to keep it, so I gave it back when I left. It looks nice on you, though.' I touch the diamond pendant as they turn the corner, two perfect people in love.

'What a bitch!' I gasp. My mind starts wildly casting about. I feel like something's pushing down on my windpipe. She ended it with Rob! So he found himself suddenly single and thought he'd come crawling back to me, giving it that 'I can't live without you' and 'I never stopped thinking of you' shit. Has she moved out already? I bet she moved out ages ago and he's using her as an excuse to worm his way back into my life. The worst of it is, I believed him. He's made a fool of me again. I take off the necklace and think about throwing it away, but this isn't a film. I can't go around throwing perfectly good jewellery away. I feel sick at the thought of Rob.

But wait a minute, what if she's lying? God – how quick I am to think badly of Rob! Of course she's lying. She would rather die than admit I've won. I've got the man she wanted and she can't take it. Ha! Briefly I'm triumphant, but then I imagine Rob standing next to the doctor Adonis and I'm less sure.

I pull apart the bread of my sandwich crusts. If I had to bet, I'd say Rob probably lied. Most likely. But does it really matter who dumped who? We're not at nursery school. He's back with me like I wanted, and as he said, with him at my side I don't need to worry about losing my job. I can do whatever I want. I could spend more time with Nana. Rob and I are getting married. That's what I wanted, wasn't it? He said we'd get married soon. Not like last time, though – no, this would have to be a small, classy do. I'd probably already be pregnant. I wouldn't have to worry about money ever again. I'd be like those Chelsea mummies with their diamond earrings, clogging up Starbucks with their Bugaboos . . . or maybe not like them, but my baby would have everything.

I try to picture a baby with Rob's pretty blue eyes, but I can't quite see it. I put my head on the table.

I'm walking through Irish fields carrying Max's baby in a sheepskin sling. He's beautiful, smiling with dimples, brown as a berry with his father's unruly black hair . . .

Next thing I know, Reg is shaking me awake.

I used to think all doctors were sexy by virtue of being heroic healers, but this one, with his red roadmap nose and leaping coffee breath, and his trainee, all stooped shoulders and trembling fingers, have bucked the trend. They talk about Nana as if they have a terrible secret and are laying out clues for us to guess it. They mention blood tests and pleural effusion.

'What are you telling us?' I interrupt.

'Well, we never like to say, "Prepare for the worst," but we're monitoring for septicaemia.'

'Is she dying?'

'Septicaemia is a complication of pneumonia more common in the elderly and it accounts for about eighty per cent of fatalities . . .' The trainee parrots his textbook.

'Is she going to die?'

'We can't say at this time. A blood transfusion may be necessary, though, and we need written permission.'

'Well, whatever you think, Doctor . . .' Reg's voice breaks as he reaches for the pen.

'I'm the next of kin,' I snap at him. 'What do you mean, you "can't say"?'

'Miss Summers, your grandmother is seriously ill. The next couple of days are critical.'

'But people don't die of pneumonia these days. You must be doing something wrong.' They exchange a 'We've got a right one here' glance. 'Look, I've Googled it. I know.'

'Miss Summers, I've Googled it too, as well as studying medicine for seven years and practising for ten. Rest assured we are doing our very best. We'll keep you informed,' says Roadmap Nose and with that they melt away like spirits, behind the curtain.

Reg is all shiny-eyed and useless. I look at Nana. She's blue pale, even her eyelids. I put my face against her cheek, whispering into her hair.

'Hold on,' I tell her. 'Don't you go, Nana. You have to stay with me. I really need you.' I don't blink away tears. I try to will her better. One short week ago I had the luxury of taking her for granted.

I feel Reg's hand on my shoulder. 'It'll be okay,' he says. 'She's not going anywhere. We forbid it, don't we?' He pulls me in to his chest. His shirt smells of soap, and his heart pumps warm. 'All right. It's all right.'

I feel him rubbing my back and I want to curl into him and cry, but instead I stiffen and pull away, wiping my face. 'I'm all right. I'm okay. I think I'll just get some air.'

'Viv, do you have anyone to look after you?' His hound-dog eyes are full of concern.

'I'm a grown-up, Reg. I don't need looking after,' I snort. How old-fashioned. Looking after! I stalk away with my grief flapping around me like an open coat.

Outside a humid evening is settling over the suburbs. Dark clouds bulge with rain. The road already smells of it. I set off towards the station – being at the hospital is doing me no good, sitting around there with Reg as my shadow. No, I need to get away. I need to think. I know I've neglected Nana recently. I mean, Rob was certainly never interested in her, and since we split up I've been absorbed by the break-up. I've been thinking a lot about the website. I've made heart-break a kind of project: I've researched it, written about it and wallowed in it. I tried to make it more commonplace – funnier, even. But that's the very nature of heartbreak, isn't it? It's unique to the sufferer; everyone feels the pain different-ently. It's personal.

Now I'm facing losing Nana. Now I know how it really feels and the cold of it enters into my heart and settles like fog. Everything seems messed up and I have the creeping feeling that it's all my fault. I'm not sure how I've managed it, but it seems I've turned everything that was good into shit. I wish I could see Max. I wish I had a friend or a career or something meaningful. I search for something and the only real thing I have is 'getting married'.

But I am getting married. I shouldn't be feeling sorry for myself. I'm getting married! That's what I wanted. I didn't think it would feel like this, though. I feel as if I've sacrificed my whole life to make that one wish come true and now I'm left with that empty feeling you get when you realise something expensive you saved for is now in the sale for next to nothing. I plod on, feeling worse and worse, as I mull this over.

But really, I can't let myself feel low – I should have more faith. I'm getting married. I do love Rob. Nana will get better, she will. Max will forgive me and so will Lucy. I'll try harder at work, even get a promotion or something, and everything will be fine. It will. It *will*.

A waft of cooking floats over from the houses near the station. I glance into a garden where two children abandon their paddling pool, running across a thirsty lawn with grass cuttings stuck to their legs. I pause to watch. Their mother meets my eye and smiles and shakes her head as she bends to gather toys. Maybe she presumes I'm a mother too, thinking I know how it is to pick up after kids. I look like I should know, but I suddenly get a glimpse of a terrifying truth: I'm miles away from having children, and marrying Rob would take me away even further . . . I'd be spending all my time patching up the relationship and looking after him. God! What if being a mum is all I've ever wanted?

Back in London my mood sinks and the rain finally falls. Big wet drops splatter the pavement and it's slick within seconds. I board a bus at Victoria station, just to ride and think. Okay, time to face the fear. What if she dies? My lovely, kind, funny nana. She'd leave me to cope with the million times I've taken her for granted, the times I've snapped at her or been ashamed of her. I'll never be able to tell her I love her or see her smile again. She can't die, can she? Not my nana! I feel a sob welling up and turn to the window to avoid people staring. I rub a little space in the condensation so I can see out, and wipe my eyes. The bus shudders through Victoria's wedding-cake squares, and on to Hyde Park. If she'd just wake up, I could be a better granddaughter. I'd visit more. Be kinder.

We leave behind Green Park station where a tramp sits in a wet sack. Commuters dodge his begging hat. God, London is so unforgiving. It's hopeless if you're not strong. I take a big, shuddering breath and blow my nose. I have to control myself and stop crying. We're moving slowly down Piccadilly now, stuck in traffic. Shop fronts slide by. We pass the Royal Academy, and we lurch on again towards Piccadilly Circus.

The Royal Academy! I'm up, frantically pressing the bell, but the bus sails on to the next stop. I jump off into the rain and my hair sticks to my face almost instantly. My dress clings; my boots turn dark. I run back to the gallery, pushing through the pavement crowds; water from a passing umbrella showers cold onto my neck. If I can see his paintings, I'll feel near to him – and what if he's there? He might even be there! He might have popped in to see if they've sold or something and then we'll bump into each other and . . . he'll see that I need him. I get to the entrance and squeeze water from my hair and try to imagine Max inside. Tourists stroll and gather. If I go to the place where I last saw him, I'm suddenly convinced he'll be there waiting, like in a film or something.

My feet slip and squeak in wet leather. I think I'm in the right place; this was the very room. I look around and my eyes fall on something familiar. I look again. Lula. My heart aches remembering the time I saw her in Max's studio. I stand close to the picture, studying the brushstrokes, imagining his hands. A card displayed next to the canvas reads, 'Envy, *oil and acrylic. Max Kelly.*' She's still breathtaking, even in a room full of beautiful art. A sticker shows the painting's been sold. I feel thrilled for him. I run my finger over his printed name: Max Kelly. Clever, talented, sexy Max Kelly. Then I see another painting and I'm suddenly looking into my own face. Me, the day after Jane's wedding, wearing the Arsenal T-shirt.

I'm curled awkwardly in the chair, looking sulkily beautiful and cool with messed-up hair and smudged eyes. He's painted light in my eyes, so I look on the brink of laughter. I'm thrilled. I wish I looked like this. Imagine if I really looked like this. This is how I wish I looked all the time. I stand, looking into my face and scrutinising my eyes, and I feel flooded with hope. He's painted me how he sees me. This is how I feel when I'm with him. He's called it *Love*. I drip onto the floor in the hush of the gallery, gazing at this painting of myself. I can hardly breathe. I look again and again at the feet, at the hair, at the folds of red cloth. It's like Max has reached into my heart and lit the pilot light. I stare at the painting. People pass by. The rain stops. Everything falls into place.

25

How to Say Sorry

1. *Be sorry. Never apologise when you don't mean it.*
2. *Make the apology in person.*
3. *Take full responsibility for your actions. Do not blame the other person or make excuses for yourself.*
4. *Don't expect an apology or forgiveness in return.*
5. *If you're saying, 'I'm sorry, but . . .' or, 'I'm sorry you feel that way . . .' then you're not really sorry.*
6. *A true apology will make you and the other person feel better.*

I'm home. I let the door close behind me. 'Hello?' I call, just in case. There's no answer. I peel off my wet clothes and get in the shower, letting the hot water drum my shoulders. I tip back my head and lather and rinse the shampoo. Steam rises and fills the room. I stretch my neck, lift my arms and turn round under the flow, thinking about the painting. If that's how I can be, like that amused, sexy girl in the painting, then there's hope. I like that girl. That's how I want to be for the rest of my life, and the artist is the one who makes me feel it. No man could paint that girl and then leave her, so I will find him.

But first I have to get rid of Rob, that's what. I feel a faint pang of pity for him so I replay a few old disappointments – how he's never once bought me a bunch of flowers, never cooked me dinner, never given me a massage . . . or a proper orgasm, when I come to think of it. He acts like I'm lucky to know him and I believed I was. The showerhead dribbles as I shut off the tap. I step out of the shower, wrap myself in towels and rub steam from the mirror. I look myself right in the eye. I am completely calm. I dress in jeans and a black tunic dress and comb out my hair. I get my make-up bag and find black eyeliner. It makes you powerful – I read that. I'm just putting on a second coat of mascara when I hear his key in the lock. I realise I've been holding my breath.

'Bunny! Are you in?'

'In here.'

He leans on the doorframe, head on one side, watching me with those eyes full of his version of empathy.

'How was your day?' he asks.

'I spent it at the hospital, so how do you think it was?'

'O-kay.' He takes off his jacket and turns towards the kitchen.

'I met a friend of yours there.' This brings him back to the doorway.

'Oh yeah?'

'Yeah. Sam.' He looks blank. 'You know, Sam. The woman you were going to marry?'

'Oh.' He looks wary. 'You talk to her?'

'We had a little chat.'

'Uh-huh. What did she say?'

'Oh, she spoke very highly of you.' He looks relieved and confused at the same time and starts fiddling with his hair. 'She dumped you, didn't she?' I look at him in the mirror. 'She met someone else.' He studies his feet, taps one of his Church brogues against the other. I turn back to my reflection and slide on some lippy.

'Is that what she told you?'

'Is that what happened?' I look at him and it's as if his forehead is transparent, the clockwork mechanism of his lies visible in the making. Lucy's right: he's thick.

He rubs the end of his nose. 'Well, not exactly. I—'

'Actually, don't explain. I don't want to know.'

'I think she met him just before we started having problems, but I wasn't aware she left me for him.'

'Oh, who cares, Rob?' I stand and go to the wardrobe, looking for my highest heels. 'I can't believe anything you say. For a minute there you really had me. I was ready to believe you wanted me back, that you left her for me.'

'I—'

'To think I actually thought you loved me and wanted to marry me and have *children*!' I hear the trace of a wobble in my voice. Breathe. Control yourself. If you cry, he'll wheedle his way back in. He narrows his eyes and stares out of the window. I throw the diamond necklace on the bed. 'You bought that for her, didn't you?'

He looks from it to me, right into my eyes, and nods. He doesn't even bother to deny it. I swallow the shock, slipping on my shoes. I lean against the window, watching him. He stares back. It's very, very quiet.

'You going out, then?' He looks at my feet.

'Yes.' Our eyes meet and all the unspoken feelings and unfinished arguments buzz between us. I look away. I can't even be bothered to row.

'So what do you want to do?' he asks quietly.

'What about?'

'Us.'

'Us? There is no us.' I pick up my handbag. 'I think I just want you to go.' He looks down. This isn't working out the way I planned at all. I thought I'd be like Scarlett in *Gone with the Wind*, all righteous and powerful, but I just feel sad and a bit sorry for him.

'I know this looks bad, but I do love you.' He gathers up the necklace. His eyes glisten.

'And I used to believe that. I've only just realised you don't love anyone but yourself.'

'Bunny, don't say that!' My God, he's actually crying. He

sobs and gulps. I think there was a time when this would have worked. I couldn't have stood seeing it. Now I know I'm just watching another great performance. He moves towards me with his arms held out like a toddler. 'I'm sorry!' he sniffs. 'I'm sorry, Bunny! Maybe I haven't been truthful enough. Let's talk about it. I love you. You love me. We're good together.'

'No, see, we're not.'

'I can change . . . I can.'

'Rob, I don't want you to change. There's nothing you can do. It's too late. I just don't love you any more.'

He cries loudly like a child, shaking his head and letting his nose run, showing me the effect I'm having. 'Don't do this.'

'I'm going now,' I say quietly, 'and when I get back, I want you to be gone. Leave your keys, okay?' Tears are streaming down his face. I feel a bit sick.

'B-bunny!' He reaches out, but I dodge him and grab my jacket.

'Okay?' I repeat. He nods slowly through the sobs. 'I'm sorry,' I add, feeling a bit guilty. 'Bye, Rob.' I turn and walk out, letting the door slam behind me.

I run to the end of the street before I look back. He hasn't followed and I suddenly realise he never follows. He has never, ever followed me after a row. I can't believe it. Five years and he has never followed. And I won't feel bad about him. He's the one who did this. He pulled out of our wedding. He lied to me all along. I feel a rush of energy; I'm finally free of him, over him, out from whatever spell it was he had cast over me.

I take a deep breath. I feel powerful; I feel like shouting something. I walk past a West Indian lady and smile. She smiles back. I'm shaking with relief. A taxi rounds the corner and I suddenly decide to wave it down. I jump in and the driver makes a U-turn towards Lucy's.

*   *   *

She opens the door a crack, sees it's me and sets her face accordingly, but she steps out.

'Well, look what the cat—'

'I'm sorry,' I blurt. She folds her arms and tilts her head, listening. 'You're right, I'm boring. I'm always in a crisis and I might have been wallowing in it a bit.'

'Might have been?' she prods.

'Definitely have been. Wallowing . . . and going on about it.' I look at her, but there's nothing to read in her face and for a second I get the horrible feeling that she isn't going to forgive me. 'I've been a really shit friend,' I say softly. 'I miss you.'

A moment passes. We stand on her front step, looking at each other; then she smiles.

'No, I'm sorry. I'm the shit friend.'

'No, I am. I'm always banging on about Rob and boring you.'

'No, I'm always talking about sex.'

'You're not! Well, not all the time.'

'Oh, come here.' She opens her arms and I step into a perfumed hug. 'Want to hear my news?' she squeaks in my ear.

'Yeah.' She releases me.

'You won't believe it!' she squeals.

'Okay, only dogs can hear you now.'

'It's too exciting!'

'What?'

She holds up her left hand and there sparkles a diamond. Her face freezes in a silent scream, waiting for my reaction. I half laugh, she looks so silly.

'Lucy! Congratulations.'

'Reuben the fuck buddy is going to be Reuben the fuck husband!'

'Congratulations!' I hug her. 'I never thought I'd see the day!'

'I know!'

'This is unbelievable news . . .'

'He's here! Come on.' She dances down the hall. I follow into the white kitchen. This is weird – she's marrying someone I've never even met. Latin music plays and Reuben is making cocktails at the counter. He's small and slim-hipped like a boy, black hair closely cropped and brushed forward, beautiful nut-coloured skin and flashy teeth. She sidles up to him and they salsa a few steps, his hands on her waist. I begin to feel like I should leave. He dances over and they make a salsa sandwich with me as the filling. I stand awkward and ridiculous; I'm not really sure what's going on. I wriggle out and they dance away.

'Hey, how long have you guys been celebrating?'

'All fucking day!' screams Lucy.

'Viv, you wanna caipirinha?' he shouts, juggling two limes.

'Okay.' I smile.

'Come here, come here.' Lucy pulls me into the living room and down onto the sofa. 'I'm so sorry about everything. I've hated not seeing you. Tell me about you.' She squeezes my hand.

'Oh, you know, a lot's happened. My nana's in hospital.'

'Oh no! Is she okay?'

'Pneumonia.'

'Oh, Viv, I'm sorry.'

'Yes, so that's been . . . difficult, but I know she'll be okay. She'll get through.' I stop myself from explaining more. I don't want to rain on their festival. I take her hand. 'Gorgeous ring.'

'Isn't it? It's just mad, me getting married. But I'm so happy!' she shouts at the ceiling, drumming her hands on the sofa. Reuben comes in, bringing drinks. He kisses Lucy as he hands her hers. I glimpse a tongue and look away.

'Vivienne! I been hearing all about you! What's going on

with this Rob dick shit?' he says as he kneels on the floor
and hands me a glass.

'Ah, nothing really . . .'

'Good. Kick that asshole out of your life!' He raises his
glass to drink to that. I smile at Lucy; she shrugs.

'Do you know what, Reuben? You're absolutely right! I'll
drink to that.' I down the cocktail.

'You're going to dump him?' asks Lucy, all hopeful.

'Just did. He's gone. History.' They stare and I give a little
wave. '*Adios*,' I add for Reuben's benefit.

'Oh thank God!' Lucy roars. 'I *hated* that guy!'

'I know – you quite often said.'

'All those years! You just waiting for him to make up his
mind. It just wasn't like you, Viv. He took your shine.'

'Well, I'm getting my shine back,' I say in a hero's voice.

'Hooray!' she shouts. 'I want to dance. Let's sing
something!'

'Ding dong, the witch is dead . . .' I begin, but she's already
at the iPod and dragging me up for a dance. It's Goldfrapp,
'Rocket'. We join in with the chorus and Reuben claps along.

'She needs another drink,' Lucy shouts.

'*Amor*, don't worry, I made two jugs.'

Salsa is an amazing kind of dance. Really, all you do is shuffle
your feet and swing your hips and you're doing it! Reuben's
a great teacher. Lucy did a sort of salsa pole dance without
the pole and he filmed her. Then I had the idea of being the
pole so he filmed us both. Now, I'm not into threesomes
myself, but if I were, I think I could do a lot worse than
those two. I think I'll go and tell them that right now. I flush
the toilet and knock over a dried-flower thing. It falls in the
bowl. I try to flush, but it keeps reappearing like a withered
hand.

Back in the living room they've turned the music down

and I join them on the sofa. Reuben is a very, very nice man, stroking Lucy's knee and – oh, hello! – mine as well.

'So when are you going to do it?' I ask.

'We been doing it all day,' Reuben quips.

I slap his leg. 'The wedding!' God, he's so funny.

'Next month,' he says. 'Before summer ends.'

'We're having a sex theme,' Lucy tells me. 'I'm thinking white tutu, corset, white fishnet stockings.'

'Nice. Classy.'

'And for me, nothing but a bow tie and a smile,' says Reuben.

There's a pause as we imagine it. I have to say it's not that bad.

'Maybe put a little sock on your knob?' suggests Lucy.

'Or wear trousers?' I say.

'Yeah, wear trousers, Reub,' agrees Lucy.

'Okay. Hot pants.' He squeezes my knee. 'An' hot pants for you as well.'

'Me? No. Not a good look.'

'White hot pants and boots for Viv!' Lucy laughs.

'Not while there's breath in my body. You can't tell guests what to wear, anyway.'

'But Viv, you're not just a guest. I wanted to ask you this, but I . . . haven't seen you recently.' She suddenly sits up and squints at my face. 'Viv, you've been such a great friend to me over the years . . .'

'Bless you, and you've been a good friend to me.' I take her hand.

'Vivienne Summers, you've been with me through thick and thin,' she says, all solemn.

'We haven't had that many thins,' I reply.

'Well, there was that time you went off with Julie . . .'

'Oh yeah . . . and your deportation mix-up thingy in Spain.'

'Look, shut up, I'm trying to make a speech! What I'm saying is, you're a faithful friend . . .'

'Like a dog,' Reuben chips in.

'Like a very, very, very faithful dog, yes.' She smiles at Reuben. 'So I'd like to ask you to be my best man . . . well, best woman.'

'Or best dog!' exclaims Reuben.

'Yes, all right, Reub . . . Will you, Viv? Please?' She sniffs and gets wet eyes.

'Luce . . . I would consider it an honour to be your best woman.' I feel a ball of emotion in my throat. I throw my arms around her.

'Love you,' she whispers into my hair.

'So! Let's make a toast,' cries Reuben, getting to his feet. 'To great friends!'

I think of Max. I see his smile when I close my eyes and finish my drink.

'To great friends,' I say.

And to finding him.

26

A Poem for the Day

Poetry Appreciation Society

Oh, Max, if only you knew
What is lies and what is true,
You'd come back and kiss me.
Tell me you miss me,
'Cos bloody hell, Max, I miss you.
                    Vivienne Summers

It's past midnight and I know it looks a bit weird me snooping about outside Max's building, but since he isn't responding to emails or calls, I'm not sure where else to start. Could this be construed as stalking?

I look up at the window. No lights on. I look down at the pavement. No motorbike. I sway in the night breeze, staring up like a Romeo. I throw a pebble; it misses, but sets a dog off barking. 'Where the fuck are you?' I mutter, and listen as if he'll reply. I recognise the thump of 'Disco Inferno' from the nightclub round the corner. There's a clatter as a can falls near the bins, making me jump. I spin round and peer into the darkness with the eerie sense of another presence.

'Hello?' All the horror movies I've ever seen combine in my head until I'm sure a doll/scarecrow thing with knives for fingers is about to thunder out into the light. I'm listening intently and hear a high raspy squeak; something's moving. Just as I'm about to run away, screaming, 'There are evil clowns living in the drains!' a small cat trots out, tail high. He approaches my legs and weaves himself through them like a ribbon. I clutch at my chest in relief, partly to calm myself and partly because they do that in horror films. 'Dave!' I bend to tickle his throat, feeling his speedboat purr. I scoop him up and he hangs on my arm, eyes half closed, legs dangling. 'Poor little Dave. Poor pussycat. He left you behind!' The front door opens and a rectangle of light frames a woman wearing a Minnie Mouse nightshirt. Dave scrabbles free and disappears through her ankles. The woman squints my way for a second and goes to close the door.

'Er, hi, excuse me?' I step forward; she holds the door slightly open. 'Hi, I'm looking for Max Kelly. I wonder if you know where he is . . . That's his cat . . .'

'Huh! Aren't we all looking for Max Kelly?'

'Are we? Do you know him?'

'He asked me to have the cat, gave me a hundred quid and said he's going away for a while.'

'And he didn't say where?'

'No. If I knew where, I'd send this bloody cat there. It's a pain in the arse.'

'When did he go?'

'Look, does he owe you money?'

'No. He's a friend.' I notice a cat scratch on my arm, a line of blood-red pinpricks.

'He went on Wednesday. Here, if you're his friend, can you take the cat?'

8 August, 01:07

From: Vivienne Summers
To: Max Kelly
Subject: [None]

So you've gone away. Very dramatic. When you coming back?
  Love from Dave

9 August, 14:22

From: Vivienne Summers
To: Max Kelly
Subject: Re:

Max,
You've made your point now with this not-speaking thing.
How can we resolve this? It's completely and totally inconceiv-
able to me for us to not be friends.
V x
P.S. Please find attached my photo album of us. I particularly
like the graduation pictures. What had you done to your hair?
And that jacket – you have always been a knob, see?

9 August, 14:37

From: Vivienne Summers
To: Max Kelly
Subject: Re:

Max,
If you ring me in the next five minutes, I'll take you to the
Chinese all-you-can-eat place for dinner. On me. I'll pay. You can
have one of those red cocktails with the umbrella too.
V x

9 August, 14:46

From: Vivienne Summers
To: Max Kelly
Subject: Re:

I can explain . . . everything. x

9 August, 15:07

From: Vivienne Summers
To: Max Kelly
Subject: Re:

Please, Max. Would you see me for just half an hour, even?
   x

9 August, 15:28

From: Vivienne Summers
To: Max Kelly
Subject: Re:

Don't be a knob. I miss you. x

9 August, 15:41

From: Vivienne Summers
To: Max Kelly
Subject: Re:

Shall I leave you alone? Okay, this is it, then, last message.
   Goodbye.
   dramatic pause
   Goodbye, Max.

9 August, 16:09

From: Vivienne Summers
To: Max Kelly
Subject: Re:

You have a real stubborn streak. It's not attractive in a person.

9 August, 16:17

From: Vivienne Summers
To: Max Kelly
Subject: Re:

And the beginnings of hairy ears.

The dialling tone in Ireland is weird. Is their phone permanently engaged? If not, it's taking ages to answer. What kind
of place must they live in to take this long to get to the
phone? I'm here in London, listening to a dialling tone, while
somewhere in Ireland there's a castle and an old-style phone
shrilling to an empty room . . .

'Hello?' says an impatient voice.

'Hi there, is that Mrs Kelly?'

'Is that Sun Life insurance again? I told you we've had no
accidents!'

'No. I'm a friend of Max's. I'm Vivienne Summers . . . Is
that you, Mrs Kelly?'

'Might be.'

'Well, I don't know if you remember me . . .' No answer.
'We met when you visited Max at university?' Silence. 'I
stayed with you on New Year's Eve once?' God, this is
difficult.

'What d'you say your name was?'

'Vivienne.'

'No, no, doesn't ring a bell.'

'Oh. Did he not mention me? We've been friends for years.'

'No.'

'Okay. Well, it's just that I'm looking for Max. He's left his
flat and gone somewhere and I wondered if you might have
heard from him.' No response. God, it's like pulling teeth.
Maybe she's hung up. 'Hello?'

'Yes.'

'So if Max gets in touch, would you just say that Viv called?'

'Ah, hold on, Viv. Yes, I know you.'

'Yes. Hi.'

'You're the dark-haired one he holds a candle for, aren't you?'

'Yes! Does he?'

'He does talk about you.'

'So you've heard from him?'

'Not this week. I'll tell you it's as if he hasn't heard of a telephone. I told him to ring every week at least. And he never visits. Last July we saw him – he was back for Siobhan's wedding. She married the cousin of our neighbour . . .'

And on and on for a full twenty minutes: the list of his auntie Hilda's ailments; his eldest sister's back hasn't been the same since she had the caesarean. They love the bones of him. They miss him like mad. Just like me.

27

Endings/New Beginnings

Facebook Group – Where's Max?

Basic info: Search for lost lover
Category: Love, heartbreak

Description: Is it better to have loved and lost? I don't
think so. My name is Vivienne Summers and I've lost my
love because I didn't realise what I had. There was a
misunderstanding; he thinks I betrayed him and now he's
gone. I have to find him. If you know him, have seen
him or meet him, would you let him know I'm sorry and
I love him.

Subject Profile

Name: **Max Kelly**
Sex: **Male**
Nationality: Irish
Birthday: 5 April 1980
Hometown: London
Description: Six foot two-ish, dark curly hair, scruffy-looking
Dresses: From the floor – jeans, track pants, T-shirts;
sartorially out of step
Interested in: Poetry, art, motorbikes, guitar, telling long,
often pointless stories
Favourite word: Slot
Favourite colour: Vermilion

In the airless box of the thirteenth-floor meeting room, Christie's bubble gum pops. She winds a pink-grey string and stretches it in front of her face before nibbling it back.

'I like your hair,' she says. 'Have you had it done?'

'Ages ago.'

She walks round my chair. 'Oh yeah.' She pops her gum again.

'Can you not do that?' I smooth my hair at the back.

'Is that a version of a mullet?'

'I don't know what it's "a version" of.'

'Hmm.' She sighs and slumps into her chair, stretching her arms across the desk.

'So, Christie, let's have a little think. How are we going to sell ten thousand unethical candles?'

'We can't. We're doomed.'

'Shall I just put that in the report for Mole, then?' I pretend to write down, 'We're doomed.'

'Why does everything have to be ethical? Nothing is ethical any more. No one cares.'

'Except the slave labour children hand-stitching buttons twenty hours a day.'

'Yeah, but we're talking about prisoners making candles. It's not like they have lives.'

'Shall I put that down as well?'

Christie rolls her eyes.

'It's Barnes and Worth; they do everything properly, remember? Anyway, Snotty and Mole don't know about the unethical part yet.' I glance at my notes. 'Or the ten thousand part, actually.'

'Oh.' Christie starts picking off nail polish.

'Christie! Come on, they'll be here in half an hour. This is our last chance to show them that we're not crap.'

'Oh God . . . I don't know. I don't know. Maybe we just are crap,' she says, rubbing her face.

'We could divert the stock to the online warehouse; then they could be sold online for ever. Then we just have to tell them where they're made.'

'Let's do that!' she shrieks, slamming the desk. 'It's genius!'

'Okay, I'll call IT and see what we have to do.'

Ten minutes later Michael arrives, wearing a purple silk shirt and crushed-velvet drainpipes. I introduce Christie; he casts an expert eye over her rump like a gypsy at a horse fair. He sits beside me, ankles crossed, feet jiggling. The room fills with his musky scent. He takes my laptop and brings up the online store.

'Where d'you want them placed?'

'I don't know, Christmas?'

'Unless you want them to sell through all year . . .' He leans back, cradling the back of his head in his hands. His knees begin to jump like drummers' elbows. 'In which case they should be in homewares.'

'Oh well, yes, homewares, then.'

His fingers scamper across the keyboard. 'I need a photograph,' he says.

'I'll email one.'

'Well then, *c'est possible*. It'll be tricky, though, to just put them in – I'll have to imply it was an IT error and we don't make 'em. I'm only doing it because it's you.'

'Thanks, Michael. I owe you.' I smile. 'A drink, I mean,' I add, noticing his tongue cover his lips.

He moves towards the door. 'No can do, Vivienne. This is one opportunity that has well and truly passed you by.' He strokes down his body with the back of his hands.

'Really?'

'Yup. This guy's wanderlust seed-sowing days are at an end.'

'That's a real shame.'

'Correct, Viv. For all the girls I've not got around to.' He looks pointedly at me.

'Are you taken, then?' asks Christie.

'I am indeed, young Christie, and I think you well know the queen of my heart and loins.'

'What?'

'I'm engaged to Marion Harrison.'

The announcement hangs in the air, with Christie looking vacant for ages before the penny drops. 'Oh my God! You mean Mole!' she squeals. He stops jiggling as he considers the nickname.

'Congratulations, Michael! I had no idea you two were . . . uh . . .' I say.

'Doing the wild thing? Yeah, for a few years now, off and on.' His eyes get a faraway look. 'It's funny how it catches up with you. No matter where I go, I just keep coming back to that sweet—'

'Good, good! Congratulations . . . again.' I stand up and usher him to the door.

'Laters.' He points a finger-gun at me, before aiming at Christie and firing.

As I try to close the door after him, he takes my hand. 'You're invited to the engagement party, doll,' he says, and winks.

'Thanks so much, Michael.' I smile at the door until he steps into the lift. Then we try to freshen up the room by turning up the air conditioning. The windows don't open on the thirteenth floor, in case of suicide attempts.

'I can't believe it. Mole is getting married!' says Christie.

'I know.'

'She must be ten years older than him.'

'I suppose it takes all sorts.'

'Viv, if she can get married, there's hope for you.'

'Thanks, Christie.' I smile, sinking back into my seat. 'Look, in ten minutes they'll be here. So we'll update them on all the ranges and slip the candle thing in at the end.'

'Right.'

'Let's have a look at the folders, then.'

We're halfway through when Snotty and Mole sweep into the room. Mole smiles and they sit down at the top of the table in silence. Snotty is wearing some passable purple seventies wedge boots. She eyes me coldly.

'Vivienne.' She nods. 'Christine.' I notice there's no engagement ring on Mole's chubby finger, so I decide against congratulating her. 'We'd like you to begin by updating us on these Scandinavian candles, please,' Snotty continues. I feel my heart jolt. I'm well used to this panicky feeling. I take a deep breath.

'Scandinavian candles?' I murmur.

'Yes.' She looks up. The light glints off her little glasses and into my eyes like some sort of torture.

Confess, I think. Spill. Sing like a canary. 'We have ten thousand in the warehouse.'

Mole looks up sharply. '*Ten* thousand?' she asks.

'Yes. That's correct.' I pretend to check my notes, shuffling a few papers. 'Also, they're made by Norwegian prisoners.'

'Prisoners?' asks Mole.

'Yes.'

'Prisoners?' echoes Snotty. What are they? Hard of hearing?

'Petty-criminal prisoners, not murderers or rapists or anything,' I say. They stare at me carefully. 'I think just shop-lifters and maybe a few tax dodgers . . . So yeah, that sort of thing.' I suddenly feel liberated. I meet their eyes and smile.

'You knew this.'

'Yes I did.' God, this is so cathartic! The truth – what a novelty.

'But you ordered ten thousand?'

'Actually, it was me,' Christie confesses. 'I was supposed

to check the prisoner thingy. I ordered the ten thousand.' She looks like she might cry.

'And I was supposed to supervise her, so it was me as well.' I smile, beginning to see why Catholics go to confession. A silence follows, during which Snotty's ears go bright red.

'Well. I really don't know what to say. You are aware of your position? Having had all the warnings we can give?' she asks.

'Yes, we are aware, I think. Are you aware, Christie?'

Christie nods; then Snotty points at her dramatically. 'Christie, you're fired,' she announces. Christie gasps as if she's been struck.

'Oh, very good. Very good.' I clap. 'I bet you've been dying to say that.' I stand up as inside my head a little warning bell rings. 'Well, you won't get to say it to me, because I resign.' They gape like frogs. 'Yes, I quit!' I throw my bag over my shoulder. 'I'll have you know, Christie and I have been head-hunted several times by competitors. We are known in this industry as 'the dream team'. So we don't need to sit here and be bullied by the likes of you. Come on, Christie.' She hesitates before scrabbling up her things and taking ages to put them in her bag, leaving me standing glaring at the expectant faces of Snotty and Mole. 'Come on, Christie. Let us go and seek out friendlier skies.' I'm not sure where that came from – *Les Mis*, I think – but it has just the level of dignity I'm looking for. Finally she scuttles round the table and stands beside me and we stalk out together.

Later we sit despondently in the Crown with our celebratory bottle of Chardonnay. The wine is warm and yellow as wee.

'Still, if we're being headhunted . . .' begins Christie. She looks like a lost fawn.

'We're not. I just said that.'

'Oh. So . . . we're not the dream team, then?'

'Not as such.' I take a huge gulp of wine. It's like liquid headache.

She clasps and unclasps her hands in her lap. 'You didn't need to do that,' she says. I wait for her to thank me for my act of altruism. 'I mean, we'll get shit references now, won't we?' I hadn't thought about references. We sit side by side, staring into the cavernous pub. An old man sitting at the bar keeps shouting, 'We won the Gold Cup!' and lifting his pint of stout in a toast. I watch until I can't stand it any more.

'Look, Christie, we don't need references.' I turn to her. 'We'll set up on our own. Dream Team PR!'

She looks a bit doubtful. 'What, just me and you?'

'Why not? We have the knowledge and the contacts. We can promote anything. We can sell edible knickers.'

'I suppose we could approach Ann Summers,' she says.

'Good one! We can do a whole range of saucy accessories.'

'Yeah.'

'And we'll be better than we've ever been before because it will be just us.' I lift my glass. 'So, to Dream Team PR.'

'To us!' She chinks with me; then we sit mulling it over. It's terrifying.

'I have an idea for our first project. It's a PR campaign.' I turn to face her. 'I need to find someone.'

It's late when we leave the pub. I call the hospital and speak to a nurse who doesn't think Nana is on her ward. I ask to speak to Reg, but she says she hasn't seen him. It's weird. I decide to call back later and hopefully speak to someone who knows what they're doing. I just want to go home. Last night when I returned, struggling with Dave, five tins of Whiskas and a litter tray, I was so tired I went straight to bed. I'm looking forward to spending time alone in my own space again.

I turn the key with a huge sense of relief. The flat is silent. I peer into the living room.

'Dave! Where are you, kitty?' There's a folded note on the coffee table. I throw my bag on the sofa and scoop it up, recognising Rob's anal handwriting.

> *Viv,*
>
> *I want you to know you've made a big mistake. You're a very silly girl. I'm the best thing that has ever or will ever happen to you. I want you to know two things:*
>
> *1. You'll never find another man like me — one who was prepared to give you everything.*
>
> *2. This is definitely goodbye. Don't think I'll be back — you've blown it. It's over.*
>
> *Don't try to come crawling back. Good luck with your life. When you think of me, remember that I was the one who loved you, and you were the one who threw it all away!*
>
> *Rob*

I let my head fall back against the sofa, looking up at strips of street light filtering through the blind. Dave pads in and sits by my feet, curls his tail neatly around his paws, blinks and begins to purr.

'You're pleased with yourself. What've you been doing all day?' I crumple up the note and chuck it across the room. Dave suddenly pounces after it, skidding onto his side and tapping it under the coffee table with a front paw. The phone rings and the answer machine kicks in.

'Viv? It's Rob. Listen, Bunny, we need to talk. Call me.' Dave blinks.

'I know . . . tragic,' I say.

He springs up, kneading the sofa with white hook claws. I push him to the floor, but he jumps straight back, rhythmically scratching at the leather.

'Don't do that.' He stops, seeming to reflect before starting again. 'Can't you go and lick your bum or something?' I flick him off and go to get changed.

The bedroom is carnage; a feather pillow has been ripped like the savaged belly of a bird and my silk kimono dressing gown is shredded to ribbons. Dave follows quietly behind. He sits by my feet looking surprised. I pick up the kimono. 'Bloody hell, Dave! This cost nearly a hundred pounds!' Lemon eyes follow the swaying strands of silk. 'How're you going to pay for it, huh?' I kick the pillow. 'And that was my favourite pillow.' He bats at a floating feather as I kneel to pile the pillow remains on the bed. 'Listen, stupid, you can't do stuff like this, okay?' A feather sticks to his lip and he tries to eat it. 'Do you need a scratching post or something?' I consider the best way to clear up, deciding to sweep the whole mess into a bin bag. 'Go on, scat!' I chase him out; he scarpers, tail down, and hides under the coffee table.

I walk around the flat looking for traces of Rob. It's such a relief to be rid of him, I can't believe it. I loved him . . . No, I was obsessed with him. I thought I'd be upset, worried about the future. The future I'm actually facing right now – jobless, soon to be penniless, almost without a friend, single. I allow the 'spinster' word in and mull it over . . . No, still huge relief. It's actually lonelier to be with the wrong person than it is to be on your own. See – alone you have hope, and peace of mind. Alone anything can happen; you're in the driving seat: you can learn trapeze, get that piercing, travel to Guatemala in a van, have a fish finger sarnie for dinner.

I move to the fridge, experimenting with thoughts, seeing if they hurt. Rob with someone else . . . nothing. Pushing a pram? God, he'd be a terrible father! Bumping into Rob while I'm single and he's with some supermodel and their baby and I'm all sweaty from the gym? I pour a glass of water. Ow, yes, something hurts in that scenario, but it's only a scratch; it's okay without the sweaty part. Dave appears, looking hopefully up at the fridge, white front paws placed neatly together.

'What? I'm not speaking to you.' I glare at him and he gives a soft squeak. I scoop out cat food onto a saucer and he purrs, pulling chunks of meat onto the floor.

'You've no manners at all,' I tell him. 'Like your owner.' Your delicious, sexy owner. How would it feel to lose Max? To bump into him when he was with someone else? Devastating. Unimaginable. Well, I'm not going to lose him. I hurry to the laptop, open up the website and begin a blog to him.

By the time I've finished typing, I'm wiping tears from my eyes. If he were here, everything would just be better. I post the blog and wait. But what am I expecting to happen? Some kind of magic? He's not going to appear at my door with a huge bouquet of roses. I flick on the TV to drown out the silent phone and search the kitchen for snacks. I find some out-of-date cheesy biscuits and a bag of Twiglets and lie on the sofa flicking through channels. Dave settles himself on my tummy and we share them. I feel myself relax as I stroke the back of his head; a comforting feeling settles around us. We're just getting interested in a programme about embarrassing body hair when the phone rings. I freeze. Could it be Max? It could be him. He's read the message and he's coming over. I rush to answer.

'Vivienne?' says a familiar voice.

'Nana!'

'Hello, love.'

'How are you?'

'I'm all right. How are you, my darling?' Her voice sounds weak.

'I'm so happy to hear you.' She laughs and it turns into a cough. 'When did you wake up? I wanted to be there.'

'This morning. I didn't know where I was. They had to do some tests so I was pushed from pillar to post. I'm in a different ward now. It's a bit nicer, not so many old codgers, you know?'

'I can't believe it's you. I've been so worried.'

'I know. Sorry, love.'

'No, no, I didn't mean . . . It's not your fault. Oh, I can't wait to see you.'

'They say I might be going home tomorrow.'

'Are you sure? I mean, isn't that a bit soon?'

'God, no. I can't wait to get out of here, and anyway they need the beds for all the old fogeys. Soon as you're awake they tip you out.' She sounds like her old self, just croakier. I want to cry with relief.

'Well, if you think you're strong enough . . . but don't you need the doctor to keep an eye on you?'

'Dr Begg is only round the corner.'

'But will you call him if you need him? Reg said you wouldn't let him get a doctor before.'

'Oh yes, I think I've learned my lesson.'

'Good, because there's no point being stubborn. When you're ill, you're ill.'

'Viv?'

'Yes.'

'I have something to tell you and I don't want you to be cross.'

'Okay.' What has she done? Bequeathed her house to the cats' home?

'I'm getting married on Saturday.'

28

BLOG TO MAX #1 – WHERE ARE YOU?

It's been four hours and four days. Remember how you said if either one of us didn't contact the other for twenty-four hours, it would be because one of us had died, so the other one should go and break their door down? Well, I've been to your place but the door is heavy iron with double locks, I only had an emery board on me, and anyway your bike is gone so I know you're not dead. Where are you? Not knowing is killing me, and if I die, who'll break *my* door down?

I've filled your voicemail box . . . and your inbox. I called your mother. She says can you call her, by the way? You have your very own Facebook group! I know you'll hate that, so if you come back, I'll close it. I've kidnapped Dave and I regret it already – he's evil and semi-feral. Maybe he just misses you. I miss you so much. I'd do anything just to hear your voice. I'd eat liver. I'd sing in public.

If you are reading this, look how hard I'm trying! Let me off? Or if you can't forgive, maybe you could call and shout. Just please don't take your love away like this. I love you. I know that now and I'm sorry I didn't know it before. I really do love you, Max.

V x

I get to Nana's early. It's still cool and quiet in the street. I knock a couple of times and try the door; it's unlocked so I go inside.

'Only me!' I check myself in the fluted hall mirror and straighten my hair. Is it my imagination or has the place acquired that old-person smell? Sort of TCP and mildew. I take chocolates and a net of oranges out of my bag, ready to present to Nana. 'Hello?' I start downstairs to the kitchen and I'm met halfway by Reg. There's an embarrassing moment where we both step aside together.

'Shall we dance?' he says.

'Not on the stairs, hey, Reggie?'

He turns and makes his way down more carefully than I thought he'd need to. I look at the crosshatched skin at the back of his neck and suddenly he appears somehow vulnerable. I feel a pang of shame at how I've treated him.

'She's in the garden,' he says as we reach the kitchen. 'Shall I take those for you?'

I hover, unsure of what to say. 'Is she . . . is she all right?'

'Right as rain. Bossier than ever!' He laughs and our eyes meet; he looks wary.

'Congratulations,' I say.

'Thank you, Vivienne.' He lifts his chin as if waiting for a punch.

'I mean it. I'm very happy for you both.'

'Thank you. That will mean a lot to her.' He looks me straight in the eyes and I notice that his are a lovely dark blue.

'And I wanted to say . . . I'm sorry. Those times in the hospital, I know I wasn't nice to you. I think it was, you know, the shock of it . . .'

He clasps my shoulder. 'No need to explain. Go on out. She's been looking forward to seeing you.'

The garden has been transformed since the hot July day when Max and I were here last. The patio is swept, the lawn is mown, and the roses are in full bloom. All along the neat edges of the grass, new flowers and shrubs have been planted, the colours bright as paint. A new arbour has been built over the patio with roses climbing over it. Even the stone angel is clean. Reggie has been busy. I hesitate at the doorstep as my eyes get accustomed to the sunshine and then I see her, a small, thin figure in a wheelchair under the shade of the pear tree. I feel a lump in my throat remembering the last time – her and Max, their cocktails and silly hats. I go over to her, checking my face to hide my feelings. Her shrunken, brittle body against the backdrop of this vibrant garden adds to the shock; she's like a skeletal leaf blown onto a new lawn. I notice her curled fingers and thin hair. Despite the heat, she has a bright crocheted rug over her legs.

'Nana.'

She turns, the side of her face waxy like soap. 'Viv!' I kneel in front of her, taking her hands. 'Hello.' She smiles and moves a strand of my hair from my face. I don't know how to be with her.

I tap the wheelchair. 'What's this, then?'

'Oh, I know. Not exactly the height of fashion for a bride-to-be, is it?'

'It could catch on.'

She smiles and her eyes flick over me. 'You've lost weight,' she remarks.

'Not as much as you.' I circle her wrist with my thumb and forefinger.

'No. Well . . .'

I lean up to kiss the soft skin of her cheek. 'Welcome home, Nana. And congratulations.'

'Thank you.' She pauses. 'I'm glad you're pleased for us, Viv.' I look into her eyes and catch a glimmer of her spirit. A spark of fun.

'I mean, it was a bit sudden, but . . .'

'Well, sometimes you need a scare like this to kick you up the bum.'

'I suppose you do.'

Reg is coming across the patio with a tray of drinks. He puts it down on the steps and they bicker about bringing a table before he goes off to get one, humming to himself. Nana notices me studying Reg as he shuffles away.

'He's a very good man, you know. Kind.' I smile at her. 'And he's a few good years in him yet.'

'I'm not worried about him.' I squeeze her hand.

'And don't worry about me,' she says with some indignation, as if she's never been ill in her life.

'Okay, because you say so, I won't. I had thought I'd be getting married before you, though.'

'Well. Yes. Any news of that Rob fellow?'

'No, that's not happening.' I smile at Reg, who is now shuffling back, carrying a small card table. He places it next to Nana's chair and turns to collect her drink.

'Not that table, Reg! I meant the one from the kitchen.'

He rolls his eyes at me. 'Fruit punch, anyone?' he asks, holding up the jug.

'Isn't it Pimm's?' she asks.

'No, my love, they said no alcohol for you – as well you know.'

She sniffs and gazes out over the lawn. 'Look at the plums!' We turn to see where she's pointing. 'That tree's laden.'

I stand, take a glass from Reg and hand one to Nana.

'Well, I'd like to propose a toast,' I announce. 'To you, Nana, and to you, Reg, and to love.' They look at each other and smile, and in that smile I see a glimpse of a great friendship, a real knowing affection. I raise my glass. 'And to me finding my love . . . wherever he is.' We all drink.

'That's not bad, actually.' Nana drains hers. 'Although a bit of gin wouldn't go amiss.'

'So, this wedding, then,' I say. 'Have you booked the hot-air balloon?'

'Ah!' She laughs. 'The wheelchair is a little heavy, I fear.'

'Where're you having it?'

'Well, for the legal stuff we'll nip to the registry office, but the real ceremony will be right here. This is our cathedral.' Reg waves his arm around the garden. 'We'll make our own promises under the arbour; seats for guests along here, you know, making a sort of aisle.'

'Perfect.'

'Viv, you'll give me away, won't you?' asks Nana.

''Course I will.'

'You'll have to wheel me, I'm afraid.'

'I can do that. Shall we practise?' I grab the handles of the chair and go to wheel her across the patio. It's lighter than I expected and at first I use too much force and she lurches forward. 'I can do your first dance too, if you like.' I rock her sideways. 'What shall we do if you get cold feet? We could have some sort of signal, like you hold up your bouquet and I'll turn you round and we'll scarper?'

'That won't be necessary!' she shouts and it makes her cough. She coughs for a long time. Reg passes her a napkin and she holds it to her face before folding something inside it carefully.

'How long will you be in the chair?'

'Just till I'm strong again.'

'Soon, then,' I say.

'Oh yeah, very soon.' She smiles.

I open the door of my flat late in the afternoon. I left early to get to Nana's and the curtains are still closed. It smells of cats. Dave comes running and makes an escape attempt, darting between the door and my legs. I catch him in the stairwell and haul him back. The litter tray is overflowing. There are dishes in the sink.

I open the bedroom curtains and the sun pools through the dusty glass. At least nothing's been savaged, I suppose. I feel irritated by the place. The washing basket with the lid that doesn't fit, the windowless bathroom and leaky shower. It's not that it's a bad space; it's just not where I expected to be. I'd imagined a big square kitchen with a huge table and kids and dogs. Well, I'd imagined that with Rob. Now that I know I love Max, life seems golden and exciting, stretching ahead and glittering with possibilities. If I could just find him and if he still loves me . . . I sit on the arm of the sofa.

What if he doesn't love me any more? I imagine him the last time we were together – not at the gallery, before that when things were good. He said he'd always love me. But when I think of his face at the gallery, I feel a hot dart of shame. I hurt him. I never wanted that. I feel a rush of self-loathing looking around at the low-level mess and begin to pick up crisp packets from beside the sofa. I never thought I'd be giving my own nana away – but then what does it matter what I thought? I thought I wanted Rob. I thought Max was a skint loser. I thought this place was cool and edgy. I notice scratch marks on the chair leg. I thought it'd be fun to have a cat. Obviously I can't trust what I think.

I wander into the kitchen. I hate that there's never any food in here. I open the fridge and pull out a tub of something that could once have been taramasalata. I lift the edge of the lid, unleashing an unholy stench. I throw it into a bin bag and search around the flat throwing other stuff in, topping it off with the contents of the litter tray. I grab my purse and drag the bag downstairs, flinging it on top of the pile in the sweaty rubbish bay. I head round the corner to the mini-market and start to fill a trolley with coffee, milk, biscuits, carrots, tomatoes, I don't know – whatever I can find that might be made into a meal. It's time to grow up; it's time to start looking after myself. I get proper wine, not just the cheapest I can find. I throw in some cleaning stuff with the word 'Bang' on the side. That's exactly what I need – a bit of Bang in my life. I add some scourers and get to the checkout.

I wait as a young woman with severe scraped-back hair and a tattoo on her neck slowly passes each item over her scanner.

'That's ninety-two pounds twenty,' she mumbles without looking up.

'Whoa, cleaning stuff is expensive, eh?' I say, feeling suddenly hot. She chews gum, slack-jawed, as I put my card in the reader and press in the PIN, trying to calculate if there's enough money in this account. 'PIN OK,' it says. 'Remove card.'

I get the shopping home, put the kettle on and start to clean up. I'm taking control of the situation now, so things will be better. I straighten out the bed and squirt Bang in the toilet, the fumes making my eyes water. I am in control. I will find him. I fill the kitchen cupboards with packets and tins. I make tea and turn on the laptop to check Facebook. The 'Where's Max?' group has 102 friends already! Mostly very romantic people thinking I'm sweet and wishing me well.

I check my own Facebook page. I've been invited to Michael's engagement party. I can't go and face Mole, can I, after my dramatic exit from work? But some strange loyalty to Michael makes me accept. I check my mail. Nothing from Max, anywhere. If he's on some art road trip brooding and sulking, he might not see my blog or the Facebook page and realise that I love him. He doesn't have a clue about Facebook, and I doubt if he'd visit the website after what happened. I need something else, something bigger. I call Christie, and we arrange to meet at a tea shop she knows.

Whoopie pies are big at the moment, I notice. Here in the window they're piled onto vintage glass cake stands in pastel-coloured towers. Inside there are floral oilcloths on the tables and painted wooden chairs with heart-shaped seats. The place is called Mad Hatters; all the teapots are oversized. It's full of women of the same type, slightly dotty and girly. Among them sits Christie in denim cut-offs, a long sequinned waist-coat and boxing boots. Her hair's arranged on top of her head, wrapped in some sort of orange bandage.

'Christie, you've really got to stop reading *Vogue*.'

'Oh, hi! Hi!' She kisses the air, both sides. 'No, Viv, you probably don't understand this look; it's direct from the catwalk. Remember my friend Nigel?' I think of the ruined feather dress, the one I'm paying for in instalments for the rest of my life. 'Well, he's doing a show at the college – this is one of his.'

'Hmm, well, I guess you carry it off. Will I be wearing it a year from now, then?' I eye the bandage headdress.

'Maybe. In a really watered-down way. Anyway, all the buyers go to the shows. Topshop were at Nigel's . . . Ooh, let me get you a cake.' She jumps up and I watch her animat-edly ordering. Other people are watching too. Christie has this ability to attract attention wherever she goes. She is a pretty girl, but it's not that . . . She startles people; they just don't *expect* her. I wonder if there's a way to harness this talent. Nigel the designer has recognised it, obviously, giving her his outfits to model. The sequins of the waistcoat sparkle as she picks up the tray with a ridiculous polka-dot teapot balanced in the middle, and wiggles back to the table.

'Those sequins . . . they should say something,' I comment.

'They say, "Twinkle twinkle!"'

'I'm thinking they could say something for us, for the campaign to find Max.'

'"Wanted . . . tall Irish man,"' she muses.

'Yeah or something simple like "Where's Max?"'

'What, we wear eight-hundred-pound designer waistcoats with "Where's Max?" written in sequins? Cool.'

'No. Obviously not sequins, something else.'

'These are hand sewn.' She plucks at a loose thread and the fabric shimmers like fish scales.

My mind is racing. I'm thinking of a huge campaign, a fashion show, TV coverage . . . but with no money. Christie pours the tea.

'T-shirts.'

'Right.'

'T-shirts with a "Where's Max?" logo. Not in sequins but something shiny. Your mate Nigel could do it for us and put it in his show.'

'Hmm . . . I wonder if he'd do that.'

'Then Topshop will buy them and the campaign will be huge.'

'Why would Topshop buy them?'

'I thought you said your mate does catwalk shows for Topshop?'

'Yes, but—'

'And they're always championing new talent.'

'Well, I could ask him.'

'Beg him, Christie. Sleep with him.'

'He's gay.'

'Get your flatmate to sleep with him.'

'He's not gay.'

'Oh, I don't know, just . . . think of something! It's too good an idea to miss.'

'All right.' She takes a Hello Kitty notepad and matching pen from her handbag and begins to write. Hello Kitty's head lights up every time she starts a new word. I sit in wonder.

'Nice pen.'

'Oh, I just love stationery and Hello Kitty is so cute!' She frowns at the page. 'Just "Where's Max?" That's all you want it to say?'

'Maybe on the back it could have our company name, or just the initials DTPR?'

She wrinkles her nose. 'Sounds a bit like herpes.'

'Okay, not that, then.'

She closes the pad, lightly stroking the cover. We sip tea and Christie tackles a lemon bun.

'Right, next we need to chase those Sunday papers and get them to write about this search when they cover nevergoogleheartbreak.com . . . I'll do that.' I take out my phone and tap in a note to myself. Then I look out of the window of Mad Hatters and focus on a guy outside. I feel a hit of excitement. He's tall with dark curly hair and he's looking in the shop window opposite. The faded jeans, the old boots . . . he's just like Max. Actually, it *is* Max. Could it be? I stand up in the window. Yes . . . the broad shoulders, the way he's standing with his feet squarely planted. God, it's him. I bang on the glass. 'Max!' I shout. 'Max!' I bang again one, two, three times and scramble towards the door, pulling chairs out of my way. Then the guy turns and smiles as he takes the hand of a small girl coming out of the shop. He glances towards me, a little confused, obviously wondering whether to wave. He decides against, since he doesn't know me and they walk on, leaving me standing with both hands pressed against the window like a demented mime artist.

I turn slowly back to the café, finally able to speak. I nod over to the frilly-aproned woman at the counter. 'Sorry, I . . .

I thought I knew that guy.' She smiles in mock sympathy. Two women at a window table stare. 'All right, show's over. Get back to your cupcakes,' I snap as I step around them back to my seat. The chatter resumes as I sink down.

'Okay,' says Christie, 'we really need to find your man.'

29

I Thought He Was You

Days since I saw you: 26

I thought I saw you yesterday. The guy had your kind of style. That implies you have style and we both know you don't, but he had some of the essence of you, and I made a fool of myself in a café shouting your name. And when he turned round and it wasn't you, I was so gutted.

I have to see you. Do you fancy the pub? We could get gin and tonics and crisps. Or stay in . . . Whatever. I want to do everything with you, but I'd settle for just hearing your voice. Do you think you could call? You won't believe it but Nana is getting married to Reggie. You're invited. It's this Saturday.

You know how I'll never take no for an answer, and how you love that about me? Well, I'm starting this campaign to find you. I know it sounds melodramatic and like something from a bad romance, but I have to do something. I have to make you see the truth. You said you would always love me and that I'd be the one to decide, but that's not true. You will be the one. It will be you, Max. I love you.

V x

PS: You have 500 Facebook friends.

Lucy stands in front of an enormous gilded mirror in a strapless wedding dress. I'm on the chaise with our complimentary half-bottle of champagne – well, not exactly complimentary, since we paid twenty quid for the appointment. Shania Twain sings 'You're Still the One' on a loop.

'I thought you were going for a corset and white fishnets?' I remark. Lucy turns and looks into the mirror over her shoulder. The dress is laced at the back with satin ribbons. She holds up her hair and pulls her wide-eyed mirror face. A round woman in a navy suit rushes forward and billows out the skirt.

'This is a beautiful dress,' says Lucy.

'It is,' I agree. 'Do you want your champagne?'

She gazes at her reflection, clearly pleased, holding her arms slightly away from her body like a ballerina.

'What's it made of? This fabric is gorgeous.'

'It'll be silk or satin, won't it?'

'It sort of glows, doesn't it? What's this colour, would you say? Shell?' She strokes the skirt.

'Shell? What's that, then, a kind of off-white?'

'What's wrong with you?' She frowns into the mirror.

'Nothing. What happened to the corset idea?'

Round Woman is back with a pearl tiara and a veil, and Lucy bends a little for her to pin it on. Stiff lace now hangs from Lucy's head like a half-opened umbrella. She brushes the edge of it with her fingertips. Round Woman climbs on a sort of carpeted pedestal and arranges the veil over Lucy's face. Lucy steps towards the mirror and her skirts have to be arranged and billowed out all over again.

'Excuse me,' I say, 'could we try a more sparkly tiara?' Round Woman scuttles over the plush pink carpet to the accessories room.

'Do you think it needs more sparkle?' asks Lucy.

'No, I just wanted to get rid of her for a minute. She must

be knackered with all that billowing.' Lucy peers at me through the veil. 'Can you see out?' I ask.

'Look, the lace has tiny shell pearls sewn into it.'

'Oh yeah. What is a shell pearl?'

'Dunno. It's beautiful, though, isn't it? Do you love it?'

'Do they sell bridal corsets here?'

'Viv! Shut up about the bloody corset idea, will you?'

'Just trying to keep you real.'

'We were off our heads when we said that! Do you really think Reuben is going to wear hot pants?'

'Dunno, I don't really know him. I've bought mine, though – and the boots.'

She starts to laugh. 'Christ, get this thing off my head!'

When Round Woman returns, I'm on the carpeted pedestal trying to untangle the tiara from Lucy's hair. She takes over and Lucy eventually emerges a bit cross and red in the face, her hair looking backcombed and wanton.

'Viv, please will you try and concentrate? I know it must be hard for you to be in here after you were jilted . . .' I shoot a look at Round Woman. She looks quietly pleased. 'But this is not about you and you're supposed to be helping me.' Lucy looks on the verge of tears and I suddenly feel bad.

'I'm sorry. It's probably because I'm a spinster. We don't do well in wedding emporiums.'

'I know you're a spinster!'

'All right. Keep your voice down.'

'But couldn't you just postpone feeling sorry for yourself for half an hour? I'd really like your opinion.'

I heave myself off the chaise and stand behind her at the mirror. 'You want my opinion?' Secretly I'm pleased she cares what I think; in darker moments I had thought she might have invited me along to rub my nose in it.

'That's why I asked you to come.'

'Well, with your hair messed up like that, this dress looks amazing. It's not too "done". With the veil I think you need a raunchier dress – that way it's edgy.'

She pushes her hair back. 'You're right.' She half turns and studies herself. 'When you're right, you're right.'

I look her up and down and nod. 'You do look amazing and beautiful in a sexy way, but not trying at all.'

'This is the dress, isn't it?'

'Looking at you now, I think it is.'

Her eyes fill with tears. 'Oh my God,' she cries. 'This is the dress!'

Smelling a sale, Round Woman rushes forward. She reaches up and holds her hand over Lucy's eyes.

'I want you to imagine it's your wedding day . . .' she breathes in a sort of storytelling, half-American accent. 'The most important day of your life. Your hair and make-up are perfect, you look beautiful, you smell your favourite perfume.' She spritzes a bit of something into the air at this point. 'You are holding a stunning bouquet and standing outside the door of the church.' I see in the mirror that my mouth is hanging open, so I go back to the chaise and finish the last of the champagne. 'Your husband-to-be is standing inside; he can't wait to marry you and he's nervously looking towards the door. That door now opens and *this* is what he sees.' She removes her hand with a flourish and Lucy looks at herself, dumbfounded.

'I'll take it,' she gasps.

And *voilà*! Two thousand pounds later she is the proud owner of a beautiful Vera Wang wedding dress.

'Will you come for a cocktail to celebrate?' she asks. 'That place across the road with the really long bar does amazing watermelon margaritas!' she adds, as if that's all I've been longing for my whole life.

'Well then, let's go!' I link her arm.

We seat ourselves at one end of the very long metal bar. The place is all blond wood and weathered leather chesterfields. Our drinks arrive looking like works of art, draped with berries and set on silver paper mats.

'Can you imagine the job spec to work here?' I ponder. 'They're all so good-looking. Ex-models required to tend very long bar. Must not be able to smile.'

'Must be able to shake a cocktail,' she adds.

'That would be on their actual job description.'

'I know.'

I look at her for a moment, then decide to change the subject. 'So what will Reuben think of your dress?'

'Oh, he'll love it.'

'Are you not going with the sex theme at all, then?'

'Yeah, but in a more toned-down way from what we said the other night.'

'What, a phallic wedding cake?'

'Exactly!' She laughs.

'How about pants with saucy slogans on?'

'I like it. Are they Barnes and Worth?'

'No, but I could get some for you.'

'What slogans?'

'Whatever you like. You could have them as part of a sex-themed cracker. Like instead of a joke, it could have a position to try.'

'Yeah, with the pants instead of a hat and maybe a little thing of lube.'

'Or a novelty condom.'

'Or a sex toy.'

We laugh and drink our margaritas. I'm starting to think about the viability of the sexy wedding cracker. It could be Dream Team's first product launch. We could supply Lucy's wedding as a starting point and then get into the whole wedding market from there.

'We'd probably want something about love in there too . . . packets of Love Heart sweets or little heart-shaped fortune cookies or something,' I suggest.

'Oh yes, love, definitely . . . love-heart glitter.'

'Okay.' I'm already thinking of suppliers, working out costs and thinking of a realistic price for a wedding favour. I realise I've missed what Lucy's been saying about her wedding.

'. . . will you?' she finishes.

'Of course.' I smile.

'Well, let's drink to that.' We clink glasses. I drain my drink with an uneasy feeling and notice the oversized digital wall clock. It's already eight and I was supposed to be at Michael's engagement party at seven. Maybe I won't go. Lucy is reading a text message on her BlackBerry.

'Reuben's on his way down here.' She smiles and I think, as I often do, how pretty she is. 'Don't tell him about the dress.'

'Of course not. Actually, I'll stay to hand you over and then I have to go. An engagement party . . . someone from work.'

The Ga Ga bar is the last doorway down a tiny back street in Soho, the kind of place you need a special door-knock code to get in to. It's half empty tonight and Michael's sitting at a central bar, lit dramatically from below by purple spot-lights. A banner sags over a small dance floor: 'Congratulations M and M!'

Something is wrong with this picture. Why is there no music? Where's Mole? A few little groups of well-wishers are gathered around the tables of nibbles, some clearly Michael's acquaintances in their *Dawn of the Living Dead* garb. They turn to watch as I approach the bar. Michael doesn't turn round. I take my engagement present and plonk it down in front of him.

'Congrats on your engagement,' I say. He spins round, hands at the ready, in some sort of jujitsu move.

'Just fuck off, will you . . . Oh, it's you.' He slumps again. I wait, but he remains silent, so I pull up a stool.

'How's it going?' He makes a triangle with his fingers and rests the bridge of his nose on top, slowly shaking his head. 'That good? Can I buy you a drink?'

'Ssa free bar.' He checks his plastic digital watch. 'Till nine.' I get a white wine from a barmaid with a platinum-blonde asymmetric bob.

'Nice place,' I say. He glances sideways so I look around. People are leaving. Michael suddenly sits up, then sways backwards and to the side before grabbing on to the bar to steady himself. He slides my gift over and starts to unwrap it like an eager child. The paper's off. It's a card-board box. He hesitates, sniggers and then opens it, pulling out a little metal donkey with side panniers. He stands it on the bar.

'That's a spice donkey. What you do is put salt in one of his baskets and pepper in the other.'

'That is fucking amazing.'

'I'm glad you like it.'

He turns to stare at me with booze-soaked eyeballs. 'What?'

'Michael, is everything okay?'

'She's not coming. She left me.' He sucks his bottom lip, blinking very slowly.

'Oh. I'm sorry.'

''S'not your fault!' Chairs scrape and I turn to see the last of the guests heading for the door.

'Cheers, mate!' one of them calls. Michael raises his hand without turning, but as the door closes he spins round and hurls the spice donkey. It bounces on the concrete step and rests on its side.

'Thanks for coming,' he says.

'Right, that's it, he's had enough,' declares the barmaid.

''S'a free fucking bar!'

'Not any more. Not when you start chucking things. It's time to go.'

'What? This's my engagement party!'

'Come on, sunshine . . .'

'I'll take him home,' I say. 'Just give us a minute, would you?' Michael rests his head on the bar. She looks at him with such pitying disgust, it makes me hope for the day her platinum-blonde heart gets broken.

'Michael?' I say gently. 'Michael?'

He turns his head, eyes closed. 'I love you,' he murmurs.

'Michael, shall we go?'

'Hmmmnnn?'

'Let's go, hey?' I nudge his elbow slightly and he starts to move off the stool, eventually standing with both arms around my neck.

'Dance with me, Marion.'

'I'm Vivienne, Michael.'

He opens one eye. 'Dance with me.' He shuffles me towards the dance floor. 'You, music.' The barmaid rolls her eyes and presses 'play' on the iPod. Herb Alpert echoes into the empty room. 'This guy's in love with you,' Herb sings. We shuffle round in a tight circle while the barmaid clears up. 'She loves this one,' he mumbles. 'Marion!'

'Let's go. Have you eaten?' I manage to shuffle him towards the door.

'Wait, wait!' He stoops to collect the donkey and I haul him out onto the street where the cool air hits us both like a slap. 'Marion. Marion,' he says, over and over. We make it to the main road.

'Look, I'm going to try and get you a taxi.' I raise my arm at a yellow-lighted cab, but the driver takes one look at the swaying Michael and drives on. Michael tries to step into the road and stop a car, but I wrestle him back to the pavement where he stands quietly crying and clutching the donkey.

'Don't cry, Michael.' I give him a hug.

'She left me.'

'I know.'

'She doesn't want to marry me.'

'You don't know that. She might just have stage fright or something.'

'She sent a text. Wanna see it?'

'Not really.'

'I've been dumped by text!' he shouts at a group of passing girls, making them giggle. He cries in thin little whimpers.

'Aw, come on, Michael. Look, the best thing is to go home now.' I put my arm around him again.

'She's gone.'

'I know.'

'She's gone.' He's crying quite loudly now. 'My Marion.'

'I know, come on. I really know how it hurts, but you'll be okay.'

'And I've got nothing,' he sobs, 'nothing. Except this shitty salt-and-pepper donkey.' It occurs to me that my engagement present may just have tipped Michael over the edge. We stand in the breeze, him crying softly and me half holding him up, desperately trying to wave down a cab.

Finally a car pulls up alongside and I throw money at the driver to take Michael home. Michael stumbles forward and makes to climb in, but suddenly stops, holding on to the door for support. 'Vivienne, I don't suppose you'd . . . help me make it through the night?' He gestures to me to get in.

'No, Michael.' He looks into my eyes, his face all blotchy

with tears. 'It's a lovely offer, but no, it would be wrong. Good night,' I say, and he nods and sinks into the back seat. I watch his ponytailed head disappear as the taxi turns the corner, thinking it's true what the song says: everybody hurts, sometimes.

30

BLOG TO MAX #3 – OTHER PEOPLE'S
BREAK-UPS

Days since I saw you: 27

I'm starting to wonder whether the whole marriage and
wedding thing just complicates love. I know it's a big
deal for someone like me to think that – being as how
I've owned three wedding dresses and had a subscription
to *Bride* magazine for three years. But really, where did
the concept come from that causes us all to go around
expecting another person to commit their whole lives to
us and then practically selling our souls to create one
perfect day on which everyone we know can witness us
doing just that? Why can't we just love until we don't
any more, whether it be death that do us part or the
gym instructor? Sorry, I realise I sound mad, but it's been
a tough evening.

I love you pure and simple and I don't need any of
the trimmings.

V x

PS: Your Facebook group has 800 friends.

It's 30 August, Nana's wedding day, and I'm waking up in
the single bed of my childhood. No Take That posters any
more, but the collection of miniature pottery animals remains
intact, and God, how I still really love the squirrel.

I pull on last night's jeans and T-shirt and open the window. It's one of those promising mornings – hazy blue with just a hint of a chill to be burnt off in the heat of the sun. There's a van on the drive – 'Special Days Caterers' are here. I go downstairs to find them already busy in the kitchen, being directed by a short woman in knee-length white jeans and a striped shirt with the collar turned up. I get in the way trying to make coffee.

'The chicken wings, Dominic!' she calls to a floppy youth, and rolls her eyes. I smile. 'My son,' she says.

'You don't look old enough,' I reply, being kind. How old would she be, maybe forty-five?

'I'm thirty-seven,' she says. Christ! Only five years older than me and with a grown-up son. Actually, looking at her now, she's a bit rough for thirty-seven. Her eyes look baggy – well, baggier than mine. I realise she's waiting for me to say something.

'Well, good on you!' I nod in what I hope is a friendly way and take my coffee into the garden.

I suppose I'm the unusual one, really, for not being married with kids at thirty-two, and the caterer woman is normal. I'm 'not normal'. I walk across the lawn and up to the statue and think of my mother having me at seventeen. It was very brave of her, really, even if she couldn't finish what she started. Having a teenage mother probably damaged me in some way. I'm probably unconsciously pushing love away. I'm sure I read that in *Find Your* Own *Way, Be Free*. I touch the statue's wings. My mother is on tour in South America, apparently, so she won't be coming today, which is a relief really as she'd only cause some kind of scene like a wicked fairy godmother and spoil everything. I sip my coffee and I suddenly feel a kind of forgiveness towards her that I've never had before. What did she know at seventeen? What do any of us know at any age?

I turn back towards the house. Chairs are already set out

on the patio – simple wooden chairs, each with a satin ribbon
tied to the back, just as we planned. I walk slowly down the
aisle and stand under the arbour of roses. I asked the florist
to deliver extra roses along with the bouquet. I want to deco-
rate Nana's wheelchair with them as a surprise, but I need
to get her out of it first. I look up at the house shining in
the sun with its climbing honeysuckle and ramshackle charm.
Nana appears at an upstairs window, peering down at the
garden.

'Morning!' I call, and she waves.

'Any sign of the tables?'

'Not yet. The caterers are busy, though.'

'They're supposed to be here. I want the tables setting up
under the apple trees.'

'It's only nine o'clock.'

'I can't do a thing stuck in this chair.'

'Hold on. I'm coming up.' I weave my way back through
the smell of garlic chicken roasting in the kitchen and
climb the winding staircase, the sun-bleached pink carpet
now threadbare on the edge of each step. I find Nana in her
little private bathroom trying to get the plug into the plughole
from her wheelchair. 'What are you doing? Let me help you.'

'Damn it! I can't do it on the crutches, either – can't get
down low enough.'

I press the plug in and turn on the taps.

'Would you put some of that bath oil in?'

I take the bottle and pour, and a sweet earthy scent fills
the room. I wheel Nana over to the mirror. 'It's a lovely day
for a wedding.'

'Look at the bride, though – a skinny old woman in a
wheelchair.'

'Don't say that.' I start to brush her hair to set it in rollers
before her bath.

'Ow, you're pulling!'

'Sorry,' I say as she winces. 'Sorry.'

'I don't want it all bouffant at the back. I don't want to look like a pensioner on a coach.'

'You won't. You'll look beautiful.'

'I used to be able to *get* beautiful with a bit of effort. Not any more.'

'You'll always be beautiful – look at those cheekbones.'

'I'm thinking that dress is a bit much now.'

I look at the dress hanging on the wardrobe door. It's a long, simply cut gown in a sort of pearl colour, with half-length sleeves and a bit of draping at the back. Perfect. 'It isn't "a bit much". What are you on about?'

'A bit young?'

'No. What's this crisis of confidence all of a sudden?'

'Nerves . . . and not being able to move; it's driving me mad. And I hate this fucking ugly chair!' Tears spring to her eyes. I stop mid-curler and put my hand on her shoulder. 'And I know it might seem odd because I'm getting married to Reggie and everything, but I miss your granddad very much today.' Her voice cracks.

'I know.'

'I thought by now I would have stopped wanting to share things with him.' I sit beside her and take her hand. 'I mean, I know he's gone and I've faced it, and I'm fine . . . It's just sometimes I forget and I'll make him a cup of tea or think I'll tell him about this or that and it's a shock all over again to know he's not here any more.' She pauses to blow her nose and I give her a little squeeze, blinking away my own tears. She's never really talked about this before. The last thing she needs is me blubbering, but she notices.

'Don't you start!'

'I can't help it.' Now we're both weeping like a pair of lost children.

'You know, I wake up and my mind is still programmed

to what it knows, to life as it was with him, so for a split second I think he's still here. Then I realise, because I'm doing something so totally unexpected.'

'What, like marrying Reggie?'

'Yes!' She laughs and wipes her eyes, and we look at each other.

'He makes you happy, though, doesn't he?'

'Yes, he really does.'

'Good, because I want you to be happy. Granddad would want you to be happy.'

'I know.' She leans forward and hugs me. She smells my hair and squeezes the back of my neck, then takes a breath and exhales. I feel her gathering herself up and when she looks at me again, all the vulnerability is gone. She gives me back my hand.

'Anyway, I'm fine. I'm fine. What about you, though, Vivienne? And where's Max?' I feel a jolt of excitement at hearing his name.

'Well, that's the big question.'

'So I read.'

'You read?'

'In the *Gazette*.' She points to the dressing table. 'Apparently your Facebook search has caused a stir.' The paper's open at page seven and at the bottom is a small column. I glance at the headline.

'"Lovestruck Woman Uses Facebook to Find Her Man."' There's the photo of Max holding me up at Jane's wedding, along with some of the text from my blog. I read out loud:

'"The search for Max Kelly has captured people's imagination as far afield as Australia and Mexico. The 'Where's Max?' group has a thousand friends and counting . . ." Wow.'

'I was rather surprised to see your face in the paper.'

'I'm surprised. I didn't know about this.' She waits for an explanation. 'I mean, I am doing a kind of campaign to find

him and I sent a press release out, but I didn't dream it would
be in the paper this quickly.' I feel quite excited to get the
story in a newspaper. Media interest! He'll be found, he'll
see how much I love him, and we'll sail off into the sunset.

Nana smiles and looks down at her hands. 'A campaign?'

'Well, the press release and a couple of Sunday papers
promised to cover a website I set up, so I told them about
searching for Max as well, and we've had some T-shirts
designed with "Where's Max?" printed on them. Hopefully
they'll be on sale in Topshop soon.'

'Topshop. Gosh.'

'What?'

'Well, do you think he'll like all this fuss? He might have
just gone on holiday.'

'We slept together.'

'Naturally.'

'He told me he loved me; then I turned up to the "Meet
the Artist" night of his exhibition with Rob.'

'Oh dear, I missed a lot in hospital, didn't I?'

'And, Nana, I love him. So much. But he thinks I betrayed
him. I didn't. I'd never hurt him and now he's disappeared.
I just want to find him and this is what I know.' I wave the
paper. She nods slowly as if I'm six and have just put on a
puppet show. 'What?'

'Nothing. You're just so dramatic, I admire you.'

'I don't think I'm being dramatic.'

'Most people just accept things as they are and go merrily
along, but not you. Always searching for something . . .
wanting to change the world since you were a little girl,' she
says, half to herself, and I feel the words settle sharply around
my heart.

'Well, maybe I'll find what I'm looking for one day.'

'Or maybe you'll just stop searching and let it find you.'
Her eyes dart to my face; there's a moment's silence.

'But probably not,' I laugh to get her off my case. 'Anyway, enough about me. Are you getting hitched today or something?'

She smiles with her halo of rollers. 'I am,' she says. 'I am.'

I wheel her back to the bathroom and there's an awkward moment as I help her into the water. Your nana naked is not something you ever expect to see. She holds onto my neck as I take her dressing gown away at the last possible minute, trying not to look at the bones of her hips and jutting shoulder blades. She sinks beneath the bubbles and we're both relieved.

'I'll just go and check how everything's going, then,' I say, and scuttle out.

Back in the bedroom I down more champagne and read the newspaper story again. Am I being dramatic? Could the whole campaign to find Max actually be making things worse? I look at his picture, at his smiling eyes. I don't know what else to do but try to find him. What if I did nothing and regretted it for the rest of my life?

'Viv?' Nana calls through the bathroom door. 'Would you check if the tables have arrived?'

'Okay.' I go back to my room, taking the wheelchair with me. I'll cover it with roses and ribbons now while she's safely stuck in the tub.

31

BLOG TO MAX #4 – NANA'S WEDDING

Days since I saw you: 28

Do you remember when we got pretend married? Admittedly it was after you rolled your first spliff, put the entire packet of grass in and thought the stapler was evil, but I think it could still count. The ring-pull ring? The fish and chip wedding breakfast? The honeymoon day-trip to Stockport? I wish I'd let you kiss me on the ferry now.

So what to tell you? Today I gave Nana away to 'Reggie from next door'. I'm okay with it – she's happy. I cried, though, when she made her vows. I think it was when she said, 'Live all of your days with the certainty of my love.' That set me off. Don't you think that's a beautiful thing to say? Then after the buffet she made a speech about love and made a toast to Granddad and then everyone was crying. There was a little jazz band and coconut cake and all the champagne you could drink. You'd have enjoyed that part. It was a perfect day except for you not being there.

They're off to Spain in the morning for a few weeks and I asked her to look out for you in case you were there. You're probably sitting in a café in one of those Spanish squares right now, thinking you look interesting ordering *café solo* in a tiny cup. I bet you're pretending

to read Jean-Paul Sartre. More likely you've been forced
to sell caricatures of tourists for money.

Anyway, it's not cool to disappear.

Can you come back? I miss you, Max.

V x

PS: A thousand friends now.

'Hello?'

'Hello, Miss Summers?'

'Yes?' Christ, what time is it?

'Hi there, my name's Ruby North. I'm a researcher for
Romance Radio.'

I sit up in bed; it's light outside. 'Hi.'

'We're interested in your search for Max Kelly.'

'Oh.'

'I've just read your article in the *Sunday Read* and I think
your story would interest our listeners.' The *Sunday Read*? I
scrabble on the bedside table for my phone. It's eight o'clock
in the morning and it's Sunday. What kind of hot property
have I become? 'Sorry for ringing so early, but I'm sure you'll
get lots of press calls today and I wanted to get in quick and
book an interview with you for our station.'

'An interview?'

'Yeah, just a few questions about Max – it's part of a "Lost
Love" feature. Have you found Max yet?'

'No.'

'Aw, bless you. Would you like to come and tell our listeners
about him?'

I feel my heart speeding with adrenaline. I suppose any
publicity is good. Radio is good. You can hear radio anywhere.
Max might be listening and I could speak directly to him.

'Okay, yes, please.'

'Great!'

I take down the details – Romance Radio, Love Lane, Battersea, tomorrow at one, Ruby North – and hang up. Bloody hell! What have I started? I get up and pull on clothes from the floor – jeans and a shirt that Dave has been sleeping on, judging by the cat hairs. I put on my sunglasses and trot out to get the papers.

Ten minutes later I'm back with coffee and a copy of the *Sunday Read*. I take out the magazine supplement and turn to Donna Hayes's page. The headline reads, 'What Becomes of the Broken-hearted?' There's a little photo of Donna looking windswept and much better-looking than she does in real life. The article runs over two pages and I scan down:

It's a lonely place to be when you find yourself freshly dumped and heartbroken. Friends and family start to glaze over, colleagues avoid you, and invitations dry up. It turns out no one likes misery. So where can you go for solace when it's been weeks, months or even years and you still can't think of your ex without sobbing? You can read about it, attend self-esteem courses, even hypnotise that man right out of your hair (see details below). From now on, though, I'll be directing broken-hearted friends to www.nevergoogleheartbreak.com, a spiritual home for the lost and lonely. You can wallow in the company of fellow dumpees, join thread discussions, read real-life experiences to make your toes curl and tap into 'top tips' such as 'How to tend your lady garden for love'. Guaranteed to make you feel better, the site is less a web address and more a club – and if you did the dumping, ease your guilt by bigging up your ex on the 'Date my ex' page. This site is funny, easy to navigate and, most importantly, hopeful.

Pssst! If fairytale romance is your thing, check out site founder Vivienne Summers's blog to her own lost love, or 'like' the 'Where's Max?' group on Facebook – thousands already have . . .

Good for Donna Hayes! She only went and did it, like she said she would. What a total legend. I can't believe it – my site and my blog in the Sunday papers! I check Facebook. 'Where's Max?' suddenly has 2,000 friends. This is getting huge.

My mobile phone buzzes across the table. Christie.

'Have you seen the paper?' I ask.

'What paper?'

'The *Sunday Read*. I'm in it! Well, not me, but my site and it mentions "Where's Max?"'

'No, haven't seen it.'

'Sorry, I thought that's why you were ringing.'

'No.' There's a long silence; I think she's been cut off, but then I hear her breathing.

'So, what can I do for you this fine morning, Christie?'

'Well, I just wanted to tell you, Nigel's come up with two designs and printed a few T-shirts.'

'Great! So he didn't mind?'

'No.' Her voice seems distant.

'Right, so do we need to choose one?'

'No.'

I wait for her to explain, and wait. 'Christie? Are you all right?'

'Yeah, I'm here . . . Sorry, just painting my toenails.'

'So about the designs . . . ?'

'Yeah, Nige did two and I liked one of them, but all his fashion mates have started wearing the other one.'

'What's it like?'

'Oh well, Nige can be such a prat sometimes. He's only gone and done it in French!'

'French.'

'I know! And it's just words, just *"Où est Max?"* in sort of boxy black capitals on a white T-shirt. I don't think you'll like it, Viv . . . The other one had much more to it – it was more fancy and in a language we actually speak in this country! Anyway, Nige is mates with that model – you know, Betty George?'

'Yeah?' The crop-haired, impossibly tall, incredibly pouty *model du jour* Betty George?

'Well, the silly sod gave one to her and she's been papped wearing it, so we'll have to go with that design now.'

'Betty George was photographed wearing an "*Où est Max?*" T-shirt?'

'Yeah . . . I was just thinking, you didn't get to okay the design.'

'It's genius! Where's the picture?'

'In the *Post*.'

'I'll call you back.'

Oh my God, oh my God, oh my God. I'm running up the road to get the *Post*. Betty bloody George!

This is crazy! There she is, arm in arm with some other gorgeous human, wearing nothing but a belted T-shirt – and emblazoned across that T-shirt is the name of my love. I have a fleeting uneasy feeling to do with Max's name being near the breasts of Betty George, but I'm quickly over it. This is so cool it's unbelievable. I check the Facebook site; it's up to eleven hundred friends. The blog has a thousand subscribers all of a sudden. I call Christie.

'I love it, Christie. It couldn't be better.'

'French is foreign, you know, Viv.'

'It adds mystery; it's amazing. Nigel's amazing.'

'Oh, well, if you think it's okay . . . That's a relief.'

'I want one. I want to wear it tomorrow. I'm going on the radio, Christie!'

'People can't see you on the radio.'

'I just want to wear one!' I want to squeeze her and kiss Nigel.

We arrange to meet at a bar in Smithfield and she says she'll try to get Nigel to come. I'm excited by this. I'm going to a cool bar in Smithfield to meet an up-and-coming designer. A designer who knows Betty George. God, I wish Max was here! He might be soon with all this publicity . . .

I'm in the grip of a massive clothes crisis. I was thinking black skinny jeans, forgetting my legs look like two parsnips in skinny jeans. Now I can't find a single thing that is cool enough to meet a fashion designer in. The door buzzes. It can't be Max. It won't be Max. Could it be? My heart races. I press the intercom.

'Hello?'

'Hi,' says a male voice.

'Hello?' I repeat.

'Viv, it's me . . . Rob.'

I release the button. What's he doing back here? Didn't I tell him not to darken my door again? The door buzzes. Oh shit! I don't know what to do. What shall I do? I press the intercom connecting us.

'Rob, can you bugger off, please? This is not a good time.'

'Have you got someone up there?'

'What? No.'

'Because if you have, I swear I'll—'

'What do you want?'

'I want to see you.'

'Well, you can't at the moment.'

'I have to see you, Viv.'

'I'm letting go of the button now, Rob. Will you go away?'

'Don't—' he begins, but I lift my finger and he's gone. Seconds later he begins the buzzing again. I run to the bedroom and try to drown it out by drying my hair. When I think he's gone, I switch off the dryer and listen. Silence. Thank God. The last thing I need is a scene with Rob.

I decide on a black dress. I step into it and zip up the side, but it looks too boring so I add some leggings. I hold back

my hair thinking it might be better tied up today; then the
buzzing starts again, this time in a rhythm, like Beethoven.
Argh! It's unbearable. I rush to the intercom.

'What?'

'Well, I can't go without seeing you. I've brought you some
flowers.'

'I'm going out.'

'Just let me give you the flowers.'

'Did you get them from a petrol station?'

'No, they're expensive roses. A dozen. Pink.'

'And you actually bought those with me in mind, did you?'

'Oh, come on, Viv!'

'Well, I'm busy getting ready to go out.'

'I'll wait.'

Oh hell. I can't stop him waiting on the street, can I? 'It's
up to you. I won't be ready for ages, though.'

Now I'm hassled. I try to pin my hair up artfully, but it's
too tricky: the top is so short. In the end I leave it messily
down. Now shoes . . . Would heels be trying too hard? I go
for flat pumps. Flicky liner, lip gloss and I'm ready. I put my
phone and purse into a huge green tote that I hope is cool
in a Hoxton-type way and try to get a glimpse of Rob from
the kitchen window. I can't see him. Dave jumps onto the
kitchen worktop and rubs his tail against my arm.

'Look, I've told you – don't go on here, okay?' He head-
butts my arm, rubbing his face against my skin and purring.
I drag him down and scrape disgusting fish mush from a
can into his saucer. He crouches next to it. 'Right, be good
and I'll see you later.' I grab my keys and slam the door.

Outside the day is hotter than I'd imagined. I wish I
hadn't bothered with the leggings. I let the building door
click shut and Rob immediately steps up with a stunning
bouquet.

'Hello, Viv,' he says very seriously. As usual he's devastatingly good-looking, smirking in a 'forgive me' way like something from a perfume advert. I should probably throw my arms around him and he'd let the flowers fall to the ground; then there'd be a close-up of the perfume bottle and a flashback to us kissing. The voiceover would say, 'Forgive: the new fragrance from . . .'

Anyway, none of that happens. What actually happens is we stand there looking at each other and I wonder how I'll get rid of him.

'How are you?' he asks.

'I'm okay.'

'Good. That's good.'

'Yes.' I gaze off down the street.

'These are for you.'

'I can't accept them.'

He looks shocked then genuinely sad. 'Okay. No, that's . . . I understand.'

I nod and look at my shoes.

'What have you done to your hair?'

'I have to go,' I say, but he holds my arm.

'No, Viv, don't.' I pull away. 'Can't you just give me ten minutes? Can't we go for a coffee or something?'

I have all kinds of righteous thoughts about the times I begged him to see me, and how cold he was. 'Rob, can you just let go of me?'

He drops my arm. 'Sorry,' he says, patting me now. 'Sorry, sorry.'

'Okay.' I make to leave and he tags along.

'Vivienne, please! We were spending the rest of our lives together; what do ten more minutes matter?'

'I can't. I'm busy.'

'But, Viv,' he wails. Tears spring to his eyes, stopping me in my tracks. I can't stand a crying man.

'Jesus, do not cry!' I shout at him.

'I will cry, Viv. I'll follow you crying if you don't have a coffee with me!'

We end up in the coffee shop by the tube, him with a skinny latte and me with a cappuccino. He watches me empty two sachets of sugar into mine.

'So you think you're in love with Max,' he says eventually.

'I am.'

'What makes him Mr Perfect, then?'

'Lots of things.' I consider telling him some of them but think better of it. 'You don't want to know.'

'No,' he concedes, looking around. 'You're in the paper, I see.'

'Yeah.' I feel a pop of excitement.

'I suppose you must really love the bloke to do all that blogging and everything.'

'I guess so. What're you doing reading my blog?'

'I'm not going to sabotage you or anything – I mean, I just wanted to tell you that.'

'That's big of you.'

'Hmm.' He takes a few good gulps of his drink and wipes off a milk moustache. 'Do you think he'll come back?'

'Dunno. Hope so.'

'You know I could start a big media campaign to get you back,' he says.

'You won't, though.'

'No,' he admits. I smile and so does he and it feels really grown-up to be able to sit together like this after everything that's happened. I suddenly come over all magnanimous, taking his hand and giving it a little squeeze.

'You'll be all right, Rob.'

'Oh yeah, *I* will. But *you're* probably going to end up alone. Want to know why?'

'Tell me.'

'You don't know what you want.' I finish my coffee so he

can't see me smiling. 'But what I'm willing to do is offer an opportunity to you now,' he says. 'I'm willing to wait for you for a month or so while you mess about with this Max thing, but after that, Viv, I'm going to have to move on.'

'Okay, Rob.' I stand and put my bag on my shoulder. 'Well, I have to go now. Please don't wait a month for me. I'm not wasting another minute on you.'

'I'm not taking that as your final answer,' he says as I pass the back of his chair. 'You're probably pre-menstrual or something, low on oestrogen!' I walk towards the door. 'Think about what I said!' he calls.

'Bye, Rob.'

As I pass the window I glance in at him: an inordinately good-looking man with a bunch of roses already scrolling through his phone numbers for his next victim. I can't help feeling a little pang of affection. To think he was the reason for so much heartache. To think he could be the reason I've lost my best friend and the love of my life. But I won't let that happen. I head underground and board the tube to Farringdon.

I arranged to meet Christie in a bar near Smithfield meat market and here I am outside the huge decorative half pipe entrance. This is one of London's real old trading places. It actually is a market where they sell meat every day. It's closed now but the evidence is around – pigeons picking at a flabby scrap, a rosy puddle by the drain, a stray eyeball coming to rest by my shoe. Okay I imagined the eyeball. The street ahead is windy and deserted like an after hours film set. There's a feeling of having missed the party. I search for a bar along the low line of buildings opposite and spot Christie sitting in a square of window under a corrugated-iron sheet on which the word 'zoo' has been daubed in pink. I cross the road and push at the studded door. Inside everything is painted black even the concrete floor. There are huge tables

and benches with black plastic upholstery, some of it ripped.
One wall appears to be covered in graffiti, but actually I see
it's a menu with things like egg and chips and bacon butties.
Fluorescent lights along the skirting boards cast fingers of
shadow, and clubby chill out music washes in a calm, after
party feeling. An enthusiastic waitress in dungarees with one
of the legs rolled up greets me.

'I'm meeting friends,' I enjoy saying as Christie waves.

At the table Christie stands to air kiss, and I see she's
wearing some sort of romper suit of snow-washed denim
and shiny pink high-top trainers. Her head is bandaged in
black and her white-blonde hair pokes from the top like a
yucca.

'Viv. What ever you do don't mention the dress he lent
you,' she gasps in my ear. I look over her shoulder at Nigel.
He smiles and raises his hand in a kind of wave. Christie
makes the introductions: 'This is Nige; Nige, Viv.'

'Pleased to meet you.' I say keenly. I must say he's not
what I expected at all. He's scruffy in an Iron Maiden T-shirt
and pinstripe trousers that look like they came from an old
Oxfam suit. His sandy hair is close-cropped, I guess in an
effort to disguise the receding hairline, and he's wearing
wire-rimmed circular glasses. I realise I have no idea. I am
in no way cool. I don't get it and suddenly feel naked because
I've tried to look nice. I've tried to match stuff and no, it's
all wrong. I mustn't let Nigel know what a mainstream geek
I am.

'Drink?' He asks. I glance at their glasses filled with something red. What could that be? A red drink on a Sunday
morning?

'Bloody Mary, please.' I smile, sitting between them.

'Retro,' he says rolling the r. I look to Christie for guidance,
noticing her white mascara and glitter lipstick. She's smiling
encouragingly.

'I hope I'm not late,' I say. Nigel shakes his head. I look from one to the other: it's as if he's watching a very compelling soap opera and she's his adoring girlfriend. I order my own drink when the waitress comes.

'More watermelon juice?' she asks Nigel, but he declines with a shake of his hand. We sit in silence. Christie smiles and shrugs my way. Should I take charge? Are they sitting here wondering why I asked to meet?

'So . . .' I begin. They both turn to me mildly surprised. 'Nigel. I'm so thrilled that you agreed to design something for us. I've seen the papers this morning and I love what you've done. It's really, well, it's genius.' Nigel has turned his ear to me and is slowly nodding. There's another pause. 'Can I see a T-shirt?'

'For sure,' he reaches into a rucksack and lays a white shirt over the table. The big capitals cover the front. I touch Max's name.

'I love it,' I say sincerely.

'Yeah, as a brand I think it's got legs,' Nigel replies. He takes other stuff out of the bag, laying a sweatband and a cap with the same logo out on the table too.

'A brand?'

'I'm thinking a lot of different merchandise. The logo's really visual, it's strong.'

'Imagine that, Viv – "*Où est Max?*" everywhere!' Christie sounds excited.

'I'm seeing it . . . but what about when he comes back? The search would be off and how would that work then? I mean, if you're thinking of building a whole brand?'

'This is rooted in reality, but not linked to a specific person,' says Nigel.

'Except it is, because it has his name on,' I point out.

'The name is universal.'

'Oh.'

'It can be multidirectional. It can mean the ultimate, as in "where is the max?"'

'But it says "Where is Max?", though – the person, Max.'

'In capitals. People can bring their own meaning to it. It's not necessarily about your friend, except that it is for you. It's actually in and of itself.' To be honest, I don't know what the hell he's on about and I'm feeling a little out of control. I have a gulp of Bloody Mary. Why did I order this? I hate tomato juice.

'Hmmm, right. What do you think, Christie?' I ask.

'I hear what you're saying, Viv. I do. But I love the existentialist nature,' she replies dreamily.

'Oh, you do? Could you explain that to me?'

'Not right now, Viv.' She shoots me a look.

'I mean, I love the design. Thank you for designing it.' Nigel nods. 'Can I take one?' I pick up the T-shirt.

'Sure,' he says.

'I think it's great. Amazing that Betty George wore one!' Don't gush. Don't gush.

'Cool.' Nigel nods.

'It is about finding Max, though,' I persist.

'Sure thing.' He smiles. What does this mean, then? Another silence falls over us all.

'Hmmm,' says Christie, grinning away. I look at Nigel, waiting for him to explain.

'Did you design Christie's outfit today?' I ask, just to say something.

'No. What are you channelling today, Christie? Eighties fitness?'

'Eighties fitness meets space,' she explains.

'Cool,' he says.

'So is Betty George your friend, then?' I feel compelled to ask.

"She's such a stupid cow.' He says and turns to me and

laughs. Christie laughs too and so do I and we are all laughing at nothing.

'Any how . . .' I say, 'Yesss,' I'm making a total arse of myself and I don't even know how I'm doing it. Is he über-cool and therefore I'm not worthy? Or is he just up himself and a bit rude?

'So, Top Shop placed an initial order of one thousand shirts,' fires Nigel. 'But they want exclusivity. You okay with that?'

'Okay? Of course!'

'I won't charge you for my design, so I take all the risk, and profits.'

'That seems . . . okay I think. Is that okay?' I frown over at Christie.

'See if the whole thing bombs Viv, then Nige's reputation could be damaged,' she explains. 'So I said, didn't I Nige? I said, Viv won't be interested in money. She's all about love.'

And so speaks my business partner. Oh this is tricky territory. I've heard about legal wrangles over this sort of stuff.

'Well I am looking for my love yes. But I do need money!' I laugh. They don't. 'I mean, don't we all?'

'Hmm' says Christie, looking at Nige who's bumping a clenched hand against his chin.

'I know it's your design Nige, but it was my idea. So . . .' I begin. He turns to scrutinise me, his little eyes bright and clever.

'I can pay you a fee for the idea if you like, a one off. We'll work something out,' he says casually.

'You do owe Nige money,' interrupts Christie, pointedly widening her eyes, 'for the feather dress you wrecked I mean.'

'The one we weren't going to mention?' God who's side is she on?

'How about this, I'll take all the profits for the "*Ou est Max?*" brand, and you keep the dress,' offers Nigel.

'I don't have the dress, it's ruined.'

'How about you make her another dress?' says Christie.

Nigel sighs and throws himself back in the chair.

'I don't need another dress Christie . . . I mean how big will the Max brand become? I'm sure you're not ripping me off but . . .'

'Okay,' says Nigel, 'final offer. I will make you one couture dress of your choice and get you both front row tickets to my show in London Fashion week.'

Christie looks at me longingly, probably already imagining us at the show. She nods slowly, looking into my eyes with a 'watch this' glint in her eye.

'And we would want all-we-can-drink champagne at the show,' she says triumphantly.

Nigel agrees, and the deal is done. I leave, confident I've just been fleeced. But I can only worry about so much.

Later when I'm settled on the train I peek into the bag at the T-shirt. I look at Max's name and although I'm excited about the whole Top Shop deal, I feel a tiny point of doubt. I wonder have I overexposed myself? What will Max think? Have I sold us down the river? Turned our love into some sort of circus to add insult to injury? I shake that thought away and concentrate fully on the original goal. The main thing is that I find Max. And I have to find him, don't I? I have to do whatever it takes.

32

BLOG TO MAX #5 – WE'RE FAMOUS

Days since I last saw you: 29

I guess everyone loves a romance. Things have gone crazy. There will soon be T-shirts for sale with your name on. You're fast becoming a brand that will take over the world! Nha nha ha!

It might be a bit out of hand, actually – everyone's after you. It's in the paper. I'm going on Romance Radio tomorrow. Me! On Romance Radio – the Stuart Hill show.

What would be really great is if you could ring up while I'm on and ask me to marry you. I'd say yes. We'd probably have to get married on TV or something, though, that could be naff.

What would be really awful is if you never came back. I'd be the sad girl who publicly didn't find her man. Also, I'd be alone for ever because you are the only one for me. I didn't betray you, Max, and this would all be worth it if I just knew that you knew that.

I won't tell you about the Facebook page any more. I don't want to freak you out.

V x

'You're listening to Stuart Hill on Romance Radio 101 FM. I'm here with Vivienne Summers, who'll shortly be telling us about her search for a lost love. That's right after Michael Bublé and "Haven't Met You Yet" . . .'

Stuart Hill takes off his headphones and rests an elbow on the bank of switches between us. He sounds all right on the radio, but in real life I think he might be a bit insane, like a weird Willy Wonka of the airwaves. I'm sitting here in my '*Où est Max?*' T-shirt, wondering at the place. The studio is a bit run-down, with fading posters of eighties pop acts like Belinda Carlisle and Debbie Gibson. It smells of old food and farts, and it's a million miles away from the sleek media pod I'd imagined, but still I feel really overexcited. I hope I'm going to come across okay; usually I hate my voice on videos – I always sound a bit slow.

'Are you ready, you lovestruck young fool?' asks Stuart, his eyes a-pop. I wonder if he's on something. 'After this track, my darling, you put the headphones on and I'll fire the questions!' He flashes a Cat in the Hat-style grin. 'Okay?'

'Okay!' I say, matching his enthusiasm.

He looks at me intently for a moment. 'Have you set your pretty little heart on this Max fella-me-lad, then?'

'Yes, I—'

'You think he'll just come running, then, do you? Well, good on ya!' I start to say something, but he holds up a hand and slides on the headphones.

'I'm Stuart Hill and I'm here with a charming young lady, Vivienne Summers. Hello, Vivienne.'

'Hi, Stuart!'

'Now, Viv, you're looking for a lost love, are you not?'

'Yes I am, Stuart. I'm looking for my friend, and the love of my life. His name's . . . Shall I say his name?'

'I should say so.'

'It's Max. Max Kelly.'

'Oh, I know him – I saw him in the pub just now.'

'What?'

'Only joking, my darling. Go on, go on.'

'Well, I'm trying to find him and I started this Facebook group called "Where's Max?"'

'And it's gone bonkers, hasn't it?'

'Yes.' I laugh.

'Right, and what makes you think this Max Kelly wants to be found?'

'Well, we were just getting together and he said he loved me, so I'm hoping when he finds out how much I love him, he'll realise we—'

'You love him?'

'Absolutely. Completely. So much.'

'What does it feel like?'

'It feels great. It would feel even better if he was actually here.'

'Is it like flying without wings?'

'Flying without wings?'

'Does he complete you?'

'Yes, I guess he does – well, if we were together he would!'

'I see your quest has been in a couple of newspapers and you're wearing one of the campaign T-shirts today. What have you got there emblazoned across your chest?'

'It says, "Where's Max?"'

'It doesn't say that, though, does it?'

'Well, it's written in French, so "*Où est Max?*"'

'Is he French, then?'

'No, he's Irish.'

'Well, as long as you're following this, folks at home! Ha ha ha!' He laughs and I feel the first pinprick of foolishness. 'So have you had any luck? Have you heard from this Max fella?'

'Not so far, but here's hoping! Here's hoping!' I guffaw.

'And tell us about your blog, Vivienne. Have you put your heart online, literally, do you think?'

'Well, yes, I suppose so. I've been writing a blog to Max,

so he can, um, you know, so he'll realise that not a day goes by when I don't think of him.' Oh no, I suddenly feel my throat getting thick . . . I can't cry!

'And has your Max ever replied?'

I try to collect myself. 'No. No, he hasn't.'

'So maybe, Viv – and I don't want to be cruel to you when I say this – but just maybe he doesn't want to be found. Have you thought of that?'

I start to notice some sad music floating in the background. 'I just hope he does, I suppose.'

'Of course you do, my love. Can you tell us why he went off in the first place?' he asks gently.

'Yes. I . . . We had a misunderstanding and he thinks I was with someone else, but I'm not and I wasn't.'

'Now if it was me – and bear with me, because I *am* a bit old-fashioned – I'd just ring him up. Why the big campaign?'

'He didn't answer my calls. This is my way to show him how I feel and . . .' The sad music swells.

'Because it might be just that he wants to get away from you, sweetie pie. I'm not being rude; I just wondered if you'd considered that.'

'I don't believe it.' I suddenly get a vision of myself sitting in this shabby studio in my T-shirt with these stupid head-phones on and I have the urge to run out of here. I know I will find Max. But not like this. Not by being publicly humili-ated or by humiliating Max. This is not how I thought it would be. I don't know what I was thinking. I'm trying to explain something so personal to this Stuart guy and it just seems hopeless and silly.

'Well, it seems a lot of people are interested in the search for Max – I mean, over ten thousand friends of the Facebook group. Hell, I'm even one of them! Why do you think that is?'

'I think it's to do with people needing to believe in love.'

'Do you think they do? Isn't love a failing force in our cynical and materialistic world?'

'Not for me . . . or a lot of other people.'

'And not for me. We're believers, aren't we, Vivienne? We believe in the power of love.'

'The thing is, I just want to find my friend. That's all.'

'Okay, then! What's next for you, Vivienne, if you don't find your man?'

'If I don't?'

'Yes . . . let's just imagine, he's reading all your blogs and Facebook stuff, even listening to us right now, thinking,' Stuart affects an Irish accent, '"For God's sake, woman, will you ever just leave well enough alone!" . . .'

And then I consider it for the first time. What if he *is* thinking that? I'm doing all this to show him I love him, but what if he hates me for it? I think back to the conversation with Nana. 'Always searching for something,' she said. 'Wanting to change the world.' I suddenly see myself not as a lover writing messages across the sky, but as an arrogant, selfish person who won't let someone she hurt get away.

'What will you do then, Vivienne?'

'I haven't thought that far.' I try to smile through the crescendo of violins in my headphones. I haven't thought at all. As usual I ploughed ahead regardless. I thought it would be fun. I thought he'd respond. This is Max I'm talking about. My lovely loyal friend, and here I am turning everything into a circus. I feel my chest tighten. I've got it all wrong. How have I ended up here with everything all wrong, again?

'Actually, Stuart . . . can I say something?' I blurt out.

'You're on Romance Radio, we *love* to talk.'

'Well, I'd like to stop the search for Max.'

'You want to stop?' The sad music quietens.

'I want to call it off.' He waits, looking down at the decks. There's a fizzing in the headphones. Is this radio silence? It

can't be good. Is it my fault?' 'I want to stop looking for Max,'
I say again to fill the gap, looking desperately over at the
bird's nest of grey hair on Stuart's bent head. He says nothing.
'I . . . I'm not looking for him any more. I think I'd like to
respect his privacy now. He clearly doesn't want to be found.'
Stuart raises his head; a look of triumph glitters in his eyes.
He nods sagely. 'So I'm sorry to all the members of the
"Where's Max?" group. I'm stopping now, so please could
everyone just stop as well?' I take off the headphones, making
a muffled scratchy noise into the microphone. I take off the
T-shirt and fold it carefully in my bag and I sit there in my
vest. Stuart scrabbles about, pressing buttons.

'Well, listeners, there she goes! That was the extremely
lovely and perhaps a little confused Vivienne Summers, who
wants to call off her search for Max Kelly. And in a way I
think she's right, because you can't force love and you can't
hurry love either, as we all know! Hey, you heard it here first,
exclusive to Romance Radio.' He plays a jingle that merges
into Adele singing 'Someone Like You'. He slides off his
headphones and pinches the bridge of his nose, seeming a
bit deflated now. Ruby rushes in to escort me from the studio.
I look over my shoulder at Stuart. His eyes are closed.

'Is he okay?' I ask.

'Oh yeah, fine. He'll just be getting ready for the next bit.'

'Well, sorry. I don't think it was what he expected.' Ruby
just smiles. 'Thank you for having me,' I say, like a child at
the end of a party.

'Aww, you're welcome!' She shows me the door and I
stumble down the dirty stairwell into the street, a bit stunned.
I turn into the wind and start walking and thinking, and the
more I think about calling off the search for Max, the more
I know it's the right thing to do. With each step I feel a kind
of calm, flowing through the workings of my mind like oil.

*   *   *

At home I take a very long hot bath. I lie in the steam, letting my fingers shrivel. People can change. I'll change. I'll be a serious person, a calm person, like the kind of person I've always admired. I won't be off on wild-goose chases. No more funny ideas. No more partying. I won't even read poetry. I mean, poetry! Where has that got me?

When the water starts to cool, I get out and put on my fluffy dressing gown. The one that reaches my ankles. The only one I have now since Dave savaged the sexy silk one. Still, I won't be needing a sexy dressing gown anyhow, will I? I switch on the laptop in the living room and begin to type.

33

BLOG TO MAX #6 – IT'S OVER

Days since I last saw you: 30

Oh God, I was a disaster today on the radio. It started okay and I was really excited and then Stuart Hill kept asking, 'What makes you think this Max wants to be found?' and I was thinking, Well, it's obvious: we love each other. But the truth is, I don't know how you feel any more. I'm presuming I can win you round, but what if I've hurt you too deeply? What if you never want to see me again? It doesn't bear thinking about. It kills me to say this, but maybe I need to face the fact that if you wanted to be found, you'd be here by now.

So. Now. Max.

I want to say sorry. I want to tell you that when you saw me that day with Rob, it wasn't what you thought. I want to tell you I know I'm a stupid arse. And I want to say this will be my last blog.

I'll always be hoping for you and looking for you and loving you, but I'm calling off this crazy big search. This campaign is over, and if you want me . . . well, you know where I am.

V x

I stare at the cursor blinking there until my vision begins to blur. This is the right thing, though. It's time for me to go quietly about my business and stop searching for things, just like Nana said. I'll be calm. I'll be at peace. Serene. I stifle a little sob.

I read some of the messages posted by members. I suppose I should write a little thank-you message to them, sign off properly. I look out of the window at the twilight sky. Now the nights are drawing in, it's getting nippy and my mad summer's over. I think of those few hot days spent with Max. I missed my chance for love, I guess. I look back at the screen, take a tissue and blow my nose. Dave appears and curls around my ankles. A new message appears.

> Hey V, it's me.
> M x

My heart briefly leaps, until I realise it's some joker. There have been a few pretending to be him. I'll ignore it. I stare at the words . . . What if it is him and I miss my chance again? Of course it isn't, though, because he'd phone, wouldn't he? This'll be some weirdo.

It wouldn't hurt to check, though.

> If that is you, Max, phone in five minutes.
> V x

I wait. Nothing. I wait some more. Who am I trying to kid? I go to the kitchen and pour myself some orange juice. No more boozing. I'm changing my ways. I walk back into the living room, deliberately not looking at the laptop screen. I sit on the sofa and flick through the paper. Dave starts mewing and scratching at the chair leg. Bloody cat.

'Stop that or I'll have you stuffed.' He jumps onto the chair and then the table, rubbing his face against the laptop screen and purring. 'I'm not joking,' I warn him, and then it occurs to me that Dave might be trying to tell me something, like

Lassie. I say, 'What's that, boy? There's a message from your owner? He's stuck down a well?' Dave stares. He blinks. I go and check.

> In Spain. Big mountains. No signal.
>   M x

I'm not going to get myself all excited about this. It's obviously some fool thinking he's hilarious. But . . .

> How do I know it's really you?
>   V

I wait, scratching the top of Dave's head. He purrs like a buzz saw. A message appears.

> What u on about? It's me, look!
>   M x

I stare at the screen. I dare not hope. My heart is in shreds as it is; if this is a joke, I'll be tipped over the edge.

> Prove it.
>   V

I can't sit and wait. I walk around a bit and check. Nothing. See? This is not Max. I pull my dressing gown tighter and tuck my hair behind my ears. Nothing. I look at Dave still sitting by the screen, purring. 'It's not him. Don't get your hopes up,' I say, and take my glass through to the kitchen.

I check on my way back. Still nothing.

34

SOME THINGS I KNOW ABOUT VIVIENNE SUMMERS

By Max Kelly

She has a birthmark the shape of Ireland on her right arse
cheek.
She has the dirtiest laugh I've ever heard.
She's stubborn as a mule.
She doesn't like motorbikes or Arsenal or tattoos, but she
does like me, and her mad nana and English roses.
She likes tea in the morning, coffee after lunch and dry
white wine any time.
She has always been crap at poetry and she can't draw.
I fancy her most when she smiles.
She can't handle her booze.
Her favourite colour is pink but she thinks it's blue.
She's bossy and impatient but kind and lovely.
I nearly died of a broken heart when she walked into an
art gallery with someone else, but I can't live without her,
so I'm having to look her up again.
If I think she might love me, I'd take on the world.
She's the sexiest thing I've ever seen.
She's my beautiful, hilarious, clever friend.
I fancy spending some time with her.
I heard she might be looking for me and I wondered if
she'd like to come to Spain for a bit.
Believe me now?
    M x

It's you!
  V x

So how about it?
  M x

35

Adios, Amigos

1 September, 19:14

From: Ryanair.com
To: Vivienne Summers
Subject: Flight confirmation

Thank you for choosing to travel with ryanair.com.
    This receipt is not valid for travel.
    Your ticket will be emailed to the address you provided.
    Please check the details below carefully and click to accept.

Name of passenger: Vivienne Summers
Date: 2 September 2012
Airport From: London Stansted, UK
Airport To: Barcelona (Girona), Spain
One way/Return: One way

Click.

Acknowledgements

Thank you, Steve Garcia, for tirelessly being my muse and making me write this.

I'm extremely grateful to my agent Madeleine Milburn for all her encouragement and wheeling and dealing. Thanks to everyone at Hodder, especially Isobel Akenhead for her hawk-eyed editing and her lovely assistant Harriet Bourton, who is not at all like Christie. Thanks to Charlotte Maslen, Tessa Ditner and Danielle Shaw for repeatedly reading my writing and being so cool, clever and honest. Thanks to everyone who ever broke my heart and apologies to all my funny friends whose one-liners I've pinched. Thanks, Mum and Dad, for everything.

Author Emma Garcia has enjoyed plenty of her own romantic misadventures over the years – some hilarious, some just . . . weird. She spills the beans to her editor in this exclusive Q&A.

In NGH, Viv has a knack for rather embarrassing herself at entirely inappropriate moments in the name of love. What is the craziest thing you have ever done for someone you loved?
Erm, I'm a bit shy and nerdy so not as brave as Viv, but I once followed a man because I liked his coat and we ended up going out for brunch. Also I made a necklace with a shoelace and one of my teeth for a boy at school . . . but that ended badly. Then ultimately I got married and had three babies . . . That's a totally bonkers thing to do when you think about it.

When you were writing NGH, was there a particular heartbreak of your own that you had in mind?
Might have been. You know who you are and I want my juicer back!

I think we all fell in love with Max pretty instantaneously. He had us at 'Hello'. He really is a very fine specimen of a man . . . Sorry, back to the question. Do you think being in love is at its best when it's with your best friend?
Well if you want to have a total laugh and an easy life I'd recommend falling in love with your best friend because a) they actually like you, and b) they get you, which is a good start.

You leave us imagining Max and Viv's reunion at the very end (darn you!). What do you think the future holds for them?
Well the last I heard of them they were rolling along trying to make it together and Viv is already pregnant so they are about to become parents, which will be fun all round.

Lastly, I heard a terrible rumour that there is an astounding similarity between Christie and your fair editor. Surely this is paparazzi fodder?
All I'll say to that is this; Christie can sometimes be amazingly efficient.

The best books live on in your head long after they are finished. As you read, you are turning the pages faster and faster to find out what happens next, only to feel bereft when you reach the end.

If that is how you feel now, you might like to join us at www.hodder.co.uk, or follow us on Twitter @hodderbooks, and be part of our community of people who love the very best of books and reading.

Whether you want to find out more about this book, or a particular author, watch trailers and interviews, have the chance to win early limited editions, or simply browse our expert readers' selection of the very best books, we think you'll find what you're looking for.

And if you don't, that's the place to tell us what's missing.

We love what we do, and we'd love you to be part of it.

www.hodder.co.uk

 @hodderbooks

HodderBooks

 HodderBooks